THE DYING LIGHT

A totally enthralling psychological thriller
with a stunning ending

JOY ELLIS

Detective Matt Ballard Book 3

First published 2020
Joffe Books, London
www.joffebooks.com

ISBN: 978-1-78931-475-5

This book is dedicated, plain and simple,
to my incredible, amazing readers!
It's been a tough time, right across the world,
but it's given me the chance to get to know so many
of you through the books. We've buoyed each other up,
shared good and bad experiences, and taken time out
to laugh, yes quite a lot of that! It's been like one great
big universal hug with wonderful new and old friends.
I'm delighted and humbled to hear that the books
have kept some of you going through lockdown.
Well, you've kept me going too, with all your support,
good wishes and care. You are all very special!
Joy

CHAPTER ONE

Matt Ballard allowed a smile of satisfaction to spread across his face. He turned to his partner. Liz Haynes was smiling too.

'We did it! Our first case solved! And paid for!' Liz squeezed his leg. 'We really cracked it, didn't we?'

It had been a gamble, but in the end, turning private had been the only course the two of them could take. Liz had been forced to give up working in the police force after an attempt on her life had left her unable to meet their medical requirements. As for Matt, he had served his full time, but at fifty-three years old he was still fit, and far from ready for the allotment and the bowling club. Opening a private investigation business seemed wholly appropriate. They could pick and choose their jobs, and Liz could adjust her work according to the requirements of her condition.

Now they had a cheque in their hands, a happy client, and the man they had been investigating was with their former colleagues in the custody suite at Fenfleet police station, waiting to be charged.

'Textbook, wasn't it?' He chuckled. 'Not that I think all the cases we get will be that clear-cut.'

'Very satisfying,' said Liz, then added almost wistfully, 'but in a way, I'd like a bit more of a challenge.'

'Be careful what you wish for, my darling!' Matt warned her. 'We used to say things like that when we were on duty, then the next shout would see us up to our elbows in one of the shittiest cases we'd ever had.'

'True, but . . . oh, you know what I mean. That was a bit tame, wasn't it?'

Before Matt could answer, his mobile phone rang.

'Will! How's tricks, my friend?' He switched to loudspeaker so that Liz could hear. They had both worked alongside DI Will Stonebridge and had been saddened when a severely damaged elbow had seen him step away from the job he loved.

There was a long silence, then Will's voice filled the car. 'I have to admit things have been better. Any chance of me popping round for a cuppa and a chat? I'm beginning to think living on this fen is making me mildly neurotic. I need a dose of Ballard and Haynes's common sense, if you have some to spare.'

If he was trying to make light of something, he wasn't doing very well. Matt glanced at Liz. She was frowning.

'We are on our way home right now. How does half an hour suit you?'

'Kate's in her studio so she'll be working until late,' Will said, 'so that's perfect. I'll see you soon.' He hung up immediately, as if he were afraid they'd change their minds.

Matt took a deep breath. 'Well, that sounds rather ominous.'

'I hope Kate isn't slipping back,' said Liz softly. 'That girl has suffered enough.'

They had become close friends over the years, so Matt and Liz were among the very few people who knew the Stonebridges' true story. Kate Stonebridge was a very successful children's book illustrator. She had been working on a series of books called Fairy Dreams, featuring fairies and elves, and other magical beings. They had been so popular that now the accompanying merchandise was outselling the books. Kids all over the globe were wearing T-shirts, using pencil cases and sleeping under duvets that featured Kate's creations. She and the author had cleverly introduced a new character into each latest publication, which had kept sales of the books and merchandise at record levels. Along with Will's glittering career in the force, they seemed to be living a charmed existence. However, beneath the surface, there was little magical about their life.

Will and Kate had lost their baby. Kate had almost died in labour. She survived only after a life-saving hysterectomy robbed her of the chance of giving birth again. Naturally, Will had been devastated but he held on to the fact that he still had his beautiful wife. Kate, on the other hand, had been terribly affected, needing countless months of counselling. Depression had followed, culminating in a short period in a psychiatric unit, and then a regime of drugs whose side effect was a debilitating ennui that made doing the work she loved impossible. Just as Kate was starting to improve, reduce the medication and begin painting again, Will had been attacked by a crackhead and his arm had been badly broken in two places.

As soon as he had recovered enough to drive again, they had decided it was time to move away from their old home and all its bad memories. They hoped, in new surroundings, they could move forward. They could hardly believe their luck when they found Holland House, an old property on Whisper Fen. They had now lived there for almost six months.

'I'm not sure fen life is suiting our Will, are you?' said Liz thoughtfully. 'He's alone so much when Kate is working. Perhaps it's getting to him.'

Matt agreed. 'Will has always been active and, let's face it, suddenly having to leave the career you'd been expecting to follow until you were pensioned off is very hard to swallow.' He looked at her. 'Well, you know all about that, don't you, my love?'

'It's certainly a shock, but you can't go back and change the past, so you just have to move forward.' Liz winked at him. 'And sometimes things turn out better than you ever expected — huh, Mr Ballard?'

'You're so right, but we've been lucky. Even though we went through some very dark times, we aren't as fragile or sensitive as Kate. She was always delicate, and as Will is the first to admit, she has never really got over losing their baby. Probably she never will.' Matt eased the car into the lane that led to Tanners Fen and home. 'I wonder why Will wants to talk to us so urgently? I'm beginning to get a bit anxious.'

'Me too.' Liz stared out over the miles of lush green fields of vegetable crops. 'Matt, what do you think of their new home, Holland House?'

He exhaled. 'Well, I've known it all my life, so I've never really thought about it. It's in a beautifully remote spot, and it was an absolute steal at the price they paid. I've always thought it an imposing sort of place. It still needs a lot of updating, probably hasn't been touched since old lady Holland was younger, but—'

'No, I don't mean the practical things. What do you *feel* about it?'

Matt shrugged. 'I don't feel anything, really.'

'Mmm. Maybe that's what I mean,' Liz mused. 'Our home always makes me want to smile, but Holland House seems, well, lifeless.'

Matt laughed out loud. 'You didn't smile when you first saw the old Ballard family pile. As I recall, you told me it looked like a museum — no, *mausoleum*.'

Liz tried to look contrite and failed. 'True, but I didn't hate the place. It was simply that I could see what it was crying out for. We've stamped our mark on it now, and it's warm and welcoming.'

Matt pulled into the drive of Cannon Farm. 'Well, they haven't really been at Holland House long enough to make it theirs, have they? Will is still restricted by that damaged arm, and Kate spends every waking hour working, or so it seems. Give them time. It will be their dream home one day, you'll see.'

Liz didn't seem convinced. 'I think it will take more than a few paint charts and an order from Wayfair to make that place a dream home. But that's just my opinion.'

Matt had barely got his front door key in the lock when Will Stonebridge's car drew up behind theirs. One look at his face told Matt that his friend was far from okay. His smile seemed forced, and his eyes definitely weren't smiling.

'Come on in, I'll get the kettle on.' Liz hurried off in the direction of the kitchen, while Matt ushered Will into the lounge.

'We'll wait for Liz and the coffee. You look like you need to offload a bit, Will.' Matt smiled somewhat anxiously at his old friend. 'You've got that look we used to have when a crappy case got really exasperating.'

Will gave a humourless laugh. 'I recall the feeling well. Life is a bit like that right now, but the thing is, I'm not sure if it's me and I'm reading too much into things, or whether I have every right to be bothered.'

'Well, we were coppers for a long while, and we do tend to see the negative side of things. And you were one of the most intuitive detectives I ever worked with, so if there is a rat, you will definitely have smelt it.'

'A while ago I would have agreed with you, but since I had to give up the job and we moved here, I just don't feel like that man any more.'

'Why don't you talk to Liz, Will? After all, she went through exactly the same thing. She too was retired out of the job she loved. She might be able to help, and if nothing else, she's a damned good listener.'

'Oh, I'm not going to lay all this on her, she's got her health problems to contend with. And the two of you are happier than I've ever known you to be. Take no notice, I'm probably just feeling sorry for myself. Anyhow, it's got nothing to do with what I want to talk to you about.' Will lowered his voice. 'I'm starting to realise that I don't think I ever came to terms with how ill Kate became after losing the baby, and the effect it still has on her. She's so vulnerable,

Matt! And so mercurial — she changes in the blink of an eye.'

Matt nodded. That couldn't be easy to cope with. He was about to respond when Liz arrived carrying a tray of coffee and chocolate biscuits.

'I thought this sounded serious enough to hit the Hobnobs.' She placed the tray on the coffee table and flopped into a chair.

Will chuckled. For a fleeting moment Matt caught a glimpse of the old Will.

Matt handed his friend a steaming mug. 'Okay, Will. What's bugging you?'

Deliberately, Will set the mug down on the coffee table. 'Actually, I want to hire your professional services.'

Matt sat up straight. 'What? As investigators? Why?'

'Something is not right on Whisper Fen, and I'm a bit too close to start digging around myself. Added to which, Kate is on a deadline and working all hours, which means I'm running the home, shopping, feeding us and trying to work on the house at the same time. I'm run ragged.' He raised his hands. 'Oh, I'm not complaining, honestly. What Kate is doing is amazing, and I fully support her, but I don't have the time, or the inclination, to embark on an unofficial investigation.'

Absentmindedly nibbling on a biscuit, Liz had her gaze fixed on Will.

'So, what do you think is going on?' she asked.

Will took out a small notebook from his inside jacket pocket. 'Several small, seemingly unconnected incidents. It's possible that they mean nothing, and I've blown them all out of proportion, but listen to this.' He looked down at his notes. 'Whisper Fen is only a few miles from Tanners Fen and having lived here all your life, you might know a couple of the people concerned. Have you heard of a woman called Emilia Swain?'

Matt nodded. 'The German lady, lives quite close to you. Husband died quite a while ago. Nice woman, as I recall. I had some dealings with her husband way back, after his business was broken into.'

'Ah, good, that could make life easier. Well, recently, someone has been aiming a series of malicious acts at her. I only found this out last week. She has put them down to prejudice, but I don't believe that for one second.' Will sipped his coffee. 'The thing is, she doesn't want to bother anyone, and she certainly won't make an official complaint, so I wondered if we could engineer an accidental meeting with you both, so you can get her to talk about it.'

'What kind of malicious acts?' asked Liz, offering the biscuits to Will.

'For starters, someone killed her cat.' He pulled a face. 'Disgusting. Then someone snapped the lock off her shed and trashed everything inside, and . . .' He paused, frowning. 'And I think there is something else, but she clammed up on me.'

'Well, you certainly don't need to hire us, Will.' Matt looked at Liz and raised an eyebrow. 'We'll see what we can find out, but as your friends.'

Liz nodded vigorously. 'Of course! And we've just concluded the case we were working on, so we can pitch in immediately. Tell me, how do you propose to set up this "accidental" meeting?'

'She'll be going to the farmers' market in Fenfleet tomorrow. Her old car has packed up, so she'll take the bus from Whisper Corner. If you were to bump into her and give her a lift home . . . ? I know the bus times, and she never misses market day, so you're sure to find her there. Sound okay to you?'

'Yup,' said Liz. 'And if she already knows Matt, that should work well. We'll tell her we were on our way to see you.'

'I'm happy with that,' Matt said. 'So, what else is bothering you?'

'A man named Gerald Grove. Ever heard of him?'

Matt frowned. 'The name doesn't ring a bell. How about you, Liz?'

She shook her head. 'Nothing.'

'I have seen him before, I know I have. It must have been to do with work.' Will's expression darkened. 'And I don't like him.'

'Ah, we might need a little more than that,' Matt said.

'I don't recall anything he actually did, he just gives me the creeps. He lives a quarter of a mile away from here in a lonely, ramshackle old place on the edge of the marsh.' Will looked at them both. 'You guys know that feeling, don't you? The one that screams out "not to be trusted."'

They did.

'He turned up about eighteen months ago, and he seems to spend an inordinate amount of time wandering alone along the sea bank and marsh paths. Which brings me to the other thing.' Will frowned. 'The pain from my elbow and my arm sometimes keeps me awake at night, and I've taken to getting up, trying not to disturb Kate. Some nights I go for a walk. I've seen a vehicle heading down the marsh lanes — as you know, they go nowhere other than the marsh and the estuary, or that old mill that's waiting for demolition. No one lives out there, so where is it going, and why? Add to that the lights right out in the Wash, in the area around the Fenfleet Deeps, and I'm getting pretty twitchy.' He munched thoughtfully on a Hobnob. 'Thing is, I've asked around, and it seems I'm the only one who has ever seen the vehicle or the lights.'

'This is getting interesting,' murmured Matt. 'Though it sounds as if the three are probably not connected.'

'Maybe not . . .' Will sat back. 'Look, I really am happy to pay you. We are pretty comfortable since my injury, and Kate rakes it in from the illustrations and all their spinoffs. In fact, I'd feel much happier if you took it on as a proper job.'

'Let's just make a few enquiries first,' Matt said, uncomfortable with the idea of charging an old friend. 'Test the waters, see if there really is anything to investigate, and we'll take it from there. Maybe just expenses, if we need to lay out any cash.' After all, they had embarked on their new career to keep themselves occupied rather than to earn a living from it.

'Deal. If anyone can put my mind at rest, it's you two.' Will sat back, evidently relieved, and they began to chat about inconsequential things. 'You'll have to come for lunch. You'll be amazed at my newfound culinary skills.'

Liz laughed. 'Ah yes — the King of the Microwave. If it didn't finish cooking with a ping, then according to you, it wasn't real food.'

'All in the past.' His smiled faded a little. 'When Kate was so ill, I had to take charge of feeding us, and she needed good food, not some reheated microwave dinner. It was a wake-up call. I must say, I quite enjoy cooking now. So, how about Thursday, the day after the market? Then you can fill me in on how you got on with Emilia. I'd say call in after you drop her off, but Kate's agent and author are coming down to pick up the draft images of Kate's new character, so we'll be pretty tied up.'

'Thursday will be lovely. It'll be nice to see Kate again,' Liz said.

'Er, look, I have to warn you, she could be absolutely fine . . .' He sighed. 'It could be just us for lunch. If she's in the middle of working on something, she might not want to interrupt it. No disrespect to you, I promise. It's just the way she is at the moment. The deadlines don't help with her stress levels and I'm inclined to let her do what she has to.'

'Of course.' Matt beamed at his friend, secretly disturbed by what he had just heard. 'If we see her, great, but no pressure, okay?'

Will drained his coffee. 'I suppose I'd better get back. I'm so pleased you can check all this out for me.' He stood up and smiled at Liz. 'And you were right about the Hobnobs. We clearly did need them.' He pointed to the half-empty plate. 'I'll see you Thursday. Come at around one.'

They waved him off and went back inside.

'What did you make of all that?' Liz asked.

'He's strung out like a washing line,' Matt said. 'And I get the feeling that all at Holland House is not sweetness and light.'

'I'll be very interested to know how our lunch date goes.' Liz, carrying the tray, backed through the kitchen door. 'But in the meantime, we have our rendezvous with Mrs Emilia Swain. Tell me what you know of her.'

Matt shrugged. 'Not much. She lives in a cottage called Little Anchor on the road that leads to Holland House. She's Will and Kate's nearest neighbour, has a very pretty garden, you've probably seen it.'

'I know the one, we commented on it last time we visited Will.'

Matt nodded. 'She must be in her early seventies but still looks pretty tough. She has an air of determination that I rather admire. I hope we can help her — if she opens up to us.'

'Use your charm, my darling. Women are putty in your hands.' She grinned at him, fluttering her eyelashes. 'Resistance is futile where you're concerned. I should know!'

'Strumpet! Away with you.'

How he loved her! They were planning to marry at some point but felt no need to hurry. They were happy as they were, enjoying their new freedom. They had spent years living for nothing but the police force — juggling shift work, overtime, broken sleep and missed appointments. It had been a life governed by crime and its perpetrators. This new life was a revelation. Even so, Matt was certain that they had made the right choice in not giving up work entirely. He was determined that he wasn't going to keel over into a newly dug compost heap. Anyway, he was no gardener. Unlike Emilia Swain. Thinking of her, his buoyant mood sank. Having her garden shed ransacked and, worse, her precious pet wantonly killed, would have been traumatic for anyone, let alone an older woman living alone.

Maybe this was the sort of thing they would become good at. Not solving murders any more but making peoples' lives a little bit better. They would start by helping Mrs Swain.

CHAPTER TWO

The small town of Fenfleet held an outdoor farmers' market every Wednesday. Matt and Liz arrived early and found a parking space that gave a clear view of the bus stop. The local bus meandered around the more outlying villages and hamlets and brought those people that did not drive into the town, returning two hours later. There were only two buses a day, but the more remote areas the service covered considered themselves very lucky, as some had no public transport at all.

Matt and Liz felt like they were back on "obo," and while they waited, they reminisced about the long hours they had spent watching and waiting in far less salubrious surroundings than these.

Matt spotted Emilia Swain stepping down from the bus. 'See her? Greying hair, glasses, purple half-jacket, check shirt, black slacks and walking shoes.'

'Got her.' Liz stared at the woman. She was upright, well built, with a weathered skin that spoke of hours spent outdoors. 'Doesn't look like a shrinking violet, does she?'

'She isn't,' said Matt. 'I understand the lady has been through a lot in her life. Her husband intimated as much when I spoke to him. He was fiercely proud of her.'

'So, we let her get her shopping, then, er, intercept her?' She watched the woman head directly for a large greengrocer's stand.

'We'd better follow at a distance, and pick up a few bits and pieces to justify being here.'

'Good. I see the Cheese Man is here today — his Lincolnshire Poacher is to die for. Plus, we could do with some fresh veg, so the trip won't be wasted.' Liz pulled a list from her pocket. 'I came prepared.'

They spent the next twenty-five minutes wandering from stall to stall, keeping Emilia Swain in view. Finally, Matt announced, 'Okay, she looks pretty well laden with bags. Time for my Bafta-winning performance.'

'Right, and who are we today? Kenneth Branagh? I see a vague resemblance.'

'He'll do. Not as good-looking, of course.' With a grin, Matt hurried towards the unsuspecting woman.

'Well, I'm blowed! It's Mrs Swain, isn't it?' He turned to Liz. 'Liz, this is Will and Kate's neighbour on Whisper Fen.' He stopped in front of the surprised woman. 'Matt Ballard, Mrs Swain. I knew your husband, Leonard. Back then, I must have been DS Ballard. Now, I'm a retired DCI.'

Light dawned. Emilia Swain beamed back. 'Of course! That nice police officer who was so helpful to my dear husband. How are you?'

'Very well, thank you, Mrs Swain. This is my partner, Liz. We worked together at Fenfleet police station.'

'I'd shake hands, but . . .' Liz laughed, holding up her shopping bags.

'Actually, we are just about to head off home. Can we give you a lift? It's almost on our doorstep, and we are only parked over there.' He pointed across the square.

'That's very kind,' said Emilia. 'If it's not too much trouble, that would be wonderful.'

Liz smiled to herself, hearing the "v" in wonderful. Emilia might have lived here for the greater part of her life, but she had never lost that accent.

Matt took some of her bags and they made their way to Matt's Toyota hybrid. After loading everything in the boot, he helped her up into the car.

'I hate using the bus,' she said, 'but my old car is finally kaput. I knew it would happen one day. My husband, he told me so many times that I should get a new car every three years, but my Petunia, she was running so well that I kept her longer than he suggested.' Emilia shook her head. The passing of Petunia had obviously been a great personal loss.

'How long did you have, er, Petunia then, Mrs Swain?' asked Liz.

'Ah, let me see. We bought her in 1967, brand new, of course, one of the last they produced.'

After a quick calculation, Liz came to the conclusion that Petunia had had an incredible run for her money — she had to have been well over fifty.

'What kind of car was she, Mrs Swain?' asked Matt.

'An Austin A40 Farina Mark II in Horizon Blue,' Emilia declared proudly, then opened her capacious handbag and rooted around in it. 'Of course, I shall get a replacement. You cannot exist out in the fen villages without wheels. While I was at the market last Wednesday, I also went into a couple of garages.' She extracted two brochures and handed one to Liz. 'I'm torn between that . . .' she indicated the first, 'and this one.'

Liz found herself staring at the spec sheet for a Lexus ES saloon. She coughed to hold back a laugh. 'Nice cars.'

'My husband always had a Lexus. It was just me that liked my little bit of history. I sold his motor when he died, one old lady and two cars was a bit extravagant. Do you know anything about this one, Mr Ballard?'

They had pulled up at some lights, and he glanced across at the other brochure. It was for a Ford Mustang Fastback. 'Oh, that one's a bit classy for me, I'm afraid. The only Fords we ever drove were police transit vans, and a Focus traffic car.'

Emilia pushed the pamphlets back into her bag and sighed. 'Perhaps I should buy a, ah, what are they called, a banger?'

Liz smiled at her. 'If you are used to nice cars and can afford one, why not have one?'

A dark look passed over Emilia Swain's face. 'I'm not sure now is the right time.' She paused. 'Mr Ballard. Liz. You were both police officers, were you not? I can tell you this. Last week I found my cat dead. She had been thrown into my flower bed, the one with the geraniums and the marigolds, just outside the front door.'

'Oh, I'm so sorry to hear that,' Liz said. 'Perhaps someone ran her over and didn't want to leave her out on the road.'

'Road accidents do not generally leave an animal with a cleanly slit throat, do they, Liz?'

'Are you sure about that?' Liz said.

Emilia Swain gave her a withering look. 'And the week before that my potting shed had the lock snapped off.'

'Was anything taken?' asked Matt.

'Everything was thrown outside, trampled. A terrible mess, terrible, but I think that nothing was stolen. It was hard to say with all the chaos.'

'Did you report these incidents, Mrs Swain?' Matt asked.

'What could anybody do about it? Nothing was taken and the cat is dead. Even your wonderful local constabulary cannot perform miracles, can they?'

'Still, you should have told them.' Liz said kindly. 'They could keep an eye on things for a while.'

'I'm sure that they don't have the time or the manpower. There must be plenty worse things than that going on.'

Emilia was right, but a couple of private investigators might be interested in following it up. 'Any idea who it might be?'

'I cannot begin to think. I know nearly everyone in Whisper Fen and the surrounding villages. There are a few newcomers, but they seem good people. There is old Robert Lenton's son, he is not what my husband would have called quite right in the head, I think, but the poor soul has the mind of a child and he loves animals. No, I cannot think of anyone.'

'Do you know a man called Gerald Grove?' asked Matt, easing the big car on to the road leading to the villages.

'A rude and ill-mannered man. Certainly. However, I think that he is too intelligent to ransack garden sheds and garrotte domestic pets.'

'Where's he from? Do you know?' Matt asked.

'He has never opened his mouth to me. It was the post-mistress in the village who told me he has some sort of degree or other — you know, letters after his name — and he has a lot of publications sent to him, academic journals and the like.'

'I've been told he looks like a tramp,' said Matt.

'Do not be deceived by his looks, Mr Ballard. There is a good brain beneath those greasy locks, believe me.'

Liz decided to chance a suggestion. 'Mrs Swain, as Matt said, we are both retired and have time on our hands. We would be more than happy to keep a discreet eye on your lovely cottage for you. If we gave you a card, then if anything should worry you, ring us and we can be with you in ten minutes.'

'Oh no! I couldn't be such a nuisance, honestly,' Emilia protested, but Liz caught the relief in her eyes.

'Liz is right, Mrs Swain,' Matt added. 'Why should some mindless moron get away with it? It's totally unacceptable. We'd be happy to keep our eyes and ears open for anything suspicious.'

They stopped at her cottage and helped her in with her bags. Liz was full of admiration for the garden.

'It's my one passion now,' said Emilia Swain. 'I used to have many different hobbies and interests but now it's just the garden — and reading. I do love my books.'

'While we are here, Mrs Swain, could we take a look at the damage to your shed?' asked Matt.

Emilia frowned. 'If you want. Such a mess! I haven't had the heart to sort it all out yet.' She led the way around the back of the cottage and down a neatly trimmed pathway.

Approaching the large wooden structure, Liz saw exactly what Mrs Swain had meant. The lock had been wrenched off, the door itself damaged. The contents had been thrown out and most of them, it seemed, had been trampled. Emilia had retrieved a few things and taken them back into the shed, but most of it was fit only for the bin.

Matt set his jaw, angry. 'I'll come round tomorrow, Mrs Swain, and try to fix that door for you, and I'll fit a new lock. We are coming over to have lunch with Will and Kate, so we'll call in afterwards.' He held up a hand. 'And no arguing. I'm no master carpenter, but I can sort that for you.'

'It's a very good thing you ran into me, Mr Ballard, and you too, Liz. You are turning into my guardian angels.'

'And it's Matt, please, Mrs Swain.'

'Then please call me Emilia.'

They went back to the car and Liz handed her their card. 'Don't take any notice of the private investigator label. We are offering to help simply because we care about what happens out here on the fens. After all, you are our closest friends' neighbour. Please promise to ring if you are concerned about anything at all. You might not want to call the police, but you can call us, anytime.'

After some hesitation, Emilia finally accepted the card, adding, 'But don't you waste your precious time looking out for me. I'm what my husband called a tough old bird.'

That was probably true, but Liz had seen the gratitude in her smile.

Back in the car, Liz asked whether they should call at Will and Kate's place, as they were only two minutes away.

Matt said no. 'If you recall, he said Kate's agent and the author of the books that she illustrates will be there today. They won't want us intruding.'

'You're right,' she said. 'I'd forgotten about that. Just seems a shame to be so close and not drop by. We haven't done that in quite a while, and I feel bad about it. When they first moved in, we used to see quite a lot of them.'

Matt turned the vehicle around and they made their way back to Tanners Fen, Liz gazing out of the window. 'It's a very different landscape here to where we live, even if it is only a few miles away. We are pretty remote, but this place is in another league altogether.'

Matt nodded. 'We are that bit further inland, into farming country, and our part of the sea bank runs alongside the river. Whisper Fen leads directly on to the marsh and then the Wash and the North Sea. My gran on my mother's side lived here. In fact,' he pointed out of the driver's window, 'see those two small cottages in that tiny copse close to the marsh lane?'

Liz saw them. To her they looked sad, lonely, weather-beaten, and in desperate need of some TLC.

'Don't know who's there now, but she lived there for most of her life.' He grunted. 'Deserved a medal in my book. Cannon Farm, my paternal grandparents' home, was warm and dry and a good place to grow up in, but I'm not sure I would have liked to spend years of my life here.'

'I'm damned sure I wouldn't.' Liz gave an involuntary shiver. 'Although I have to say, Mrs Swain's place is very attractive.'

'Must get lonely being so far out, though she'll probably be mobile again soon — in her new Mustang or her Lexus.' He laughed. 'What a woman! You have to admire her, don't you?'

'I do, but she's still very vulnerable, living alone.' Liz could foresee the problems that would accompany advancing years in a remote location. 'I'm glad Will is not too far up the road. He could be a lifeline as she gets older.'

Matt sighed. 'I think our Will is struggling to cope with his own problems, darling, without taking on other people's. I'm sure that's why he wants us on the case. He feels slightly responsible for the old duck but doesn't have the energy to be on call for her.'

'I wonder how Kate's going to behave tomorrow? Will seemed terribly edgy about her, didn't he?'

'Oh well,' Matt said. 'Not long to wait. And I'm dying to see Will actually cook something. What's the betting it's a Pot Noodle?'

Liz elbowed him. 'I'm sure you'll be utterly amazed.'

'If he cooks at all, that'll be enough for me.'

They drove back to Tanners Fen, laughing about times past. There had been some horrific cases, but there had been a lot of fun too. Liz was happy that they were beginning to leave the bad things behind and recall the good times. Life was finally moving on.

She rested her hand on his leg.

* * *

Angela Lazenby, the author of the Fairy Dreams series, and Hubert Price, who was agent to both Kate and Angela, had phoned ahead to say they had been held up but should be there within the hour.

'Damn and blast! Don't they realise I could be working! I can't sit fannying around waiting for them to get their arses into gear,' Kate said.

Will didn't even try to stop her tirade. She'd been on edge all morning, constantly telling him what a pain it was, having to put everything on hold for this "royal visit." He hadn't liked to remind her that it was she who had insisted they collect the new designs because she didn't want to trail up to London with them. 'But, sweetheart,' he ventured, 'you've finished this new character now. Why the rush to get back into the studio?'

'Because,' she emitted a harsh exhalation, 'if you must know, I'm sick of Angela's bloody fairies and I've started a book of my own.'

Will stared at her, open-mouthed. She had always said she wanted to create something that was not some other author's brainchild, a work for adults, something that was entirely her own making. 'Well, that's brilliant! But why the secrecy? You always used to show me your work.'

Kate fiddled with her watch strap. 'Er, well, they are a bit different to my usual style. I've been experimenting, and I wanted one finished painting for you to look at.'

Will gazed at her with interest. Her style had been developing since they moved, and he could hardly wait to see her latest work. 'So, can I see?'

'Give me three or four days, baby, will you?'

His face fell. 'But . . .'

'Please?'

He'd give in of course, he always did, but he couldn't resist one last try. 'Then show me this new fairy that Angela and Hubert are collecting. I can't believe you haven't even let me inside the studio while you were designing it. Please let me see it before them?'

This new habit she had of working behind a closed door caused him considerable pain. For years, he had loved to watch his beautiful wife work, but since she'd taken possession of a new studio upstairs, he had not been allowed to enter. She told him her concentration was not as good as it used to be, and she would work better alone. He had had to accept it.

For a moment Kate looked irritated, and then she nodded. 'Of course you can. Come on.' She held out her hand and led him up the stairs.

Kate opened the door to her studio. It appeared to be empty, apart from a single painting displayed on an easel.

The painting depicted a boy fairy standing under a rowan tree. It took Will's breath away. 'Incredible! Kate, you are getting better and better. The detail in this will be lost on children. It's really beautiful.'

Kate explained that fairies considered the rowan to be a very special tree, and they always protected the garden in which it grew. It was a "witch" tree, which meant it belonged to the goddess. 'There is a spell you can cast to make your bedding plants flourish. We must try it, darling, now we are proper country people. It involves burying old leather boots and shoes along with a handful of rowan berries. You repeat a little charm over them — I've got the words here somewhere. You do it by the light of a waxing moon, either a Friday or a Wednesday as they are the nights of the guardian angels,

Anael and Raphael. Oh yes, and the berries have to be collected on Rowan-tree Day, that's 13 May.'

'Hate to tell you, honey, but May is long gone.'

'Rats! There go my hopes for winning the village "Best Garden" competition.'

Will looked at her, amazed. In a matter of minutes, she had gone from angry and belligerent to his old enthusiastic Kate, waxing lyrical over her latest creation. 'How do you find out all this weird stuff?' he asked.

'Research. I read the copy of Angela's story and obviously illustrate that, but the extra detail comes from researching the subject. Like this. Her new fairy is called Runa, that's Norse for a charm, or Sanskrit for magician. I'm not sure which she meant, they both fit the bill. The rowan is greatly revered for its protective qualities, it's meant to ward off harm.'

'That's a bit of luck. We have a splendid one in the back garden. It's a lovely tree.'

'The Welsh planted them in their churchyards, where we used to plant the yew. They are supposed to watch over the spirits of the dead.'

'And this young chap?' He pointed to Runa, standing under his rowan tree.

'He's her new hero for this next book, *The Protector of the Magical Garden of Gort.*'

'I've a feeling we'll be seeing his face staring at us from quite a few grubby T-shirts next year.'

'Who knows? But he *is* a handsome little devil, isn't he?'

They stared at the painting. It was definitely too good for children. It had a magic about it, but it was more than just a pretty picture for kids. The colours were deep and rich, and the attention to detail reminded him of the Millais painting of Ophelia. Runa himself possessed a charisma that shone like a beacon.

'Who on earth did you model this boy on?'

'He's not a boy, Will. He's a fairy.'

'Okay, but you had to model that face on someone.'

'No, I didn't. It's just how I see Runa. Now it *is* Runa. I just hope he's everything Angela is hoping for.' Kate sounded unsure of herself all at once.

'I'm certain he is, and a whole lot more besides. Angela will be thrilled when she sees this. It's your best yet.'

'I'm glad you think so, but still, I really am tiring of Angela's fairies. It's this place. Having been here for a while, I now know that I can do much, much better.'

Will saw a strange, intense light in her eyes that he had never seen before. 'Well, you are only contracted for one more book, so why not get that out of the way, then take a break and concentrate on your own work?'

'I can't wait that long!' She almost spat the words back at him. 'Don't you understand, Will? I need to be rid of all this!' She stared accusingly at her rowan fairy, and for one awful moment Will thought she was going to sweep it from the easel and hurl it to the floor.

Then the doorbell rang.

Kate closed her eyes and took a deep breath. 'Oh shit. Well, we'd better get this over with.'

CHAPTER THREE

Liz stood in the garden of Cannon Farm and gazed around her. It wasn't picture-postcard pretty, like Emilia's colourful cottage garden, but it was rather beautiful in an overgrown sort of way. The numerous trees and shrubs fought for supremacy, forming a glorious border of thick mature plants with little or no space between them. Liz rather liked this jungle of variously shaped leaves and colours. Neat and manicured was pretty, but she definitely preferred this natural look.

'Not exactly the Eden Project, is it?' Matt appeared beside her and handed her a mug of tea.

'I like it. And seeing Emilia's passion for her garden has inspired me to think about how we can make more of this lovely space.' She pointed to a corner of the lawn. 'I can see a summerhouse over there, can't you? With those lovely trees behind it? And maybe a trellis arch with climbing roses at the bottom of that path?'

'Uh-oh! She's turning into Charlie Dimmock.'

Liz laughed. 'Hardly! It's just that there's never been any time for these kinds of thoughts before, has there? It's almost intoxicating.'

'Like you.' Matt was gazing down at her.

'I guess it's time we turned our thoughts back to our new unpaid job before we become, er, side-tracked.'

Matt grinned at her lasciviously. 'Damn! Oh well, I suppose you're right.'

They went back into the house and sat down at the kitchen table.

'I'm really worried about that woman,' said Liz flatly. 'If it had been just one occurrence, like the garden shed, I'd have put it down to some idiot bored kids who'd probably pinched a few cans of Dad's lager and then got stupid. But two incidents, both in the same place, in that remote spot, and only a few days apart? No way. Someone's got a grudge against Emilia Swain, don't you think?'

Matt nodded slowly. 'Whoever attacked that lock did so with real venom. And her stuff wasn't just thrown around, it was trashed, systematically.'

'So, how are we going to play this, boss?'

Matt chuckled. 'That sounds like the old days. We're partners now, remember? I'm not the boss any more.'

'I'd still like to know what plan of action we are considering.'

'First, I suggest we get on the computer and see exactly what we can find out about Gerald Grove. I think we can afford to take a couple of runs a day out to Whisper Fen, just to keep an eye open. That part of the marsh is a great spot for bird-watching, so we can take some binoculars and not look out of place.'

'Sounds like a plan,' Liz said. 'Shall I hit the internet?'

'Perfect. I'll drive down to the big B&Q on the Saltern-le-Fen road and get our Emilia a new lock and some timber to strengthen that shed door. Are you okay with that?'

'Sure, and it's good to know you're so handy.'

He stood up, kissing her lightly on the neck. 'Oh, you have no idea.'

After Matt had gone, Liz went to her laptop and googled Gerald Grove. Apart from a lawyer in the United States, and a quantity surveyor in Co. Durham, the only possible Grove was mentioned in an old newspaper article from around two years ago. It was from the West Country and referred to someone of that name appearing in court over a breach of the peace. It gave no further details. Liz frowned. Could be him, but she would need to know more about him before she dug deeper. Emilia had said that according to her friend the postmistress he was educated, possibly an academic. Liz wondered what his subject was. Why would an academic want to live in a tumbledown cottage on the marsh? Maybe he needed seclusion to write some paper or professional article. But why was Will so certain that he'd come across him before, and in his professional capacity?

Liz groaned. She was used to accessing the police databases, legally tapping into a wealth of information. Now she was on her own. What had once been a simple request for information was going to be a whole lot more difficult now she was a civilian. What she could not do was ask her old colleagues for help. For a start, the Data Protection Act prevented the sharing of information with the general public. Years ago, a quiet word in a friend's ear could produce a wealth of information but these days it was more than their job was worth. As registered PIs, she and Matt could legally access all public records, including criminal records and court documents. What they couldn't do was get hold of details of a person's phone, their financial, medical or sealed court records. No, she'd have to do it the hard way, get out and talk to people. And of course, she needed to see Grove for herself, to see his face.

Matt would be about an hour, but as soon as he was back, she would suggest they go over to Whisper Fen and perhaps do a bit of surveillance.

Liz pulled a notebook towards her and wrote the words, "Know Your Target," and underlined them. She then put down four bullet points:

- Speak to post office re his academic interest.
- Try local pub.

- Check out his cottage and get full address.
- Try to get a look at him.

It wasn't much, but it was a start. She closed the book and stood up. Working independently was going to be a steep learning curve for them, but she was sure that once they found their feet, they would turn out to be damned good private detectives.

* * *

The late lunch had been a bit of a rollercoaster as far as Will was concerned. He found himself constantly watching Kate and listening out for any sudden outbursts. Angela could be a bit of a handful at the best of times, and although Hubert always had Kate's best interests at heart, he was somewhat in awe of the larger-than-life author, and tended to defer to her demands rather too quickly.

They managed to survive the cold buffet meal without any disasters, and as Will had predicted, when Angela saw the painting of Runa, she was stunned by the mastery of Kate's work.

The agent, Hubert Price, told Kate that he was certain the publishers would tell her to go ahead immediately with the full set of illustrations for the book.

Before she left, the author confided in Will that she felt the move had inspired Kate to higher things. And then she stood in the warm midday sun, stared across the desolate marshes and shivered.

'I can see where she would get her inspiration from. This is a wild place indeed. Look at all that sky.' She turned away. 'But not for me, I'm afraid. I find this spot just a little too remote, too lonely.'

She seemed almost overcome with melancholy. Then she shook herself. 'I'm so sorry, William. I'm a bit susceptible to atmosphere, and you have quite a lot of it here, don't you?'

She laughed, but it was a hollow sound.

Will was greatly relieved to see them depart, but Kate seemed almost elated. She poured them both a glass of wine, and they wandered out into the garden and sat on the bench in the afternoon sunshine.

Will told Kate about Angela's reaction to their new location.

'Oh, I'm not surprised, darling. She is a great writer, but she loves the social whirl, the parties and the hubbub of the city. My wonderful marshes would send her into a depression after a couple of hours.' She smiled mischievously. 'And there isn't an off licence for six miles! That would never do.'

They giggled like children.

'I was rather glad to see Hubert take the car keys, considering how much wine Angela put away with lunch.' Will laughed, enjoying this rare moment with an uncharacteristically relaxed Kate. 'So, my clever darling, another deadline ahead. I told you they'd love your illustrations. I've never seen Angela look so in awe. She seemed almost stunned by your interpretation of her character.'

'Yes, it's great, isn't it?' Kate nodded, looking suddenly pensive. 'But there is so much I want to do here. I feel a bit trapped by my work.'

'Then finish this volume and take a break. Take some time out. If you feel like working, then concentrate on your own book. You have plenty of time before that final novel will be ready. Angela admitted that she hadn't even started it yet and was struggling to come up with fresh ideas.' He spoke hesitantly. Just recently, the most innocent comments had been misconstrued, causing his moody wife to snap at him.

Kate sipped her wine, watching the sunlight glint in the crystal glass. 'You're right. I'll buckle down and get this one put to bed as soon as possible. I've already done a whole load of preparatory sketches, so I'm ahead of the game.' Absentmindedly, she reached across and laid her hand on his leg. 'Then I'll turn my attention to our home. I want it to be perfect, just as it used to be. Which reminds me — would you mind if I do a bit of research on the history of Holland House?'

'In your spare time, I suppose?' He tried not to show it, but he was somewhat surprised that with her deadline for the publisher, her own work, and her wish to revamp an entire house, she would even consider another time-consuming hobby.

She smiled and looked out across the salt marsh.

'So, what do you want to know about the house?' he asked after a while. 'Do you think it has a grim past? Murder, mystery and mayhem?'

'I sincerely doubt it. It's hardly Medmenham Abbey.'

'Or Borley Rectory, for that matter.'

'I'm interested, that's all.' She turned and looked at him. 'It is our home. Surely you want to know all about it, don't you?'

'I know that it's been in the Holland family since it was built. Old Mr Holland's grandfather built it as a wedding present for his son and his new wife. And that's enough for me.'

'Don't be boring, Will.'

'You can investigate to your heart's content, my sweet. Just don't start reciting the Holland family tree. I don't want to know who begat who, thank you. In any case, it'd just go in one ear and out the other.'

'That's fine,' she murmured, gazing out over Whisper Fen. 'This is *my* project.'

She turned and looked up at Holland House as if she and this construction of bricks and mortar had an understanding between them. Will wondered when she had last looked at him like that and experienced a pang of what could only be described as jealousy.

* * *

Matt and Liz returned from a very profitable sortie to the tiny village of Whisper Fen. Emilia wasn't alone in being friendly with Gladys Conway, the local postmistress. Matt, too, was on first-name terms with her, and they learned a lot about Gerald Grove.

They went over what they had learned while preparing supper.

'So now we know why he spends so much time wandering around the marsh. He's a lepidopterist, an expert on moths and butterflies.' Matt lowered two pieces of fillet steak into a pan, which soon began to sizzle.

'And he's studying this area as a hotspot for rare specimens.' Liz was rinsing salad leaves under the tap. 'Maybe Will is wrong about recognising him from before? He might be a bit of a ragbag, but I can't see him falling foul of the law over a few old moths, can you?'

'Ah well.' Matt shrugged. 'You know as well as I do that he could still have a murky past or be hiding dirty secrets, even if he is a scholar.'

'True. And it is also true that no one has had a good word to say about him.'

They'd had a drink in the Silent Coachman, a tiny pub situated midway between Tanners Fen and Whisper Fen. The landlord, along with a few locals had been more than happy to share their views on Grove — and hadn't held back.

Matt laughed. 'I'll say. The entire clientele awarded him the prize for "Rudest Man on the fens."'

Liz put their dinner plates to warm, and sniffed the delicious aroma of peppered steak, while, in another pan, Matt was cooking mushrooms and tomatoes.

'Can you check the oven chips, sweetheart? These won't be too long now.'

Liz looked at the timer. 'Five minutes.'

'Perfect.' He frowned. 'I wish we could have got a sighting of the man himself.'

'Me too,' she said, 'I need to have a picture of him in my head. Still, we have his full address now, which will help us with our background check. I must say, it's a huge bonus that you know so many people around here.'

'Well, I am a local, after all.'

'What are your thoughts on those hostile acts against Emilia?' Liz asked. 'Now you've had time to consider them. Do you think it could possibly be someone with an ancient grudge against Germans?'

Matt sat down at the kitchen table. 'I can't see that being the reason. Sure, there's probably one or two old-timers who still hark back to the war, but why now? Even before Leonard died, the Swains had been living here for donkey's years. Why leave it until now to start hounding her?'

Liz helped herself to mustard. 'That's just what I'm asking myself too. I mean, the war ended in 1945.'

'Supposing while I'm doing my "Bob the Builder" bit tomorrow, you have a chat with Emilia?' Matt said. 'Maybe she hasn't told us everything yet. And if you recall, Will thought that maybe something else was bothering her. See what you can find out.'

'That's my plan. Leave it to me, boss. Meanwhile, I'm still intrigued about what's going on in Holland House. I hate to see our Will looking so edgy. It's not like him at all.'

Matt stopped eating. 'To me, he looked just like he did after they lost their little girl, and when Kate was undergoing treatment. I don't ever want to see them going down that route again.'

They ate on in silence.

* * *

Kate had spent the last part of the afternoon up in her studio but came down for a late supper. When that was finished, they went outside to their vantage point in the garden and sat looking across the saltmarsh.

The sky was still a soft blue, dotted here and there with islands of grey and peach. On the horizon a dark band of night cloud moved slowly across the sky, like a flagship heralding the close of day.

'This is the best time of all,' whispered Kate, and started to hum a haunting tune. Will recognised it as one he often heard coming from her studio late at night while she worked.

Will put his arm around her and held her tightly. 'Rather apt, don't you think?'

'Mmm?'

In a soft, surprisingly melodious voice he sang the familiar lyrics. They told of two people, comfortable in each other's company, looking forward to spending the rest of their lives together, no matter what life threw at them. He stopped, unsure of the next words.

Kate took up the song, until he silenced her with a kiss. 'No more. I seem to think the next bit is sad. Isn't it about something parting them? That's never going to happen.'

'Never,' she echoed.

As a moving-in present, Matt and Liz had given them a wonderful old watercolour depicting a cottage and a mill at sunset on the edge of the marsh. The title was *Dying Light*, and it hung in pride of place above the fireplace in the lounge.

Gazing at the evening sky, Will was reminded of the painting. They touched their glasses together.

'Will?' Kate asked. 'Do you really like it here?'

Her question surprised him. 'Yes, of course I do. Why? Do I give the impression of not liking it?'

'No,' she said softly. 'It's just that I love it so much I'd hate for us to move on again.'

'My darling, after all the hard work we've been putting in, they'll have to carry me out in a wooden box before I uproot from here.'

'Angela worried me rather — all that talk of too much solitude. I hoped that she hadn't put you off the house.'

Will laughed. 'Nothing Angela Lazenby could say about it would influence me in the slightest.'

She took his hand. 'And you don't miss the force too badly?'

'You haven't given me a chance. I work harder now than I ever did at the nick. And it seems you have a lot more in mind.'

Kate was silent for several minutes. 'I'll be doing a lot of the work on the interior myself, Will — wallpapering and painting and the like. It has to be . . .' she seemed to drift off into her own thoughts for a moment, '*exactly* right.'

He held back his quip about her lack of faith in his workmanship and returned to her question about leaving the force. 'As to my early retirement, no, I really, truly, enjoy spending all my days with the one I love. All those scrotes and drunks . . . I can't say I miss them at all, thank you.' He was lying, and she probably knew it, but it sounded as if he meant it. The mention of scrotes brought him round to Gerald Grove. Kate spent hours wandering the sea bank, as did that unsavoury character. 'Kate? There's a man who walks the marsh a lot, he's called Grove. Should you see him, please steer clear. He's not the nicest man in the world.'

'Oh, you mean Gerald. He's no trouble.'

Will took a breath and held it. 'You know him?'

'I've spoken to him a few times. He's studying the wildlife in the area, mainly butterflies and insects. He's quite interesting.'

This didn't sound anything like the man Emilia had mentioned. She had described him as unbelievably rude, an opinion endorsed by Emilia's friend in the Post Office. So why was Grove chatting pleasantly with his wife? 'He really bothers me, sweetheart. I'd appreciate it if you kept your distance.'

Kate pulled a face but promised to give him a wide berth in future, adding that in any case he did smell rather.

Will reminded himself to mention it to Matt and Liz.

* * *

Somewhere around two in the morning, Will awoke to see the dark shadow of his wife slipping silently out of the bedroom. Moments later, he saw the light go on in her studio and heard her sorting through her painting materials.

He was tempted to go in, ask her if she would like a hot drink or something, but fearing her reaction, decided to let her be.

He moved over to her side of the bed and breathed in her special flowery smell. He'd never been able to tell what it was — a mixture of flowers, sea breezes and washing that had been hung out to dry. It was uniquely hers.

He began to drift off to sleep, trying, as he had so many times before, to name the flower that she reminded him of. Lily of the valley? Roses, or sweet peas? Was it lilacs . . . ? He woke up at first light, as Kate slipped in beside him and immediately fell into a deep slumber.

CHAPTER FOUR

On arriving at Holland House, Liz and Matt stood outside for a few moments, taking in the old building and the vista across the fen. Not having been here for a few months, they noticed at once how much work had been done outside. For years during the residence of old lady Holland, the garden, greenhouse and outbuildings had all been neglected. Now Will was doing a heroic job, considering his injuries, in restoring them to their original order.

'Hey, you two! How are you doing?' Will hurried out to join them.

Matt noted that Kate wasn't with him. 'We're fine, Will, thank you. Lovely day again.'

'You've done a really good job here,' said Liz admiringly. 'I hadn't realised you had a proper wishing well. It's beautiful.'

'Seems odd, but that's one of the reasons why this place was so reasonable.' Will went over to it and laid a hand on the rim. 'Did I tell you about the clause Mrs Holland put into the conditions of purchase?'

Matt shook his head. 'No, I don't think you mentioned any clause.'

'Did you ever meet Mrs Holland, Matt?'

'Oh yes, she lived here all the time I was growing up. I remember a strange old lady with pursed lips and beady eyes. We kids stayed well away from this place. Even when she was younger, she was a right tyrant if she caught any of us hanging around. She really did not like children. We called her a witch and invented all sorts of scary stories about her.'

'So, you won't be surprised when I tell you what she built into the sale agreement.' He slapped the brickwork. 'I had to try not to laugh when the estate agent read it out, I really wondered if the old girl was the full ticket. The clause stated that she would not sell to a family. According to her, the house was not suitable for children, and the prospective buyer must be either retired or permanently childless.' He stopped.

Matt and Liz were aware that after her breakdown, Kate and Will had been told that she was in too fragile a condition to even consider adoption. They had been advised to put all thought of having children out of their minds for ever.

'We signed and got a ridiculously good deal.' Will spread out his arms. 'All this, for the price of small three-bed newbuild on an estate. No brainer.'

Liz wrinkled her brow. 'I wonder why she felt so strongly about children.'

'Officially, she considered it dangerous for kids, with the old well, the ancient outbuildings and the treacherous tides that could sweep across the marsh. In truth — and please, keep this to yourself because Kate is unaware of the fact — it probably originated from the fact that her two-year-old daughter had been lost on the marsh. Apparently, one minute the child was playing in the garden, and the next she was gone. The papers were full of it. People suspected murder, abduction, all sorts of theories, but it was almost certain that she got lost and swept away in the tide. Do you remember it, Matt?'

'Of course! Well, not personally, I was too young at the time, but I remember my dad saying there were search parties out all over the area, looking for a missing little one. I'd forgotten that it was Mrs Holland's child.'

'And Kate is unaware of this?' Liz looked concerned. 'How do you think she would react if she did know?'

Will raised his eyebrows. 'Probably very badly.' He looked anxious. 'Mind you, I think she'll find out soon enough. She's started researching the place, and she's bound to dig that one up.'

'Where is she?' Matt asked tentatively. 'Working?'

'Actually, she worked for most of the night. I left her sleeping this morning, but she said she'll be down for lunch.' He shrugged. 'Well, I hope she will, but no promises. She wants to finish her current book as quickly as possible, then spend time redecorating the house.'

They went inside. Matt sniffed the air. 'Hey, what's that? It smells delicious.'

'Spicy chicken and avocado in a tortilla wrap. It's nothing special, but it's one of Kate's favourites. Ten minutes and we're there.'

Matt felt Liz elbow him in the ribs. 'Knocks spots off a Pot Noodle!'

Will looked at them blankly.

Matt laughed. 'Private joke.'

Will poured Liz a glass of wine. 'I'll go and give Kate a call. I hope she hasn't gone back to sleep.'

While he was out of the room, Liz gave Matt a long look. 'He's making a big effort, but he's still edgy as hell.'

Matt nodded. If only Will would drop the pretence and tell them everything that was worrying him, no matter how harrowing.

A few minutes later, Kate came in.

Matt was shocked at her appearance. In just two months, she had lost weight and looked almost gaunt. She was very pale, as if she lived in the dark. She gave them both a hug and said how good it was to see them again, but there was something not right about Kate Stonebridge.

The food was as tasty as it smelt, and Matt took delight in ribbing his old friend about his metamorphosis into Jamie

Oliver. Meanwhile, considering it was supposedly her favourite lunch, Kate ate almost nothing.

Liz tried to draw her out about the illustrations she was working on, but Kate brushed her questions aside. All she wanted to talk about was Holland House and Whisper Fen.

As soon as they had finished, Kate jumped up. 'Liz, could you come and give me some of your thoughts on wallpaper for the dining room? I've got heaps of pattern books but it's not easy to find one that fits this house.'

Matt took advantage of their absence to tell Will about their meeting with Emilia Swain. 'We are calling in after we leave here to fix the lock on her shed. While I'm busy with that, Liz is going to try to find out what else is worrying her.' He lowered his voice. 'We are well in with her, I think. I reckon she's relieved to have someone to talk to. Why don't you ring me later, and I'll update you?'

Will said he would.

'Kate really loves this house, doesn't she?' Matt said.

Will nodded unenthusiastically.

'Is she okay, Will? Only she's lost a lot of weight since we saw her last.'

'She's overdoing it, mate.' Will kept his voice low. 'She's working all hours and sometimes well into the night. She's desperate to finish this book for her publisher, she's working on new paintings of her own, and then there's the house, which seems to be becoming something of an obsession.' He ran a hand through his hair. 'I want it to look good too, of course, but Liz is dead set on it being exactly as it was when Mrs Holland first married. She's sourced wallpaper designs from the thirties, researched paint colours and had them specially mixed, she's even tracked down some authentic fabric for drapes. Hell, Matt, by the time she's finished I'll be living in a museum.'

Matt recalled Liz telling him his home was a museum, then had made it into the lovely place it was now. It seemed that Kate wanted to do the exact opposite.

'Don't you have any say in it, Will? After all, it's your home too.'

Will laughed. 'Sometimes I wonder. Oh, I don't mean that, it's just that she's become so fixated on her idea of Holland House that I don't really feature. She thinks that because I love the property, I'll love what she does with it. End of.' He sighed. 'And she wanders off all over the marsh and the sea bank. She says she's looking for inspiration for her work. Sometimes she's gone for hours.'

'And she's worrying you sick.'

Before Will could answer, they heard Kate and Liz coming back. Will went off to make coffee.

They stayed for another hour or so, until Matt sensed that Kate was growing restless. 'I think we should make a move, guys. It's been really lovely seeing you both again. You must come over to us next week. It's our turn to cook.'

A slight look of irritation passed across Kate's face, but Matt chose to ignore it.

'Yes,' added Liz, 'although I'm not sure we're up to the standard of Master Chef here.' She grinned at Will.

'We'd love to,' said Kate, with a wide, forced smile. 'We certainly mustn't leave it so long next time.'

As Matt and Liz drove down the lane to Emilia Swain's cottage, Liz let out a long low whistle. 'Oh my!'

She said nothing further. She didn't need to.

* * *

Will had just started clearing the dishes and stacking the dishwasher when he saw Kate sitting at the table with a large glass of wine, staring at a wallpaper sample.

'I thought you didn't want a drink, honey,' he said affably, 'or I'd have poured you one.'

She stared at him coldly. 'I changed my mind. There's no law against that, is there?'

'Of course not,' he said carefully. 'Uh, what's the matter, Kate?'

'You really don't get it, do you? Why on earth did you invite *them* round? You know how much I have to do, but you make me waste all this time.'

Will was dumbstruck.

'Oh, don't stand there with your mouth open, for heaven's sake. I just don't have time for people and idle chit-chat right now. I thought you would have realised that. And anyway, sure they were very helpful when we moved in, but they aren't really my kind of people.'

Will suddenly found his voice. 'What on earth do you mean by that? We've spent more time with Matt and Liz than anybody. Hell, you've spent enough hours with Liz in the past, drinking her wine and having girlie days out! They've been damned good friends to us!'

Kate, her back rigid, stared unblinkingly at the heavy book of wallpaper patterns. 'Oh, don't make a song and dance about it, Will. I only said I wasn't that keen on them. I don't have to like all your friends, do I? Now, what do you think of this stripe for the hall and stairs?'

Will turned his back on his wife, stormed out of the house and went to the woodshed.

* * *

Kate came by twenty minutes later. He was still hurling the axe into the big, round logs, reducing them to kindling, and himself to a sweating, gasping, mess.

He knew she was there, but he refused to acknowledge her presence immediately. After a while, he let the axe fall and looked at his wife with hurt in his eyes. 'I'm sorry my friends aren't good enough for you. You never said as much before, so I really wasn't to know, was I?'

'Will, Will, I'm so sorry. I don't know what got into me. There's nothing wrong with Matt and Liz. I love them, really I do. It's me. I'm stressed, and really overtired, I suppose. Forgive me?' She ran to him and held him close, running her fingers through his wet hair.

Will said nothing.

'I panicked.' She paused, while he wondered why. 'I could see us getting into a round of social gatherings again — out for dinner one night, lunch another day . . . I simply can't handle trying to talk to people, pretending to enjoy myself when I just want to be here, making the house special again, and working in the studio. I have to finish Angela's bloody fairies! I need to be rid of them, and their damned Magical Garden of Gort! Then, and only then, can I do some real work.'

He realised that she was crying. Still seething with anger and hurt, he said, 'Shh, it's okay, sweetheart. But you can't go on like this, you know. You have to slow down. This isn't you. And you know as well as I do that Angela's "bloody fairies" have made you — us — a lot of money. You've always loved doing them, so why this change of heart?'

'Because I resent them. They are taking up my precious time. I just want this assignment to be over, so I can get on with what I really want to do.' She sniffed. 'I don't mean to be so horrid to you, but I can't stop myself. I just seem to get so angry.'

'You need sleep, Kate, a whole lot of it.' He released her grip, held her away from him and stared at her. 'You are exhausted. If you don't recharge your batteries, you will crash, and then there will be no work done at all. Now, I'm going to get a shower, and if you want to go to your studio, fine, but no late nights, understand? And then tomorrow we'll try to work out some sort of routine — one that won't kill you.'

She nodded, squeezed his hand and murmured that she was sorry.

Will hung the axe up on its hook, realising that he had done his injured elbow no favours by attacking half the woodstore in a frenzy. Now it was killing him. He trudged back to the house to find painkillers, get a hot shower and continue worrying about Kate.

* * *

While Matt sawed wood for the repairs to the shed door, Liz and Emilia sat in the cottage kitchen.

'I couldn't sleep last night, Liz. I lay awake and came to the conclusion that since you are so kind as to take an interest in me, I really should tell you everything,' Emilia said.

Liz could have punched the air. 'There have been more things?' she asked.

Emilia went to a kitchen drawer, took out an envelope and passed it to Liz. 'Look inside.'

Liz opened the envelope and removed a single sheet of white paper. On it, in black marker pen, were the words, YOU ARE NOT SAFE HERE.

Liz swallowed. This was a real threat. It took the whole thing to a different level. 'When did you get this?' she asked.

'The day before I found my beautiful Heidi dead.' Emilia hung her head. 'It was like they killed her to make sure I understood that they were serious.'

'You really should have gone to the police, Emilia. You must be terrified out here on your own.' Liz didn't mean to frighten her, but she had to appreciate that this was no gang of bored kids. Someone intended her real harm.

'I am not frightened, Liz, but I am very angry.' Emilia sat down in a chair opposite her. 'I have experienced far worse than this, believe me. As I am Jewish, and my family came from Germany . . .' She shrugged. 'You can imagine, can't you? Even though I married an Englishman, my life has not been a bed of roses, I assure you. This makes me livid. I have done nothing to upset anyone. I do not deserve this.'

'Is there anyone you can stay with, just for a while?' Liz asked.

'I will not leave my home. For one thing, they would have free rein to do what they pleased, and for another, I refuse to let them think they have won.'

Emilia set her jaw, and Liz realised that there would be no arguing with her. 'Then, would you mind if I tell one of my old colleagues at Fenfleet police station? As you said before, it's unlikely they can do much to help, but they really should know about this. Maybe the occasional visit out here in a marked car might deter whoever is threatening you.'

'I'd rather you didn't.' Emilia shrugged again. 'I cannot think why anyone would want to do this to me. It doesn't make sense.'

Liz agreed. 'When I was in the police, I came across cases of unscrupulous property developers putting the frighteners on people who refused to sell them their homes or land, but let's face it, no one would want to build out here on the marsh edge.' She rubbed her chin thoughtfully. 'No one has made you an offer for your property, have they?'

'Never. As you said, it's not in a particularly desirable area. Yes, it's beautiful in its way, and I love it, but people want amenities, regular transport, shops, schools . . . We have nothing here other than a tiny post office cum village store, and a pub a mile and a half away.'

'Some people would love it for that very reason.' Liz looked around. 'It's a beautiful home and a spectacular garden, Emilia, and there are people who really do want peace and quiet. I'd hate to have a school and pub next door to my home!'

'But there have been no offers from anyone, I promise you.' Emilia sighed. 'Now I'm wondering what they have in mind for their next little assault.'

Liz didn't want to start speculating. 'We'll show this to Matt as soon as he's finished doing a Tommy Walsh in the garden.' She pointed to the note, the police officer in her observing that the envelope was plain and obviously hand-delivered and was of the self-seal variety that did not require licking the flap down. 'May we keep it, Emilia?'

'With my blessing! It will be a relief to have it out of my home.' Emilia straightened up. 'Now, I think it's time your lovely partner had some tea.'

She went to the fridge for milk, and added, 'Actually I do have to go away quite soon. I have a yearly meeting with my accountant, who is based in London. We are old friends, so I generally go up on a Friday night, stay over and travel back the following Monday morning. The thing is, I'm picking up my new car on Thursday, and I dread leaving it here unprotected while I am away.'

'Then why not leave it with us? We are only a few miles away,' Liz volunteered. 'What car did you choose, Emilia?'

'A Volvo V60 estate. It was love at first sight, and it's not as ostentatious as the Lexus, or one of those super Mustangs.'

Liz's concern escalated. A brand-new car would be a bloody great magnet for anyone wanting to cause Emilia distress. 'Then you really must bring it to Tanners Fen. And while you are here, lock the garage every night without fail.'

'Oh, I will! My timing isn't exactly flawless, is it?' Emilia said ruefully. 'But living here I have to have a reliable vehicle.'

Maybe that banger would not have been such a bad idea after all. A sparkling new Volvo and a person with mischief on their mind didn't mix too well in Liz's book. 'Of course you must. Meanwhile, we really do need to find out who is doing this and stop them, Emilia, so if you see either of us, or our car hanging around, don't concern yourself. We'll be keeping a close eye on you from now on.'

For a moment she thought the "tough old bird" might give way to tears, but Emilia took a deep breath. 'You are very kind, both of you.'

Taking that as an assent to their unofficial investigation, Liz smiled at her. 'Let's go and tell Bob the Builder that he's earned himself a cup of tea — and that we're upping our game.'

CHAPTER FIVE

Will and Kate's argument on the day of Matt and Liz's visit had left a shadow hanging over them. It would take them some time to get over it. For now, they maintained an uneasy truce.

Kate spent a lot of time behind the closed door of her studio, but at least she made the effort to join Will for meals, and to eat more regularly. Will soldiered on with his renovations, while Kate, when not painting, spent the rest of her time walking the marshes, or planning and researching her project for the renovation of Holland House. She seemed to have become stronger, and even helped with the design aspects of the garden.

The following weekend was humid and stormy, but despite this, Kate seemed almost restored to her old self. Will began to relax again. Perhaps the worst had passed?

Initially, they took great delight in watching the jagged forks of lightning zigzagging down into the Wash, but after a while the constant storms became tedious and now Kate was becoming unsettled and irritable again.

She had begun revamping the kitchen and was at the same time trying to oversee his efforts at restoring the Victorian greenhouse *and* get parts of the garden back under control.

'Damn and blast! Bloody weather! Another hour and I could have finished that bed around the well.' Kate flopped down on a kitchen chair and rubbed her hair angrily with a hand towel.

'There is always tomorrow, sweetheart. Don't forget what we said about not pushing yourself too hard. Anyone would think our time here was limited. We have all the time in the world, remember?' Busy with the tea, Will missed the look of annoyance that she threw his way.

'Have you fixed those windows yet, Will? I thought you said the fanlights were almost done.'

'That greenhouse is a nightmare, Kate. Every time I fix one thing, something else falls to bits. I've practically had to rebuild those frames — they're all rotten.'

Kate's tone was tetchy. 'Well, it needs to be weatherproof for the winter. I'm hoping to get some seedlings in before the frosts start.'

'It's not a simple job, Kate. Trying to re-hang window frames with a dodgy arm is not exactly easy, you know.' He tried to keep his tone even, but he had been doing his best, and it rankled that it wasn't appreciated.

'Well, if you're not up to it, then I'll get someone in.'

'I never said I wouldn't finish it, did I? I meant don't push me. It's not a simple job.' He went silent. Kate, apparently realising that she had been, in his words, out of order, took the mug of tea from him and ruffled his hair.

'Sorry, Bear.'

He smiled. She hadn't used his pet name for ages. When they first met — on a fun run to raise money for a local children's hospice — he had been dressed as a teddy bear. He had nearly expired beneath the heavy costume, and Kate had given him a cold drink. He became her Bear from that day forth.

'I know. I'm being a total pain in the bum.' She sat down again and looked at him. 'I just want everything *right*, and there just don't seem to be enough hours in the day.'

'Is it the book? Are you behind with the illustrations?' he asked tentatively.

'No. In fact, because I'd done so many sketches, and because they want to use my original paintings as the plates, I'm well ahead with Angela's bloody book.' She gave him an apologetic grin. 'I know I promised to slow down but I want the damn thing finished, so I have been pushing it a bit.' She paused. 'I have also told Hubert I need a break before the next one and, joy of joys, he reckons Angela's nowhere near ready yet. If she's got writer's block, that's fine with me. Long may it last.'

Will looked anxiously at his wife. She was suddenly edgy and bad-tempered, "mardy-faced," as his mum would have said. He feared that she was going to slip back into her unpredictable frame of mind again, where he no longer recognised his lovely wife.

'Actually, talking about getting someone in to help us,' Kate's voice was suddenly soft and back to normal, 'I want to have a word with the builders' merchants just outside town about some more gravel for the side entrance to the garage, and I was thinking of getting some of those circular paving stones for the patio. The concrete is breaking up badly. One of us will fracture an ankle before long.'

Will groaned. 'That sounds like pretty hard and heavy work for me and my wonky arm.'

'I have no intention of letting you do the patio, Bear. I thought I'd see if one of the workmen at the builders' yard might like to earn himself a few pounds. The old rubble would have to be taken up and carted away before the new stones could be laid, and your arm wouldn't stand up to it. Hopefully, I should be receiving a nice fat cheque in the post soon, so we'll let someone else get a hernia — if that's alright with you?'

'I'll say it is. If you are okay about spending the cash, let's save me and my arm for more meaningful tasks.' He was relieved, but also concerned about some cowboy turning up and charging them a fortune for a crap job. However, this wasn't the time to mention it. Her good mood seemed to have returned, and he wanted it to continue. He smiled.

'Let's take the rest of the day off. It's still early. We can go and see your builders' merchant, then, if the weather clears, drive up to Gibraltar Point for a walk in the sea air. Or what about lunch in Stamford, nose around the shops, then on to Rutland Water?'

She didn't answer him.

'Okay, then what about a wander around some garden centres, get some of the plants you want for the garden, then go on to Skeggie? I'll buy you a candy floss if you're good.'

A smile slowly crept across her face. 'And a plate of cockles?'

'Deal!'

* * *

The day out did them both good, and by nightfall they were relaxed and happy.

Kate seemed to have left behind her mission to be rid of Angela's fairies and had got some of her projects into a better perspective. She had spoken to someone at the builders' yard, who had said he would call the following morning.

Will found some citronella candles and they took them out to the garden. They sat together on the seat overlooking Whisper Fen, beneath a sky filled with a million stars, sipping glasses of Sancerre. All the recent worries and tantrums seemed to have slipped away, leaving them peaceful and at ease.

'This is beautiful,' Kate breathed softly. 'I wonder if old Mrs Holland used to sit out here and watch the night sky over the marshes? I bet she misses all this now she's in a nursing home.'

Will looked doubtful. 'It was her home all her life, but I don't suppose she had much love for the marshes.' As soon as he'd uttered them, he regretted his words.

'Why? To have lived here all that time surely you'd have to love it?'

A tiny stream of disquiet trickled between his shoulder blades. He hadn't intended to mention the missing child.

'I heard there was a bit of a family tragedy years ago.' He glanced towards the fen. 'Someone got lost out there.'

'You never said! How come I don't know about it? Come on, you tight-lipped copper, spill the beans.' Her tone was still light, however. Will knew that the story would come out sometime, so maybe it was best that it came from him. He told her what he knew about the child who had gone missing.

She stared into her glass, watching the candlelight glimmer in the pale sparkling liquid and said quietly, 'So her daughter died out there. No wonder the old lady didn't want children around.'

'She disappeared, Kate. There is a difference. They never found her. It is supposition that she died.'

'All that rigmarole about the well and the dangerous outbuildings was a cover. Her real worry was the fen.'

'I should think so.'

'Whatever, she was right. This place isn't suitable for children. In fact, I don't think Holland House likes children at all.'

Will was well aware of how sensitive Kate was, but her words caused him to shiver. How could a house — mere bricks and mortar — have feelings? He was a down-to-earth plod, and such fancies were beyond his comprehension. He admired her fairy paintings but to him, they were nothing more than play. He changed the subject quickly. Sometimes her odd fancies gave him the creeps.

'Have you seen that weird guy Grove again? You know, the stinky bloke that lives in that ramshackle old cottage down by the sluice?'

She raised an eyebrow, evidently amused at his too obvious change of tack. 'Once, although I hadn't meant to after you warned me about him.' She looked at him enquiringly. 'Are you sure you're right about him, Will? Sure, he's not very chatty, but he does love the marsh. And there's nothing he doesn't know about all the birds that pass through here, even though he doesn't come from this area.'

Though annoyed that she had ignored his warning, Will was loath to spoil their peaceful evening. 'You found out quite a bit from someone who doesn't say much. I could have done with you as my snout when I was working.'

They fell into a companionable silence. After a while, Will asked Kate to point out some of the constellations to him. He could never remember them. He enjoyed his beautiful wife's enthusiasm as she pointed them out.

'There's Cassiopeia. See that "W" shape to the left of the cottage chimney? And that's Orion, the Hunter, with his belt and sword. That really bright star in the belt is Rigel, it's a blue-white supergiant. The other slightly less bright one is Betelgeuse — that's a red supergiant.'

As she continued to point out her favourites, telling him their names and their impossible sizes and distances from Earth, his eyelids began to droop.

'I love you,' he said. 'You're my brightest star, brighter than all of these.'

'Thank you, my Bear. I love you too.'

* * *

The night wind sent a cooling breath over their naked bodies. They lay on top of the bed, entwined.

As he drifted down into sleep, Will heard her ask, 'Do you think she had any other children, or just the one, the one who died?'

Not wanting to answer, he pretended to fall asleep, real sleep following soon after.

* * *

The following morning, Will rolled over and reached for her, only to find a cold empty space beside him. He struggled up against the pillows and tried to massage a bit of life back into his aching right arm. He peered at the clock radio whose green digital numbers proclaimed it to be six thirty-five, so he flopped back down again.

For the whole of the previous week, Kate had adhered to their new regime. They enjoyed a morning snuggle at around seven o'clock, then they made tea and drank it in bed, planning the day ahead before they got up and showered. Today, though, she was back in her studio, and more than likely trying to make up for lost time.

Out in the garden, Will had been working for an hour or so when he heard the growl of an engine. He put down his hammer and saw an old battered white lorry pull up a few yards from their drive. His eyes narrowed. Everything about the vehicle shouted "cowboy." It might just as well have been a covered wagon. Will was relieved not to have gone out this morning. This was not the first time he had had to save his wife from being ripped off.

He set off down the garden, but Kate was already coming out of the front door.

'So glad you made it,' she exclaimed happily. She turned to Will and called out, 'This is Barry, darling.'

The young man extended a hand and bestowed a friendly smile on Will. 'Pleased to meet you, sir. Nice 'ouse you have 'ere. Your wife said you've not bin 'ere long?'

His accent declared him to be a fens man, and he had a surprisingly pleasant voice.

'Yes, we lived in Fenfleet before,' Will said.

They went around to the back of the house.

'So, Barry, what do you think of our dilapidated patio then?' he asked.

'Shouldn't be too difficult to get it up, sir — it's pretty crumbly to start with. We'd get a skip in to take away the 'ardcore but use a bit of it for the base of the new patio, that'd keep the cost down.' He looked at Kate. 'Yesterday you said you wanted the job done asap, Mrs Stonebridge. Well, we are really booked up for at least the next two months . . .'

Kate's face fell.

'But,' he continued, 'if the estimate is acceptable and you wouldn't mind a lot of noise pretty early in the morning, we could start tomorrow. Thing is, I'd booked a couple of extra chaps for a big landscaping contract over Wainfleet way, but there's a two-week hold-up on it, so rather than put them off—'

'Excellent. We don't mind at all, do we, darling?' She left no room for Will to reply. Kate was in full flow. 'That's perfect. Well, we'll let you get on with the estimate. Will you need to send it to us? Could you just tell us, so as to save time?'

Will took her gently by the arm and led her towards the house. 'Barry will want to check the price of materials, sweetheart. Let's leave him to it, and not rush him, shall we?'

The young man nodded and began taking measurements.

Back in the house Kate was buzzing with excitement. 'Wow! What luck that they have a cancellation!'

'Babe,' Will said, 'they probably *always* have a cancellation. It's how they work.'

'Cynic. I'm just pleased that they can start so soon.'

'You haven't even seen the quote yet. Perhaps we should get more than one. Don't get ahead of yourself.'

He had hardly got the words out when Kate turned on him. 'I want that work done, and I want it done soon. If the estimate is even halfway fair, I'm going to let them start tomorrow morning.'

'What the hell has got into you, Kate? We used to discuss things. Now all the decisions seem to be made between you and the bloody house. What about me? What on earth is all the hurry for?'

'Because it needs doing, and if I wait for you, we'll still be dithering around at Christmas.'

'Kate! We are arguing again. We *never* argued before we came here.' His voice trembled and tears welled up in his eyes.

'Oh right! You're going to blame the house for everything that goes wrong, are you?'

'If I think it's to blame, then yes,' he said.

'Well, I suggest you don't.' She spat the words at him. 'It has nothing to do with the house.'

'Then what is it?'

She stuttered, searching for words. 'It's, it's . . . oh!' She ran from the room. He heard her steps on the stairs, and a door slammed. Once again, she was in her studio.

He pictured her sitting on the window seat looking out over Whisper Fen. He desperately wanted to go to her, to hold her close. He wanted to bury his face in her sweet-smelling hair and breathe her fresh, clean scent. He wanted things to be as they had been before they came to this beautiful, lonely place.

He held his head in his hands.

A voice from the back garden called his name. He swallowed hard and went out to Barry.

'Thank you for giving me a bit of breathing space, sir. I do need to price this up properly back at the office. Your wife is really keen to get it done yesterday, isn't she?'

Will managed a forced laugh. 'You do what you have to. Don't let her rush you.'

'I'll get it done by four and give you a ring, if I may? These chaps I've got on 'old, they'll be wantin' to know. Must be pretty grim, not knowing if you've got money coming in or not.'

Will nodded. The guy actually seemed honest. 'I know I sound like my wife, but any rough idea on a price? I promise not to hold you to it.'

The man rubbed his chin. 'Off the top of my 'ead? Somewhere in the region of a grand, say one thousand two hundred tops. I get the materials at trade price, and I'll pass that on to you.'

Will remembered one of his mates at the station paying far more than that for a patio area the year before. A skip alone cost over a hundred pounds.

'Look, if the estimate comes out near that figure, you can go ahead. My wife seems to have set her heart on getting this done. If it's a lot more, perhaps we may have to think again, but—'

'It shouldn't be more, Mr Stonebridge. That was my outside cost, but I'll ring you later.' He glanced at his watch. 'Gawd! I 'ave to go! The lorry is my uncle's. My own truck is in dock and I've pinched his vehicle for the morning. 'E'll kill me if he don't 'ave it back by dinner time. Thank you for the possible business. I'll ring you later.'

Watching the old lorry disappear in a cloud of dust, Will stood wondering what to do. He looked up at Kate's window but there was no one there.

He went inside, climbed the stairs, and stood outside her room. He called her name softly, hesitantly.

She bade him come in. Her back was to him, and she was frantically sketching. As he approached her, she closed her pad and turned to him, wearing a strange smile.

'Hello, Bear. What do you fancy for dinner tonight? I'll cook.'

* * *

Liz threw down her pen and looked at Matt. 'Gerald Grove *does* have a skeleton in his cupboard! I knew it!'

When they weren't watching over Emilia Swain, they had spent the past week making covert enquiries into the man that Will had found so troubling. Now, after exchanging countless emails with the West Country, Liz had finally found what she'd been looking for. 'He was involved in an investigation regarding a boy of nine who was abducted.' She read from the printout that was just coming through. 'Grove lived in a village on Exmoor, and he fell under suspicion because he'd been in a spot of trouble a while before this case. It was peeping-Tom activities, nothing he could be nicked for, but because of it, he was questioned on suspicion of abducting the lad.'

Matt whistled. 'So, our Will's copper's nose was spot on.'

'Well, even if he was innocent, and no one seems to think he was, as a peeping Tom he's certainly not Snow White.' She referred to the printout. 'The boy turned up alive and unharmed. He said he'd got lost on the moor, spent a couple of days in an old barn. He also swore that Grove had nothing to do with it, but a badge that the kid always wore was found in Grove's cottage. Grove said children were always calling in so he could identify butterflies and moths they found, and he could have dropped it on one of those visits. As the boy denied having been abducted, there was nothing to hold Grove for, and there was no charge to answer. But the detectives on the case were certain that the kid had not been holed up in any barn. They also thought Grove was lying through his teeth.'

'How did you get hold of all this?' Matt asked.

'I found a journalist who had been following the police inquiry into the missing boy. Nice bloke, very helpful. He coughed it all up on the understanding that if Grove steps out of line down here, I give him the lowdown.' Liz grinned. 'And I'd be very pleased to do that, should Grove turn naughty on us.'

'But so far he hasn't done anything on this patch, or as far as we can ascertain,' Matt said thoughtfully.

'Apart from be rude to everyone, nothing.'

'Everyone except for Kate Stonebridge, according to Will.' Matt sat down and crossed his legs. 'Will said she met him while she was walking up on the sea bank. She said he was perfectly fine with her and told her about the wildlife and the birds.'

Liz wrinkled her brow. 'That's worrying. I hope Will told her to steer well clear.'

'In no uncertain terms, apparently. Kate said she would, mainly because the man smelt.' He rolled his eyes in disgust. 'At least we've seen him for ourselves now, thanks to our little snout the postmistress letting us know when he collected his magazines from her. I can't wait to tell Will what you've dug up.'

'And tell him to make sure Kate understands that Grove is not to be trusted.' Liz sat back. 'Any luck with talking Emilia into getting a surveillance camera installed at Little Anchor?'

Matt shook his head. 'She still says it reminds her of bad times — and the stories her parents told her of being watched and spied on. I can't push her too hard, we don't know what she's been through in the past, but I won't give up trying.'

'Shame,' said Liz. 'I know whoever it is has gone quiet, but I'm sure they haven't finished with our Emilia yet.'

Matt nodded. He felt the same. The question was, what had they in mind for next time?

CHAPTER SIX

The week had been a series of ups and downs for Will and Kate. In the main she had been a bit calmer. Barry and his workers had started work on the patio, and as it turned out, he had proved to be the exception to the rule. Will was obliged to admit that he and his workers had done an excellent job for a very reasonable price. So much so that, as Barry's next job had been held up yet again, they had begun clearing an overgrown area to the back of the well, with a view to constructing a series of small terraces and a pond. It was actually quite reassuring to see them working outside. Having them there made the place feel kind of normal, and they were certainly working far faster than him. Even better, it clearly pleased Kate.

Even so, despite the good days, Kate oscillated between being the loving woman he had married and a preoccupied, impatient and bad-tempered stranger. Her mood swings left him tired, unhappy and unable to sleep.

Kate's sleep patterns had altered too. More often than not she would rise in the dead of night and spend hours in her studio, and she never volunteered to show her husband the fruits of her labours.

Once, after constant requests from him, she produced a finished image. It was powerful and cleverly painted, but it lacked the fine detail that normally characterised her work. It was shadowy and somehow frightening. It showed some kind of underground dweller, a troll-like being crouched at the entrance to his cavern and looking out suspiciously. He was depicted slightly turned to one side so that you saw his deformed back. Outside the cave, like a window looking into the light, was a mountain meadow. That was sunlit and colourful but it only occupied a small portion of the painting. It seemed to Will as if this glimpse of a meadow was the only part of the picture that Kate had painted, the rest being the work of someone else. That other artist was undoubtedly brilliant, but sinister.

She refused to show him anything else, which made him wonder anxiously what the other paintings might be like. Will longed to talk to Matt and Liz about Kate, but he felt that this would be a betrayal. He was sure she was deeply depressed. He recalled the breakdown she had suffered following the loss of their child. It was some time ago now, but still she found it impossible to talk about the baby.

Little Emma Stonebridge had lived for one day. Kate had haemorrhaged so badly after the birth that they thought they would lose her too. But she survived, coming out of it minus her torn and damaged womb. The shock of losing Emma before she could even hold her, and then discovering that she could bear no more children, had pushed her one heartbreak too far. It had been a long road back for them both.

Matt and Liz knew the bare bones of what had happened, but Will had never gone into detail about the full extent of Kate's emotional disorder.

Now Kate seemed to be operating in overdrive, working all night in her studio and decorating by day. She accomplished miracles. Along with her reluctant workhorse, Will, she painted and papered, bringing the old house back to its former splendour. Will's more relaxed routine long abandoned, she even found time for longer walks on the marshes and the sea bank, sometimes disappearing for hours at a time.

Will could only watch in horror, waiting for the inevitable crash.

On this particular day he was carrying some empty paint cans to the garage when he heard someone call out to him.

'Sorry to bother you, Mr Stonebridge. Have you got a moment, sir?' Barry's foreman, an older man called Neville, was coming towards him along the drive.

As he went out to meet him, Will experienced an odd disquiet. His gut began to churn, as it had when he was still in the force, a sure sign that something was not right.

'You know that natural bit of higher ground behind the well — the mound we cleared last week and planned on cutting the terraces out of?'

Will nodded.

'It's not actually natural at all, sir. It's an old air-raid shelter, left over from the war. We don't rightly know what to do now, sir. Would you come and take a look at it?'

He and Kate had often wondered about that piece of raised ground. Lincolnshire gardens were predominantly flat. In the end they had decided that it must just be old topsoil piled up and ready for a job that never got done. Weeds and brambles had covered it completely.

'Well, I'm damned!'

'It's built a bit like an Anderson shelter, dug down into the ground and with them curved sheets of corrugated iron over the top. I remember playing in the one my gran had — she lived in the East End of London during the blitz and used her shelter as a sort of garden shed for donkey's years. Good fun for a kid, too. My brothers and I used to love it.' Neville chuckled.

'I am surprised there's one on the fens,' Will said. 'London certainly, but out here?'

'Well, Greenborough's not far away, that was considered a prime target — East Coast port, you know, and this *is* Bomber County, Mr Stonebridge. The Lancasters flew out of here every night on their missions. Didn't yer dad tell yer about 'em?'

But Will's dad had died when he and his younger sister, Eva, were kids.

Neville, well up on his local history, went on to tell Will about the thousands of evacuees who had poured into the rural villages after war was declared. Will had to stop him after a while and bring him back to the matter in hand. 'So, is it intact?'

'Dunno yet, sir. Thought you better see it first. It has a proper solid door, which is a bit unusual. Lots of folk used to just hang a curtain up — doors meant no air and would have made it pretty uncomfortable. Our young Steve is still digging down to get it free.'

A young man with a selection of colourful tattoos and a shovel was moving great heaps of rich soil away from the old, damp wood. Sweat glistened off a ferocious-looking tiger and dripped across the heart-encircled *Mandy*.

'Nearly there.' He raked away some loose earth and threw his spade down with a gasp. ''Ot work, an' no mistake.'

'Open her up, Steve, and I'll get you a cold beer,' Will called out.

The lad dragged on the old door. It opened with a squeal, and the three men peered in.

As their eyes adjusted to the gloom, they made out two beds at either side of the shelter, with a small wooden table in between. A rickety bookcase stood just inside the door with a rusty bucket next to it. The bedclothes had long gone, but a hurricane lamp still stood on the table alongside a tin box, and when Will prised it open, he found a pack of dog-eared playing cards and a mildewed prayer book.

No one spoke for a moment. Just as Will was about to make a comment, he looked back and saw his wife standing behind them. She looked gaunt, deathly pale.

She was staring past them into the shelter.

Slowly, as if in a trance, she moved forward between them. Then Will saw what she was looking at.

On the roughly constructed duckboard floor lay a toy, a handmade rag doll with scrappy woollen hair and an embroidered face. It was filthy.

With something like reverence, Kate picked it up, tried to smooth its tattered and dirt-stained smock and, holding it like a baby, turned and walked away.

The workmen looked at each other uncomfortably. Unable to offer an explanation for his wife's odd behaviour, Will turned and ran after her.

She had gone to her studio, of course, and he dared not follow her in.

He stood on the landing, unsure of what to do. No sound came from behind the door, but he knew she was in there. He called her name, softly at first, then a little louder, but she did not reply.

He wanted to beat on the door, kick it in if necessary. Drag her out and scream at her to pull herself together. But he stood where he was, mute and powerless to act.

After a while, he returned to the garden with a can of lager for each of the men. He had nothing to say about Kate's behaviour, but he didn't want the village hearing that the woman at Holland House was crazy, so he mumbled something about her being very overtired after completing a gruelling assignment, and working so many late nights had stressed her out a bit. Then he attempted to turn their attention back to their rather strange find.

Neville said that the air-raid shelter was set low in the ground with an awful lot of soil heaped on top of it. They could still continue with their original design, or they could pull the whole thing out and get rid of it. What did he think?

To Will, there was no question. Get rid of it. It was a sad reminder of a horrible and frightening time. For a moment, he heard the drone of the enemy bombers and saw the flashes as the baskets of incendiaries fell. He heard screaming.

He shook himself. This was not like him. Heavens, when he was born the war was just a memory. While realising that Kate was not going to be happy with a decision concerning her precious Holland House that she had not been privy to, he told the men to rip it out and get shot of it.

Neville glanced skywards and said it looked as if it would have to be a job for the following day. Great boiling black clouds had gathered, and before the men could collect up their tools and run for cover, a violent storm had descended upon them.

Will shouted that he would see them the following day, but his words were lost in the wind. By the time he reached the kitchen, his clothes were soaked, and water was streaming from him on to the tiled floor. He ran to their bedroom, stripped off his wet clothes and towelled himself down. Wearing a dry sweatshirt and joggers, he went back out on to the landing.

'Kate. Darling, come out and talk to me. Please.'

The silence ate into him. He wanted to scream, to break something. But instead he slipped slowly down the wall until he was sitting outside her door. 'Kate, I'm staying here until you come out. If it takes a week, fine, I'll still be here.'

Some ten minutes later he heard footsteps moving towards the door. He listened to the bolt being drawn back. His wife came out. She stared down at him, frowning. 'You look pretty silly sitting there, Will. Let's go and have some tea, shall we?'

She began to walk away from him. 'And there will be no talk of getting rid of the shelter. It stays. Understand? Now, tea or coffee?'

* * *

The shelter stayed.

Will looked down from the bedroom window, where he was busy fitting a sash cord. He couldn't forget those glassy, unblinking eyes and the expression on his wife's face when she had said, 'Understand?' He shuddered whenever it came back to him.

Now, the shelter was covered with fresh soil, which Kate had planted with a carpet of late summer flowers.

'Just as it was. That's how it should be.' She had spent a morning clearing it out. She'd brushed dirt from the floor, rust from the metalwork, rubbed down the old woodwork and oiled the creaking hinges. She had refused his help on the grounds that if he were prepared to destroy it in the first place, he had no reason to assist her in its restoration.

He had been in touch with Matt and Liz during the days since the discovery of the shelter. He sensed that they knew something was terribly wrong, but he hadn't had the heart to talk to them. On one occasion they had called in to tell him that he had been right about Gerald Grove, and Kate had made a brief appearance. They had barely been able to disguise their shock.

Yesterday he had gone to their new GP on the pretext of needing stronger painkillers. He had gone fully intending to ask the doctor for help with his troubled wife, but once he was seated in the slightly shabby surgery, he had found himself incapable of discussing her. He couldn't do it. He couldn't betray her.

He tightened the sash cord and tested it.

They had come through it before and would do so again. Their love for each other would sustain them. He had recently discovered that the nicer he was to the house, the more he did, even the smallest of chores, the better Kate's mood became. Thus, he continued to busy himself with useful jobs.

Two things did disturb him, however, and one of these was the doll.

A few evenings ago, Kate had been working in her room when she suddenly went off to the bathroom, leaving her door wide open. Will had taken the opportunity to snatch a glance inside, in the hopes of seeing something of her latest painting. All he had seen were covered benches and, to his surprise, sitting on the long window seat looking blindly out over Whisper Fen, the doll from the air-raid shelter. Not filthy as it had been, but freshly washed, its woollen braids carefully untangled and its smock neatly ironed. He had hurried into their bedroom, where he had sat on the bed feeling slightly queasy. She had even re-stitched the face. It was just a hasty glance but long enough to see it. His wife had cleverly embroidered it in such a way that instead of the usual blank face, it wore a very adult expression — the rather too full lips were now twisted into a sort of sneer. Surely, he reasoned, it had to be a trick of the light, but for a second, he had seen something distinctly corrupt about that face. And worse, it immediately brought Gerald Grove to mind.

Then there were Kate's occasional excursions. She had made it abundantly clear that he was not welcome on these trips, which she said were either research for her paintings, or to look for items she needed for the restoration of the house.

She was out again now, but this time he was slightly less anxious. The following day was his birthday, and Kate was good at birthdays. She knew that he was a big kid where birthdays were concerned and without fail, she made his day one to remember. He recalled the time she had treated him to a trip in a hot-air balloon. It was unforgettable. Even if she was embroiled with Holland House, Kate would have thought of something special for him. She always did.

He gathered up his tools and went downstairs. Maybe this was a good time to ring Matt and ask if they could meet up. His anxiety was becoming too much to bear. But maybe he should just take a look at her latest paintings before ringing his friend, so he had something more concrete to tell him.

Slowly, he mounted the stairs and stood in front of the studio door. Kate's studio had been a medium-sized bedroom that she had chosen for its unusual window and the uninterrupted view over the marsh.

The lock was old and stiff. He would never be able to pick it. The only way in was from the outside. He knew the long floor-to-ceiling window did not open, but there was a smaller window next to it with a sill. He had noticed earlier that it was on the latch.

Looking up, he remembered promising to clean the windows this week. Now seemed an excellent time to start.

From his vantage point at the top of the ladder, he looked out at Whisper Fen. Here and there the sun, reflected off the dark waters of the lagoons, produced stars that flashed and sparkled. A line of seabirds flew into the marsh on silent wings. How beautiful their new home was. If it weren't for Kate's obsession with the place, it would indeed be a perfect place to live. With a sigh, he turned his back on the view and began to clean the window.

Once that was done, he pulled the side window open and stepped in over the sill, keeping his gaze away from the doll. Kate's studio looked as it always did, tidy and orderly. Her brushes were all clean and arranged in pots according to size. Fresh pads, books and boards were stacked neatly under the benches and her workbench was clear.

But there were a tremendous number of finished canvases stacked with their faces turned towards the wall. Glancing back out of the window, Will pulled round the first one to face him.

He gasped.

It was horrible. Staring back at him was a dark form, indistinct except for a pair of pale hollow eyes with yellow irises. It seemed to be leaving a cellar by way of some steep and rotting stairs. Will swallowed hard. Beneath its arm, tucked in close and almost hidden in its pitchy vestments, it carried a child. All that could be seen of it was a white arm and hand, chubby fingers grasping a teddy bear, and a slight glint from a lock of golden hair that fell over the partially concealed shoulder.

Where did this nightmare of a painting come from? Will thought of Kate's fairy pictures — so full of light, vivid with life and colour. Now this monstrosity, oozing decay and evil intent. What was going on in her mind?

With a beating heart and full of trepidation, he began to take out the others. They were all similar to that first one, and each featured a dead child.

He ran back to the window and climbed out. As he placed a shaking foot on to the first rung of his ladder, he caught sight of the doll. The face, even in the sunlight, wore a sneer, as if it watched him in secret amusement. That look chilled Will to the marrow.

He hurriedly descended the ladder and sat down heavily on the seat that overlooked the fen. The scene had lost its magic. All at once, it had a sinister quality. His wife had told him that she could think better out in the desolate marsh. Well, now he knew what those thoughts were about, and he shuddered.

He had just half risen to go and ring Matt and Liz when he saw Kate's car swing round the bend in the lane. Wondering how he was going to face her, he realised that she had stopped the car in the tiny layby where the rough path out to the sluice and the far end of Tylers Lane branched off.

Someone got out of the passenger seat, and to his horror the unmistakable figure of Gerald Grove slammed the door and made its way out on to Whisper Fen.

Will's fear and concern for Kate turned to anger. He had warned her to stay away from Grove, and now she was giving him lifts. It was the final straw.

Seething, he strode towards the car, but his anger melted when he saw her get out. She looked as ghostly as one of her pictures. For the first time, he noticed that she had lost so much weight that her clothes no longer fitted her. She looked at him through dark-rimmed eyes and said forlornly that her trip had not gone well, and please would he make her a cup of tea?

So, without saying a word about her passenger, he took her bags and went inside to boil a kettle.

Kate sat with her fingers wrapped round her mug of tea, tears slowly running down her face. He put his arm around her, and she looked up at him pathetically.

'There was another child, you know. Another Holland child died here.'

His initial reaction was to shout, shake her out of this nonsense. Instead, he drew his chair closer and calmly asked her to tell him about it.

'She fell into the well. She used to sit on the wooden cover, which was perfectly strong, so no one ever considered it a dangerous thing to do. Well, one day it gave way under her — or so everyone believed. She was alone at the time, so no one saw what actually happened.'

'How do you know all this, sweetheart?' Will asked, keeping his voice steady.

'I went to see Mrs Holland today, in the nursing home. I had to. I had to know more about Whisper Fen. It has secrets, Will, and we should know what they are. Otherwise they could be dangerous, especially to the people around us.'

It had never crossed Will's mind that Kate would visit the old woman. 'How do you mean, Kate? What danger?'

'Children have no place here, Will. That's all. You have friends at the police station with children. They mustn't ever come here, never.'

Once more Will was tempted to shake her. Knowing that this would only drive her away from him, he assented to what she had said. He had no idea how to deal with this. He had to talk to Matt.

Having told him, she seemed much calmer. She went on to tell him that the child had been seven, a tomboy. Her name was Ruth, the only daughter of Mrs Holland's sister. After a while, he saw her eyelids drooping. She was fighting off sleep.

'Right, Mrs Stonebridge, you are going upstairs, to spend the rest of the afternoon in bed. Look at you, you're exhausted.'

Kate got to her feet wearily. 'Come up with me.'

He took her up to the bedroom and watched her undress. She flopped down on to the bed and slept almost immediately.

Will pulled the curtains, shut the door and tiptoed down the stairs. Outside in the garden, he sat beneath the rowan tree and pulled out his mobile phone. It rang, startling him.

'Will, I'm not sure how you're fixed, what with Kate and all that, but I am down at Emilia Swain's cottage. There's something here you really need to see,' Matt said.

'On my way, Matt. See you in five.'

* * *

Knowing that Kate would probably sleep for hours, Will locked up and jogged down the lane. As soon as he got closer to Emilia's cottage, he saw why Matt had called.

Emilia's garden had been wrecked, her precious plants ripped from the soil and trampled. The runner bean sticks had been torn down and snapped in pieces. Even the trees had not escaped the carnage — the lower branches had been snapped off and left to sway in the breeze. Petals from Emilia's bright flowers lay bruised, trampled to shreds in the mud.

Will stood for a few moments, staring in horror, until Matt came up and stood at his shoulder. 'Where is Emilia?' he said.

'With Liz, back at Cannon Farm. She's naturally terribly upset, so we took her out of the way. I rang it in as soon as we saw it. It's gone too far now.' Matt stared around. 'This is more than mindless thuggery, isn't it?'

Will looked at a big terracotta pot, shattered, and the damp potting compost spread over the broken remains of the flowering shrub that had been growing in it. 'Definitely. Tell me, has Emilia had any more of those threatening notes?'

Matt shook his head. 'No, and it's been quiet all week. Liz and I have been keeping a pretty close eye on the place. We were just beginning to think the bastards had called it a day when this happens.' He exhaled and shook his head angrily. 'That poor woman. She was away for a couple of nights — left her car with us — and came back to find her beautiful garden totally trashed. I feel responsible, Will. We said we'd watch the place and we failed her.'

'It's not your fault, Matt. You could hardly camp out in the garden. She's my next-door neighbour — you'd have thought we would have heard something, given the damage they did.' Will pointed to Emilia's cold frame. The vandal had picked up a heavy stone bird bath and hurled it into the glass lid of the frame, smashing the glass and buckling the metal framework.

'Next-door neighbour, but certainly not close. You can't even see Little Anchor from your house.' Matt shook his head. 'No, we let her down, and I'm damned well going to see to it that whoever did this faces a bloody judge.'

Will had never seen Matt so upset. 'What time did you come out here last night?' he asked.

'Around nine, and then again just after midnight. We even waited a while, about half an hour, but the place was deserted and quiet. I'm guessing this was done just before dawn.' He bent down and picked up the broken branch of some flowering shrub. 'Look, it's a recent break. The stem is still oozing sap.'

Kate must have driven past on her way to the town. She had to have noticed it. So why didn't she stop and ring him, or come back to the house and tell him herself? You couldn't not notice, the old woman's garden looked like a warzone.

He heard a car approaching. 'We have company.'

Matt nodded. 'DC Bryn Owen. We are honoured — we have a detective, no less!'

Will smiled. 'I'm not surprised, considering it was Fenfleet's former DCI who rang them.'

Bryn greeted his old boss warmly. 'Didn't expect to see you again so soon, sir. How are you?'

Matt accepted the outstretched hand. 'I'm fine, Bryn, and it's not "sir" any more. I'm just plain Matt now.'

'Sorry, but you'll always be the guv'nor to me.' The young Welshman looked around. 'Good Lord! What on earth happened here? A runaway JCB?'

'No, lad,' Matt growled. 'Some vindictive little bastard, and I can't wait to lay my hands on him.'

'Okay, what's the background?' Bryn took out his detective's notebook.

Matt told him everything that had happened.

Bryn pulled a face. 'Any ideas? You two know her. Has she said anything to give you some clue as to what is going on?'

Matt shrugged. 'We actually don't know her that well. She seems like a strong and capable woman. She keeps her place nice and her garden was a work of art.' He grimaced. 'Was.'

‘You said she’s foreign. Where is she from?’

‘Her parents were German Jews, but she’s lived in Lincolnshire most of her life, so I’d say she counts as a local by now. She hasn’t spoken much about her parents, or her childhood. I had some dealings with her late husband when his business was broken into, and he intimated that her father was on our side during the war.’

Bryn absentmindedly picked up the overturned bird table. ‘Doesn’t sound as if it’s an anti-German thing, then. The war’s been over a long time now. Mind you, I do know that the Nottingham police have been having a bit of trouble recently with some really nasty fascist group targeting people with Jewish connections. It’s unlikely but I’d hate to think they had a cell in our area. In any case, I think it would be a good idea if she went to stay with someone for a while. This has been done with considerable venom, and if they could slit the cat’s throat . . .’ Bryn pulled a face. ‘That’s gross.’

‘I totally agree, but even though she’s upset right now, getting her to move out could be tricky,’ Will ventured.

‘And another thing,’ added Matt. ‘She owns a brand new Volvo, less than a week old.’

‘Oh shit, sir. I can see the paint-stripper eating into some superb bodywork as we speak.’

‘So can we.’ Matt groaned. ‘We were supposed to be looking after this place for her, and the scrote managed all this! That car stands no chance, even if we are doing a regular drive-by.’

‘Well, apart from sitting in her coal-shed twenty-four hours a day, what can you do? Oh, and security cameras, maybe? Have you suggested that to her, sir?’

Matt nodded. ‘First thing we did. She held back initially, but we managed to convince her just before she went away. They’re already ordered — should be here today, although it’s looking a little like shutting the stable door after the horse has bolted.’

‘Good. I’ll report this as criminal damage, especially as her shed was broken into and a threat was made.’ Bryn made some more notes. ‘I’ll get uniform to do a regular drive-by and also keep their ears and eyes open on the streets. Some little toe-rag may just start mouthing off in the pub when he's had a few bevvies. It's about the best we can hope for — unless he takes it a step further, of course.' He frowned. 'But that threatening note does bother me. I'll make sure this doesn't get swept under the carpet, sir, but as you will appreciate, it doesn't warrant a forensic sweep, what with the budget and all that.'

'I realise that, Bryn, but do you mind if we take a look around? There might be something. Someone has expended a terrific amount of energy doing all this — he could have dropped something or left some nice clear footprints. Liz and I are treating this as a private investigation. Not that we'll be charging Mrs Swain.'

'Be my guest, sir. I'll even leave you some evidence bags. Just in case. And if you are as successful with this as you were with your first private case, we'll be slamming a door on him in no time.' The young police detective's smile faded, and he suddenly looked sad. 'If I had my way, I'd do more for the poor old soul. These bastards want the book throwing at them, terrorising an old lady like this.' He kicked at a broken flowerpot and swore. 'Anyway, must get back. I'll do all I can. Nice to see you again, boss, and you too, sir.' Giving Will a little salute, he went back to his car to fetch the bags.

As soon as he had gone, Will and Matt took a careful look around. For half an hour they searched unsuccessfully for anything that might give them a clue as to who the vandal was.

The only thing that Will found was a tiny scrap of creamy white linen. Matt found the broken tip of an old scythe, but that could well have already been in the ground. They bagged it and the cloth, although he did not believe either would be of any help.

'I reckon we're wasting our time,' said Matt after a while. 'I guess I'd better get back and fill Liz in on what Bryn said, and try to convince your neighbour that the time has come to take a little break away from Whisper Fen.'

Will reached out and touched Matt's arm. 'Before you go, have you got just a few minutes? I really need to talk to you.'

Matt looked at him shrewdly. 'Of course, mate. I'll just ring Liz and put her in the picture, then I'm all yours.'

Will felt an overwhelming desire to cry.

CHAPTER SEVEN

Matt had never seen Will look so distraught. They walked back to Holland House so that Will could check on Kate. She was still asleep, so they went out on to the new patio and sat down.

Will seemed at a loss as to how to begin, but then the words tumbled out in a torrent. Matt had a hard job to make sense of it all. The Will he knew was a tough, level-headed DI, down to earth and practical. The man sitting opposite him was almost a stranger.

From what Will was saying, Matt made out that Kate was subject to violent mood swings, going from the gentle person that he loved to a vitriolic horror, and then back again, in the space of a single conversation. He told of the strange, disturbing paintings she was making, and her obsession with the house and its morbid history. Finally, the flood came to an end, and Will stared at Matt with a glazed, exhausted expression.

'My God, man! You have to get her professional help. You can't go on like this. It's killing you!' Matt said.

'No doctors. After what she was subjected to when the baby died, the drugs that turned her into a zombie and the endless psychotherapy, Kate made me swear that I would never call a doctor. I can't do that to her, Matt.'

'Well, we have to do something or it will get worse.' Matt paused, thinking. 'From what you've told me, I am certain that it all comes back to the original problem, her grief over losing your baby daughter. Oh, Will. Out of all the properties in this huge county, how could you have picked the one with a history of child deaths?'

'I never knew!'

'Now I feel I'm to blame. Trouble was, when you were buying Holland House, Liz was in intensive care and I was still reeling from the terrible case that almost destroyed us. Your buying this particular property and what it might mean just wasn't registering with me. Even when you were ready to move and I was so much better, I didn't give the history of the old place a second thought. To be honest, I thought the stories about it were old wives' tales — other than the girl who got lost on the marsh, of course, but that could have happened anywhere. I had no idea that two children had died at Holland House.'

'No, it's me who's to blame, Matt. Every day I kick myself for not looking further into that weird clause or even wondering what was behind it. Now that's just what Kate is doing but she's looking too deep.' Will stared down at his feet. 'I wish we had never set eyes on this place.'

'Oh, Will, it's not the house. It's Kate's illness that's turning everything into a nightmare. Holland House is beautiful, and you're doing an amazing job on it. We have to try to make her see the place for what it is, and to forget all the macabre stories.' He drew in a long breath. 'Listen, you say she's into tracing its history, so maybe I really can help there. I have photographs and all sorts of stuff relating to Whisper Fen and Tanners Fen, so what if Liz and I offer to help her with her research? I don't mean the macabre stuff, just interesting local history. We could try to gain her trust that way? It might help, and at the very least, you'd know that there are other people looking out for her and you're not alone.'

'If you would,' Will said, 'that might just work. She refuses to socialise, but she'd bite your hand off for any piece of information about this place.'

'Let me talk to Liz. We'll formulate a plan, and then I'll text you and we'll take it from there. After all, we'll be in your neck of the woods quite a bit from now on, trying to help out Emilia.'

Will exhaled. 'Thank you, Matt. You're a bloody good friend!'

Matt stood up and hugged him. 'I'd better go.'

Will accompanied Matt to the lane and then returned to the house. Feeling as if he'd just been poleaxed, Matt continued on to his car. Before getting in, he stood for a while looking out over the marsh. In the distance, he could make out Gerald Grove's cottage, a black silhouette against the huge sky. Though it was a warm day, a trace of smoke filtered up from the chimney. The damp out there must be appalling if Grove needed a fire. Tylers Lane ended at the cottage, as near as you could get to the Wash without being inundated when the notorious autumn tides swept over the marsh. He pictured that man hunkered down in his shack and shivered. As he stared, he saw a point of light out on the fen. Odd. It wasn't even dark yet. So that was the light Will had seen.

He recalled some of the old-timers' stories about a local phenomenon called the hobby lantern, a will-o'-the-wisp that drew unsuspecting travellers to their doom on the lonely marsh. He shook his head. 'More like bloody poachers. Someone up to no good, anyhow.'

He got into his car and with a last look at Emilia's decimated Eden, drove back to Cannon Farm.

* * *

Liz was relieved to finally see Matt's car draw up. She had tried hard to persuade Emilia to go and stay with a friend for a few days, but Emilia had dug her heels in. She was going nowhere. Now she was over the initial shock of finding her garden trashed, anger had taken over, followed by a determination to get to work and salvage what she could from the destruction.

One look at Matt's face told Liz that all was not well, but she decided not to ask any questions until they were alone. She made tea and they sat around the kitchen table.

First, Matt told Emilia what the police had said, along with their advice to move out for a while. He got the same answer as Liz. Emilia was staying put. When they had finished their tea, she declared it was time to go and face the carnage.

'I can get a few hours' tidying up in before dusk. I think it will be therapeutic. Oh, and I need to call in to my friend from the Post Office too. It's our evening for a sherry and a gossip, and I don't want her to hear about my garden from anyone else.' She stood up. 'And I will call you if I'm concerned about anything, I promise.'

'I'll come with you,' said Matt.'

'No, no, I've troubled you enough. I'll be fine, I promise. And as you say, I can always call you.'

'Day or night, Emilia. We can be there in no time. Just make sure you lock up and keep that lovely car in the garage,' Matt said rather sternly. 'At least it's a solid building. You couldn't knock that down in a hurry.'

Emilia laughed. 'Well, that's not surprising, is it? You remember what my husband did for a living?'

Matt looked puzzled for a moment, then smiled. 'Ah, yes, of course. Construction of purpose-built outbuildings and garages.'

'No one would break into that, I assure you,' said Emilia proudly. 'He was a craftsman.'

Liz accompanied her to the door. 'I can't tell you how sorry I am about what happened,' she said. 'We still feel responsible and that we let you down.'

'You couldn't be there all the time, Liz. Whoever is doing this is clever. They'd have picked their moment carefully, and

I'm certain that they knew I was going away — although I have no idea how.' She squeezed Liz's arm. 'It wasn't your fault, my dear, so please, think no more about it.'

'We know a very good gardener, Emilia. I'm sure he wouldn't be averse to a few extra hours' work, just to help you with the heavy stuff? I can ring him if you like.'

'I might take you up on that, but first I'll see what needs doing. I'm going to tackle it as if it were the aftermath of a natural disaster, then, once it's cleared, I will have a blank canvas to play with. It could be a new project for me.' Emilia went out to her car.

Liz stood and watched her drive away. Just as she'd told them, she was a tough old bird. Even Liz, a retired copper with a good few years under her belt, would have thought twice about staying in a house that was under attack.

She hurried back indoors and found Matt still sitting at the table. 'Okay, what's happened?'

Matt shook his head. 'I hardly know where to start.'

'Like we used to say when we interviewed people — from the beginning.'

Matt began. As he spoke, Liz grew more and more disturbed. When he'd finished, she said, 'You're right, darling, we have to help them, especially if doctors are out of the question. We need a plan of action.'

'It seems to me that my local knowledge will be our way in, along with your expertise on the computer. Plus, we have the time to spare, so if Kate is burning the candle at both ends, she might be glad of a couple of willing foot-soldiers to help her out.' Matt nibbled on his thumbnail. 'Will warned me about her appearance. She's still losing weight and, to put it bluntly, she looks like the walking dead, so we need to be tactful. Plus, she might be pretty ill-disposed to our presence to start with, possibly even hostile, so we need to get her onside, no matter what it takes. Will is struggling, Liz. I mean, really struggling. I've never seen him like this, never. Even with some of the most harrowing cases we had to deal with, he was never anything but in control.'

'Ah, but those cases weren't personal. They didn't involve the woman he loves.' Liz reached out and touched Matt's hand. 'We'll find a way to help, and if things get too bad then we might need to be there for Will if he has to make a hard decision like bringing in professional medical help against Kate's wishes.'

Matt drew in a long breath. 'Right, then. First, I need to get up in the attic. I have a stack of boxes and cases, all coated in decades of dust, that contain photographs and diaries and other papers concerning my family and the history of this area. That should be our starting point.' He stretched. 'Sure you're up for this?'

'Bring it on,' she said. 'But we mustn't lose sight of Emilia. We're going to have to do a bit of juggling with our time.'

'Well, I did say I didn't want to get bored in retirement.'

'And like you also said — be careful what you wish for.' She grinned at him. 'Okay — up in that loft. I'm quite looking forward to getting a sight of the Ballards of old.'

* * *

Kate slept solidly until supper time, but even when she woke up she seemed lethargic and sleepy.

Will had prepared a simple meal, guessing that Kate wouldn't be very hungry. He was right, but she did make some effort to eat what he put before her. As he was clearing away the plates, she said, 'I'm so sorry about earlier, sweetheart. But the simple fact is, I can't do it, Will. I don't want to go into town any more. I felt terrible. I can't seem to face crowds, people, or even traffic.' Her look at him was so pathetic that it hurt.

'Okay, love. Tell me what happened,' he said gently.

'There's nothing to tell. I can't face the town, that's all there is to it.'

He squeezed her hand. 'I think it's time we had a word with the doctor, Kate. Look at you, you're losing weight by the hour, you're pale — and now this. What do you think?'

She pulled her hand away. 'No doctors, Will. We've been there before, remember?'

He needed no reminding. 'I'm not talking about like before. I meant a quiet word with the GP. Perhaps you just need a tonic? You may be a bit anaemic, or just generally run down. A blood test might be all that's necessary, and then some iron tablets or vitamins.'

If he could just get her into that surgery, hopefully the doctor might notice her deterioration and take things further.

But her look dispelled all hope of that. Her eyes took on a steely glint. '*No* doctors.'

There was no arguing.

For once, Kate didn't go to her studio. Instead, she sat with her laptop on her knees and yet again began a search on the history of the area.

'Not fed up with all that?'

'No way. Look at this — it's fascinating.'

He stared blankly at some dull document that he presumed to be a parish record.

'The Holland family have been on this fen since it was full of mists and eels,' she was saying.

'Still is, isn't it?'

'Mists, yes, but I mean a time when eels and wild birds were the staple diet of the folk that lived in this watery no-man's-land.'

'Sounds gloomy.'

'It was. The fen people must have had a pretty meagre existence, living on wild food, plants and fruits, fish and fowl.' She looked up at him, her face reflecting the silvery glow from the screen. 'Outsiders used to reckon they had webbed feet, you know.'

'I noticed you've been keeping your socks and shoes on a lot recently, maybe you've been spending too long out on Whisper Fen,' said Will smiling.

She cast him a withering look and resumed her search.

Will saw that if Matt and Liz were to give them any help, it would have to be through Kate's research. Thank goodness

Matt was a true “yeller-belly,” and had lived all his life on this stretch of the marsh. But how would Liz cope with Kate’s strange mood swings?

And how, he wondered, had Kate managed to drive past Emilia Swain’s wrecked garden without noticing? He decided to try and find out. ‘I thought I’d take a walk down the lane and check on Mrs Swain. Fancy a stroll?’

For a moment Kate looked confused, as if struggling with something. ‘Oh dear. I . . . I meant to say earlier,’ she bit her lip, ‘but when I came back past her place, something seemed to have happened in her garden.’ She looked at him anxiously. ‘I meant to tell you but I was so upset, I forgot.’

‘Happened?’ he asked blankly, careful not to let on that he already knew what had happened. Neither did he say what he was thinking — that she hadn’t been too upset to give that scumbag Grove a lift home.

‘Sorry, Bear, I don’t really know, it just looked like some animal had got loose in it.’

‘Then I’ll definitely go and check it out.’ Will left before he could say something he would regret. He didn’t need to go back there, he’d seen enough already, but perhaps an evening walk would clear his head a little, and if Emilia was home, he’d call in and tell her to ring him if anything worried her in the night.

Not finding her at the cottage, he sat on the wall for a while in the last rays of the late afternoon sun. What was happening on Whisper Fen? From a peaceful haven, an idyllic retreat, the place had suddenly become sinister, almost menacing. He hurried home.

As he entered the garden, Will saw his wife running down the path. Her call was almost lost, carried away in the breeze off the marsh.

He broke into a run and nearly fell through the gate. When he reached her, he saw that her face was wet with tears. Surely it wasn’t another dead Holland child?

But the news she gave him was totally unexpected. She held both his hands tightly in hers and gazed at him compassionately. 'Will, darling, it's Eva.'

He stared at his wife, uncomprehending. Eva? He rarely heard from his sister. As a Royal Canadian Air Force wife, Eva travelled all over the world and was hardly ever back in England.

'Darling, come inside.' She led him into the kitchen and pushed him gently into a chair. 'Eva and Guy . . .' She paused, swallowing hard. 'Guy's commanding officer rang for you. There has been an accident. They don't know any details yet, but . . . they are both dead, Will.'

As a police officer, Will had often been the bearer of tragic news. Almost invariably the recipient told him he must be mistaken. "It's all a terrible mistake" was what people said, over and over.

'When? Where?'

'He's going to ring you back, darling. I said you'd only be a minute or two. I'm sorry. I was so shocked I didn't ask the right questions, and you weren't here.' Her tone was almost accusatory.

Then she was holding him, hugging him to her like a baby.

The phone rang and he rose unsteadily to his feet.

Thankfully, the man knew his job. He was sympathetic but factual, offering Will and his family every assistance. He would of course ring back as soon as he knew more himself.

Keeping his voice steady, Will thanked the man. He was about to hang up when a thought struck him.

'Sophie! What about Sophie? Was she with them?'

The officer assured him that his eight-year-old niece was safe and well, being cared for by her best friend's family. Will exhaled noisily. At least Eva's child was unhurt. He sat back down at the table and put his head in his hands. 'She was only in her thirties, Kate. That's no age to die. And Guy. I couldn't have wished for a better husband for my little sister.

Both dead. He said it seems that their vehicle came off the road. I didn't even know they were in Germany.' Kate held him while he cried. As the sobs subsided, she told him she loved him, was there for him. Her smile belonged to the old Kate, even if he barely recognised the gaunt and pallid face that wore it.

They talked about Eva well into the night.

Later, just before he finally drifted off into an exhausted slumber, he thought of Sophie. 'I wonder what will happen to her, Kate? Guy was an only child and his parents are getting on in years. I suppose I'm her only close relative.'

Did the arm that held him tighten?

CHAPTER EIGHT

After a fitful sleep, Will finally got up at five and went to the kitchen for tea. He recalled bitterly that today was his birthday. Poor Kate. She had made the effort to go out and organise something to give him, and now her surprise would be ruined. Now the initial shock had worn off somewhat, he saw his sister's death in a clearer light. He loved her dearly, of course, but they had seen so little of each other. They were not close now, not as they had been as children.

He poured a second cup of tea and took it up to his sleeping wife. He quietly put the mug on her bedside table and slipped back into bed beside her. She stirred and nestled into him.

'Morning, my Bear. Did you manage to sleep at all?'

'A bit, babe. It's just difficult to take on board.'

'I can't believe it either. I spent half the night thinking about their wedding day. All those uniforms! Who would have thought . . . ?' She fell silent.

Every time he thought of Eva, Will's mind was crowded with images from their childhood. Eva on her three-wheeler, him on a racing bike. Eva sitting on the garden wall, him balanced beside her on one foot. Eva as a bridesmaid, smiling out from beneath the wreath of flowers in her gleaming chestnut hair, he scowling, uncomfortable and stiff in the best suit he hated.

'If you had to sum up Eva in a single word, what would that be?' Kate mumbled, half asleep. 'I think I would choose vibrant. Yes, vibrant.'

Kate was right. Eva dressed in colours that no one else ventured to wear. She went out to dinners in dresses like butterfly wings, drawing the admiring glances of everyone in the room. Even her wedding dress was a bright Aegean blue. Will sighed, turning his thoughts to more practical matters. Where would the funeral be? Probably Canada. When? Flowers! He must organise flowers — his brilliant little sister would have to have something bright. And then there was Sophie.

His thoughts were interrupted by Kate extricating herself from him and reaching for her tea. 'Did the air force people say when they'd be ringing again?'

'Uh, no, he just said he would keep us informed, so probably later today. Not exactly the kind of news you want to hear on your birthday, is it?'

For a moment Kate said nothing. He waited, fully expecting her to leap from the bed, run out and return with his present. Surprise!

Instead, she turned towards him slowly, and a huge tear welled up in her eye and rolled down her cheek. 'Oh, Will! How could I forget?'

For the first time in their relationship, he felt truly alone. Her tears were real enough, so he consoled her, meanwhile bitterly resenting her total preoccupation with the house. He couldn't help remembering his birthday of ten years before. It was the last time Eva and Guy had been able to get to England for a short holiday. They had all gone to Lincoln for dinner in a top restaurant, and Kate had arranged for a birthday cake in the shape of a police car. There had been balloons, sparklers and party poppers, and the four of them had behaved like teenagers.

Having sent his red-eyed wife off for a shower, he lay back against the pillows, finishing his tea and trying desperately to suppress his hurt. In the light of two tragic deaths his pain seemed petty and selfish. He felt it all the same.

He went down to prepare breakfast, still half expecting to see the card propped up against the toaster. Surprise! Surprise!

* * *

The following week gave Will little time to think about his forgotten special day, or Kate's problems. Indeed, apart from a strange remoteness, she too seemed to have been caught up in the change brought about by this unexpected death. She had promised to make up for her blunder, but it was too late.

A high-ranking officer had called from Germany to inform Will of the circumstances surrounding the accident. It appeared that his sister and her husband had been returning from an evening function in a village near Heidelberg. They were temporarily attached to an air base just outside Mannheim and were on their way home. Since this was an official gathering, Sophie had stayed the night with her friend. Guy had been driving and as he never drank, alcohol was not an issue. A freshly killed deer lay not far from the crash site. Examination showed animal blood and hairs on the car's front bumper — or what was left of it. The BMW had ploughed head on into some trees, both of its occupants killed instantly. Endeavouring to be as tactful as he could, the officer told Will that by an odd fluke — the angle of the decline and the positioning of the trees — Eva's airbag had inflated but had broken her neck. Guy's airbag had been punctured by a massive, jagged branch entering the car. 'There is no suspicion of foul play at all. Frankly, it was the best we could hope for, sir, considering the kind of accident. It would have been over in seconds. They would never have known what hit them.'

Will had seen enough RTAs to accept this. The bodies were being flown back to Saskatchewan, Guy and Eva's home, where a funeral would be held with full military honours.

'I hope this is acceptable, sir? It is on record that they wished to be buried in the same plot. Naturally, we will fly you and your family out, sir. The date is not fixed yet. Captain Hogan's parents are in a pretty bad state, as you can appreciate. Meantime, sir, if there is anything the RCAF can do for you, please don't hesitate to ask.'

Will could think of nothing. What could they do? He was hardly going to object to his sister being buried with the man she loved, was he? He had been assured that his niece would be staying with Françoise's family until a permanent home could be found for her. Apparently, the little girl was devastated. She was being monitored carefully and given the full support of the base medical team. The Fauve family were giving her love and a good home environment to assist her to come to terms with her loss. It was thought prudent to leave her where she was. Philip and Annette Fauve had insisted that Sophie stay with them as long as necessary. They had been Eva and Guy's closest friends and were devastated by the horrific news.

Will rang them. He had been dreading speaking to Sophie, but when he did, although she seemed quieter than he remembered, their conversation was far less emotional than he had expected. Annette Fauve spoke to him shortly afterwards, and said the little girl was being remarkably brave, although the smallest of things could bring on floods of tears.

He was dreading the funeral. The last one he and Kate had attended had been their daughter's.

He would have to go without her, but the thought of Kate alone in Holland House filled him with concern. On the other hand, the thought of Kate in black again was beyond contemplation.

They had not yet broached the subject, but Will put off discussing it with her until a date was set.

On the Wednesday, he went into town and bought himself a new dark suit. He couldn't bring himself to put on the one he had worn to his daughter's funeral, and he wondered why he had kept it.

When he returned, Kate was sitting on the bench, waiting for him. She beckoned to him and patted the seat beside her.

Will kissed her forehead and sat down.

'I can't go to the funeral, Will. I just can't face it.' She was staring at the ground.

'I don't want you to go, sweetheart. I know it would be too much for you, but you can't stay here on your own either. Perhaps you could spend a few days with your cousin Judy. She'd love to see you again.'

'Oh, I couldn't leave the house, darling. I'll be fine here. I'm not scared. After all, I spent enough nights alone when you were on shift.'

'Not on the edge of a desolate fen, you didn't.'

'And what, officer, is the crime rate here, compared with the town?'

'There is no comparison, Kate!'

'I rest my case.'

'Come on, babe! I'll worry myself sick. What if we got someone to stay with you until I get home?'

'Who, exactly?'

'I don't know. There must be someone.'

'William! How long do you think Mrs Holland was alone here? An old lady with pots of dosh around. If anyone was going to get burgled, it would have been her, right? And was she? No. If she could be happy here alone, then so can I.'

For a second, he didn't care what she did. He was tired of all this. If she wanted her precious house to herself, then so be it. Then he thought of those awful paintings in her studio.

He rubbed his tired eyes. At least he had a little more time. He hadn't yet been given a date for the funeral. Maybe they could reach a compromise by then. Maybe.

That afternoon Will drove out to Tanners Fen. He had already rung Matt and Liz to tell them what had happened, and they had offered to do anything they could to help out. Now he wanted to see them in person.

When he arrived, his friends were engrossed in sorting through the contents of an ancient battered suitcase. The kitchen table was piled with yellowing documents and dozens of old photographs.

'We've just found this case — it was stuck on top of a wardrobe,' explained Matt. 'We've been putting together an archive on this particular area of the fens. I've been meaning to sort all this stuff for donkey's years, and Kate's research has given me the push I needed. It seems that I really do know quite a bit about Whisper Fen.'

Liz led Will through to the dining room, where he saw another table covered in papers, folders and clear plastic envelopes all labelled in black marker pen.

'Hell-fire!' Will exclaimed. 'This looks like the case notes from a major investigation.' He looked at some of the files of photos and was surprised to see one marked "Holland House." The pictures were in black-and-white and sepia.

Liz gave him a grin. 'It's the only way we know how to work. Once a copper always a copper, I suppose.' She reached out and squeezed his arm. 'How are you doing, Will? Are you coping alright?'

He gave her a tired smile. 'I'm okay, Liz, thank you. In a way it's been made easier by the fact that I saw so little of Eva since she married. We had very different lives. Even so, it's hard to believe I'll never see her again.'

'And Kate?'

What to say? He didn't know himself. Before he could answer, Matt joined them carrying three mugs of tea. They sat at the table amidst the piles of documents.

'Kate isn't going with me to the funeral.'

'Oh, thank heavens! That's a huge relief. We were worried about that.' Matt took a deep breath. 'Which brings us to the next thing we were going to say. You can always say no if you think it would be inappropriate but considering the circumstances, I would be very happy to go with you for moral support, and Liz will keep an eye on Kate.'

Overcome with emotion, Will couldn't speak for a few moments. He had been dreading having to make the trip alone. 'You would?'

'Of course! Sometimes you need a mate close at hand,' Matt smiled, 'even if it's just to pour you another drink and listen to yet another story about when you were a kid.'

'I've subjected Kate to enough of those recently,' said Will, laughing. The laugh faded. 'But as to looking out for Kate, I'm really not sure if she'd agree.' He stared into his tea. 'She almost seems to relish having Holland House to herself for a while.'

'Well, at least she'll know I'm just a phone call away and could be with her in minutes if need be. And whether she likes it or not, I will keep an eye on her, one way or another.' Liz looked at him seriously. 'But I'll be clever about it, don't worry. I won't intrude.'

'Liz can use some of these snippets of Holland House memorabilia as bait to draw her in,' Matt added. 'The closer we can get to her, the more help we'll be.' He paused. 'This couldn't have come at a worse time for you, Will, could it?'

'No,' Will said. 'Although, strangely, I've seen more of my old Kate in the last week than all the time we've been here. There've even been a few times when I began to wonder if I'd been getting it all out of proportion and worrying over nothing, and then I remembered those awful pictures.'

'I'm sure you're right. Don't be lulled into a false sense of security, my friend.' Matt sounded grave. 'Have you had a date for the funeral yet?'

'Not yet, although the circumstances surrounding the accident were quite straightforward, so it should be fairly soon.'

'Well, I can be ready at short notice. Liz and Emilia are in touch a couple of times a day, although once again it's gone very quiet at Little Anchor.'

'I've seen a police car drive past several times, and Emilia is already beginning to get her garden back to what it was.' Will drank his tea. 'I must say, I do admire that lady.'

'She's such a nice person,' added Liz, 'and very interesting to talk to.'

'But still no clue as to who could have done all that damage?' Will asked.

'Not a thing,' she murmured. 'It's really frustrating.'

Will left shortly afterwards. 'I'll let you know immediately I hear from Canada. I'm so grateful to you both, I can't tell you what your offer means to me. But I'll leave it until I know the date of the funeral before I tell Kate of our plans. I don't want to give her time to start formulating excuses to keep Liz away.'

* * *

The call came on Friday. The bodies had been flown to Moose Jaw, Saskatchewan, where Guy had worked at the Canadian Forces Flying Training School. The funeral was arranged for the following Thursday, and a representative of Guy's squadron was to collect him early Tuesday evening. The official had sounded surprised to hear that there would be just two of them attending — they had been expecting a large family party. Will had explained that he and his wife were Eva's only remaining close relatives, and that his wife wasn't well enough to cope with the long flight, so his closest friend had volunteered to accompany him. He would return the following day.

The mere thought of Kate all alone in Holland House, and Whisper Fen on a dark night sent shivers of dread down his spine.

Guy's family had requested that their son and his wife be buried in the family plot in Regina, his home town, rather than the military cemetery, and Will agreed. His nomad of a sibling had loved the coniferous forests and the plains of Saskatchewan.

Will wanted to take a present for Sophie but had no idea what to buy for an eight-year-old. He tried to ask Kate, but she seemed not to want to even think about it. Finally, he asked her if she had a fairy painting they could give the child. Eva had begged him to send her Angela's next book as soon as it was published, saying Sophie adored them. An original painting by her aunt would be a special gift that he was sure his niece would love.

Kate had not been particularly interested in his idea. It took him a lot of coaxing until she was reluctantly persuaded to look through her old work. Eventually, she produced a watercolour of one of Angela's early characters, a fairy called Snapdragon. 'You can have this, if you like. It's a painting they didn't use in the book.'

It was perfect. The character's impish face grinned cheekily from between some tall, brightly coloured flowers.

'Seems a long time ago that I painted that.'

Indeed, when he compared it with the sinister and macabre work that she was making now, Snapdragon might have been painted by another artist altogether.

He still had not told Kate about Matt accompanying him, or about Liz being on call. The right moment had not yet presented itself. Trying to work out how best to go about telling her, he prowled around the kitchen, opening cupboard doors and peering hungrily into the fridge. Kate had forgotten about lunch again. No wonder the weight was falling off her.

He called up the stairs asking if she would like a sandwich, but she answered that she needed to finish something and would grab a bite when she was through. He wondered what malevolent figure was emerging from her dexterous fingers and began to wish he'd never sneaked a look at those awful paintings.

As he swallowed the last mouthful of his lunch, she came into the kitchen and stood before him, holding up a painting.

'Well? What do you think?'

After a moment's hesitation, he raised his eyes and beheld not some vile goblin but a magical landscape. Imaginary flowers surrounded a waterfall, all rendered in glorious colours. Mythical birds with vivid plumage flew among the blossom and in a pool at the base of the waterfall, a gathering of water sprites frolicked in sunlight. What on earth was she up to?

'You keep saying I don't show you my latest stuff, so here it is. Opinion, please?'

But when he looked closer, Will realised what she had done. The picture had seemed vaguely familiar, and it was. She had resurrected an old painting, adding more flowers and birds and the sprites. It was years old and she must have thought he'd have forgotten it by now. But Will remembered them all. Not one single brush stroke had ever escaped his attention.

What should he say? He stalled for time, taking it to the window and holding it under the light. She was going to extraordinary lengths to keep her new work hidden from him. He decided to go along with the charade. 'Great, babe! I love it. But what about the new, powerful approach you told me you were using for your own book? This is more your original style.'

He detected a flicker of panic — or was it anger? 'Oh, that. I've put it on hold for a while.'

Okay, two could play at that game. He smiled at her and asked if he could come and watch her paint, like he used to.

She suddenly found something of great interest on the toe of her trainer. Without looking up, she produced her habitual excuse. 'I'd love you to, Will, but my concentration is shot at the moment. I've no idea why, it's just the way I'm feeling right now. Give me a bit longer, can you?' She raised her eyes to his, beseeching.

'Of course. It's just that I love to be near you — well, you know that.'

'I *do* know, Bear.' Her eyes stayed on him. 'And I love you. You know that too, don't you?'

Will nodded. Despite everything, he had never doubted it. He held out his arms to her.

* * *

The following morning, Will rose at dawn and slid out of bed, leaving Kate asleep. Donning a sweatshirt and jeans, he went downstairs and pulled on his walking boots. Out in the garden the air carried the fresh chill that heralds an approaching change in the seasons.

It was time he discovered for himself just what it was that continued to draw his lovely Kate out on to that desolate marsh.

The ground leading up to the sea bank was soft underfoot. It had rained the night before, and the slender stems of the grass formed miniature arches to which clung countless droplets that shone like crystals. Mist hugged the trees, whose black trunks disappeared into an enveloping grey. Soon the trees gave way to scrubby, deformed shrubs, to be succeeded by coarse tussocks of reedy grass and sea lavender.

Aware of the danger of the rising tide, which swept in fast over this part of the marsh, Will kept to the path. Eventually, he sat on an old, broken gate and stared out over the flat, tide-washed landscape. It was a strange place, unlike any other he had seen. It seemed ancient, aeons old. Primeval.

He shook himself. This fanciful mood wasn't like him. He tried to imagine what it would be like to be artistic and could see how this wild stretch of coastline might cast a spell over a creative mind. What did Kate see? The black water in the lagoons, slithery beings that moved through the reed beds, the brooding atmosphere of the darksome marsh. But there were breathtaking cloud formations in the endless sky, tiny snow-white fen violets and the song of the skylark that hovered far above.

Not so long ago, she had thrived on such small details, imbibed them and then sprinkled their beauty into her paintings. Fairy dust.

Will slid down off the decrepit old gate and slowly made his way home. So now he understood. He had felt what she must feel on her endless wanderings across the marsh. They had made a terrible mistake in moving to Whisper Fen.

He kicked absentmindedly at a dandelion head. He would be crossing the Atlantic, far away from Kate. Part of him was relieved. Perhaps, at some distance from her, he would be able to see their problems from a new perspective. Mostly, however, he was full of trepidation.

His gaze moved to Holland House, standing alone on the edge of the marsh. From this far away, the big old house looked like a dream come true. Only the foundations were unstable, and nightmare creatures resided in the studio.

He waited for a while, not wishing to return to what had become a place of dread. Some wading bird watched him suspiciously from a reed bed, and he noted the statuesque figure of a grey heron surveying him from the muddy mouth of an inlet.

'Stupid birds. It's not me you should be wary of, it's this bloody place,' he muttered. 'Go and fish elsewhere, somewhere healthy!'

Acquiescing, the great bird rose majestically, its enormous wings beating soundlessly in the morning mist. With a single cry, it turned and flew inland, away from Holland House.

As Will, too, would be flying. But what would he find on his return?

CHAPTER NINE

Will left it until the Monday morning to tell Kate that Matt would be accompanying him to Canada. He said it had been a last-minute offer. Kate had little to say about it, appearing far more interested in all the jobs she had lined up for herself in his absence. As the time for his departure grew closer her moods were swinging like an out-of-control pendulum.

It was weird. One minute she was her old loving self, telling him she would miss him terribly, and the next she was nagging him to get everything ready for all the jobs she was determined to do. Instead of calmly preparing for his sister's funeral, Will found himself moving heavy furniture into the centre of the lounge so that she could begin decorating, sweeping the chimney and carrying unwanted items up into the loft.

By Tuesday morning, he was exhausted, while Kate seemed full of energy. Will realised that while he was distraught at their enforced separation, Kate was actually relishing the prospect.

At last the car the RCAF had sent for him was winding its way up the marsh lane, and Kate was crying and clinging to him like a child. Will experienced a moment of sheer panic. He shouldn't be leaving his wife. He could do nothing for his sister, he certainly couldn't bring her back, so why hadn't he remained where he was needed, with the living?

But it was too late now. He kissed her gently, told her he would be back soon and would phone often.

As the car moved off down the lane, he looked back. Kate was standing in the porch, outlined by trailing leaves of clematis and a few late roses. She seemed to be part of the building itself — the pale spirit of Holland House.

By the time they reached the end of the lane, he found he was crying.

They collected Matt. As he and Liz said goodbye to each other, Will couldn't help comparing this farewell with his and Kate's. They were so close, so unreservedly in love. Will felt a pang of envy.

With a young officer called Mitch as their escort, they soon arrived at the airstrip and the military plane took off. As the wheels retracted, Will's fear of what might happen to Kate almost overwhelmed him, but Matt turned the conversation to practical matters. He questioned Mitch about the plane, while Will tried hard to follow their conversation.

Mitch described the CC-150 high-speed jet they were travelling in, and told them about Moose Jaw being home to the Snowbirds aerobatics team and also the NATO Flying Training Programme that Guy Hogan had been attached to. While he talked, a young man approached carrying three trays laden with a delicious-looking supper.

They passed the rest of the journey eating, drinking and dozing. Will found that the further he got from Whisper Fen, the clearer his mind became.

He slept again, waking to find Mitch gently patting his arm. 'Welcome to Canada, gentlemen.' It was a long way to travel merely to say goodbye.

* * *

The hotel was comfortable and functional, typical of those bland conference hotels that specialised in short stays for business travellers. Will and Matt had been given rooms next door to each other.

The first thing Will did was to ring Kate. With the time difference, it was seven in the morning on Whisper Fen.

Her sleepy voice soothed his worries instantly. 'Bear! You're safe?'

'I'm safe, sweetheart. We're being treated like royalty. How are you? What was your first night like?'

'Apart from worrying about you, fine. I worked until quite late . . .'

He drew a breath, immediately thinking of her recent artwork, but she went on, alleviating his concerns.

'. . . not painting, though. I've started on the lounge. I thought something physical would occupy my mind better, stop me thinking about my husband, high up in the night sky over the Atlantic. I was stripping wallpaper until two in the morning!'

'Hey, you! Don't go overdoing it! I'll be back before you know it, and I'll help you.'

'I know, Will, but it's good for me, therapeutic and all that.'

'Okay, but get some rest as well.'

They talked for a while, until he said he was going to try to sleep. There was little to do as it was the middle of the night there, and might as well try to acclimatise himself to local time. They had their mobiles, but knowing the intermittent signal on the fens, and Kate's propensity for forgetting where she left hers and forgetting to charge it, he gave her his room number and the hotel telephone number for emergencies, and promised to phone her again before she settled down for the night. He reminded her to ring Liz if she felt at all worried about anything, but she just laughed at him.

'Stop being an old woman, Will! I love Holland House.' There was a pause. 'And the house loves me.' She blew him a kiss down the line and told him to take care.

He whispered that he loved her, but she had hung up or been cut off.

He prepared for bed, frowning. *The house loves me*. She had not finished her call with her usual, 'Love you, Bear.'

Will told himself he was becoming paranoid. She had blown him a kiss and told him to be careful, what more did he want? He rearranged his pillows and tried to get comfortable.

He missed Kate so much. She was his world, his life, more so now that Eva had gone. All he had left was Kate — and little Sophie, of course.

Without warning he was suddenly overwhelmed by grief for his sister. The realisation that she would never again walk into a room wearing one of her brilliant dresses, and turn heads all evening, was just too much to bear. The world had lost a bright light, and it was a duller place now for her passing.

Will cried into his pillow. Memories of a happy childhood came to him, one after the other, and still the tears fell.

After a while he rallied, and he realised that all these raw emotions had been held back, suffocated by his constant, twenty-four-hour worrying over Kate. Now that he was away from her, he was free to grieve.

He undressed and climbed into bed, fully expecting not to sleep a wink, but instead, he drifted off almost immediately, surrounded by images of Guy and Eva's little daughter, Sophie.

* * *

Matt talked to Liz for ages, loath to hang up despite the cost of the call. They had been together from the moment he retired, and he felt as if he had lost a limb suddenly.

'I feel like I'm making up for lost time, don't you, Mattie?' Liz asked. 'We came rather late to the party and I don't want to miss one minute with you.'

He told her he felt the same way. He couldn't wait to get back to her. 'Have you seen Kate yet?' he asked.

'Not yet. I rang and told her that I was here for her and would be happy to drop by at any time, but she was somewhat cool.' She laughed. 'Until I casually mentioned that we had some old pictures of Holland House that she might like to see. Then I threw in that you knew a whole lot about the area and that I was helping you research it. After that, I was suddenly her best buddy.'

'So, are you going to see her?'

'Tomorrow, after lunch. She says she's decorating, but she'll take a break for an hour or so at around two. I'm going to tie it in with a visit to Emilia.'

'Don't take on too much, my love. I know you're so much better, but you mustn't get overtired.'

'Don't worry. We come first. I'll do all I can to help our Whisper Fen neighbours but not at the expense of my health.'

Liz told him that she loved him and very reluctantly he hung up.

* * *

The two men ate breakfast together. Matt offered to let Will go alone to meet his niece and her friend's family, but Will was having none of it. He was far from certain how he was going to cope with meeting Sophie again under these tragic circumstances, and he wanted Matt's calming presence.

They set off for the Fauve home with Mitch as chauffeur. Will had no wish to meet his niece for the first time in years while standing by two gaping holes in a cemetery lawn.

His heart was racing as they drew up outside Philip and Annette's big family home. He had rehearsed a million things to say to the little girl, but as they stepped out of the car, he forgot them all.

Before he could collect himself, Sophie had run down the path and thrown herself into his arms.

'Uncle Will! I'm so glad you've come!' she said.

She clung to him for what seemed like hours. When she finally let him go, he held her at arms' length to look at her properly.

He was astounded. It was as if he were looking down at his little sister.

'Sophie! You're the image of your mother!' Will said.

She lowered her head and quietly began to cry.

'Your mum was a very beautiful woman, and you are going to be just the same. Be proud of that, sweetheart.'

'I am, Uncle Will. But I miss her so. I miss Daddy too, but he was away so much. Mummy was always here, and now . . .' Her voice quavered.

He kissed the top of her head. 'First, I want you to meet my friend Matt, then perhaps you'd like to take me to meet your friend Françoise?'

Sophie smiled at Matt and stuck out her hand. 'You look nice! Thank you for coming all this way with Uncle.' She turned back to Will. 'You'll like Françoise. She's funny. My doctor says she is just what I need right now. Come on, Uncle.' She pulled him towards the house.

A slender blonde woman of about Eva's age smiled at him from the entrance hall. She wore jeans and trainers with a baggy pink sweatshirt emblazoned with the words "Sloppy Joe." Behind her stood her husband, tall and broad. He had a clipped moustache and his auburn hair was cropped in military fashion. He would have looked severe if he hadn't been smiling broadly.

'Hi! Come on in! Sophie has told us so much about you, it's great to put a face to the name. And good to meet you too, Matt.'

The big man pumped his hand in welcome. 'Terrible thing, Will.' His grip tightened and he turned away for a moment. His wife took Will's hand. Her voice was soft, and there seemed to be another accent beneath the Canadian vowels.

'We are hanging on in there for Sophie's sake but it's pretty tough. Philip is, well, gutted. I've never seen him so hard hit. Guy was his closest buddy — he was our best man, Fran's godfather . . . And Eva.' Her voice broke. 'I don't know what to say to you, Will.'

'There is little any of us can say, is there, not at a time like this. But I can't thank you enough for what you're doing for Sophie.'

'It's the least we can do. The two girls are inseparable anyway. Hey, let's not hang around here on the doorstep. Come on in.'

Mitch stayed with the car, while Matt and Will, who was carefully carrying the painting of Snapdragon, went inside. They were introduced to Françoise, a chubby and bespectacled version of her dad, followed by the dog, the cat, the rabbit and the guinea pig, and finally given a tour of the house, conducted by a very grown-up Sophie. On their return to the others, gathered in the family room, Will produced Kate's painting and gave it to Sophie.

She undid the paper slowly, painfully so, very carefully winding the string into a ball, then folding the brown paper, while Fran bounced about impatiently, desperate to see what was inside.

Sophie held the picture up with an excited gasp. 'Look! Fran! Ann! Philip! Snapdragon is my very favourite. I'm sure I've never seen this picture in the books.'

'Auntie Kate says it is a one-off, especially for you.'

The child rose several inches, bursting with pride. 'I want to ring Aunt Kate. Will that be alright, Philip?'

The big man laughed and said of course she could, right then if she liked.

'Oh, later, when I've calmed down, I think. Thank you, Uncle Will. It's wonderful, I shall treasure it.' She propped the picture up on the table and hugged him again.

The two girls went off to play on Françoise's computer and Philip went into the kitchen and made his guests some coffee.

'Is she going to the funeral tomorrow?' Matt asked.

'Yes. She wants to go,' Annette said. 'We had a long talk with her, and so did the base doctor and her counsellor. She knows what to expect and we will all be there to support her. The doc thinks it's a good idea. We couldn't let Sophie see her parents. We went to the Chapel of Rest, and well, Guy was,' she swallowed, 'ah, pretty badly injured. Eva looked sort of asleep. Let's just say we thought it best she remembered them as they had been, full of life and happy.'

Will agreed. 'I saw my mother, and I wished I hadn't.'

'Mmm, well, the doc says because of that, she will need some kind of closure, so it's good that she wants to go to the burial. Kids are very resilient. He reckons that after tomorrow, and with plenty of support, Sophie will be able to get on with her life again.'

Will nodded. 'I suppose so, but it's a lot for a youngster to cope with. Losing one parent is bad enough — Eva and I lost our dad when she was really tiny. Luckily, our mum was a tower of strength, but not a day goes by that I don't think about him and wonder . . .' He paused. 'So, what will happen after tomorrow? The air force chap who rang me in England said she should stay with you for a while longer, but is that okay? I mean, it's quite an undertaking, isn't it?'

'We wanted to speak to you about this, Will.' Philip looked at him directly. 'We wondered if you were wanting to take her back to live with you. Apart from her grandparents, who are in their seventies and both in poor health, you are her closest relative.'

Will said nothing. For a second, all he could hear was Kate saying, 'Holland House doesn't like children, they must never come here!' With an effort he pushed the memory away.

There was a slight feeling of tension in the air.

Annette was looking at him intently. Philip stared at the froth on his coffee. Will wondered how they would react to his reply.

Glancing at Matt for reassurance, he said, 'I will be perfectly frank with you both. It would be very difficult for me to take Sophie. Personally, I would love to, but my wife is far from well at the moment and, well, she is showing signs of getting worse, not better. It would be impossible to give Sophie the care and attention that she needs at this terrible time.'

There was a noticeable relaxation of the atmosphere in the room. Philip, speaking slowly, said, 'We sure are sorry to hear about Kate. That's really tough and we both wish her well. But in that case, if it's alright with you, we'd like to continue to look after Sophie.' There was a long pause, then he added, 'And depending on what the future brings, maybe consider something more permanent? We are talking about adoption. Would you have a problem with that, Will?'

For a moment he couldn't answer. It was a mammoth decision to make. Then he saw Kate, that almost ethereal, painfully thin and desperately sick woman that was his wife. He saw the mist off the marsh surrounding Holland House with its chilly damp tendrils. Compare that to this warm and friendly family home where he sat. He could have wept all over again. He had no choice at all, did he? No option whatsoever. 'I'd have no problem with her staying with you. She deserves the best, and she will get that with you, I can see that.' Indeed, Will's heart suddenly sang at the news. Sophie's fate had been eating into him since he had first heard about the accident.

Annette went to her husband and kissed him. Matt smiled at Will and patted his arm.

Philip, his voice choked with emotion, said, 'I loved Guy like a brother, and I know he would have done the same for our Françoise if it had happened that way.'

Sophie would be safe with these good people, her future would be assured. For once he had to agree with his wife. Whisper Fen was no place for a child. Kids needed stimulation and other kids to play with. He thought of the brooding atmosphere of the marsh.

* * *

Next, they had to find a florist. Will easily found a bouquet of those brightly coloured flowers that his sister had always loved, but when it came to writing the card, he came to a full stop.

Matt saw his blank expression and pitied his friend.

'There's no hurry, sir,' the florist said. 'It's the worst part, I always think. I'll leave you for a few minutes.'

Will looked helplessly at Matt. 'What do I say?' He sounded like a little boy rather than a retired crime fighter.

'What would you like to say to them if you could?' Matt said.

'I guess that I loved them, and I'm going to miss them. I didn't see them often, but the world won't be the same without them.'

'Well, there you are. That sounded perfect to me. Just write it as you would say it.'

Will wrote, *To darling Eva and dearest Guy. The world has lost one of its brightest flowers and a giant redwood of a man. We will always love and miss you. William and Kate.*

'I'm sure Kate would have put it better, but . . .'

Matt squeezed his arm. 'No one could have put it better, mate. You said it all.'

Back in the car, Mitch asked if they would like to go on to the Chapel of Rest.

Will shook his head firmly. 'No thanks, Mitch. I appreciate your offer, but I prefer to think of them like this.' He took a photo from his wallet and handed it to Mitch, who passed it to Matt.

It was a holiday snap sent from a vacation in the Bahamas showing Guy and Eva sitting on the edge of a sparkling azure pool, laughing at their toddler daughter, who was splashing happily around in an inflatable baby floater.

'Probably for the best, Will,' said Mitch. 'Good-looking couple, weren't they?'

'Yep. Eva had all the looks in our family. Sadly, she had the brains as well. I got left with very little in either department.'

'Don't you believe him,' said Matt. 'This man was one of the smartest detectives I ever worked with.'

Mitch said he didn't doubt that. He then asked if he could give them a sightseeing tour instead.

Matt thought that would be a great idea, something to keep Will occupied, but surprisingly, Will declined. 'Would you mind if we went back to the hotel? If it's okay with Matt, I think I will take advantage of the swimming pool and the steam room. It's all been a bit traumatic, especially seeing Sophie, and I've still got tomorrow to get through.'

'No problem. I'll give you my mobile number. If you fancy a trip downtown this evening, or just want some company, call me. My commanding officer has put me at your service 24/7.'

Will took the man's number and thanked him. 'A drink or two later might be just the thing. If so, we'll give you a call.'

After the airman had left them, Will said, 'Are you okay with this, Matt? I should have asked what you wanted to do.'

'The pool sounds perfect. I assume there's a shop on site where we can buy bathing trunks?'

'Yes, I read it in the hotel info.' Will looked apologetic. 'I drag you all this way and don't even let you see the sights. Some friend I am.'

'Look, I'm fully aware that this is no jolly boys' outing, so don't beat yourself up. If you need to unwind, where better? Let's go check out that pool.'

* * *

After half an hour of swimming, Will was starting to feel some of the tension leave his muscles. Swimming always relaxed him. As a kid he had loved the water, and after his accident he had been encouraged back into the pool as a form of therapy. He would think of nothing but his breathing, and the rhythmic strokes of his limbs. He guessed it was his form of meditation.

'Shall we hit the sauna?' he suggested to Matt.

Luckily it was empty. Will closed his eyes and exhaled. 'Surreal, isn't it, Matt? All of this.'

Matt sighed. 'You can say that again. How are you doing, my friend? You looked really worried when Mitch asked you if you wanted to go to the Chapel of Rest.'

'I simply couldn't do it, mate. I made the mistake of seeing my mother at the funeral home, and I went crazy. I can still hear myself screaming, "This is not my mother! What have you done with her? Where's my mother?" It was awful. I swore then that I would never do it again. My memories of the dead when they were alive will suffice.' He sat up. 'But it wasn't just that, I just felt so stressed and I didn't understand why. I mean, my great worry was Sophie's future, and that couldn't have turned out better, could it? So why was I feeling so panicky?'

'Because you want to get it right, for Eva's sake. You want to do what your sister would be happiest with. And your grief is getting in the way of clear thinking. And then there is Kate, of course.'

Will shook his head and gave another sigh. 'Yes, Kate.'

They sat for a while in silence. 'I keep seeing those awful paintings, and they scare me.'

'People do use art therapy to express their darkest fears on canvas, Will,' said Matt practically. 'Perhaps she's doing that. Perhaps it's a *good* thing. Perhaps it's a channel for all the bad stuff in her head.'

'Maybe. And it's true that artists can have "black" periods. Come to think of it, some paint that way all the time.'

Matt looked confused. 'Art's not really my thing. Didn't crop up in police training.'

Will chuckled. 'Didn't in mine either, but Kate was always dragging me round the art galleries. I went under sufferance, but eventually I began to look a bit harder. I found some paintings fascinating, while others bored me rigid, and some were simply beyond my understanding. There was one artist called Hieronymus Bosch. I seem to recall he painted some pretty hellish creatures.'

'Actually, I had a case once, involving a major insurance fraud. The guy we were investigating was an art collector. The stuff he collected really gave me the creeps. I can see it now, and the case was years ago. He said it was inspired by the Holocaust, so you can imagine what they were like.'

'Something similar happened to me,' Will said. 'Kate was invited to go to New York with Angela on a promotional tour of Fairy Dreams. We were in this mammoth bookshop where Kate was looking for some art books she wanted. I found a book on this photographer who liked to work with dead bodies. His pictures turned my stomach. I put the book back quick before Kate could see it. The plate on the last page showed a dead baby. Imagine how Kate would have felt if she'd seen it.'

Matt wiped sweat from his eyes. 'Well, then. In light of all that, perhaps Kate's new work isn't so disturbing after all.'

'Maybe, but they are so unlike her usual work. They're dreadful pictures, Matt, but I could see how well executed they were. Anyone who likes that sort of thing might think them works of genius. The sense of darkness and foreboding she conveyed was so powerful. It was just that it was my darling Kate that had made them. And they weren't the Kate I knew.'

'I'm looking forward to hearing from Liz how she got on with Kate today. From what she told me, our plan might just be working.' Matt grinned at him. 'Apparently, Kate can't wait to hear how our research is going.'

'I bet she can't,' Will said. 'Holland House and Whisper Fen are all she thinks about.'

'I wonder if Liz might be able to get her to show her some of her artwork? Shall I ask her to try?' Matt suggested.

'You can try, but I'll bet she won't get far.'

Matt mopped his face again. 'I think I've had all the heat I can take, Will. I'm off for a cold shower.'

'Me too,' said Will, climbing down from the bench. 'I'll call Kate and then we can decide where to eat and what to do for the rest of the evening.'

'Good idea. Come to my room afterwards and we'll have a think.' They stepped outside. 'See you later.'

Reassured by their conversation, Will began to look forward to talking with Kate. He went up to his room and called her on his mobile.

And waited. Her phone rang and rang, but there was no answer. All his anxiety flooded back. Where was she? Out on the marshes, without her mobile? On top of a ladder painting a ceiling? Will sat on the bed and idly flicked through the different channels on the TV, worrying about his wife.

Unease about Kate turned to apprehension about the following day's funeral. How could he cope with it all?

After a few minutes, he tried ringing Kate again, this time on the landline. Just as he was about to give up, she answered.

'Kate! Where were you earlier? I was worried about you.'

'For God's sake, Will, I can't hang around the telephone in case you choose to call me! You said you'd ring before I went to bed. It's not even nine yet!'

'Sorry, babe. It's just that I really miss you. You seem so far away, and I hate it. We've never been this far apart before.'

'You sound like a big kid.' Softening a little, she said, 'How's it going?'

'Okay, I suppose. It's not the nicest thing I've ever had to do, but Matt is a rock. I'm so thankful that he offered to come. Still, once tomorrow's over, I'll be thinking of getting home to you.' He paused, waiting for a response that didn't come. 'I did see Sophie today. She is the image of Eva. It's quite uncanny. Oh, and she is going to ring you, if she hasn't done so already? She adored your picture. Snapdragon is her favourite, so it was an inspired choice on your part.'

'Oh, good,' she said without enthusiasm.

Since she said nothing more, Will went on to tell her that the Fauve family were going to continue to care for Sophie, with a view to formally adopting her at some point in the future.

Now she did sound animated. 'Really! What lovely people. And they actually told you that, did they? They said they wanted her permanently?' Her tone had changed completely.

'Well, yes. They asked if I was planning on bringing her back to England to live with us.' He heard a slight intake of breath. 'I told them it would be very difficult for us and they nearly broke open the champagne.'

'Yes, yes, you were quite right, darling. It would be no good her coming here, no good at all. And of course, she has her friends, her school, the support of the air force. Everything she needs is right where she is now.'

For a moment he wanted to argue. It wasn't Whisper Fen that was out of the question. It was Kate. Stifling his retort, he changed the subject. 'So what have you been up to today?'

Eagerly, she listed the tasks that she had tackled already and those that were lined up for the next day. If she were missing him, Will thought, she was certainly showing no signs of it. She seemed to be thoroughly enjoying herself. Then she added, 'Oh, and Liz called round. Do you know, Matt has lived on this stretch of the fen all his life, and they are researching it! Isn't that exciting? She brought me some photos of Holland House in the twenties. They're awesome.'

After that, they seemed to run out of things to say to each other. Kate muttered a perfunctory, 'Love you,' and said she had better hang up before her paintbrush hardened. He said he would ring her after the funeral and that he loved and missed her. He put the phone down.

The room felt oppressive. She had made it plain that she had been dreading him bringing his niece to England with him. And again, no 'I love you, Bear.' It was something she always said. The call had left him feeling sad, empty. Will stood up. Damn it! If Kate was enjoying herself, then so would he. He burst through the door to Matt's room. 'Okay, buddy, let's ring Mitch and say we'll take him up on that offer of seeing the sights, and we'll have a bloody good dinner. I feel like a drink.'

CHAPTER TEN

Matt walked back into his room, shut the door and exhaled noisily. He loosened his tie, wrenched it off and threw himself down on the bed. He had no idea what time it was in England, but he didn't care. He needed to talk to Liz.

'Mattie! Is it all over? How did it go? Are you alright?' Liz said.

'Sweetheart, I've been to quite a few funerals in my life, but that was one of the most distressing and most beautiful I've ever attended. Simply hundreds of people came to say farewell to the pilot and his wife.'

'And Will? How did he cope?'

'Brilliantly, all things considered.' Matt got up, went to the minibar and took out a small bottle of bourbon. 'I think he held it together for Sophie's sake, and it'll probably hit him later.'

'I can't say I'm totally in agreement with young children going to funerals,' said Liz softly. 'It's so traumatic for them.'

'She was about as brave as a child could be.' He took a swig of the bourbon. 'It was pretty heart-wrenching, especially when she laid a rose on each casket.'

'Glad I wasn't there, Mattie. I'm sure I'd have cried my eyes out.'

'A lot of people did. I guess it was all those uniforms that made it so powerful. And there was a military band and a choir to add to the charged atmosphere.' He gave a little chuckle. 'On the lighter side, the chaplain painted such a glorious picture of life in heaven that I quite expected the entire congregation to agree one massive suicide pact and all march off to the promised land!'

'Stop it, Matt! That's awful.'

He chuckled. 'Enough of funerals. How did your visit to Holland House go?'

Liz didn't answer immediately, as if she was trying to find the right words. 'Well, our Kate's a very confused woman. I don't know how Will lives with her the way she is right now. She's changed so much in such a short time. It's scary.'

'Simple. He loves her.'

'He must.' Liz lowered her voice. 'Matt, I'm no shrink, but I reckon Kate is suffering from some form of bipolar disorder. Her mood swings are unbelievable. She flips from almost comatose to manic in the blink of an eye. I spent an hour and a half with her earlier this afternoon, not long, but long enough for me to know that Kate needs professional help.'

'He promised her there'd be no doctors.'

'Sometimes you have to go against what a loved one wants. *Especially* in the case of a loved one. I can see something tragic happening if he sticks to his promise.'

'But at least she spent time with you, didn't she?' Matt said. 'That's something. According to Will, she doesn't let anyone over the doorstep.'

'Your photos were my passport inside. She loved them and said she can't wait to talk to you about the old place.'

'And Mrs Swain? Any more from her?' asked Matt.

'I helped her tidy up for a while after I left Kate. She's treating it like a new project but seeing all that devastation must be hard for her to take. At least there've been no more incidents, and the police have been out here a couple of times. I saw both Swifty and PC Barney Woods this morning. Emilia's so utterly stoical! Talk about keep calm and carry on!' Liz paused. 'Oh, I do miss you, Matt Ballard!'

'Ditto, Liz Haynes. I can't wait to get back to you.'

'Any idea of when?'

'None at all. We are at the mercy of the RCAF. Will is hoping it will be tomorrow, but I'll let you know as soon as I hear.' He drank a little more bourbon. 'I guess I'd better go check on Will. I don't want it to hit him when I'm not around. He managed well, but he's not at his strongest right now.'

'Give him my love,' said Liz, 'but keep most of it for yourself.'

Matt hung up. He realised that he was smiling. But then Liz always did make him smile.

* * *

Will was also phoning home, and once again Kate didn't answer her mobile. He texted her, and now he was trying the landline, but all he got was the answerphone. With a sigh, he took two bottles of whisky from the minibar and poured them into a glass.

He lay on the bed and thought about little Sophie. He didn't usually have much to say to children. They made him feel rather shy. Since the death of his own baby, Emma, he had had little to do with any youngsters, so it had come as a huge surprise to find that he had really warmed to Sophie. He found himself wishing things were different at home.

Home. He picked up the phone and dialled again. This time Kate answered almost immediately. She said she had no signal on her mobile, and then she listened while he told her about the funeral and said she would be glad when the trip was over. She sounded sad. She said almost nothing about her decorating and there were no more little gems from the history of Whisper Fen. Will put this down to the solemnity of the occasion.

She asked him when he would be flying home, but Will couldn't say. 'I'll text you, but in case the signal's down again, put the answerphone on, babe, then if I find out anything and it's night time over there, I can leave you my flight schedule.'

She agreed, which saddened him. Once, she would have told him that she didn't care what time of the day or night it was but only wanted to hear his voice.

'Are you okay, Kate? You sound a bit down.'

'I'm fine. I expect it's all this talk about funerals. Not the most cheerful subject, is it?'

Well, I'm so sorry my sister died, Will wanted to say but swallowed his sarcasm along with the bourbon. 'I'd better let you go. Will you ring me before you turn in for the night?'

There was a pause. 'Well, yes, of course, but I may be working tonight, so if I get carried away you will have to forgive me. You know how I lose track of time if things are going well.'

'Please try, sweetheart. It's been one hell of a day and I could do with a transatlantic hug.'

'I'll try, I promise. I love you, my Bear, and I'm glad today is over.'

'Me too.'

Will shook his head. Well, he might as well make the most of his time away from the marsh. They were going to Philip and Annette's this evening for supper, the last time he would see Sophie, possibly for years.

Once again, he wondered what it would have been like if the Fauves hadn't offered to adopt Sophie. Could he have ever taken her home to live with him and Kate? Could he have made it work? She might have made a difference to their lives, given Kate a new direction. Then he saw again that picture, the malevolent goblin with the child under its arm.

* * *

Will, tired and drained, had to turn down Philip's offer to sample some of the local beers. He made up his mind to bring Kate to Canada for a holiday as soon as she was better.

'Hey, if you do come out again you guys have to stay with us! And you too, Matt! And bring that Liz of yours, we'd love to meet her. We have some great places we can take you all to, and Sophie would love it.'

Sophie clung to Will all evening, until she was too tired to stay awake. He kissed her goodnight and promised to ring her often, and as Annette led her up to bed, she began to cry.

Before he left, Will went to her bedroom to see her. Sophie lay in bed, her chestnut hair spread over the pillow, and he saw his little sister again.

Mitch picked them up just before ten. 'I just had a call from the base. You are on a flight tomorrow. It has been delayed a bit though. Take-off is now at twenty-two hundred hours. You should be in England by about three in the afternoon, local time. Which gives you almost a day here. I could run you out to Moose Jaw, if you like, show you around the base.'

Will glanced at Matt, who nodded. 'Great, we'd love it. I've said my goodbyes here, and I don't want to upset Sophie again.'

Soon, they were back at the hotel. Will was shattered. His back ached and his arm throbbed.

'Come to my room and we'll have a snifter before we turn in,' said Matt. 'It'll help you sleep.'

Will agreed. Despite his fatigue, he wasn't looking forward to climbing into a cold hotel bed. He wanted his wife and their own warm bed in Holland House. A whisky might deaden all sorts of pain.

After Matt had poured the drinks, he said, 'I'll just give Liz a quick bell, even though it's around five in the morning there. She sent you her love when I spoke to her earlier, by the way.'

Will settled into an armchair, listening to Matt's conversation with a pang of envy. No conflict, no silences, no trying to read between the lines. Why couldn't his conversations with Kate be like that?

Matt's face became more serious, and he said, 'I'll pass that on to Will, darling. Now, I'll let you go, and hopefully I'll see you later tomorrow night.'

He hung up and frowned at Will. 'Liz said that she'd forgotten to tell me earlier, but she thought you should know that when she arrived at Holland House with the photographs, Kate wasn't there. Then she saw her walking back from the sea bank, and that Gerald Grove character was with her. Kate told her that Grove had given her some butterfly wings that she wanted for a new painting. Liz tactfully suggested that he wasn't the nicest of men to hang around with, but Kate shrugged it off with an, "Oh, he's harmless. Everyone has it wrong about him, just because he prefers his own company."'

Will swore. 'I've warned her, and she takes no bloody notice. Maybe I should tell her what you guys have found out about him and see how she responds to that.'

Matt looked dubious. 'I'd keep that to yourself for now, mate. Once I'm back, we'll keep a really close eye on that piece of shit. Then we'll see.'

An hour or so later, Will went back to his room. He checked his phone but there had been no messages or missed calls. He decided to ring her. After a few rings, the tinny version of his own voice greeted him for the second time that day.

He sighed and told the voice that their flight was due in at around three the following afternoon. He would be home soon.

He fell into bed and dreamed of monsters with butterfly wings.

* * *

Will awoke unrefreshed and wandered over to the tray of packaged beverages. Tea wasn't on offer, so he made himself a cup of instant coffee and powdered creamer. It was better than nothing when his mouth felt like he had been on the beer all night.

Still in his pyjamas and robe, he went and knocked on Matt's door. 'Fancy going down for a swim before breakfast? I need something to clear my head.'

'Good idea. Give me five and I'll be with you.' Matt yawned. 'Might wake me up.'

They swam for half an hour, then went back to their rooms to pack their things, ready for that evening's departure. Will went down to the reception and found that their bills — including their inroads into the minibar — had all been taken care of. The Royal Canadian Air Force had collected the tab.

He was just about to go and tell Matt about their generosity when he saw Mitch hurrying in through the front doors.

'Problem, Will. The flight has been delayed again. Now it's not going until tomorrow morning.'

Will's heart sank. For a minute he wondered if he could get Matt and himself a last-minute cancellation on a commercial airline.

'But,' Mitch was saying, 'if you are prepared to forgo luxury, 17 Wing Winnipeg have a Hercules transport plane at Moose Jaw collecting emergency relief supplies to take out to Eastern Europe. It has to touch down in Newfoundland, then at RAF Waddington, in your home county. You're welcome to wait for the executive jet, but if you're prepared to rough it, the transporter will get you home today. It leaves in two hours. It isn't quite what we had planned for you, but you're looking real concerned. I can get you there if you want.'

There was no decision to make. He couldn't leave Kate alone on Whisper Fen for yet another night. 'We're already packed, Mitch. I'll go and alert Matt, then we're good to go.'

Will gave Kate a quick ring to tell her of their change of plan.

Not only was there no answer, but she had switched the answerphone off. He cursed inwardly but decided that it made little difference, he would just be home earlier than he had thought.

* * *

Within half an hour they were driving towards Moose Jaw. As they got closer, Will remembered about the hotel bill. 'Hey, Mitch, when I went to pay my bill, the hotel said that you guys had taken care of it. I wasn't expecting that. Is it usual?'

Mitch pulled a face. 'Well, it's not exactly "us guys," but one man in particular.'

Will was intrigued.

'No one has actually said that I can't tell you, but even so, perhaps you would keep this to yourselves?' Mitch said.

Will nodded.

'There was accident on the base last year. The wife and child of one of our commanding officers were involved. Captain Hogan got them both out of their burning vehicle. He saved their lives, Will. He was regarded very, very highly by the squadron. You are part of Guy's family, so the major pulled a few strings to afford you every hospitality.'

'I never knew! Eva never mentioned it,' Will said.

'That's the way he was, Will. He reckoned anyone would have done the same, but I don't think so, and neither does the major.'

Will whistled softly and looked at Matt. 'Then that would have been the officer who read the eulogy? I hadn't quite understood what he was saying about outstanding bravery, now I know.'

'Yep, that was him, Major Ted Chipman,' said Mitch.

'It was a pity that neither of Guy's parents were there to hear that service. They would have been so proud,' added Matt.

'It would have been too much for them. They are in very poor health — his mother is in a nursing home and his father is crippled with arthritis. No way could they have coped with it. I thought it was a miracle that little Sophie stood up to it so well, poor kid.'

'She's a tough little cookie alright,' said Will, with a fond smile. 'I would have loved to take her back with me, but she is so happy with the Fauve family and they desperately want to adopt her.'

Mitch nodded. 'So I hear. But she is still your flesh and blood, Will. I know it would be an upheaval for her, but in the long run she might prefer to be with you. You looked pretty comfortable with her yesterday.'

What have I agreed to? Will thought. The kid was his sister's child, for heaven's sake. He *should* have taken her, for Eva's sake.

'Hey, I'm sorry. I apologise. It's none of my business. Captain Fauve is a terrific chap and you have obviously talked it through with them. I have no right to mouth off. I don't even know your circumstances back home.'

Dead right, thought Will. Mitch had reminded him of exactly what his circumstances were. He sensed Matt tense beside him. 'It's alright. We have all agreed that there should be a trial period for Sophie and the Fauves, to see how she settles in. But I assure you, there is much more going for her here in Canada than an injured ex-copper can offer her in a backwater in the fens.'

No one spoke for the rest of the journey. Then they were there, and Mitch was offering him a hand. 'Best of luck, Will. Gonna have to hand you over to the flight crew now. Sorry there's no steward on this baby.'

They looked up at the big grey transport plane with its four powerful Allison engines. 'What sort of crew does it take to fly this?' asked Matt, clearly in awe of this behemoth.

'Two pilots, a navigator, a flight engineer and the loadmaster. It's a real workhorse the CC-130. It's used in search and rescue, and can airlift troops, cargo or equipment. It can even be reconfigured to carry fuel. It can carry ninety-two passengers, but you two are the only ones until you reach Goose Bay, Newfoundland. Then you'll have a bit of company as they are collecting a couple of medics and some medical supplies from 5 Wing. Well, it's been great meeting you both, just sorry for your loss.' Beneath the plane, a tall skinny man was hurriedly beckoning to them. 'Good luck.' Mitch saluted them, and then waved as they climbed aboard the Hercules for their less than first-class flight home.

CHAPTER ELEVEN

Matt and Will finally set foot on English soil again, each mighty glad to have joined the police rather than the air force. It was a journey they would have preferred to forget, although Will said he had a feeling that his back was probably not going to let him do so for some weeks to come. There had been hold-ups and unforeseen problems at Newfoundland that had delayed them for hours, but at least they were now home.

RAF Waddington was only a short distance from Lincoln, and Matt said he would happily blow some money on getting a cab back home. Will agreed and was just about to ask for the use of a phone when a rather rotund officer approached him, his hand outstretched.

'Hello there. Mr Stonebridge, isn't it? Interesting trip, huh? Bet you wish you'd waited for the exec jet!' the man said.

Will took the proffered hand. 'It would have been nice, but to be honest, we are just happy to be home, thank you. Everyone has been very kind to us.'

'Yes, they are a good bunch, the Canadians. Now, I'm just off to Fenfleet myself. Can I give you a lift? You are going that way, aren't you?'

Will looked at Matt and grinned. 'If it's not too much trouble, we'd really appreciate that. Thank you very much indeed.'

* * *

Soon they were turning into the lane leading to Holland House. Matt waved to Will and told him that he would call around after breakfast the following day. They would start immediately on Kate's research into Holland House and the marsh.

When he arrived, Liz was standing in the doorway, waving happily to him.

Matt thanked the officer and lifted his bags from the boot. Cannon Farm had never looked so good, and he suddenly realised that some of Will's tension had rubbed off on him. Matt's home was his haven, where he found peace and happiness. Will's was full of conflict and unease. At the sight of Liz hurrying down the path towards him, all the stress of the last few days evaporated.

Matt dropped his cases and took her in his arms, kissing her long and hard. Liz was smiling broadly at him.

'You're really early! I was thrilled when I got your text! That's marvellous! Oh, Mattie, I've missed you so much. Come on inside and tell me all about it.'

Matt dumped his things in the hallway and followed her through to the kitchen. The kettle was already on with two mugs waiting beside it. 'Oh, God!' he exclaimed. 'A proper cup of tea! I've missed that almost as much as I've missed you!'

'I hope not.' Liz smiled.

'I did say *almost*. And you know how I love my tea.' His smile faded. 'Oh, Liz, it's been a nightmare. I hadn't realised how much Will is suffering, and just how disturbed Kate has become since they moved.'

They sat down and held hands across the table.

'I too was shocked when I saw her. I didn't know what to do or say. It was like she was a different person to that lovely girl we used to spend so much time with.' Liz bit her bottom lip. 'I wanted to offer to help, but it was as if I didn't know her.' She sighed. 'You'll see for yourself when you see her.'

'Liz?' Matt said seriously. 'I want two things now I'm home.'

'Yes?'

'I want that bloody cup of tea that you threatened me with.' He gave her a wicked grin. 'And I want you.'

She licked her lips lasciviously and stood up. 'Then I'd better get a move on with the tea, hadn't I?'

* * *

Will stopped at the gate and looked back over the marsh. He had never wanted to see Whisper Fen so much in all his life. The last few days had been a surreal nightmare. Now, all he wanted was his home and his wife. He wondered what kind of reception he was about to get — the returning warrior, or an indifferent, "Oh, you're back."

He got neither. The house was empty.

He called her name but there was no reply. He had forgotten the time difference and wasn't sure if it was morning or afternoon. A glance at the kitchen clock told him it was only a little after ten. Wherever she was, she couldn't have read his text, or she'd be here surely?

He dragged his cases up the stairs and put them on the spare bed. More than anything he wanted a shower and a change of clothes.

He made quite sure that Kate was not working in her studio and hadn't heard him and went to see how far she had got with decorating the lounge.

The furniture was still covered with dust-sheets, but work was well underway. She had finished the ceiling and painted the coving and all the woodwork. The old wallpaper had been stripped away and the walls above the wooden dado rail had been painted in a warm shade of terracotta. One wall was completed, with the bottom part papered in a heavy, and slightly ornate, striped pattern in deep burgundy, dark terracotta, ivory and gold. Will had not particularly liked the design but was forced to say it looked wonderfully rich on the walls of the old room. He smiled to himself. Kate had been right, as always, with her colour choices.

Sick and exhausted, he needed a shower, or maybe a bath. Everything else could wait. He went back upstairs. He had thought Kate must be walking the marshes, but he saw that her car had gone. Maybe she had mustered the courage to go into the town, or at least the supermarket.

He opted for the bath and was soon luxuriating in one of Kate's bath foams. It smelt of lavender and the hot water soothed him.

The sound of someone opening the front door made him realise that he had dozed off. 'Kate! Up here, sweetheart! I'm in the bath.'

There was the sound of hurried footsteps and then a door closing. His brow furrowed for a moment, and he was about to get out when he heard her call out that she would be with him a minute. Then, after considerably longer than a minute, she was with him, giving him a wet hug and a kiss. 'I didn't expect you until much later.'

'I did text you.' He bit his lip. He didn't want a row. 'Long story. I came home in less than style, but I'm here, that's all that matters.'

She took the sponge and the soap from him and began to wash his back. 'It's all over now, Bear. Are you glad you made the journey?'

He hated the casual way she spoke. It had been his only sister's funeral, for heaven's sake, he'd hardly had a choice! Once again, he stopped himself. 'Of course I'm glad I went, although it was murder being away from you. We don't do "apart," do we?'

She was slower to answer than he would have liked. 'No, of course we don't.'

'I saw how much work you've done on the lounge. It looks wonderful.'

'Not bad, is it?' He lay back in the warm water and looked up at her. She was drawn and grey, quite haggard. His initial delight at seeing her burst silently like the bubbles from the bath foam. He sat up, splashing water over the edge of the tub, and took her hands in his.

'Kate. How much sleep have you had since I left?'

'Oh, don't start, Will.' She pulled her hands away and dried them on his bath towel.

'Come on,' he persisted. 'Tell me. Have you been working day *and* night?'

She looked at him in a slightly bemused fashion. 'I . . . I'm not really sure. I finished when I felt like it. I wasn't clock watching, so maybe I did work really late once or twice.'

'And have you eaten?'

'What is this? The bloody interrogation room? You've been home five minutes and listen to you!'

'You look terrible! That's why. I'm upset. Have you looked in a mirror recently? The weight is dropping off you. I'm worried, Kate, really worried. You can't blame me for caring about you.' He stood up and wrapped the towel around himself, while she stood by the door, looking utterly miserable.

He took her by the shoulders and gently drew her closer. He felt her resist for a second, and then she allowed herself to be embraced.

'I love you, Kate, and it tears me apart to see you like this. Be honest with me. Have you had a proper meal since last Wednesday?'

She sighed. 'I've picked at things. You know me when I get working, I don't have time to fanny around cooking. I've had stuff from the fridge and sandwiches. Oh, and some fruit.'

He didn't believe her. He was sure if he checked the fridge, nothing would have been eaten. He had bought her half a dozen individual ready-made meals and even made some of his special Bolognese sauce and put it in the freezer for her. He supposed it was all still there, untouched.

'This isn't good enough, Kate,' he said softly. 'You have to start looking after yourself or you're going to get ill. Then you will have no choice about seeing the doctor, will you?'

Her face contorted in fear. Her eyes widened. 'No doctors! We agreed!'

'Then you are going to eat and rest. If necessary, I will force-feed you and tie you down, understand?'

'I'm not on a hunger strike, for Christ's sake! I just . . . forgot, okay?'

'No, not okay! Oh God! What a mess!' He felt tired again. He hugged her tighter. 'Well, at least I'm here now. I can cook, make sure you get something nutritious down you again. Oh, Kate, what am I going to do with you?'

She looked up at him, her dark eyes filled with emotion. 'I don't know, Will. I really don't.'

'Will you please make an effort? Now I'm back. Will you try?'

She pulled away from him. 'I haven't done any shopping, I'm afraid.'

Will wasn't surprised to hear that. 'It's alright, we can eat the meals that are in the fridge. I'll go to the supermarket and get fresh bread and milk in the morning. I thought maybe that was where you were when I got home,' he said. 'Your car wasn't here.'

She turned and went to the door. 'I'll make you some tea, shall I?'

'Where were you, sweetheart?'

'When?'

'You know when.' He sighed. 'When I got back an hour ago.'

She bit her lower lip. 'I went to get some petrol. I forgot to fill up before you went away. I was going to go on into the town, but I'm not ready for it yet. I'm sorry, but you'll have to do the shopping for a while longer.'

'I'll shop for as long as you like, just as long as you don't give up on yourself. You have to keep trying, Kate, okay?'

Kate gave him a wan smile and nodded. 'I'll make that tea.'

* * *

That night he prepared a somewhat makeshift dinner and they had a couple of glasses of wine. Kate had resumed her work on the lounge in the afternoon but had promised to give it up before supper.

After they had eaten, he told her about Canada, and Guy's act of quiet heroism. He also said how friendly and welcoming everyone had been and asked Kate if she'd like to go there for a holiday.

She stared down into the ruby liquid in her glass. 'One day, maybe.'

'It's a breathtakingly beautiful country. It would inspire your work.'

Still she would not look up. He noticed how tightly she gripped the stem of her glass. 'As you say, one day. Want a top-up?'

She held out the glass, still in one piece. He poured the wine and sat back in his chair. 'Fancy an early night?'

He fully expected her to find an excuse, but she flashed him a rare smile and said that would be lovely.

For the first time since he got back, she told him that she had missed him.

For once, she didn't visit her studio, and was still in his arms when the misty grey light of morning filtered through the window.

CHAPTER TWELVE

Matt and Liz lingered over breakfast, not wanting the day to begin. Matt had promised to go to Holland House and see Kate, under the pretext of sharing some of his local history knowledge. He wasn't looking forward to it.

'I had an enquiry about another private investigation while you were away,' said Liz, helping herself to more marmalade. 'It doesn't sound too challenging, but I said I'd ring back today after I'd spoken to you about it. His name is Nigel Foreman, a businessman from Fenchester who owns several village stores in this area. He's concerned that one of the store managers is using his shop to fence stolen goods. He told the police, but nothing came of it. It's being going on for some time, apparently, but he hasn't managed to get a single bit of proof.' She looked at Matt. 'His problem lies in the fact that the guy who is managing the store is also his brother-in-law, and if he's wrong, well, it could cause an almighty family bust-up.'

Matt raised an eyebrow. 'Sounds like something we could handle, doesn't it?' He frowned. 'Although I feel bad that we've had no luck in finding whoever was carrying out those attacks on Emilia Swain. And then there's Kate. I have a feeling you may be right in saying that something tragic could happen unless Will finds a way to get her some professional help.'

Liz pulled a face. 'Suppose I go and talk to Mr Foreman and tell him we have a case to tie up but if he is prepared to wait, we'll look into it for him? What do you think?'

'Good idea.' Matt smiled across the table at her. 'I know we don't need the money, but if we want to build up a viable business, we need small jobs like this. I'll go and see Will and Kate, and you see what the timescale is on Mr Foreman's job. I had a text from Will, he's off to the supermarket and will be home around ten thirty, so I'll aim for then. I'll call in on Emilia at the same time.'

Liz drained her cup. 'Sounds good to me. It's only seven thirty, but I'd better go and get a shower.' She gave him a knowing look. 'Want to join me?'

Matt smiled broadly. 'I should go away more often. And as you say, it's still early, isn't it?'

They left the breakfast things and hurried back upstairs.

* * *

As Will prepared for his assault on the store, Kate pressed on with her decorating. She looked considerably better this morning, if you chose to ignore the panda eyes and the body that was little but skin and bone. Will decided that a sleep and the food had done her good. He had said he was happy for her to continue working on the house, just as long as she ate everything he prepared for her — breakfasts, lunches and dinners, and that she did not work on into the night. She hadn't been exactly enthusiastic, but she hadn't objected, so Will had some hope.

He strode out to his car and stopped. Some fleeting thing had caught his attention. Then it had gone. He stared back at the house, but it was lost to him. He sniffed. Annoying.

* * *

At twenty past ten, shopping complete, Will kicked open the back door and called for Kate to help him in with the bags.

He had unloaded the vehicle and dragged it all into the kitchen before she appeared.

'Sorry, Bear. I was on the phone. Someone I contacted through the internet had some information for me about Whisper Fen, and he had some great new websites for me to look at. How was the shopping spree?'

Biting back his comment on her obsession with Whisper Fen, Will mustered a faint smile. 'Oh, spent a fortune as usual, but at least we'll have some fresh food to eat. How's your work going?'

'Slow. Better get on.' She left him to put away the groceries and returned to the lounge.

He made coffee and took it into her. A glance around the room revealed little difference from when he had left for the shops. He guessed that her phone call had sent her scurrying to the computer, abandoning the lounge. He offered to help her, but she declined.

Not much keen on wallpapering, Will didn't argue. He said he would go and do some odd jobs. Remembering the muddy shoes, he made his way out to the porch.

He washed off the mud ready for polishing when he remembered what had bothered him earlier. As he had pulled on his trainers, he had seen Kate's best black shoes on the shoe rack, their slender heels caked in mud. Now they were gone.

Where had she been in a pair of Gucci heels?

He finished his job and decided to ask her. Then he saw Matt's Toyota pulling up outside.

'You look full of the joys of spring,' he commented as Matt strode towards him.

Matt gave him a wink. 'Oh, do I? Now I wonder why that is.'

Will thought of his own cool reception and felt empty inside. He changed the subject. 'What have you got there?' He indicated the folder under Matt's arm.

'More photos, a few old newspaper cuttings and some interesting stuff about the building of this house. Heaven knows why my parents had it, but I found it with some old deeds and documents that belonged to them. It even lists the materials used and the names of the builders. I reckon Kate'll love it. Even I have to admit it's interesting.'

'Oh, you'll be her friend for life,' said Will bitterly. 'Sorry. That came out all wrong.'

'Been a bit fraught, mate?' Matt asked softly.

'Could say that. But come in and see what she's done with the lounge. It's impressive, even if she's nearly killing herself getting it done.' He led the way into the house. 'I'll leave you two to it while I make some tea, okay?'

Matt nodded. 'Just give me enough time to do a bit of evaluating. I'm wearing my police hat today and I'm going to use some of my old investigative skills.'

'As long as she doesn't suspect anything.'

Matt smiled. 'Rest easy. I'm just a fellow enthusiast, full of eagerness to impart what I know about the marsh here.' He lowered his voice. 'The good bits, anyway, nothing too macabre, I promise.'

'Okay, well, I need to go and check my emails. I'll bring you a mug of tea later.'

Matt went into the lounge. Will listened to him making all the right noises before going into the small room off the hall that they used as a study. He logged into the computer.

He skimmed through his own mail, deleting most of the messages, then took a look at Kate's emails. He found a string of unopened messages, and dozens of websites that she had saved as favourites. All had to do with genealogy or local history.

He opened one and found it was an old story about a local eel-catcher. He left that one and clicked on another that consisted of a series of sensational newspaper articles, including a story about the disappearance of a two-year-old girl from Whisper Fen.

He sat forward, closer to the screen, horrified. There was a third child then. A third lost child at Holland House.

He read on. According to the article, it had occurred three years after the house was built. Victoria Holland, the rich farmer's daughter-in-law, to whom the house had been given as a wedding present, had given birth to twins — a boy called Albert and a girl named Elizabeth. Shortly after their second birthday, the children had been playing in the garden in the care of their nanny. This woman had apparently returned to the house in order to get her charges some cool drinks. When she came back, a matter of minutes later, the little boy was alone and crying. Elizabeth Holland had disappeared without trace.

Will groaned in dismay. Kate must not read this. He deleted the message and the link. Then he realised that she must have made a note of all these website addresses from the phone call. He sifted through the papers on the desk but found nothing. Then he searched the waste bin and found it. He removed the screwed-up piece of paper and pushed it in his pocket, collected up the bin and took it out to the incinerator in the garden, where he burned the lot.

He went to the kitchen with a heavy heart. How many more dark secrets did Holland House have to reveal? And how many of these would his wife discover?

While he made tea, Will listened to Kate's excited voice praising Matt for remembering some choice piece of information about the fen.

He carried their mugs into the lounge. Kate called out, 'Oh, I'm so glad Matt came to see me today, darling! He's a treasure trove of information.'

Will summoned a grin. 'That's our Matt for you, a right little treasure.'

'And here's the best bit. He knows an old man who has lived here all his life. And he used to work in the garden here! He's going to take me to meet him. Isn't that great? I bet he'll have some incredible stories.' Her dark-rimmed eyes burned almost feverishly.

'Absolutely, babe.' Will turned to Matt. 'Thanks for taking the time to do this. As you may have gathered by now, my lovely wife has something of an obsession with Holland House.'

'And rightly so,' Matt said. 'I'm a great believer in learning the history of your local area.'

'See!' Kate flung at him. 'I'm not the only one who wants to learn everything I can about this magical place.'

Matt stayed for another half-hour before taking his leave. 'I promised to call in at Emilia Swain's place on the way home. I'm just hoping that nothing else has happened to her.' He looked at Will. 'Fancy a ride out there? Then you can walk back.'

'Sure, then it'll be time for me to get lunch.'

'Kate, I'll ring you as soon as I can get hold of old Amos, then we can go and visit him, okay?' He smiled at her. 'And I think you're making a fantastic job of the room. It's perfect.'

Kate squeezed his arm affectionately. 'Thank you, Matt, I want to make Holland House proud again.'

'Well, you're doing incredibly well.' He patted her hand. 'And Liz and I will continue to look for anything that will help you with your project.'

Outside, Matt exhaled loudly. As soon as the car door closed, he said, 'Oh my! I'm starting to see why you're so worried about her. My friend, you have to get her some help. You just have to.'

Will groaned. 'You don't know what she suffered last time. It was horrendous. She would never forgive me if I put her through that hell again. I'd lose her, Matt, I know it.'

'You could lose her anyway. A condition like that left untreated could have terrible consequences.' Matt started the car and drove slowly down the lane. 'Look, is there any way you can get into her studio and take some pictures of her latest paintings? I really need to see them. And, Will? With your permission, I'd like to run them past Laura Archer. Besides her work for the force, she also does the occasional session in the community. At the very least, you would get a professional opinion on Kate.'

Will was torn. He didn't really need a professional to tell him that Kate needed help. 'I'll try to get the pictures, Matt. I'm assuming that's why you are carting her off to meet this Amos character? To give me time to do a bit of breaking and entering?'

'Neat, wasn't it?'

'And very convincing. But just for now, Matt, if I get those pictures, you will keep them just between us — and Liz, of course?' Matt nodded. They had arrived at Emilia Swain's cottage.

Will started to get out of the car. He stopped. 'Jesus! Look at that!'

Emilia's front door, the limewashed walls of the cottage itself, and her gate, were daubed with black swastikas.

'Oh shit! The poor woman!' Will and Matt ran up to the cottage. No one answered their knock, and when they looked through the garage window, they saw that her car had gone. Will wondered if she had already seen the desecration and had gone to the police, or whether this latest bout of vandalism was to be yet another unwelcome surprise for the old lady. They stood in silence, surveying the grim graffiti.

Matt's phone rang.

'Liz?'

'Mattie! I've got Mrs Swain here.' She sounded upset.

'I know what you're going to say. Will and I are at the cottage now. Have you called the police?' he asked.

'Just done it, they are sending a crew out. Will you wait for them, Matt?'

'Of course.' Matt shook his head. 'Hell, Liz, I was only a few metres up the bloody road! How is Emilia?'

'Distraught. As you can imagine, this has hit her hard. When you are through there, can you come home and then escort her back to Little Anchor? She's going to pack a few things and will stay with one of her late husband's relatives in Louth.'

'Best thing. And tell her yes, I'll bring her back as soon as the police have finished out here.' He ended the call.

Will photographed some of the graffiti on his phone. Then he rang Kate. 'I'm going to be a bit later than I said, Kate, and I've sent you some pictures of what they've done. Take a look and tell me what you think.' For some reason, Will sensed that something wasn't quite right about the symbols painted on the wall.

After a moment or two she rang back. 'Whoever they are, Will, they aren't fascists — well, not very smart ones anyway. The symbols are back to front. Hitler's swastika was a Greek cross with the arms bent at right angles, going clockwise, but these aren't like that. The swastika is an old Sanskrit symbol for good luck and well-being. Any real Nazi would get that right, wouldn't they?'

He grunted. 'I had a feeling you'd know, but where on earth do you get all this stuff from? No, don't tell me — research.'

'Of course. Fairies and other magical beings are all tied in with signs and symbols. Think of the unicorn.'

'So? If it's not some neo-Nazi group, then who the hell is trying to frighten this old lady to death?'

'I have no idea. That's your department, Mr Policeman. I'm just a researcher. Now I have to get back and finish what I was doing. See you soon.'

Will put his phone back in his pocket and told Matt what Kate had said.

Matt shrugged. 'Really? Would that honestly make a difference? I'd be surprised if the little shits can spell, let alone get their swastikas the right way round. What else can it be but her being Jewish?'

'Well, Bryn Owen did say there was a nasty faction operating from out Nottingham way, so if I was them, first thing I'd do is check out any fascist organisations that could have a cell round here.' It was the correct route to take, but Will couldn't shake the feeling that all this was about something very different indeed. But what?

Matt paced around the garden. 'Poor woman! She's made such an effort to sort out the last lot of damage, now this! It's so damned unfair! I'd like to knock six bells out of whoever did this.'

Will said, 'I know her going away makes sense, especially for her safety, but I hope that isn't what someone is relying on.'

'Yeah, I get your point,' Matt said. 'I must ask her if there's anything of particular value in that cottage. Something that would be easier to take if she were out of the way.'

'I thought she was getting cameras installed? They would help with this sort of vandalism,' said Will.

'Apparently, the company she chose have gone bust. Unless I'm wrong, Liz sourced another one for her and they should be setting something up later this week.' Matt sighed. 'Bit late, but if what you suggest is true, then they could still be useful.' He stared down the lane. 'Look, if you want to get back to Kate, I'll wait for the police. Then I'll get home and do what I can to sort out Emilia.'

As there was little he could do here, Will agreed. He'd promised Kate regular meals and he had yet to prepare lunch. 'Okay, but ring me later, won't you? I'll start taking regular walks down here, several times a day and maybe once late at night. I swear there's an ulterior motive for all this, and we're just not getting it.'

'Damn right we're not getting it! Bloody hell, Will, we were a couple of the Fenland Constabulary's finest, a DI and a DCI, and this piece of shit is running rings round us! Damn it, Will, that hurts!'

CHAPTER THIRTEEN

It was mid-afternoon by the time Matt and Emilia arrived back at Little Anchor. He was surprised to see Will coming towards them down the lane.

'I just wanted to say how sorry I am, Mrs Swain,' said Will. 'And to offer to try and sort this, er, artwork out for you.'

She gave him a weak smile. 'That's very kind, Mr Stonebridge, but we've already phoned a company who specialise in getting rid of this sort of blasphemy.' She threw a disdainful look at her once beautiful cottage. 'They wreck my beautiful garden, then they pollute the very bricks and mortar of my home. I'm speechless.'

They accompanied her inside and watched while she pulled clothes from an old oak wardrobe, ready to pack. 'I cannot stay and look at that . . . that filth! It will never come off, and even if it does, my home has been indelibly stained. Who is doing this, Mr Ballard? Mr Stonebridge? My God, you have no idea how much my family hated the Nazis. My dear father worked for British intelligence, for God's sake! Now it feels like history is repeating itself and they are attacking Jews again!'

Angrily, she threw open drawers and snatched at odd items of underwear and stuffed them into a case.

'Mrs Swain, can you think of anyone who may have a grudge towards you? Forget the Jewish element for a moment. Have you or your family ever had enemies for any other reason?' Will asked.

She gave a short, hard laugh. 'We were German and Jewish. We always had enemies. But no, after the war my parents worked hard at fitting in, being part of the community. It was tough, very tough, but they succeeded.' She sighed at the memory, 'Except that my poor mother struggled with the English language, I was brought up bilingual, and I still blame her for my never losing her accent.' Now her tone softened. 'My husband was a well-respected — indeed, well-loved — man, and as his wife, I was accepted too, in time. No, Mr Stonebridge, I have no enemies here.'

'I know we've asked this before, but are you sure no one has ever offered you money to move? I keep thinking about property developers. There are housing estates springing up everywhere these days,' Matt said.

'No, and I am certain that the farmer who owns the land surrounding the cottage would not let it go for building. Henry Porter is a man of the countryside. He hates the way the towns are spilling over into the rural areas. He's vehement about it. No, no one has approached me, and I wouldn't have sold if they had.' She frowned. 'Now, of course, I'm not quite so sure.'

Matt hated to think of her being ejected from the home she loved through no fault of her own. 'Look, don't make any decisions just yet. Have a break, get the cleaners to sort out the graffiti, and then think again. Will you leave me a contact address? I can let you know when the work is finished, and Will and I will keep an eye on your post, if you like?'

'I will leave you a key, if that is alright with you, Mr Ballard? If you don't think it an imposition?'

'Of course not. I'll be happy to help.' He gave her a rueful smile. 'I'm just sad that we've not managed to protect you from it all. To tell you the truth, Will and I are feeling pretty useless.'

The old woman went to a bureau in the corner of her bedroom and took out a sheet of white paper. On it, in elegant script, she wrote a name, address and telephone number, and her mobile number, and handed it to him.

'No one could have done more. And you're both being so kind. It means a lot to me. Lena is a dear old friend, as well as a relative of my husband. She used to live in the old Manor House in the village here, but it got too much for her after her family grew up and her husband died. She now has a nice little bungalow in Beckington, near Louth, and I can stay for as long as I want. She was a great friend of old Mrs Holland, too. She is a good woman, she will make me welcome.' She turned to Will and smiled. 'Oh, and do tell your wife that I will be staying with Lena Marshall. They met at the funeral. Mrs Stonebridge was quite taken with her, Lena having spent such a lot of time at Holland House in the past.'

Will froze, then stuttered, 'Funeral?'

'Yes, Mrs Holland's funeral. It was very good of your wife to attend, when she clearly isn't very well herself. There were precious few who did, I can tell you. I know it was rather early in the morning but even so, the crematorium chapel was almost empty. Just myself, Lena, a couple of representatives from the home, and your good wife.'

Matt watched as Will struggled to cover his confusion. 'Oh, yes, of course. I was in Canada at the time. I'd forgotten.'

Emilia seemed to accept that and continued with her packing. Matt caught Will's eye and nodded towards the door. 'Shout when you're through, Emilia, and we'll carry your cases down.'

He hurried Will downstairs. 'What was that all about?'

'Black Gucci shoes with mud-covered heels.' Will looked shell-shocked. 'When I came home from Canada, Kate wasn't there. I got in the bath, and heard her come in. She was ages before she came and found me. I asked where she'd been, and she said to the garage for fuel. But I saw her best shoes in the porch, the heels all muddy.' He looked as if he was about to cry. 'So much for getting petrol! She had been at the funeral. How could she, Matt? We travelled halfway across the world without her because she couldn't face going to my only sister's funeral. She couldn't be there to support me in my grief, yet she managed to dress up and drive herself to the cremation of a complete stranger! I didn't even know the woman was dead!'

Matt didn't know what to say at first. He gripped his friend's arm tightly. 'Look, Will, you need to get a hold on this. There's one hell of a difference between flying off to another country and driving a couple of miles in familiar territory. And don't forget, Mrs Holland was her only living link to the place she's obsessed with. In her fragile state, I'm willing to bet that Kate believed she had no choice.'

Will looked at him, hollow-eyed. It was going to take him some considerable time to get over this apparent betrayal.

'Come on, man! She's far from being herself, and you know it. Cut her some slack. Just don't go storming off home to have a go at her. We both know that could have disastrous consequences.'

'I'm ready!' Emilia called down. Her voice seemed to rouse Will from his stupor.

'Coming!' he called back. He swallowed. 'I hear what you say, Matt. I'm just hurt, and I think I have every right to be.' He went back up the stairs two at a time and collected the bags.

Five minutes later, the two men watched Emilia Swain's new Volvo drive away in a cloud of dust.

'Bloody shame,' growled Matt. 'We must find out what is going on here. We have to.'

Will nodded absently.

'Want me to come back with you, Will?' Matt asked.

Will shook his head. 'I appreciate the offer, Matt, but it's okay, I won't mention it — well, not tonight. Maybe another time when I'm less emotional, but I won't have a go, I promise.'

'Okay, then I'll head off home. If you see my vehicle around, it'll just be me keeping an eye on Emilia's place.

Not that I think I'll do any better than I did before. Speak tomorrow.'

He watched his friend trudge slowly back along the lane, head down and shoulders drooping. What has happened? Matt thought. Whisper Fen used to be a happy place, but now an old lady was fleeing her home and a happily married couple were disintegrating before his eyes. Oh yes, and not to forget their other neighbour, the possible paedophile, just down the road in Tylers Lane.

Shaking his head, Matt got into his car and revved the engine.

* * *

Will made his way slowly down the lane, trying to gather up the tattered remnants of his composure before going into the house. Right now, he couldn't trust himself to speak to Kate. He would be sure to say something he'd regret, words he couldn't take back.

He sat on a wooden feeding trough and stared out across the salt marsh. He had to remember that he was not dealing with a rational person, to remind himself that Kate was ill and that was why she was behaving as she was. Most of all, despite her betrayal, he knew she still loved him.

He felt drained. Empty and confused, and lonely. Then he thought of Matt and Liz. Matt was right. He should say nothing to Kate about what she'd done. After all, she had suffered a similar illness in the past and come through it. With his help and love, she would do it again.

His phone rang. It was Matt. 'I've been thinking, Will, and I had to ring.'

'You can only be five minutes up the road!'

'I know, but listen. You know how much Kate is obsessed with the house. I swear she simply couldn't stop herself from going to the Holland woman's funeral. To her mind, she had no choice. It had nothing to do with not wanting to go to Canada with you. Just think, she really couldn't have stood at a graveside, not after little Emma. It would have destroyed her. The Holland funeral was quite different. She saw it as a responsibility that she couldn't neglect. She was compelled to go. You do see where I'm coming from, don't you?'

Will exhaled. 'Yes. Yes, I think I do.'

'So, keep what you know to yourself, okay?'

Will felt a rush of affection for Matt Ballard. He was truly lucky to have such a caring friend. 'I'll do as you say, Matt. And we'll talk tomorrow. Oh, and thank you. I could have really blown it this evening.'

'Hang on in there, my friend.'

Will spent the rest of the way back to the house rehearsing what he would say to Kate. He had never been a good actor. Eventually, he decided to blame any change in his behaviour on the pain in his arm.

He opened the door to a silent house. Maybe she was in her studio again. Then she came in from the garden and gave him a hug and a peck on the cheek.

'How is Mrs Swain? You were gone ages. I was worried about you.'

He choked back his sarcastic retort and managed a grin. 'She's gone to stay with a friend. Matt has her key, and we said we'd forward her mail. She's understandably cut up. In fact, she's thinking of moving away.'

'Oh no! That's terrible. The poor thing. It's not fair!' She brushed a strand of hair from her face and he noticed how prominent her cheekbones were. He hadn't expected her to show so much sympathy for Emilia's plight, and it took him aback slightly. Recently she hadn't seemed to care much about anyone or anything other than the house.

Will tried to keep his voice level. 'I'm sure she'll see things differently if we can nail the bastards who are doing this.'

'We?'

'Sorry. I meant the police — and Matt and Liz.'

She touched his face gently. 'Do you miss it very much?'

He swallowed. Her mood swings were very hard to cope with. He didn't know who he was talking to any more, or how to respond. He was tired of having to constantly try not to upset her. 'Oh, you know, sometimes, I guess. But there is plenty to do here, isn't there?'

She looked miserably down at her trainers, and then into his eyes. 'You are having to do everything, aren't you, my Bear? You are carrying me at present, and it's not fair on you. I promise that as soon as this book is finished, I'll pull my weight again, I really will.'

He wondered vaguely why, after an encouraging start, all his good nourishing meals seemed to have made no difference to her. He ran his fingers through her hair. How dry it was. Only a short while ago her hair had been rich and shiny, full and thick. She was turning into a black-and-white negative, all colour drained from her. She, who had shone so brilliantly. He held her to him and kissed her. 'I love you, babe. I'll do it, for as long as it takes.'

She kissed him back. 'I love you too.'

He began to berate himself for his anger over the way she had sneaked off to attend that woman's funeral. If she was sick, she needed his support, not his condemnation. Perhaps it would not be so difficult to act normally after all.

'I want you to see something, Will. Come up to the studio.'

He started. She wanted him to see her work? He followed her upstairs.

The studio was unusually tidy. Only the doll, leering at him from the windowsill, jarred. He looked away.

'I have been forced to accept that if I really want to spend time on the house, and my own work, I have to get Angela's illustrations out of the way, so . . .' She removed the paper covering from her worktable. 'I admit that I *was* working all hours, but I've produced these.' She stood back.

Will approached the table, looked down and gasped. 'This is for the new book? You've done all these? That's amazing.'

The table was covered with finished illustrations, every one of them delicate, intricate. They must have taken hours to complete. Looking closer, he noticed that they seemed darker, slightly more malevolent than the ones she had done for previous books. He wondered if this was intentional, because of the storyline, or whether her depression was creeping into her work. 'They are incredible, darling. This new character is quite powerful, isn't she?'

'Mmm, she turned out just as I hoped. And seeing that Angela's next book is the last, I thought I'd ramp it up a bit. Give her Magical Garden of Gort a bit of an edge.'

Well, you certainly did that, thought Will.

'I just have the main plate to finish now, and then it's done.' She went to her easel and took the cover from her work in progress.

Again Will gasped. 'What's her name? She's amazing!'

Kate laughed, and he heard the old Kate in it. 'She's called Alyena. I think Angela drew the inspiration for her from Helen of Troy. She was supposed to be the most beautiful woman in the known world.'

'Wow. Well, she's that, alright!' Alyena was indeed beautiful, but he detected the slightest hint of cruelty around her lips.

Will stood back and couldn't help taking a quick glance around, just to see where her collection of "alternative" paintings was stacked. He spotted them at the back of the room, all shrouded in dust-sheets. Now he knew where to find them when he returned to take his clandestine shots for Laura.

'You can see why I was so tired,' Kate was saying, 'but all for a good reason. Two more sessions on Alyena here and I can kiss the bloody fairies goodbye for a while, and do what I want to do.'

'And eat and sleep and build yourself up again,' he added. 'I think your work is breathtaking.' He hugged her. 'I'm so proud of you, Kate.'

Did he feel her flinch slightly, or was it his imagination? He really must not analyse her every movement or expression. He should just enjoy having the old Kate back for a while, because it wouldn't last.

CHAPTER FOURTEEN

Matt paced the kitchen, fuming at their inability to protect one little old lady from vandals and threats. 'It has to be someone who wants that cottage, but why? There's nothing special about it. There's an empty cottage two houses before Little Anchor, it's the same size and of similar design. If they wanted somewhere close to the marsh, why not have that? It's going for a song, apparently.'

Finally, he sank down on to a kitchen chair and stared at Liz. 'Sorry. Rant over.'

She gave him an understanding smile. 'Now it's my turn. I went to see Mr Foreman about that job he would like us to undertake, and although I know you are eaten up with worry about Will and Kate, as well as Emilia Swain, I think we should accept.' He opened his mouth to object, but she held up her hand. 'Before you say anything, Mattie, listen to this. I took the address of the village store in question and drove past on my way home. I parked up opposite and sat there for a while, just to get a feel for the village and his clientele, and I saw someone I recognised going in. Remember Clem Cutler?'

'Do I ever! What a toe-rag he was!' Matt exclaimed.

'Well, he was there, in and out in minutes. I already have a slim suspicion of what could be going on, and if I'm right, I think I could get Mr Foreman the proof, or at least the information he needs to act on, very quickly indeed.'

Matt sucked in air. 'I see. My only worry is Whisper Fen. Things seem to be getting worse out there and I could easily get sidetracked. I wouldn't want to let a client down.'

'I've told him we are pretty tied up, but I'm happy to make a few low-key enquiries, so long as he doesn't need results yesterday. So far, he's just delighted that we'll look at it for him.' Liz leaned closer. 'But that isn't all, Mattie. I noticed something else. In a corner of the pub car park, where I was sitting observing the store, I saw a man talking heatedly to a shadowy figure inside a battered blue Ford Fiesta. It was Gerald Grove, Mattie!'

Now he was really interested.

'I tried to get a look at the driver of the car, but I could only make out a shoulder and a close-cropped head. I'd have had to get out of the car to see the reg plates, unfortunately, but I did see Grove back away from the Ford, remove something from his inside pocket, and pass it in through the open window. Then he buggered off. So did the Ford Fiesta, and from where I was sitting, I couldn't see much of the vehicle, other than the make and colour.'

'Drugs?' asked Matt.

'I don't think so. It was more like a large envelope than a proper package.'

'Something crooked though?'

'Oh, it stank, Mattie. He was furtive, like a rat, glancing this way and that. Luckily, he didn't clock me.' She shrugged. 'I have no idea what it meant, but it certainly proves that Will hasn't lost his ability to sniff out a wrong 'un.'

'I never doubted that for a moment,' said Matt.

'So, are you okay if I do a little sleuthing, and possibly pick up some small remuneration, while you are being psychotherapist to Kate? I'm not being dismissive of her plight, believe me, but it's you she will respond to now you are home, not me. And I'm sure Will appreciates your support.'

Matt nodded. 'Sure, and if things calm down, I can chip in and help. Don't forget, Will originally wanted us to check out Grove, and that's just what you're doing, even if it was unintentional.'

'Great. How about a glass of wine while I prepare the dinner, and we'll work out how to proceed?'

Matt put her wine on the table. 'Would you mind if I did a night shift on obo down at Little Anchor? I've been thinking that if someone has been monitoring Emilia's comings and goings, they might have seen her drive off with luggage.'

'Or they might allow the dust to settle and return when they think everyone's forgotten about them,' added Liz, cutting up vegetables.

'True, but for some reason, I think they'll strike quickly. There has to be something they want in that cottage, even if Emilia herself doesn't know what it is.'

'Well, we all know never to ignore our intuitions, but how about if we do shifts, rather than you doing a whole night? I could go down at dusk, and then you take over at around one or two?' She looked at him. 'Shall I get the flask out? I never do obo without a brew.'

'I don't want you overdoing it, my darling,' Matt said.

'I'm okay, Mattie. I know my limitations, and I'm certainly good for a few hours' observation. Where do you suggest we park up?'

'Let's ring Will and ask if we can use his drive as a base, then walk back to Little Anchor and set up camp in her garden. She has a tiny summerhouse that they forgot to trash when they wrecked the garden. That would offer some protection and give a good view of the lane and the front of the house.' Matt took a sip of wine. 'Shall I ask him? Oh, and I'll tell him about your sighting of Grove.'

'Sounds good to me. Go for it.'

While Liz pan-fried some salmon fillets and cherry tomatoes, Matt called Will. 'He's offered to do a couple of hours as well, so that none of us gets bored or overtired, considering we aren't exactly used to it any more. He said if we cover until four in the morning, he'll wait there until around seven.'

'It'll be just like the old days, won't it?' she said and frowned. Some of the old days had almost killed them both. She saw from Matt's expression that he was thinking the same. She smiled. 'I'll rephrase that. It'll be *nothing* like the old days!'

* * *

Maybe it was the thought of doing observation again that made Will think of Billie Briars. That, or the mention of Grove. Upon whom his wife still looked benevolently. Poor misunderstood victim. Pah! What a line he must have fed her! Just like Billie Briars.

Young Billie was everything the do-gooders loved. Supposedly the product of a broken home, beaten by his father and ignored by a drunken mother, he had a baby face with an angelic expression that wouldn't have been out of place in a white surplice. But instead of a hymn book, Billie preferred to carry a knife, and that cherubic smile concealed dark thoughts that no social worker could even imagine. Billie was pure evil. But what an actor! Billie was able to turn on the charm, and the waterworks, whenever they were needed. Will's darling Kate wouldn't have stood a chance, and she wouldn't have been the first to fall for his "little boy lost" routine. He had been given more chances than anyone could count, but his luck finally ran out one dark night in a stinking alley, when he encountered Will and his crewmate.

Will and his mate had been called to a fight outside a pub in Fenfleet. When they arrived, the offending parties appeared to have sorted out their differences and were nursing only a few minor wounds. They had hung around for a while to ensure it didn't flare up again. Just as they were leaving, a middle-aged man, red-faced and out of breath from running, called out that there was something going on down a service alley at the back of the parade of shops. He had heard a cry and the sound of a scuffle but was too scared to go down there himself. The two policemen had found Billie in the middle of attacking two terrified women. He went down for rape, attempted rape, unlawful possession of drugs and assault with an offensive weapon.

Will stared out of the kitchen window, reliving his relief when the judge sentenced Billie Briars to twelve years. At least he hadn't been taken in by the amateur dramatics, and even Billie couldn't sweet-talk away the forensic evidence that had piled up against him. Little bastard. It should have been life. Will shivered. There were times when he was glad to be out of the force.

But here he was, off out on obo again. He grinned to himself and shook his head. He hadn't told Kate yet, but he had a feeling she wouldn't mind one way or the other. She might even use his absence to sneak back into her studio.

Actually, things had been better this evening, Kate's mood had remained quite stable. When it was like this, he dared to hope that maybe they were weathering the storm and soon . . . soon he'd have his Kate back again.

His mind wandered to Sophie. She had phoned him the day before, and they had talked for nearly an hour. He couldn't quite believe how easily he chatted with the child. It felt like he was back with his little sister. Even Kate commented on it, albeit somewhat sardonically. The Fauves were pleased that Sophie was settling in, although Philip was worried about going back to Germany and wondered how the little girl would handle the disruption. He was to go for a year, and his family were able to accompany him. 'It's a tough decision, Will,' he said unhappily. 'I can leave them at home, but a year apart from your kids is a hell of a long time when they're growing up. But how can I take that poor kid back to the very place where her mum and dad were killed? What do I do?'

Will had no answer to give him. After some thought, he suggested that they ask Sophie what she would like to do.

Will worried about his niece. Strange, because he'd had little to do with her while her parents were alive. Now, she had become dear to him and he wanted her to be part of his life. He had no idea how he could make that happen.

He tidied up the kitchen and found that he was quite looking forward to keeping cave at Little Anchor. He went upstairs to set his alarm clock, took a deep breath and went to find Kate and tell her.

* * *

Liz had taken the early shift. Her three hours had been uneventful. The last hour dragged, and the warm night had her fighting to keep her eyes open.

She was pleased to see Matt's large frame slipping through the summerhouse door.

'Nothing to report, boss,' she said sleepily. 'Unless you count several tom cats and a couple of hedgehogs.' She handed him the night vision binoculars. 'Don't forget, mind, no wading in alone if you see someone. Bryn Owen knows what we are up to, and if we need the Fenland Constabulary's help, we ask for it.'

Matt smiled into the darkness. 'I know the drill, Liz, and I promise I'll follow it to the letter.'

'Why don't I believe that?' she whispered back.

'Can't think.' Matt pecked her cheek. 'Now, go and get some sleep, but keep your mobile with you, just in case.'

Liz slipped silently out into the night.

* * *

Matt was an hour into his shift when he heard the noise. It was a metallic sound, a single note, like someone striking a steel drum.

He crept cautiously out of the summerhouse and listened, trying to ascertain where the sound had come from. All he could hear were the sounds of the night — the breeze blowing about a plastic bag caught in the hedgerow, the quiet knock of wood on wood from Emilia's badly fitting greenhouse door, the call of a night bird somewhere out on the marsh. And something else.

He was not alone in that garden.

The wind dropped and an eerie stillness settled over Whisper Fen.

Matt crept closer to the hedge and squinted into the darkness, trying to discern any sign of movement.

Ahead, in a narrow passageway between the house and the coal shed, was a shadow, moving almost imperceptibly towards the rear of the building. Matt took his heavy Maglite torch from his pocket and braced himself.

As soon as the shape reached the far end of the alleyway, Matt broke cover and ran. He hesitated at the corner of the house in case the villain was waiting for him and was just in time to see the dark figure move swiftly towards the back gate.

Matt crashed through the gate and almost cannoned straight into him. A vicious blow to the side of his head knocked him to the ground, stunning him momentarily. When he staggered to his feet, still groggy, his assailant was already out in the lane and running.

With no earthly chance of catching him, Matt picked up his torch and made his way to the front of the house. He sank down on to Emilia's garden seat, took out his mobile and called the police station. They would never get to the lane before his attacker vanished completely, but it was worth a try.

His head felt as though he had run full pelt into a brick wall and a wave of nausea swept through him. He told himself to ring Liz, but he didn't want to alarm her. While he waited for the sickness to pass, he tried to recall if he had noticed anything about the person who had hit him. Finally, he rang home.

Liz answered almost at once. 'Mattie! Are you okay? Have you seen something?'

He told her briefly what had occurred and that he was waiting for the police.

'Matt Ballard! If I wasn't so worried about you, you'd get the bollocking of your life!'

'I took a tumble, that's all, sweetheart. Out of practice, I guess, but I'm fine,' he lied. Meanwhile, his head throbbed as if he had the granddaddy of all hangovers.

'I'm on my way. I'll wait with you, and then I'll drive you home. We can pick up your car later.'

He was still feeling nauseous when he saw the flashing blue lights of a squad car making its way along the road from the village.

Matt stood up, dizziness forcing him to hang on to the arm of the bench for a moment before he made his way gingerly towards the two uniformed officers getting out of the car.

He was pleased to see PC Jack "Swifty" Fleet, who was accompanied by a new young female PC. She smiled at him. 'So, you're the famous DCI Ballard. Pleased to meet you, sir. PC Debbie Hume. Swifty here never stops talking about you.'

Matt managed a feeble smile. 'I don't think I am quite living up to my reputation tonight. I've been keeping an eye on Mrs Swain's house for her, but so far I've achieved nothing but a thumping great crack on the head for my trouble.'

The policewoman looked concerned. 'I don't need to tell you that you should get that head looked at, sir, do I?'

'That's exactly what I would tell a victim, but I'm fine, honestly, and besides I know what they'd say — standard head injury instructions, sleepiness, vomiting, visual disturbances and all that. No, I'm okay really, just shaken up, and I didn't black out completely.'

'Concussion can cause you to fall unconscious for just a few seconds, you know. You don't have to have been out for hours. You really should have twenty-four hours in hospital, under observation. Look at you, sir, you're still dizzy, aren't you?'

'I'm okay, really,' Matt insisted, and she held up her hands.

'Well, as you know, we can't make you go to hospital, but if you have someone at home, get them to keep an eye on you, won't you? Now, why don't you sit down and tell us exactly what happened?'

Swifty Fleet went to check the passage and the back of the house and came back to report that he had found a discarded petrol can and a torn up sheet close to the coal shed door. 'Unless the old dear has taken to setting fire to her bed-linen rather than washing it, I'd say that you have just saved her from having her house burned down.'

'What the hell is going on here? That poor woman will be forced to leave for good if things continue as they are.'

'Did you get a look at him, sir?' asked Swifty.

'No. I only saw his general build as he ran away. Very slim and quite short, about five seven, at a guess. Wore dark clothes, looked like jeans and some kind of zipped-up jacket — you know, one of those light nylon sports jobs. Oh, and a beanie hat pulled down to his eyebrows.' He stopped at the sound of an approaching vehicle. 'That'll be Liz come to collect me.'

An anxious-looking Liz hurried towards them. Swifty smiled at her. 'Sarge! Good to see you!' He pulled a face. 'Pity it had to be like this. Our Matt has had a nasty bang on the head, and he refuses to go and get it checked out.'

Matt rolled his eyes. 'Thanks, Swifty. Now I'll have Liz nagging me, as well as you two! Can we just finish the interrogation so I can go home to bed?'

With an exasperated glance at Liz, Swifty continued. 'Age?'

'No idea. I'd say youngish, but he could have been a wiry type. Certainly ran like the wind. Um . . .' Matt paused. 'He must be a local, because he veered off into the marsh, and not on a footpath either. It had to be someone who knows the area really well.'

'Or a total idiot who doesn't realise how dangerous it is out there,' said Debbie.

Matt had to agree, but when he recalled the way the man had dashed off, it was as if he knew exactly where he was going.

'We'll take a run down to Gerald Grove's place and ask him if he's seen or heard anything — not that he'd tell us if he had. I reckon the bloke's long gone.' Swifty lifted his cap and scratched his head. 'Still, we have the petrol can. I couldn't see anything else round the back, but we might see something in the daylight. Why don't you get off home now, sir? We'll talk to you again tomorrow, you can make a statement then, and don't worry, we'll go over this place with a fine-tooth comb in the morning.'

'I'll need to notify Mrs Swain. Oh, and ring Will — he was coming down to take over from me just before dawn.'

'We can ring Mrs Swain, sir.'

'I'd rather Liz or I talked to her first, Swifty. I've got the number of where she's staying back at home. I'll give it to you when I make my statement.'

'Of course, sir.'

'And I've already contacted Will,' added Liz, 'on my way here.'

'And, sir,' Jack Fleet said, regarding him anxiously. 'Back off now, please. I know you're trying to help the old lady, but attempted arson and assault are in a slightly different league to daubing someone's house with graffiti and a spot of extreme gardening. You've already had a clout for your troubles . . .'

This was no time for a discussion, so Matt raised his hands. 'You're right, and I'm sensing that Liz here is keen for me to get home. Do you want me to come to the station tomorrow?'

Debbie Hume shook her head. 'We'll be back here at first light, so we can call in on you. Any particular time suit you?'

'Whenever you want. We'll be there.'

As Matt turned to walk away, Debbie Hume took his arm. 'Sorry, sir, you still look pretty groggy to me. You can change your mind about going to the hospital if you want?'

'Liz will drive me home, and I'll get to bed.' He smiled. 'But thank you for your concern.'

He climbed into Liz's car, his already aching head reverberating with unanswered questions. Something was lurking in the corner of his mind, and it was ringing alarm bells.

'Home, James, and could we leave that bollocking until I've had a few hours' sleep?' Matt asked.

'Well, just this once. It's more than you deserve, though. Pull another stunt like that again and all hell will break loose, I promise you,' Liz said.

'Sorry, Liz,' he mumbled. 'That was really stupid, a proper rookie mistake. I deserved a bang on the head for being such a plank.'

'Well, I'm not going to argue with that,' Liz said, 'although if I'm honest, I'd have probably done the same.'

'I'm just pig sick the bastard got away. Jesus, he could have burnt the place down.'

* * *

Back at Cannon Farm, Liz sent him straight to bed. He lay with his head throbbing mercilessly. At midnight, he awoke feeling sick, but it passed, and he drifted back to sleep.

At just after seven o'clock, he awoke and sat up, but giddiness forced him to sink back on to the pillows. After a while, he tried again, this time considerably more slowly. The throbbing in his head had reduced to a steady thud. He slid his legs over the edge of the bed and sat up tentatively, considering himself quite fortunate to have got away with just a headache. His sight was unaffected, and he hadn't been sick. All good signs, he told himself.

'Hey, back into bed, you!' Liz stood in the doorway and glared at him over a breakfast tray. 'Nurse's orders.'

She placed the tray on his lap — hot buttered toast and marmalade, and a cafetière of freshly ground coffee.

'This is wonderful. I must remember to get thumped more often.'

Liz leant over, touched his temple gently and kissed it. 'There is no bruising.'

'It's really tender, though. Feels as though it should be black and blue. Still, I've had worse.' He looked up at her. 'What on earth is going on at that cottage?'

'I have no idea. I mean, why try to burn it down? If you want something from it or need the old lady out of the way for some reason, you don't torch the place. It's bizarre.'

'I'm so glad this happened on my shift and not yours, or Will's for that matter. I think my skull's probably the thickest.'

Liz raised her eyebrows. 'Now, will you be alright if I go and grab a shower? And I suggest you get one as soon as you've eaten. I have no idea when our colleagues will be calling in to see you. I've got a couple of errands to run this morning, so I might not be here when they arrive.'

* * *

The police car drew up outside at nine thirty. Matt was relieved to see Swifty climb out. It was so much easier talking to someone you knew well and trusted.

Over mugs of tea, Matt duly gave his official statement.

Swifty collected up the paperwork, put it into a folder and leant back in his chair. 'I don't like this business. We found a bloody great lump of sawn-off fence post in the back garden. Looks like that was what you got clobbered with. Your assailant wasn't mucking around either, I reckon he wanted you out of the picture for a while. Lucky you've got such a bleedin' hard head! Most people would have been stretched out in the hospital after that.'

'I wasn't far off. Your PC Hume did all she could to get me down to A & E, and at one point I nearly agreed, but to be honest, I was worried for Liz. With all these weird goings-on, I didn't want to leave her alone out here.'

'Well, I can understand that.' Swifty looked worried. 'We went down to that Grove character's cottage after you left but it was in darkness. If he was there, he certainly wasn't showing himself.'

'Well, it wasn't him last night. Wrong build, wrong height, wrong everything.' Matt looked seriously at his old friend. 'Swifty, there is something I'm missing. Something came to me last night when I was talking to Debbie Hume, but it's gone again. You know that "just out of reach" feeling? I've been struggling with it since I got up.'

'Easier said than done, but it sometimes comes back if you can think about something else for a while.'

'I suppose, but it's driving me mad.'

'If you remember, ring me.' Swifty stood up. 'I'm going down to Holland House now, to make sure the Stonebridges are aware of what's going on. I'll be warning them to make sure they lock their doors at night and maybe stay away from the marsh and the sea bank for a while.'

'They are aware of the situation, but good luck with that. Mrs Stonebridge wanders off out there all the time.'

'Well, maybe Will can keep an eye on her. I certainly wouldn't advise going out alone until we get a handle on what's happening.' Swifty smiled at Matt. 'Everyone at the station misses you, you know, and the sarge. It's not the same without you both.'

Matt felt a surge of affection for his old colleague. 'Thank you, Swifty. I do and I don't miss it, but, well . . .' He shrugged.

'DC Bryn Owen told me the super reckons you should go back in. They are precious short of experienced senior officers, and although you'd served your time, they would be happy to give you another five years before saying goodbye permanently.' Swifty looked at him and raised his eyebrows. 'As I said, it's not the same without you.'

Matt pulled a face and sighed. 'Ah, Swifty, those last two cases took me to the brink. You were there, you saw what happened. I've had enough, really.'

'Time heals. Well, I've delivered the message. Just so that you know, the door isn't closed to you.' He straightened up. 'Must go. I'll keep you posted, and I'll update Bryn Owen as soon as I get back to base. See you soon.'

Matt was moved by what Jack Fleet had said, although he was glad Liz hadn't been there to hear it. If he were honest, after a flying start, he now wasn't sure that being a PI was right for him. He was so used to the way the force worked that going solo was proving frustrating. But Liz was committed to making their new venture work, and he couldn't burst her bubble. She had fought long and hard to get herself back from the bad place she had been in, and he couldn't let her down now. And he hadn't lied to Swifty — his last case had almost finished him. Why on earth would he choose to go back into that hotbed of pressure, that violence, when he had finally found peace and quiet, and a life with the woman he loved? 'Matthew Ballard, there are times when I seriously doubt your sanity,' he muttered.

It had to be frustration that was making him think this way. He was getting nowhere while some arsehole ran rings around him. It was time to up his game.

CHAPTER FIFTEEN

Will was alone in Holland House. Kate, who had been wall-papering since breakfast, declared she needed some fresh air and was going up on the sea bank for a while. As usual, she declined his offer to accompany her. He reminded her about the unknown assailant who had poleaxed Matt and asked her, for the sake of her safety, to keep close to Holland House. To his surprise, she agreed. He was about to add a warning about Gerald Grove, but thought better of it. He watched her walk away until she was just a tiny figure on the sea bank. It wasn't until he trained his binoculars on her that he saw she was carrying the doll.

He lowered the glasses. Why on earth was she taking that thing with her? He had noticed that, lately, it was no longer confined to Kate's studio, but turned up in different places around the house.

His phone rang. It was Matt. 'How's the head this morning?' Will asked.

Matt grunted. 'Still reminding me what a stupid arse-hole I was, thanks for asking.'

'Sorry.' Will laughed. 'But don't be too hard on yourself. It could have been any of us.'

'I keep reminding myself that at least it wasn't Liz, or Mrs Swain.' He paused. 'Or you, mate. You've got enough on your plate at present. How are things today?'

'Delicate. I'd never really appreciated the expression "walking on egg-shells" until now.'

'Look, I thought I'd pop over this morning with some more photos and stuff for Kate. I won't let on that I'm coming, so act surprised — if you're okay with that?'

'Of course.' Will was certainly okay with it. Having Matt around lifted the pressure off him, even if just for a short time. 'She's up on the sea bank right now. I can see her from here.'

'Not the best place for her, but I imagine you had little say in the matter?'

'None at all. Although at least she agreed to stay in sight of Holland House. I think I'm learning how to use the place to my own advantage.'

'Sensible,' said Matt. 'Will? Can I throw something at you to consider? Well, two things actually. One is Little Anchor. Do you think what's going on there could be connected to Holland House in some way? I was thinking earlier about the property a few houses down, the one that's for sale. It's almost identical to Emilia's place, so if you needed somewhere close to the marsh, why not just buy that one?'

'So, you're thinking that the particular importance of Little Anchor is its proximity to here?'

'It's a shot in the dark, but it's possible.' Matt grunted. 'Not that I know what the heck it could mean.'

'Food for thought, mate.' Will ruminated for a moment. 'So, what's number two?'

'Does your Kate know Laura Archer? Did their paths ever cross whilst you were working? Does she know that she's the force psychologist?'

Will considered the questions carefully. 'Well, I know they've never met. I never had a lot to do with Laura. And to be honest, as soon as Kate was painting again, she was so tied up with her own work that I rarely talked about mine. I can't swear that I never referred to Laura in passing, but I very much doubt it. For reasons you will fully understand, I was wary of even mentioning anything to do with doctors or psychologists.'

'I rather hoped that was the case, Will.'

'What are you thinking?'

'I've spoken to Laura, as I said I would, about the paintings. With your permission, I'd like to tell her the full story and get her professional opinion. It wouldn't go any further, I promise.' Matt took a breath. 'She's offered to come over to Tanners Fen late this afternoon for an informal chat, and to take a look at the area. It's not a place she's familiar with. So, just in case her name cropped up in Kate's hearing, I thought I'd say she's an old work friend of Liz's. How do you feel about that?'

'I'm not sure, to be honest,' said Will quickly. 'Kate is damned canny, and she's suspicious of everything. It would have to be completely without her knowledge. Laura must never come here, not even to take a look at where we live, because if Kate ever met Laura, she'd sus her out immediately. Then life here wouldn't be worth living.'

'We'll make quite sure Kate never gets to hear of it. Your problem is that while she won't entertain professional help, you are left in the dark as to how to help her. Laura and her mentor, Professor Sam Page, are bloody good at their job, Will. They put my Liz back on the straight and narrow after having been so badly damaged in her last case, and I'd trust them with my life. If Laura can give us some basic advice as to how to treat Kate, it would help you to help her.'

Will felt a rush of affection for his friend. He really cared. 'Okay, mate. But, please—'

'Say no more. Leave it to me, and I'll see you shortly.'

Will ended the call and trained the binoculars on the lone figure, now walking slowly back towards the house. He swallowed. He wanted to run out and walk back with her, but he couldn't face that leering doll.

* * *

After his disastrous night on the watch, Matt was determined to get to grips with the problem at Little Anchor and help Will to cope with the situation at Holland House. Whisper Fen had always been a good place — lonely, yes, but tranquil. All those children lost on the marsh — he had never even heard of most of them. Their disappearances had never impinged on his life, and he didn't understand why they would now.

He gathered up the materials he had selected for Kate, and called out to Liz, 'I'll be about an hour or two, darling! And don't forget, Laura will be here at around four thirty.'

Liz was busy on the computer, searching for whatever she could find on Nigel Foreman's shady brother-in-law, Kelvin Smith, the village store manager. 'I'll be here, sweetheart. Take care!'

Matt drove across to Holland House. As soon as he drew up, Kate came out to meet him. 'Matt! How lovely! Have you managed to get hold of your old Amos?'

'I certainly have, and he's going to meet us in the Crossed Keys in Tanners Fen at midday tomorrow.' Matt smiled. 'A pint or two should jog his memory, I reckon. I had some trouble stopping him chattering on about the marsh and Holland House, so he's going to love talking to the new owner.'

Kate positively beamed. Matt suddenly noticed what it was about her that Will had tried to describe. Her eyes took on an unnatural gleam whenever she mentioned the house. It wasn't a happy light either, more a kind of fervour.

The Kate of today was a far stretch from the gentle soul who had painted fairies for children. He wondered how long it had been since she'd visited a hairdresser.

Her gaze alighted on the folder he was carrying. 'More photos?'

He nodded. 'And some other stuff that you might find interesting. It goes back to when Mrs Holland was a young married woman — just village stuff, but it gives a good insight into what life was like on Whisper Fen back in those days.'

'Oh, that's marvellous, Matt, just the kind of thing that interests me. Come on into the kitchen. I can't wait to see what you've found.' She turned and hurried inside. 'Will's just gone to the garage for fuel. He shouldn't be long.'

It was clear it was the photos that she was desperate to see, so he gave her the folder. 'You can keep them, Kate. Liz has scanned them all into our computer for when we start our research in earnest.'

'But these are the originals, Matt. Are you sure?' She held them to her chest, tightly.

'Of course, especially as they pertain to here. I think you *should* have them.'

She laid them out on the table and leafed through them. 'Oh, look at all these wonderful people! I'll need to identify them somehow.'

'I can tell you a few. Luckily, my mother had a habit of scribbling names and dates on the backs of pictures, but obviously not all.' He sat down and picked one up. 'See this man? He was the local bobby who policed this area on his bike. His name was Constable Frank Herring, and I happen to know that his great granddaughter, Penny, still lives in the area. I'm told that she is very much into genealogy. I'll bet she'd be happy to talk to us if I asked.'

'Oh, really? That would be amazing!'

They spent about half an hour discussing the photos, until Kate said, 'I really have to go and do some work, Matt. I'm almost done with my illustrations for the last but one book in the Fairy Dreams series. I can't wait to get rid of them.'

She spoke of the paintings as if she hated them. Matt said, 'I'm sure they're amazing, Kate. I remember all the earlier ones you did, and they were so beautiful. I don't suppose I could see them, could I?'

For a moment she hesitated, then, 'Yes, yes, of course you can.' She led the way upstairs.

It came as a shock to see there was a lock on the studio door, but Matt didn't comment. He knew that this hurt Will terribly and seeing it for himself brought it home to him. Poor Will. He must be living in a nightmare.

Kate's desk was covered in illustrations, with two larger studies displayed on easels. They were indeed brilliant, but even Matt, who had no eye for the finer points of art, noticed something different about these pictures. They were far more powerful than the earlier depictions of the Magical Garden of Gort and had none of their insouciance. 'They've evolved,' he stated, slightly in awe.

'They needed to,' she said flatly.

'They're breathtaking.' While he was examining one of the larger pictures, he heard the doorbell ring.

'Oh, that will be Dougie, the farmer. Will said he'd be dropping off a sack of potatoes. I'd better go and pay him. I won't be a minute.' Kate hurried out and ran down the stairs.

Matt looked around. Where were those other pictures, the ones that Will had told him about? He knew he had little time. Then he saw a series of larger paintings stacked at the back of the studio and covered in dustsheets.

He sprinted across and lifted the sheet from the first one. And gasped. Will had been right.

Matt was looking at a nightmarish painting of some hideous creature digging what looked like a grave out on the marsh. Next to it, lying on the muddy ground, was a bundle wrapped in filthy dark material. Lantern light just managed to catch a tiny, child's foot sticking out from the folds of the covering. It was brilliantly executed — yet horribly disturbing.

He replaced the sheet exactly as it had been and was back at Kate's table, just in time to hear her mount the stairs.

A few seconds later, she came in. 'Sorry about that, Matt. Have you had a chance to look at them?'

Oh yes, thought Matt, *and I've seen far too much.* 'They're quite incredible, Kate. You're a very talented artist.'

He had no idea how he managed to keep his voice steady. All he wanted to do was run from that room and out into the fresh air.

As they made their way back down the stairs, Matt was struck by the realisation that it wasn't Holland House that was affecting the sensitive Kate with its sinister history — it was the other way round. It was she who was polluting the house with her unhealthy obsession and dark thoughts. Seeing that picture caused the freshly decorated lounge to reek of malevolence, where previously, Matt had seen a delightful room full of light, with a wonderful view of wild marshland.

Back in the kitchen, he said, 'I'll let you get on, Kate. Tell Will I called, and I'll pick you up at a quarter to twelve tomorrow, okay?' He hoped he sounded casual enough. At least he was good at concealing his feelings — you had to be in his old job. He even waved cheerily as he pulled away, until, out of sight of the house, he floored the accelerator.

* * *

Laura Archer arrived punctually at four thirty, to be greeted by a warm hug from Liz. Laura, and her friend Sam Page, had helped Liz enormously when she was recovering from her traumatic last case and she owed them a lot.

It was the first time Laura had visited Tanners Fen, and she gazed around in approval. 'What an idyllic spot! It's so peaceful.'

Liz thought of Kate Stonebridge's equally beautiful situation, but there was no peace there. Matt had returned from his visit to Holland House in shock. He'd had his first insight into Kate's state of mind, and it had shaken him.

They went inside and Liz offered their guest some tea. 'Matt's just tidying himself up. He won't be long. He's been stacking logs in the store, ready for next winter.'

As Liz was bringing the tea, Matt arrived. His first words were, 'Am I glad to see you!'

'That sounded pretty emphatic,' Laura said.

And the dam burst. In a torrent of words, Liz and Matt told her about Kate and the strange way she was behaving, and their concerns for Will. Laura listened intently.

After a lengthy silence, Laura set down her mug. 'I can see that your friend is in dire need of proper help. You tell me that she refuses to ask for that help, and her husband is not prepared to go against her wishes. That means we need to try and find another way to mitigate her escalating mania and hopefully break the pattern. It will be very difficult. If she is as you describe, it's unlikely that we'll succeed without the aid of medication. Is there any way I could meet her?'

'We can try, Laura, but Will is against it at present. He's afraid Kate will realise that you're a doctor.' Matt sighed. 'The poor guy risks losing her whatever he decides to do. He's walking a tightrope, with no safety net beneath him.'

'Not quite,' said Laura with a gentle smile. 'That's exactly what you are at present. Imagine having to face all this alone, with no friend to listen to you.'

'I'm afraid of what might happen, Laura,' Matt said after a while. 'As I see it, she's heading for a complete breakdown, and if that happens, he will blame himself.'

'Is there any chance she might recover without any treatment?' asked Liz.

Laura tilted her head to one side. 'She's clearly a fighter. She came back from a similar situation once before, so she could do it again. The move to Holland House must have been quite traumatic for her, especially when she found out about the children that died there, after losing her own baby not so long before. I suppose her compulsive behaviour might resolve itself if her life gets back on a more even keel.'

'Whisper Fen isn't exactly a peaceful place right now.' Matt told Laura about the attacks on Emilia's cottage and the presence of an unsavoury character living not far from Holland House.

Laura pulled a face. 'Ah. No, it doesn't make for a relaxing atmosphere.'

Matt leaned forward. 'I only saw one of her paintings, Laura, but it was extremely disturbing. Tomorrow, I'm taking Kate to visit an old-timer who worked at Holland House many years ago. While we are out, Will is planning to get into her studio and photograph all the paintings. I'll forward them to you. I think you need to see them.'

She nodded. 'I know. I've told Sam about this case and he'd also like to see them. His help will be invaluable. From what you've told me, it's my belief that Kate's condition is due to unresolved grief over the death of her baby.'

'What advice should we give to Will?' asked Matt.

'The best thing he can do at the moment is try and keep her calm. He shouldn't try to contradict her, whatever she says. That's easier said than done with those mood swings, but even if he is screaming inside, he needs to try to keep the peace. What we don't want is something upsetting her even further. He has to try to keep things ticking over quietly, which means no nasty surprises.'

'No nasty surprises,' echoed Matt. 'It seems to me that it's Kate who's dishing those out.'

'In truth, what Kate Stonebridge needs is expert help.' Laura paused. 'It might come to that, despite everyone's best efforts.'

Though Liz didn't say so, she wondered if that might be for the best. But what would it take to make it happen? And who might get hurt in the process?

They sat talking for a while, until Laura said she ought to leave.

'Thank you so much for listening,' said Matt. 'And I'll get those photos forwarded to you as soon as I get them.'

With a final, 'No surprises, remember?' Laura Archer drove away.

CHAPTER SIXTEEN

Long before Matt was due to arrive, Will was watching the lane for signs of his approaching car.

It was the morning of Matt and Kate's meeting with old Amos. A lot hinged on whether Matt could keep Kate away from the house long enough for Will to get into the studio and photograph those paintings.

He paced to and fro, ashamed of behaving in such an underhanded way towards his beloved wife. He felt like a traitor.

As soon as he saw Matt's car, he went indoors to find his wife. Kate was upstairs in their bedroom, standing in front of the long mirror and smoothing down her jeans, which she'd tied with a leather belt to keep them from falling down. With her hair scraped back in a ponytail, she looked thinner than ever.

'Ready, sweetheart?' Will said. 'Matt's here.'

She looked like a frightened teenager. 'I haven't been out for a while, have I? Still, it's got to happen sometime, I suppose. Let's hope old Amos keeps my mind occupied. Are you sure you won't come along?'

He hugged her and found she was trembling.

‘Oh, sweetheart, you’ll be quite safe with Matt. He’s really keen to introduce you to the old guy, and you know me, I’d be bored stiff within five minutes.’

‘More like two, actually.’

‘Exactly. Tanners Fen village is only a couple of miles up the road. You’ll be fine. It’ll be good for you. You can do it, I know you can.’

She swallowed hard, drew herself up straighter. ‘You’re right. I can.’

Will waved them off, went back into the house and ran up to the studio. As he had expected, the door was locked, which meant using the ladder again.

Will hurried downstairs. He stopped in his tracks. Lying on the hall table were her keys. Seeing them there, he realised just how anxious she had been about venturing into the outside world. She normally took them everywhere with her, even to the toilet.

Back upstairs, he unlocked the door and went in.

The doll.

It sneered at him from the window seat, its derisive expression making him uneasy. He picked it up, turned it to face the window and wiped his hand on his jeans. Even touching the thing repulsed him.

He took out each painting and photographed it with his phone, making sure to put them back exactly as they had been. There were more than he’d thought. Nine dark and frightening paintings, all depicting a concealed and apparently dead child with some dreadful evil entity lurking in the vicinity.

He lingered over the one that Matt had seen. His friend had said it scared him to death. Awful in its content, it was nevertheless brilliantly executed. Soft luminescence from a lantern illuminated the scene. Though the subject matter was ghoulish and macabre, Kate’s talent was undeniable.

Will quickly went through the paintings again and came across one he had missed. He stood back and stared at it. Though it contained no monster or partially hidden baby, the painting seethed with an almost palpable sense of foreboding.

A girl of about nine or ten with wavy dark hair stood alone on the salt marsh. She wore a T-shirt and faded denim dungarees and was desperately searching for a way out of the marsh to escape the encroaching tide that was already soaking her dirty white trainers.

Unlike the others, it was set in daylight. In this painting, a swirling mist crept across a watery sun, its last rays falling on the pale and terrified face. To Will it was the most frightening of them all.

He had no idea how long he stood gazing at it — probably only a few minutes, but it felt like an eternity. Suddenly he was aware of the phone in his hand and he took a couple of shots of the painting. He replaced it and left the room, locking the door behind him.

He needed air. That last painting had hit him like a punch in the gut. Gasping for breath, he sat down heavily on the wooden seat.

Oh God! The keys! He ran back indoors and placed them back, exactly where they had been. He looked at his watch. They had only been gone for just over thirty minutes but there was no telling when Kate's nerve might fail. They could be back at any moment and he needed to be found doing an outside job, nowhere near the hall table and those forgotten keys.

He ran out to the garage, dragged out the hose and began to wash the cars, and then to polish them. As the minutes ticked by and there was still no sign of his wife and Matt, he started to relax a bit and began to hoover out her boot. He had moved to the interior of the car and was almost through when his stomach tightened. Something was wrong.

He left the cars and walked around the house, pausing at the seat that overlooked Whisper Fen. It wasn't the keys, he had replaced them alright, so what on earth was it?

He heard the distant sound of an engine. Whatever it was, Kate would be home in a matter of minutes. It was too late to fix it now.

The sun glistened off the bonnet of Matt's Toyota as it turned the bend at the end of the lane.

As the car drew up, Will glanced up at the studio window. His gut tied itself into a knot.

The doll.

Remember me?

* * *

The three of them sat around the kitchen table.

'Amos is a fascinating old boy,' Matt was saying. 'His memory is still amazing even at his age.'

That jeering face still haunting him, Will struggled to look pleased and relaxed. Why had he turned it around in the first place? What on earth did he think it was going to do to him?

'You did okay, did you, sweetheart?' he asked.

She smiled wearily, saying she was glad she had gone, although it had taken a lot out of her. To his relief, she said she would like to put some of Amos's recollections straight on to the computer while he made them all a hot drink.

As soon as she had left, he nodded to Matt. 'Mission accomplished. I'll send the images as soon as you're home.'

'Operation successful?'

'One hitch. A silly oversight. Fingers crossed that either Kate doesn't notice, or that I get the chance to rectify it before she does.' While the kettle boiled noisily, he told his friend about his mistake.

Matt looked perturbed. 'She showed me that doll when I was in her studio. She thinks it's beautiful, by the way.'

'Ugh! It's disgusting.'

'I agree, but Kate is totally enamoured of it. Calls it Elizabeth.'

Will was silent. Elizabeth was the name of the stolen Holland child, the one he had tried to keep from Kate. Had she found out about her? Or was it just a coincidence? The copper in Will was deeply suspicious of coincidences.

He made tea, and Matt took Kate hers, joining her at the computer. 'I'll go back with you anytime you like, Kate. Perhaps we'll stay for a bit longer next time, huh? Amos really is a fount of local knowledge and gossip, isn't he?'

Will joined them and watched Kate's eyes soften. 'He's wonderful. It'll be easier for me next time, I'm sure. I'm sorry if I seemed a bit on edge, Matt. I think the pressure of work, the deadlines and such, have just worn me down. Add to that the move and the effort I'm putting in to get the house as I want it, and I'm quite exhausted. I might even be becoming a tad agoraphobic.'

Will listened. It hurt him to hear her speak in the singular about all the effort being put into the house. Where did he come in?

'Thanks for your help with my research, Matt, I really do appreciate it,' she added.

'My pleasure, Kate. And Liz's too. We're enjoying it. We'll pass on anything we find, and Liz told me to tell you that should you need anything following up to let her know. She has much more free time than you.'

Kate smiled and yawned. 'Thank her for me. I might take her up on it soon.'

Matt finished his drink and smiled warmly at Kate. 'Better go. Your William's hive of industry outside has reminded me that I promised to clean Liz's car for her today. Don't get up. I'll see myself out, and I'm thrilled that we had such a successful outing.'

Kate smiled at Matt, thanked him again for his help and returned to her frantic typing. Will followed him out, closed the door behind him and walked with him to the car.

'There are ten of them, Matt. All pretty ghastly, but there is one in particular that struck me. I won't say which, but I think you'll know the one I mean when you see them.'

Matt nodded thoughtfully. 'Look, as soon as I hear back from Laura, I'm going to suggest that you and I have a quiet drink together in the local pub. At least we'll be able to talk without going through all this cloak-and-dagger rigmarole.

And do let me know if she mentions the doll. And if she accuses you of going in there deny it totally. If you are convincing enough, she'll probably doubt herself. Just brush it away as irrelevant, and whatever you do, don't make a fuss.'

'Okay, but I'm not exactly the best liar in the world.' Will gave him a rueful grin.

'Then become one, mate. You know how it's done, you've arrested enough of them in your time.'

On his way back to the house, Will couldn't resist glancing up at her studio window.

The doll was gone.

CHAPTER SEVENTEEN

The pub was busy, but Will had managed to secure them a corner table tucked away beside the fireplace.

It was almost a week since Will had broken into Kate's studio, and he and Matt had finally managed to get away to "sample the local ales." Will had made it sound as if a couple of the lads from the station would also be there, a sort of boys' night out. Not that it really mattered what he said. Kate had been snappy and uncommunicative, and he was finding it difficult to get anything out of her other than monosyllables. He could only guess that she knew of his incursion into her territory.

He stared glumly into his beer. 'She hasn't actually asked me outright — in a way I wish she would. At least it'd be out in the open then. Anyway, after you brought her back from meeting Amos, and I saw the doll had been moved from the window where I'd left it, I went upstairs and found Kate in her studio with the door open. And the bloody thing was nowhere to be seen. That is, until I went into our bedroom for something and there it was, sitting on the bed. I asked her to put it back in her studio, but she gave me the most withering look and told me it was to stay where it was. I remembered what you had said about keeping everything as calm as possible, so it's still there. I have managed to get her to put it on a chair beside the bed, so at least I don't have the hideous thing staring at me all night.'

'I know it's tough, mate, but try to keep it in perspective.' Matt grimaced. 'It's just an old doll.'

'I know.' Will shook his head. 'The thing is, it's come to represent the part of Kate that I hate, the part that frightens me.'

'It's a part you don't understand, that's why it frightens you.'

Will looked up. 'Did Laura give you any hope? Did she think Kate would ever be,' he paused, 'well, normal again?'

'She said we have to hope so. Initially she recommended medication, along with therapy — both have improved since Kate was in therapy before. But when she understood that neither of you wanted to go down that route, she conceded that Kate might just be able to pull through, since she had done before.' Matt sat back. 'We spoke again yesterday, and Laura said that without being able to see Kate and talk to her, she feels like she is, quote, "trying to conduct brain surgery with a can opener and a soup ladle."' He smiled and touched his friend's arm. 'Don't look so worried, mate, no one's giving up on Kate. It's just not easy when you can't use all the usual methods.'

Will nodded slowly. 'I used to have a mate who was a paramedic. One day when he was off duty, he came across an RTA. He was in the middle of nowhere with no ambulance, no equipment or drugs and no uniform to hide behind. He said that all at once he felt inadequate and helpless. It's a bit like that, isn't it?'

Matt took a long swallow of his beer and sighed appreciatively. 'Right, pin back your ears and I'll tell you what Laura and Sam Page made of those paintings.'

Will leaned forward.

'They agreed that the death of your daughter is at the root of Kate's problems. Add to that the macabre history of Holland House.' He looked at Will. 'Me and Liz are trying to steer her towards the more "positive" historical accounts. You can rest assured that I'm sifting out anything that even hints at murder, madness and missing children.'

'I realise that, Matt. And she does trust you. Even this last week, while she has been terse and bad-tempered with me, she's still full of praise for you. But she continues to ferret out the Holland family skeletons on the web, and the stories of other people hereabouts.'

'Not much we can do about that, is there? But, right now, back to the paintings.' Matt took another slug of his beer.

'You know, when I think of her earlier work, and its light, its atmosphere of sunshine and fun, I could weep. This new work of hers is the stuff of nightmares.' Will shook his head.

'Well, Sam reckons that is exactly what they are. Her nightmares. And Kate's horrors aren't confined to the night. They are with her all the time. Did you notice that in all but the last one, that of the young girl in the dungarees, the children are covered up and partially concealed?'

'Yes, I did. What do they think that means?'

'That she cannot face them. She cannot face her problem. She has hidden them so that she doesn't have to look at them. They are there, but they don't have faces.' Matt pulled out a sheet of paper from his jacket pocket. 'I made some notes, listen. In the case of the fiend digging the grave, she is trying to bury the problem. The monster climbing the stairs with the child bundled under its arm is her trying to take the problem away without looking at it. The child hiding in the shadows from the darker figure with the evil eyes doesn't quite exist, which means Kate doesn't have to acknowledge it. There are apparently a dozen other indicators in her paintings. Fear, anger, hurt and loss, all those feelings exacerbated by moving to Holland House, a place where other women have had their children taken from them. Her grief has deepened to a point where she is taking on the loss and heartbreak of all the past Holland women. Kate isn't strong enough to cope with her own grief, let alone theirs.' Matt looked up. 'That does makes sense, doesn't it?'

It did. Oh God, Kate was obviously sicker than he had imagined, and that meant her suffering was far greater than he had believed. Poor, poor Kate. He wanted to do his best by her, but without professional help, Will had no idea how. 'Should we force her to face her demons? Make her talk about Emma?'

'I asked Laura exactly the same question, but she said no. Doing so could send her further inside herself, into a dark and tangled place where we can't follow her. I don't want to frighten you, Will, but Sam and Laura have done a kind of assessment based on both the paintings and everything Liz and I have told them, and they've said that you really do have to tiptoe around her. Kate is very poorly, quite unstable in fact, and somehow we need to support her and return some sort of balance to her life. Only she can face the cause of her illness. You can gently guide her, but you cannot *make* her do anything.'

'I really don't understand.' Will felt close to tears. 'Sometimes she is the old Kate — except for the awful weight loss. She can still be loving and funny, and she is still working! How can she do that if she is so ill?'

'How often do you see the woman you married, Will? Be honest.'

The tears began to well. In truth, he hadn't really seen that vibrant, witty and beautiful woman for months, maybe much longer. A hint of her humour, a trace of her sparkle maybe, but that was all. He was silent.

'From what Laura said, I reckon that Kate works because she has to. She has to hold on to something familiar, something she is safe with, and most of all, is in control of. It's an outlet for her pain.'

'Why can't she hold on to me?' Will's voice was close to breaking.

'She does. Although you probably can't see it, you are her rock. She can rant and rave at you, she can be moody, can vent some of the hurt and anger at you in the knowledge that you won't fail her. She knows that you love her. Her work is her anchor and you are her safety net.'

'I don't feel too strong at present. What if she falls?'

'We have to make sure that she doesn't, mate. If, God forbid, she should, then the decision will be taken out of your hands.'

'You mean the hospital?'

'If she crashes, Will, if she's a danger to either herself or anyone else, then the decision would be made by others.' Matt paused. 'If she won't go voluntarily, then she would be sectioned. You know that from all the sad cases we've dealt with in the force.'

Will shook his head.

'This is what Laura warned me could happen, and she told me to make it quite clear to you. If I kept that from you, I wouldn't be much of a friend, would I?'

'It just seems so unbelievable, so unreal. My beautiful Kate in a madhouse. It's sickening.'

Matt pulled a face. 'Come on, Will, get real. We aren't in Victorian times any more. You've seen modern psychiatric units — they're proper specialist hospitals with highly trained mental health professionals.'

'Okay, a modern-day madhouse then. She would still be pumped full of drugs and given God knows what therapy. I can't allow it, Matt, I just can't.'

'Then you need to be strong for her now, and hopefully she will never have to go down that route, although I have to say, hospital is where she would be given real help.'

Matt went to the bar for another round, while Will tried to assimilate what he had been told. One odd thing stood out in his mind. When Matt returned to their table, Will posed his question.

'What about that last picture, Matt? The girl on the marsh with the water around her feet?'

'Ah, yes. They both said that one was a puzzle. It's set in daylight, and the child is clearly visible. The kid is terrified, in danger of death from the encroaching mist and the apparently fast incoming tide, and she knows it. Sam suggested it could be how Kate herself feels, like a child, trapped by her emotions, out of her depth, scared of going under. But he said to say that he wasn't sure.' He frowned. 'He reckoned that something in that one didn't equate. It's so different to the others it could have been painted by a completely different person. Laura said that she has a colleague who uses art therapy with his patients. If you have no objection, she would like to show him the whole series of pictures, especially that one, and get his opinion. All in complete confidence, of course.'

Will agreed. 'Sure. Any help is welcome, so long as Kate never finds out.'

Matt nodded. 'I'll tell Laura first thing in the morning.' He looked seriously at Will. 'You do realise that Laura is sticking her neck out to help you both? This is very much off the record. There are guidelines that she should be following, and she really should not even have seen those paintings without Kate's permission.'

Will gave an humourless laugh. 'Kate's in no condition to give permission or not!'

'We know that, Will. But just remember, this is between us, and it's very unofficial, okay? She's doing this because she fears for both of you. Now, she also asked me about the regularity of Kate's mood swings, but I wasn't sure as most of the time I get to see the best of her, so fill me in on the darker side, would you?'

They talked for another hour, Will explaining how his wife would, in the blink of an eye, go from morose to hyperactive, and vice versa. How she got so involved in something that she forgot everything else, and then slept the clock round. And then he said how hard it was to play second fiddle to a pile of bricks and mortar, and a rag doll with the face of a streetwalker.

Chuckling at this description, Matt said, 'Laura insists you try being nice to that doll. It is Kate's connection to all the lost children, a bond between her and the other bereaved women of Holland House.'

'Then why the tart's face? You've seen it, Matt, it is positively lewd! And she is always washing it. It's a wonder it hasn't fallen to bits. It was in tatters when she found it.'

'Far be it from me to start talking like a shrink, but don't you think that maybe she has transferred a little of the evil of whatever happened to the children to the doll? Her constant washing of it is her way of trying to cleanse it, make it pure again. Bring the child back.'

It was Will's turn to laugh, even if it was a little hollow. 'You've clearly spent far too long talking to psychologists, Professor Ballard. Whatever, being nice about the thing won't be easy. Not the way it looks at me.'

Matt smiled. 'Declare an amnesty, mate. Kate will love you for it.'

'Speaking of which, I should get back to her. She might not even have noticed that I've gone, but I worry about her. I can't begin to thank you for all you're doing for us. I'm sure I'd have given up by now if it weren't for you.'

Matt leant forward and clapped him on the arm. 'Rubbish! You love her. You'd have found the strength. Anyway, it's stopped Liz and me from vegetating. And I hate to admit it, but I'm thoroughly enjoying this family history thing. I might even dig up a few ancestral roots from my own family tree when Kate is better.'

Will drove home, repeating those last four words to himself. *When Kate is better.*

* * *

For the next couple of days, Will pulled out all the stops. He thought he noticed a slight change in Kate's attitude. There were even brief moments of light-heartedness that gave him cause for hope. But they were very brief. Then he noticed her throwing him suspicious glances, and he backed off a little. He suspected that she was weighing up the reasons for his sudden about-face, especially regarding the doll. Kate was far from stupid, and there was a good chance she had put his change of tactic down to advice from an outside source. And that could mean only one thing to her — doctors. So, he reverted to acting more neutrally towards her, her ideas, and her doll.

Today she was in a strange mood. The night before, she had packed up all her work ready to send off to her agent. She had also photographed them all and sent the images electronically. The book was finally complete. She had told Will that she had never been so glad to be rid of something and had told Hubert that she needed a proper break before embarking on Angela's final volume. Apparently, he had emailed her back saying that Angela was still struggling with this last book, and it would be a while before there was any more news on that front. Kate had then gone online and booked a courier. She had put it in the hall ready for collection, muttering about good riddance to bad rubbish.

This morning, instead of being elated that the millstone had been removed from her neck, she seemed oddly disconnected from everything around her.

Will's old concerns flooded back. He stood at their bedroom window, staring out at Kate. She was up on the sea bank again, standing perfectly still and looking out across the muddy terrain. Elizabeth was clasped in her arms.

He looked away. He needed a distraction. He couldn't keep watching her like this. Maybe he'd take a stroll down to Emilia's cottage and do a quick walk round. It had been quiet at Little Anchor recently, and the cleaning company had done a great job of removing the graffiti. Now, from being adamant that she would never leave her precious home, Emilia had become reluctant to return. It was all wrong, another injustice that rankled in his head.

Will sighed. That would have to wait. God knows how long Kate would be out wandering the marsh, and the courier had not yet collected the package. He was marooned until they arrived.

He padded downstairs and tried to decide what job he could do that would please Kate, but before he could make a decision, the front doorbell rang. The courier. Good. He flung open the door and stared straight into the excited eyes of his niece, Sophie.

'Uncle Will!' She rushed forward and hugged him.

Will stood there holding her tightly. Absolutely terrified.

After stuttering out a greeting, he cast a furtive glance towards the sea bank. Fortunately, Kate was out of sight.

'We've been trying to get you on the phone all the way from Lakenheath. I just couldn't pick up a signal. Think my mobile is bust.' Philip Fauve's great hand was held out to Will. He grasped it and said, 'Come in, please.'

They made their way to the kitchen. Philip said, 'Sorry, Will, I couldn't tell you sooner. Orders only came through late last night. Germany is off until next year — some problems at the German air base so they tell me — but I have to attend a couple of important meetings at the base in Suffolk, and they gave me special dispensation to bring Sophie. When I've finished with work, we have three days' leave together!'

Their unexpected arrival had left him poleaxed. A pulse was throbbing in his neck, and all he could think of were Laura Archer's words: no surprises. What could possibly upset Kate more than a child's presence at Holland House?

His delight at seeing his lovely Sophie again was totally destroyed by fear of Kate's reaction. He made his guests a drink and ran upstairs to see if his wife was anywhere in sight. It would be some twenty minutes at least before she might get back.

Back in the kitchen, he hugged the little girl and told her how thrilled he was to see her, meanwhile flashing Philip a worried and apologetic glance. He wasted no time but began to explain the situation.

'Kate is very ill, Philip, and as much as I'd love you to stay with us here, it's just not possible. I'm so very sorry, I—'

'Hey, no sweat, Will. I remembered what you said about Kate, so we've booked into that big motel on the roundabout just outside of town. I know this all seems very strange, but Fran's having a minor op this week, nothing serious, but Annette's going to be pretty tied up looking after her, so since I have to be here, we grabbed the chance to let Sophie see a bit of her mum's home country. We knew you might be busy, but if we could see just something of you when I get back from my meetings, that would be great. Okay?'

That was a start. Will felt relieved. At least the child wouldn't be staying at Holland House. He would have to go out to spend some time with them. Kate would surely go along with that, maybe even be pleased to be alone for a while. He wondered if he should allow her to come home and find them there, or make sure he told her of their visit before she met them. He was pretty sure that whatever he chose to do would be wrong, but Philip took the decision out of his hands.

'And, I'm sorry to say that this is a flying visit too. I have to get up to RAF Waddington by two o'clock to meet with some of my superiors prior to our conference. We'll stay over at the motel tonight and return to Suffolk tomorrow morning. The conferences will be through by Friday, then I'm taking Sophie to London for a day before coming back here on Sunday. We can then spend a couple of days with you in this neck of the woods, if you can spare the time?' He lowered his voice. 'Sophie really wanted to see you again. You've become very important to her, especially since she saw you in Canada.'

The little girl had hardly spoken. She had taken Will's hand and hadn't let go all the time they were talking.

He smiled fondly at her. 'You bet! I can't wait.' He told her he wished with all his heart that she could stay with them, but that Auntie Kate was not very well at all. Perhaps when she was better, they could all have a proper holiday together.

The child's eyes shone with excitement. 'Can we, Uncle Will? Uncle Philip?'

'Sure, honey. Just as soon as Auntie Kate is better, okay? Now, we've really got to go, or they'll be sending the cavalry out to look for us. Say goodbye, Sophie. We'll see you next Sunday, Will. I'll ring from the motel and we'll make arrangements then.'

Will accompanied them to the big Ford, Sophie still clutching his hand. Reaching the car, she looked up at the facade of Holland House and said to Will, 'It's no wonder Auntie Kate is ill, living here.'

Will tilted his head to one side. 'What do you mean, sweetheart?'

She looked at Will, and then climbed into the car. 'Auntie Kate draws those wonderful pictures for children, doesn't she? Like my Snapdragon? Which means she must love kids.' She looked at the house again, and it seemed to Will that she was looking directly at the long window of Kate's studio. 'I thought you'd be living somewhere as magical as the Garden of Gort, but you don't. It must be horrible living in a place like this, and I sure can't imagine any child liking it here.'

Will stood rooted to the spot. Perhaps Kate had been right all along. This house really was no good for children.

As the car moved away, he looked at the sea bank. With her shoulders hunched and her hands pushed deep in her pockets, Kate was slowly making her way back towards the house. He kept his eyes fastened on her until she was almost at the garden gate. He was frightened, no longer in control. And more than anything, he hated Holland House. If nothing else, he knew that they had made a terrible mistake in coming to live on Whisper Fen. It had taken Sophie to finally open his eyes. The place was unhealthy, cloaked in a miasma of despair. As she drew nearer, he saw his wife's sunken cheeks. Worst of all, the place was killing her. Laura's warning that matters might eventually be taken out of his hands suddenly didn't seem so improbable.

Stepping in through the gate, his wife said, 'Who the hell was that in the big car?'

He told her about Philip and Sophie's surprise visit.

'And you didn't know they were coming?' Her tone was accusatory.

‘Of course I didn’t! Philip’s orders came through too late to ring us, then he couldn’t get a signal.’ It sounded a little lame, even to him.

‘So, you are telling me that he has come to attend some high-powered conference without any notice or preparation?’

‘The officer who was to attend was taken ill. Philip took his place. He’s had to go straight to Waddington to be briefed.’

‘And he just happened to have the kid with him? You may think I’m stupid, Will, but next time you concoct a story, make it believable, will you?’

He bit the inside of his cheek hard, forcing back the angry retort. He didn’t know whether he was more furious at her for accusing him of lying, or because she had referred to Sophie as “the kid.”

‘Believe what you want, Kate.’ He couldn’t keep the harshness from his tone. ‘But I am as surprised as you. They are coming back this way next Sunday, staying at the Fenmoor Lodge, and I hope you will be able to drag yourself away from your precious house for five minutes to meet them.’

Kate glowered at him in silence.

He heard Matt’s voice whisper in his ear. “No surprises, mate. Tiptoe on fairy feet.” He swallowed. ‘Look, Kate. They only want to see us for a bit. They won’t be staying here, and it’ll be just two days before they go back to Canada. Please come and meet them at the hotel. Just for a short while, to say hello to Sophie. Then if you don’t mind, I’ll spend a bit of time with them, show them around.’

‘They aren’t coming here.’

It was not a question, but Will treated it like one. ‘No, they’re not coming here. I know how you feel about the house, sweetheart. I wouldn’t let Sophie stay here, would I?’

Kate stared at him suspiciously.

‘Come on, sweetheart. What do you say?’

‘They can’t come here, Will.’

He began to worry. In a moment, her features had changed from angry to fearful. Her eyes had widened, and her breathing was fast.

'Kate! Aren't you listening? They're *not* coming, alright? I promise you.'

Wild-eyed, she almost screamed, 'You don't understand! She shouldn't have come in the first place! She should never have come here!'

He lost it. 'For the last time! I didn't know they were coming! But I'll make damn sure they don't come back.'

Her fury abated as swiftly as it had erupted. Kate took a slow step towards him. She studied him coolly, her face taking on a strange, almost compassionate expression. 'You really don't understand, do you, Will, darling?' She paused. 'Because it's too late now.'

'Too late for what?' His head had begun to ache.

'For Sophie.'

'Whatever are you saying, Kate? What do you mean?' How much more of this could he take?

With a sigh, she turned from him and walked towards the house.

He stood and looked at her for a moment and then came to himself.

He ran to her and grabbed her arm. 'Kate! Don't walk away from me! What the hell do you mean by "too late for Sophie?"'

She gazed down at his hand, and then up into his confused face.

'You know.' She pulled away and went inside, closing the door behind her.

CHAPTER EIGHTEEN

'Matt, I think we need a new plan of action regarding Little Anchor.' Liz handed him a mug of tea and a sandwich. 'We've ground to a halt.'

She flopped into a patio chair and looked at him anxiously. Haggard didn't suit him. 'Things aren't going particularly well, are they?'

He shook his head and took a bite out of his sandwich.

'Matt, darling, you are doing your best for Will and he appreciates it. You can't do any more. This is not a quick-fix situation, and from what Will told you yesterday about his niece turning up on the doorstep, it's about to get a whole lot worse.'

'He's out of his depth. There are times when I want to get hold of Kate and shake the hell out of her for what she's doing to him, let alone to herself.' He gritted his teeth. 'It's not exactly a compassionate and caring attitude, but that's how I feel.'

'Mmm, probably not something Laura would advise.' She smiled at him. 'But I do understand the sentiment.' She sipped her tea. 'But that aside, what are we going to do about Emilia? I spoke to her yesterday and told her the state of play at Little Anchor. She said she appreciates us watching over it, but she doesn't want us wasting our time when we could be doing something else. She's not coming home just yet. She and her friend are enjoying some time together, going out and basically doing things that you don't do when you are alone.'

'I don't blame her,' said Matt. 'But it's galling that we are no further forward now than when I got floored!'

'And neither are the police,' added Liz, 'although CID have tracked down where the petrol container came from.' She frowned. 'Pity that it had to be the biggest motor spares superstore in the area.'

'Typical.' Matt picked up his mug and stared into his tea. 'It's odd that no one has made another assault on Little Anchor, isn't it? Nor has anyone contacted her about a possible purchase, which was what I thought might happen. It's just gone deadly quiet.'

'I can't help thinking it's personal to Emilia. Now she's not there, they've left it alone.' She shrugged 'But who knows? If the idea really was to drive her out, that means there is something special about the cottage itself, or the location, but we've been over that a dozen times, so what is it?'

'Do you think we should stop checking it out?' he asked.

'Certainly we shouldn't check on it so regularly. I see little point. But we can go maybe once a day and pick up her post for her. Frankly, I'm doing much better on my observations of Linden Road Village Store. I'm finding patterns in the times Kelvin Smith's "clients" visit. Something is most certainly going on there, but I don't want to intervene too soon. I still don't know exactly what kind of illegal goods he's handling.' She smiled. 'But I will.'

'Sounds good, sweetheart. If only I could find a way to be of help to Will I'd feel much happier about everything.'

Before she could answer, they heard the house phone ringing. Matt jumped up and hurried back indoors, returning a few moments later to say that Will was at the end of his tether. 'He wants me to contact Sam Page, Liz. He wants to talk to him personally. I think he wants Sam to see Kate.'

'Oh dear.' Liz exhaled. 'That's the first time he's said anything like that. Things must be pretty dire.'

'I think that's an understatement. I'll ring Sam, then drive down there, if that's okay with you?'

She nodded. 'Shall I come too?'

'Maybe not this time, darling. I'll sound out the situation first.'

Liz didn't say so, but she was quite relieved not to have to face the mercurial Kate. 'Take care, and remember, we can't mend everything that's been broken.'

'But we have to try, don't we?'

Liz smiled. In her opinion, this particular item was damaged beyond repair.

* * *

In the two days since his unannounced visitors had turned up, Will had been in hell. He had spent a good part of that time doubting his own sanity.

Kate had stayed in her studio. She refused to reply to his constant requests to talk, or even to eat. The first day, he left her food on a tray outside her door, as he had done in the past, but she would only accept the occasional drink. The second day he left nothing, hoping that hunger would drive her out. She remained where she was. If she drank anything, it must have been water from the bathroom tap, as she certainly never went downstairs. At night, she waited until he got into bed, and then drifted like a wraith into the darkened room, slipped beneath the covers and turned her back to him.

On this particular day, he was desperate enough to ring Matt from the house, no longer caring if she heard him or not. Matt had said he would be there within the hour.

Will made a sandwich and a pot of coffee and carried it upstairs. He set the tray down outside the studio door and called out softly that he'd brought her something to eat. As he turned to walk away, he heard a perfunctory, 'Thank you.'

Hoping that her dreadful mood might be passing, he tentatively asked how she was. Her answer was a curt, 'Alright.' Thus encouraged, he kept chatting to the locked door. He sat with his back against it and talked, describing the weather, the odd jobs he was doing, finishing by telling her that Matt would be calling in shortly and asking if she'd like to see him.

To his surprise, he heard her footsteps approach the door. She flung it open.

Kate stood over him, her face a picture of amazement and a sort of sneering wonderment. 'You really don't get it, do you? I don't want people here! No one! And I don't want you sitting outside my door whining on about nothing when I'm trying to work!'

He scrambled to his feet and turned to face her. 'I'm sorry if caring about you and worrying because you're not eating constitutes whining. And as for Matt, he's our friend! He's bending over backwards to help you right now. Why would you not want to see him?'

'Oh yes, good old Matt. He's here for me, alright. I'm not blind, you know. I can see through this deception, Will. Just like I saw through your feeble attempt to inveigle your niece into our lives. Well, it's not going to happen!'

Will turned and walked down the stairs. He had had enough, and if he didn't get away from her, he would most likely say something that couldn't be unsaid. It was no good telling himself that it was her illness. His patience was at an end. He went outside and sat on the seat to wait for Matt.

He stared out over the fen, unaware that he was pulling his wedding ring on and off his finger. He was not dealing with this situation very well at all. The sound of the door latch made him jump, and he shrank down on to the seat, fearing his reaction if she subjected him to another barrage from her acid tongue. It took him a long time to turn and look up at her.

Kate stood for a minute, and then sat down and took his hand in both of hers. Her fingers were ice cold, despite the warmth of the sun. He slipped his hand from hers, took off his jacket and draped it around her bony shoulders, gently lifting her dark hair over the collar. He noticed her sour smell. She hadn't washed since that odd conversation about Sophie. This was so unlike Kate that Will could have cried.

'What is happening to me?' She sounded like a small, frightened child, and the eyes she turned to him were huge and dark.

He held her to him and rocked her back and forth. A tear made its slow way down her ashen cheek and she began to sob.

Will had no idea how long they sat like that. Kate seemed unaware of Matt's arrival, or that she was being led indoors. Will carried her upstairs, laid her carefully on the bed and drew the curtains.

Will watched her for some time before going back down to find Matt.

His friend was waiting in the kitchen, and as soon as he walked in, he put his arms around Will.

Will spoke into his shoulder. 'I can't cope any more, mate, I really can't.'

'I can see that.' Matt sighed. 'How long will she sleep for now?'

Will rubbed his eyes. 'Anything up to twenty-four hours.'

'Okay, so why don't you go up and make sure she is alright, and I'll make us a coffee. Then I want you to tell me everything that has happened, Will. Everything.'

Will dragged himself wearily up to their bedroom and looked down at the huddled shape hidden beneath the bedclothes. He bent down and kissed her cheek. As he did so, his face touched something other than the soft coverlet. He recoiled from her in horror. There lay that doll, clutched tightly to his wife's chest.

Back in the kitchen, he almost fell into a chair and put his head in his hands. 'She's sleeping.'

Matt placed a mug of strong coffee in front of him. 'Look, I've just spoken to Sam Page. He's offered to come over immediately and I said yes. Now, he can come here, or we can meet him, say, at Little Anchor? Emilia wouldn't mind under the circumstances, and I have the key.'

Will shook his head. 'No. Tell him to come here, Matt. Kate won't wake. She'll not know anything, and frankly, even if she did, I'm past the point of caring.'

Matt made the call. 'He's ten minutes away.'

'Good.'

'If anyone can help, it's this man, Will. And unlike Laura, who still works full-time, he has all the time in the world. He will help your Kate to get better, so you can both get your lives back.'

For a while, they sat in silence. Will could see no alternative but to listen to what Sam Page had to say. There was no longer anything to lose.

Soon, the old man was with them. Matt made him a drink and he sat down facing Will. He had a kind, understanding face but his eyes were shrewd.

'I've told Sam all I know about Kate's situation,' said Matt. 'But can you bring him up to date on recent developments?'

Sam listened to Will's occasionally rambling description of the events of the past few days. When the torrent of words finally ran out, he said, 'The timing of that visit from your niece and her guardian could not have been worse. I can't think of anything more likely to upset your dear Kate than having a child turn up on her doorstep.' He rubbed at a mark on his trouser leg. 'Plus, all those unpleasant happenings down at Little Anchor, especially your friend here getting attacked.'

'She's been strangely unconcerned about all that,' said Will flatly. 'As if she didn't care at all.'

'Oh, it will have bothered her. She's just refused to allow it to intrude into her own world. When someone has an all-consuming, ruling passion, other things don't have their normal significance. It's as if there is only room for one priority and everything else is relegated to the background. Do you follow?' Sam looked at Will enquiringly.

Will nodded. 'Does that account for her complete lack of interest in food and looking after herself?'

'Absolutely. She needs every minute and every scrap of energy she possesses for her work and her mission, and if we don't get through to her, she will get worse.'

'Does it have a name, this illness? Like obsessive–compulsive disorder? I mean, she is obsessed with the house and its previous occupants, isn't she?' asked Will.

Sam puffed out his cheeks and shook his head. 'It's not that, William. Sufferers of obsessive–compulsive disorder are very aware of their problem. They know that their rituals — all the counting, the hand washing — don't make sense, but they *have* to do them.' He smiled patiently. 'I could explain OCD in more detail, but believe me, this isn't it.'

The doctor took a long swallow of his coffee. 'I believe that Kate suffered from an abnormal grief reaction after the loss of the baby and her subsequent hysterectomy. She was grieving two losses, don't forget, the child, *and* her ability to conceive. She had a prolonged, difficult and complicated response to what happened. I'm aware that she underwent treatment, William, but it seems that her grief and anger were never fully addressed. I know that she managed to get back to what appeared to be normality, but unfortunately all that work has been undone by the Holland family and their missing and dead children.' He stared from Matt to Will. 'In my opinion, and without all the tests I would carry out with a willing patient, Kate is suffering from a form of bipolar disorder — what used to be referred to as "manic depression." A mania is an exaggeration of feelings that we all experience from time to time. We can all get excited about a new project, get a bit tunnel-visioned even, but we still give room for all the other things in our lives. The bipolar sufferer cannot do that. Their lives are a cycle of intense passions, from one extreme to the other, and they become highly irritated with anyone who doesn't share in them. They are unable or unwilling to sleep, until a depression sets in. In other words, the sufferer experiences a constant series of highs and lows. They are on a roller coaster, swinging between elation and the depths of despair. At low points she will feel unable to cope with anything — like now — and the next thing you know, she is painting in a frenzy and working all night. The sad thing is, my boy, that with the right medication, she could have an almost "normal" life. This illness reacts very well to certain drugs, but they need time to work, and the longer Kate goes on like this the more difficult it will become.'

'She had those drugs before, Sam, and the side effects were awful.' Will hated to even think about that terrible time.

'A lot of research has been undertaken since then. There are different medications available now, and they're not all addictive. Many doctors would treat her with lithium. I know it has to be administered and monitored very carefully, but it can give a patient their life back.'

'Forgive my scepticism, Sam, but they told us that before. She said they made her feel like a zombie and I thought we'd never get her off the damn pills.'

Sam regarded Will's worried countenance and sighed. 'I do understand your reluctance to go through it all again, but I just wonder how much longer Kate can go on without either a complete collapse, or . . .'

'Or what?'

'I don't know. But something has to give at some point. It could manifest itself in one of a dozen different ways. At the moment, she would probably be classified as neurotic — she still has a hold on reality, and sometimes her actions and thought patterns are quite "normal." She even admits to you that there is a problem, doesn't she?'

Will nodded. 'In those moments when she's fatigued and low, yes — in her own way. She says things like, "Poor love, it's not easy, is it?" That sort of thing.'

'So, at this point it can still be managed — with proper psychological care.' Sam rubbed his eyes. 'My fear is that if left untreated, it may take over her whole personality, and she will lose that contact with reality. When that happens, the problem becomes a psychosis, which is a very different ball game indeed. As things are now, Will, you can't rule out anything, and you have to remember that her "lows" are worse than anything you or I have ever experienced.'

They sat in silence for a time. Will again went and checked on his wife.

As he walked back into the kitchen, Will had a sudden thought. 'Oh no! Sophie and Philip will be back in the area the day after tomorrow. Whatever do I say to her? Sophie will be so disappointed if I cry off.' He anxiously rubbed his hands together. 'And, Sam? What was all that stuff Kate came out with about it being too late for Sophie? It sounded so threatening.'

Sam crossed his legs and sat back. 'She has this fixation about the house being a danger to children. It's simply that. Sophie has visited Holland House and that means that Sophie is "earmarked," so to speak.'

Will sat back down in his chair. 'I find this rubbish about the house having some sort of wicked desire to devour children totally ridiculous. It's a load of crap. Houses are houses, nothing more than bricks and mortar.'

Sam Page nodded. 'Of course they are, but you have to recognise that Kate isn't like you. She is sensitive, creative, gifted and idealistic, plus she is vulnerable and highly open to suggestion.' He exhaled. 'Let me give you an example of how different people react to the same situation. Did you ever get a shout, late at night, and when you got to the place, you found it really eerie?'

Will shrugged. 'Not often but, yes, it has happened once or twice.'

'Can you recall any occasion in particular?' Sam asked.

Will frowned. 'Yeah. It happened long before I went into CID. I was on the beat with a new bloke, a young chap called, er, Tony — that's it, Tony Skates. I think he was a bit nervous about being out on the streets at night for the first time. We got a call to check out a possible break-in at an old nursing home. It was a weird, rambling sort of place, set back off the road and surrounded by lawns and big old trees. Only part of the building was in use, and that was about to be closed down. We checked with the warden, who had reported someone creeping about in the grounds, and we made off in the general direction the intruder had taken. We searched everywhere but there was nothing. We were just going back to the main house when Tony thought he saw a light coming from the deserted part of the building. There was an old door that wouldn't budge when we tried it, but we found a broken window and got in that way. We found ourselves in some kind of small chapel — you know, like some big old properties had?'

'Like a family chapel?' Matt said.

'That's right. The altar and all the carved wooden pews were still there. There were even some moth-eaten tapestries with coats of arms on them and a few dirty old candle holders. It smelt dreadful, really musty. Anyway, there was no one there, and the only door that apparently led into the house itself had been nailed up.'

Will paused, back in that old chapel again. 'I don't know whether it was the young lad's nervousness affecting me as well, but we were just about to climb back out of the window when, well, I had this awful feeling of being watched. I was a hundred per cent sure we were not alone in there, even though we had searched it thoroughly. We both ran out of that place like the clappers. It was weird.'

Sam gave a low chuckle. 'So, that was the response of a "no nonsense," hard-nut copper. Now put your Kate into exactly the same situation and try to imagine how she would have felt.'

'Good Lord. With her vivid imagination, she'd have flipped!' Will puffed his cheeks out. 'And this salt marsh has a similar, ancient sort of feel to it. I am sure it's Whisper Fen that's influencing her paintings.'

'Ah, the paintings! Laura's friend was quite disturbed by Kate's pictures, and he wholly endorses our findings. I didn't tell him anything about her history, but he diagnosed the probable root of the problem in minutes. The last picture threw him.' Sam shifted around uncomfortably. 'He said they are in no way connected, and were we absolutely sure that it was by the same artist as the other "dark" ones?'

'Couldn't he give you any clue as to why she painted it?' asked Matt.

'None at all. He tried to analyse it as a piece in its own right, but because he had already seen the other pictures, he found it very difficult. He said it depicted overwhelming fear, but whether it was for herself or someone else, he couldn't tell.'

'I did wonder whether it was one of the Holland family, and Kate had put her in modern-day clothing,' suggested Will.

'That's very possible. Oh, and before I forget, the art therapist told me she had considerable talent. He said he rarely had a chance to examine such gifted work in his line of business.'

'Her work is brilliant, it's just so sad that they're all about her nightmares,' Will said.

'It could be her saving, my boy. All the time she is painting, she is expressing her fears in the way she knows best. If she can't actually talk about it, at least it's not all being bottled up inside her.'

'So, what now? I still cannot bring myself to turn her over to a hospital. I have to give it one more try.'

'Very well. But I strongly urge you not to let things go any further. If she gets any worse, you will *have* to do something about it. You have her safety and her sanity to consider.' He paused, seeming to choose his words carefully. 'It is not unheard of for patients with Kate's problems to harm themselves. I know you mean well, but just be aware that she could be a danger to herself.'

Will was silent. If only someone would come along and take all the responsibility away from him. But he knew the ultimate decision about Kate would be his. 'The buck stops here,' he whispered.

'I'm afraid so, my friend. Now, tell me what sort of frame of mind will Kate be in when she wakes, judging by her previous moods after a long sleep?'

'Well, strangely, she is usually still tired. She's lethargic and tearful for a couple of hours, and then she goes into overdrive until the next "low."'

'Is she fairly reasonable when she is in that *après* sleep state?' the doctor asked.

'Yes. She is apologetic and quite lucid.'

Sam stood up. 'I think you should try to get in touch with Philip Fauve before she wakes. Give him as much of the story as you feel comfortable with but be sure that he grasps the severity of what is happening here. There is no way Kate can meet Sophie. No way. Then when Kate is *compos mentis*, you must tell her that they've flown back to Canada. We need to free her of that particular worry, and you need to become her guiding light again. Can you do that, Will?'

Will thought for a moment. 'Damn! I don't have a contact number for him, other than his mobile, and it's not connecting. He said it wasn't working properly even though he had roaming activated.'

'Can you ring the air base?' asked Matt.

'I can try. I'll do it now while you are both here, if that's alright with you?' He looked from one to the other. 'I might just bottle it if I leave it till later.'

His call was put on hold, and after being connected to several extensions, he was finally put through to someone who knew about the Canadian captain.

'He is at Lakenheath today, sir. I can give you a number if that will help?'

Again, he was passed around until a curt voice asked why he wanted to contact Captain Fauve. He explained that it was a personal matter. He said he urgently needed to speak to him regarding his niece and their proposed visit to the fens. The man informed him that for security reasons, the best he could do was to get a message to Captain Fauve and ask him to return the call.

Will then had to spend a restless fifteen minutes before the phone rang. To his disappointment, it was the Lakenheath base again.

'I am sorry, sir, but the conference ended an hour ago and Captain Fauve has already left. I understand he is staying the night in London, but we have no contact number for him.'

Will swore softly.

Choosing to ignore the epithet, the man on the other end of the line suggested he ring Mrs Fauve in Canada. He was bound to call home at some time, and she could pass on a message for him.

Will thanked the man. After hurriedly working out the time difference between England and Saskatchewan, he found the number.

Annette sounded surprised but delighted to hear from him, although her tone became more sombre when he told her of his problem.

'Poor Kate! How awful! Yes, of course, you must speak to Philip, but his phone is down. Let me get the London number for you. They're staying at a small hotel in Bayswater. We had a few days there a couple of years ago.'

Will could hear the shuffling of papers.

'Ah, here it is.' Annette Fauve read out the number. 'It's room twenty-five, Will, and if he rings me first, I will make sure that he knows about your troubles and doesn't spring another surprise visit on you. I really am so very sorry that turning up unannounced like that has caused such an upset.'

Will assured her that it was no one's fault. He explained that Kate had become worse of late and the smallest thing made her ill. He also explained that telephone calls could be difficult if she was around, so to forgive him if there were times when he couldn't talk freely. She said she understood, wished him well, and hung up.

The hotel said that they hadn't yet arrived but confirmed their booking reservation. Will said he would ring back. His back and shoulders screamed with pain from all the tension, and his elbow throbbed mercilessly. In the past, when his injuries had played him up, Kate would massage his aching joints with aromatherapy oils. Now he went in search of paracetamol.

'Headache?' Matt asked.

'Oh, Matt. Headache. Backache. Mainly elbow ache. You name it, it aches.'

'Hardly surprising, my boy,' said Sam kindly. 'Have you managed to track Fauve down yet?'

'No, but at least I have the number of his hotel. I'll try again in half an hour.' He swallowed the paracetamol. 'Look, if you guys want to get home, I'm over my crisis. Kate will probably sleep the clock round, so if you need to go, it's not a problem. You've both got me back on an even keel again. I'm so grateful, honestly.'

Sam glanced at Matt. 'I don't know about you, but I have all the time in the world. I'll stay until you've talked to Captain Fauve.'

Matt agreed. 'No rush. Let's make sure you have this sorted.'

* * *

Finally, Will found himself talking to Philip. 'I thought there was something wrong, Will. You were strung out like a high wire. Look, I'm really sorry about all this. I feel I'm to blame. I should have found a way to call you first, but I had no idea Kate was that bad.'

'It's not your fault,' said Will quickly, 'and please don't let Sophie feel like that either. Can you assure her that her aunt is very poorly, and that it has nothing to do with her?'

He was desperate not to let his niece feel that he'd rejected her, on top of losing her parents.

Philip promised he would tell her as much as he could. 'Do you think we will see you at all?'

'I really don't know, Philip, her moods fluctuate so suddenly. I would hate to break another promise to Sophie.'

'Say, tell you what, we'll stay on here another night, then come up to the fens a day later than planned, on the Sunday night. That way, we'll be around for all of Monday. If you can get to see us it would be great, but if not, no sweat. The motel has a pool and Sophie swims like a fish, so we can chill out there before our journey home.'

'What time do you leave?'

'Twenty-one hundred hours from Waddington. It's in your neck of the woods, and less than thirty miles from the air force base.'

'I'll do my best to see you, Philip, but I can't make any promises. I'm living from crisis to crisis at present.'

'Look, you take care of your wife? After all, it was a bit of a long shot meeting up anyway, and,' Philip paused, 'and young Sophie didn't like Holland House one bit, you know? She keeps on about it, doesn't know how you guys can live there. Funny how an ordinary old house can freak a kid out.'

Will was of the opinion that Holland House was anything but ordinary but refrained from saying so.

Philip lowered his voice. 'I think I can hear her getting out of the tub. I'll sit her down and explain things to her. But hey, it sure was lucky that you decided not to bring her back with you? You would have had Sophie to deal with as well as Kate.'

'You mean she is really that troubled by Whisper Fen?'

'Sure thing, Will. She had an awful dream about it the night after we saw you. Woke up sweating and crying. It upset me too, she looked so terrified. She said she had been trying to save some bird's eggs from getting washed away on the marsh when the tide started to come in. She tried to get back to the house, but it kept moving away from her. She said the water was over her shoes and she was calling for help, but all she could hear was the house laughing at her. It must have been pretty vivid, poor little kid. It took ages to get her off to sleep again. I expected her to have nightmares over her mum and dad, but not about some old building. Well, I better go and get showered myself, we have an early dinner booked. Take care, Will, and if there's anything Annette and I can do, just ask.'

Will thanked him and hung up. He kept seeing the terrified expression on the child's face in Kate's last picture. Was he becoming paranoid too? Or had Sophie unintentionally explained what the imaginary youngster had been doing on the marsh?

He realised that Sam Page was looking at him in some concern. Will told him about Sophie's reaction to Holland House and about her dream.

For a moment Sam said nothing, then he asked Will what he remembered about the painting, especially the detail.

He sat considering it for a while, then said that he had been so fascinated by the girl herself that he had not taken in the smaller details at all.

'So, you wouldn't have noticed the small nest at the child's feet? The tide had partly filled it with water, but it contained three bird's eggs.'

Will's mouth went dry. For a moment he was Constable Stonebridge again, back in that ruined chapel and full of terror.

CHAPTER NINETEEN

That evening, Matt and Liz sat at the kitchen table and discussed the meeting between Will and Sam Page. Their supper dishes forgotten, they were sipping a welcome glass of brandy.

Matt had printed off the picture from the computer, and it lay on the table in front of them.

'To be honest, I wish Sam hadn't mentioned the bird's eggs,' said Matt. 'I know it was a fact, but poor Will is so wrapped up in his wife's neuroses, that I think he became a bit fanciful himself.'

'I can understand why,' said Liz, staring at the painting. 'It's a bit spooky that the child dreamed the same thing as in that scary picture.'

'Not really.' Matt sighed. 'Come on, DS Haynes! Look at this like a detective. It's perfectly understandable. And I took great pains to explain this to Will before I left. Hell, Liz, he looked haunted.' He took a quick sip of his brandy. 'I'm sure you remember Kate's earlier work, all those cute fairies in the magic garden? Well, one of her big things was to incorporate nature — all her main character illustrations had flowers, trees, birds, small animals, butterflies, and things like spider's webs and, you got it, nests with eggs in them!

Sophie is a massive fan of the books, and remember that painting that Kate dedicated to her and we took to Canada? It was called Snapdragon, and at the bottom, close to where she'd signed it, was a bird's nest with eggs in it, nestling in the grass. Do you see where I'm going?'

Liz nodded. 'Put like that, yes. And Will told us at some point that Sophie was keen to know all about the fen and where he lived. He will no doubt have told her about the marsh and the tides.' Liz exhaled. 'If the lass did dream about the marsh after she'd actually seen it for herself, her subconscious could well have taken all that on board, then embellished it with something from the fairy books.' She sat back. 'Typical dream, then, and not so spooky, after all.'

'I just hope that Will remembers what I said and doesn't start making flaky connections.' Matt frowned. 'All that creepy crap makes me so angry. Especially about the marsh. *Anywhere* with water, tides and remote areas can be dangerous, especially for children, unattended ones in particular.' The frown deepened. 'History throws up hundreds of accidents on the East Coast, some of them fatal, but usually the result of misadventure or plain stupidity, not because an old house has put a sodding bloody curse on them!'

Liz grinned at him. 'I love you when you're angry, Matt Ballard.'

He smiled ruefully. 'Sorry, but codswallop like that gets my goat. Oh, and I hope you love me all of the time, not just when I'm angry?'

'That goes without saying, but you are especially lovable when you are outraged.'

'I don't think some of the villains we put away would agree with that, but those days are gone, so I suppose I'll just have to get used to being lovable.'

Matt looked at the picture of the terrified child and turned it face down. He'd had enough of all that for one night.

'So, what happens now, Matt? With Kate?' Liz sipped her drink.

'Well, I guess Will has taken a big step by actually meeting Sam face to face, but he wants one more chance to salvage the situation. Sam made it abundantly clear that he's walking a dangerous road by not getting her the help she needs, but,' he shrugged, 'we can't force the issue, so all we can do is be there to support him. At least Sam gave him his card, so he can contact him immediately if things do go tits up.'

'So hopefully a little less pressure on you, darling. I'm not being unkind, but you are shouldering rather a lot of someone else's emotional baggage, and it's draining you.'

He knew she was right. He did feel drained, but even so . . . 'I can't abandon him, Liz. He's our friend.'

'And I wouldn't want you to, Matt. I love them both dearly, but you can't help people who don't want it, and Kate certainly doesn't, not from anyone. She doesn't even want us anywhere near her precious Holland House.' Liz frowned. 'She's changed beyond recognition. Let's just pray Sam can convince Will to get her to a specialist. Otherwise he's going to lose her.'

'Sam said as much. I do believe that one more serious episode will force Will to give in.'

'I just pray he doesn't leave it too late.' Liz placed her glass on the table. 'But on a different subject: I've been thinking about the night you were attacked at Emilia's cottage. Remember you mentioned that the arsonist's petrol can and some petrol-soaked material were found by the coal-shed door?'

Matt nodded.

'If you wanted to burn the place down, wouldn't you post a rag through the letterbox, or throw a petrol bomb through a window? Why light your fire by the coal-shed door?'

Matt considered this. 'Yeah, and the coal shed is a good way away from the cottage itself. That is odd. I hadn't actually thought of it before.'

'To me, that says they didn't want to damage the house at all, just give the illusion of intending to burn it down.' She raised an eyebrow. 'Which takes us back to the premise that someone wants Little Anchor itself for some reason.'

'And it also takes us back to not knowing what the hell they want it for. Do you know, last time I went in to check the post, I went over that place again, from top to bottom, and for the life of me I can't find anything that makes it special.'

'Then we do what we agreed, and back off. If Emilia is not coming back immediately, there's no need to spend too much time there.' Liz yawned. 'I'm ready to turn in. I want to get out to Linden Road early tomorrow, see if there are any more familiar faces taking their custom to Mr Smith's very convenient store.'

'Have you decided what's being passed under the counter yet?' Matt asked.

'Not yet, but it's not drugs, I know that much. If I had to make a guess, I'd say extreme pornography. Dirty magazines most likely.'

'Well, I know the internet is the main source for that kind of stuff nowadays, but apparently there's still a massive market for "old school" porn. It could be a very lucrative sideline. What makes you think that's the case?'

Liz smiled. 'All the shady-looking characters buy papers, and not the red tops either. It's the *Telegraph*, of all things. Can you picture some seedy scrote making himself a nice filter coffee and settling down to do the *Telegraph* crossword before walking the dog or playing a round of golf?'

Matt laughed. 'No, I can't see it at all. So, you reckon there's something inside them?'

'I reckon a rather special kind of insert, one that the Telegraph Media Group wouldn't be too proud of.' She grimaced. 'I just need to work out a way of getting hold of one of those "special" copies, and then we'll be able to tell Nigel Foreman that his suspicions are correct, and hand it over to our old mates at the nick.'

Matt looked at her. 'Any ideas on how you can work that little piece of magic?'

'One or two, but I want to keep an eye on the place for a bit longer. I've noticed a couple of faces that we've come across before in our previous life, and I'd really like to know whether Smith is a one-man band, or part of something bigger.'

'Don't get spotted, especially if there are a few old lags frequenting that store, men who might recognise a copper when they see one.' Matt suddenly began to wish he was working with her on this, instead of being on call for his distraught friend. 'You take care, Liz. I'm aware that you know what you're doing, but I worry about you covering this alone.'

Liz blew him a kiss. 'Don't worry, I'm a big girl now. But thank you for caring.' She stood up and began to put the supper things into the dishwasher. 'I keep thinking of what it must be like for poor Will tonight. I'd hate to be in his head right now.' She looked out of the kitchen window. 'There's one heck of a wind getting up, Matt. Was there a weather warning for tonight?'

Matt took his phone from his pocket. 'I was too late home to catch the weather. I'll check.' He found his usual app and saw an amber warning sign flash up. 'Uh-oh! High winds coming in from the east, could reach sixty miles per hour in this area. God, where did these summer storms and high winds come from? I swear we never had them when I was growing up here.'

'Climate change, dear.' Liz stared at the trees whipping back and forth. 'It's rather dramatic out here on the coast, isn't it?'

Matt laid his phone on the table. 'You can say that again. I'm going outside to see if there's anything that needs securing. Looks like we're going to have a rough night.' He paused at the door. 'Can you check where the flashlights are, sweetheart? And there are candles in the drawer in the hall. The last time we had one of these high winds, it took out the power for two days. We'd better charge our phones too, just in case.'

'Aye, aye, Cap'n! Batten down the hatches.'

Outside, Matt saw at once that this was going to be a bad one. The winds were already building, the sky wild. He just hoped that both Little Anchor and Holland House remained safe. They were even closer to the Wash than he was. It looked as though poor Will was about to get another sleepless night.

* * *

Will Stonebridge sat on a chair at the bedroom window and looked out at the wind-torn garden. This was all he needed. For a few seconds he felt that if he were dealt one more blow, he'd simply snap.

Earlier, before it got dark, he had noticed that they had left the back gate open and had gone to close it. A strong breeze was blowing in, bringing with it a sudden squall which had drenched him in moments. In the hundred feet back to the house, the rain became a solid sheet of water that soaked straight through his shirt and trousers.

He had run, jumping like an ungainly, overgrown schoolboy over muddy puddles that hadn't existed a few minutes ago. As he did, he had glanced up at the house. Kate was standing, framed by the long window in the studio, in her nightshirt, her unkempt hair hanging around her shoulders and the doll clasped tightly to her. She seemed not to see Will dashing for shelter. In fact, her face showed no expression at all.

Will had stood and gaped at her. For all the world she looked like Emilia's cottage as it was now. A pretty shell with no life in it.

He kicked off his shoes and tore off his wet shirt, then took the steep stairs at a run. Along the galleried landing he saw that the studio door was closed but that of the bedroom stood ajar. In the semi-darkness he saw Kate's shape, huddled in the bed.

So now she was sleepwalking. He had been able to at least relax when she slept. These brief periods of respite had now come to an abrupt end. What if she wandered off on to the marsh?

He decided not to think about it for the time being. A sudden gust of wind drove the rain against the window with such force he feared it might shatter. The noise was awful, but still Kate slept on.

He sat for nearly half an hour watching the trees and shrubs whip this way and that. The wind screamed and whistled, but the willowy branches refused to snap until, to his horror, the rowan gave a great crack followed by a squeal, and the beautiful tree crashed to the ground.

He heard again Kate's words, echoing back from the past. 'They are lucky trees, darling! They belong to the goddess. They give protection to the garden and keep harm away.'

He stared in dismay at the fallen tree. It had missed the outbuildings, the shed and the greenhouse but had come down directly on to the Anderson shelter, yet another thing to upset Kate.

As he looked on helplessly at the devastation, he had the irrational thought that he must get rid of it before she woke up. Kate would take this to be an omen, a bad one. She believed all that old tosh about the rowan being the witch's tree, and as Sam Page had said, it was what *she* believed that was the problem.

Oh, Jesus! Why the hell did it have to be the fucking rowan? He felt a rush of pity for that small figure hunched beneath the bedclothes. She was so vulnerable, so fragile. His precious fairy was walking on a tightrope made of gossamer. Would he be strong enough to catch her should the delicate filigree give way?

He hoped she would remain asleep for many, many hours. If only she didn't have to awaken to the sight of the garden's custodian lying broken and dying across her Anderson shelter. If only she could sleep for ever.

He stared back out of the window, wishing that the stalwart Matt and the knowledgeable Sam were beside him. This brave copper was terrified, and it had nothing to do with the weather.

* * *

At the height of the storm, two men dressed in wet-weather gear made their way along the boggy and perilous marshland path. They stopped outside Little Anchor, and with a nod, one of them slipped into the back garden. He returned a few minutes later and gave his accomplice a thumbs-up sign. All was well. No disasters.

'A slate or two has shifted at the front,' he whispered, 'but no structural damage at all.'

'Good, then let's get away from here. The wind is dropping but the ground is treacherous. Just watch your footing. I don't want to be dragging you out of a bloody bog.'

With one last look at the deserted cottage, they slipped away into the night.

CHAPTER TWENTY

In Cannon Farm, the phone was ringing.

Matt heard the anxious voice of Emilia Swain. 'I know you won't have had a chance to check yet but I'm so worried, Mr Ballard. I didn't sleep a wink last night.'

'Don't you fret, Emilia. Actually, I went down there an hour ago, and apart from a couple of tiles that have lifted, there's no damage that I can see,' Matt said.

'Ah, such a relief! It is such an exposed spot, but at least there are no tall trees near the house.'

'I'll take a closer look later this morning, but I'm sure your cottage is fine. They knew how to build in those days.'

'I'm sure you're right. It isn't the first gale to hit Whisper Fen, and it certainly won't be the last.' She paused. 'There were no other, er, *other* problems, then?'

'Nothing, Emilia. Not recently. So, apart from a sleepless night, how are you keeping?'

'Oh, you know. It's difficult to settle, even though I am enjoying Lena's company. Part of me wants to get home, and another part never wants to set foot on the marsh again.'

'If I were you, I'd stay with your friend for a bit longer. Let the police catch the person who's been persecuting you, then come home and see how you feel about things. They will get them, you know.'

'Well, Matt, you have more faith than me. They seem to come and go like the will-o'-the-wisp, sliding in like a strand of marsh mist, committing their atrocities and vanishing as if they never existed.'

'Well, he certainly has more substance than mist, I can tell you. He had no trouble flooring me.' Matt laughed.

There was a few seconds' silence, then she said, 'Oh dear, that was thoughtless of me. I am so very sorry. I feel so guilty! How is your poor head now?'

'Like my darling Liz said, I'm lucky it's so hard. But, look, don't feel bad about it. Given the opportunity, I'd have another go at the bast— Sorry, Emilia, but I'd dearly love to meet him again. Preferably in daylight this time.'

'You know how much I appreciate your looking after the cottage, Matt, but please, please do not expose yourself or Liz to any danger. And I will certainly not even consider returning home until the police come up with some answers for me. And if they don't . . .'

'Between us and the police, we'll find answers, Emilia. Meanwhile, stay put and we'll keep you updated.' Matt hoped he sounded more confident than he felt.

'Thank you, Matt, thank you so much.'

He hung up and went to find Liz. She had abandoned her idea of watching the village store in favour of sorting out some of the damage to the garden. She was already roaming about, gathering broken branches and sweeping up shattered flowerpots.

She smiled at him. 'Could have been worse. No major damage, except that a small section of fencing has blown down. Nothing that can't be fixed.' She raised her eyebrows. 'Have we heard from Will yet?'

He shook his head. 'No. That was Emilia, and I've put her mind at rest about Little Anchor.' He gave her a worried glance. 'I wanted to drop in at Holland House after I checked the cottage, but I wasn't sure if I should.'

'Was there much damage down on the marsh?' Liz asked.

'Worse than here, for sure. I could be wrong, but I think Will has a tree down.' Matt paused. 'Maybe I'll go make us a cuppa, and then give him a ring.'

* * *

Will had woken at around six to an uncanny stillness. The storm had blown itself out during the night and the fen was silent. Not even a bird sang.

After a quick shower he went down to the kitchen and made tea. He knew he should eat but his stomach was in knots. He was worried about Kate and the fact that she was now sleepwalking. Above all, he was terrified of her reaction to the fallen rowan tree. He lifted the house phone receiver, but the line was dead. He sighed. Well, he had his mobile.

He had checked the garden, in the mad hope that the previous night's damage had all been a bad dream. Sadly, it looked even worse in daylight.

He left it until around eight before going back upstairs to check on Kate. In the bedroom, he again stood at the window, desperately trying to work out what to do next.

'Will?'

He started.

'What time is it?'

'Hello, babe. It's getting on for nine o'clock.'

'Nine?'

'In the morning.'

'Oh.' She swallowed, her gaze wandering around the darkened room. 'What day is it?'

'Sunday. Don't worry, sweetheart, the sleep will have done you good.'

'Sunday?' She sounded bewildered.

'It's alright, you needed the rest. I'll go and make you some tea, then when you're ready I'll run you a bath, okay?'

She swung her legs over the side of the bed and sat for a few moments as if still confused. 'I'll run the bath. You get the drink. My mouth feels awful.' She sounded groggy and swayed slightly but made her way slowly to the bathroom.

Back in the kitchen, Will heard the sound of running water and the toilet flushing. He decided to tell her about the rowan tree and the air-raid shelter as soon as he got back upstairs. She would see the devastation soon enough, so he might as well warn her. He mounted the stairs with a heavy tread.

He stood her mug on the side of the bath and began to sponge her back. He was pleased to see that Kate had washed her hair. She looked tired, painfully thin, but still beautiful.

'You missed one heck of a storm,' he began tentatively.

She peered at him shortsightedly. 'When?'

'Late yesterday afternoon and into the evening. I don't think it calmed down until the early hours.' He hesitated. 'It did a lot of damage, Kate. I'm going to ring Barry and get him to help me clear up. Er, sadly the rowan has come down — and the phone lines too.'

She stiffened.

'I'll call Barry as soon as I can. Maybe he can get here soon, then we can sort everything out. I haven't checked everywhere yet, but I can't see any structural damage, thank heavens. And I ought to check on Mrs Swain's place.' He chattered on, conscious of how ridiculous he sounded.

In stony silence, Kate sipped her tea, staring down into the foamy bathwater.

'Can I have my towel, please?' she asked.

Her tone was flat, harsh. She stood up, and he draped the towel around her shoulders, but she snatched it from him and began to briskly rub herself down. She stepped from the bath and pushed past him into the bedroom.

With the towel around her, Kate went and stood at the window. Watching from the doorway, Will saw a kaleidoscope of different expressions travel across her face. Horror, succeeded by sorrow, quickly followed by anger, disbelief, and then she turned and faced him.

'Why didn't you wake me?' Her tone was accusing.

'I . . . I couldn't.'

'What do you mean you couldn't? You should have woken me.'

He shrugged helplessly.

Her shoulders began to shake. Great tears rolled down her cheeks. 'This is awful. Just awful.'

'I know, darling.' He went over and put his arm around her. 'I'm really sorry. I know how much that tree meant to you.'

She stepped away from him. 'You haven't the slightest conception of what it meant. You simply don't understand.'

She was shutting him out again. For hours he had been worrying about how she would feel when she saw the tree, all for nothing.

Kate turned to him. 'I'm not having a go at you, Will. It's not your fault, but you really don't have a clue what I'm talking about. Do you?'

'Well then, explain it to me. It was a nice tree. I'm really sad it has come down, but at least it didn't land on the house.'

Kate rolled her eyes. 'It might just as well have done. It was important, Will. We need all the protection we can get out here. We'll suffer for this, you'll see.' She pulled her towel tighter around her and turned away.

Will was left staring out over the marshes. Sam Page was right. It would be worth the risk of having her hate him just to get her away from this godforsaken hole. If there was the slightest chance of getting his wife back, he'd take it. Whisper Fen and Holland House were driving her insane, and he could not, in all conscience, sit around and watch her decline any further.

He twisted his gold wedding ring around and around until his finger was sore. He must ring Sam and make arrangements. And face up to his responsibilities, while he still could.

* * *

Will made no attempt to stop Kate when she said she was going out on the fen. It would give him a chance to ring Sam Page and ask his advice on how to proceed. He had managed to get her to eat a mouthful or two of breakfast before she went out, but she didn't appear to be leaving the garden. He saw her sitting by the well with one hand on the trunk of the fallen tree, as if she were sitting at the hospital bedside of a dying relative.

Finally, she went out through the gate and made her way slowly up on to the high path. Will waited until she was a tiny figure on the horizon before he got his phone out.

Sam listened while Will somewhat incoherently described what had happened since the previous day. Sounding relieved, Sam assured him that he was doing the right thing. 'But you must do all you can to persuade her to speak to someone voluntarily. I've already discussed it with Laura Archer, and we agree that Kate should see Lawrence Hassel. He has a specialised private clinic near Wainfleet. He is prepared to see Kate tomorrow for a consultation, and then treatment, if he deems it necessary.'

'Private?'

'Don't worry about the cost, my boy. There will be no bill, and if there were to be a charge, Lawrence wouldn't take advantage of you. We were at university together. He is not just an excellent doctor, he is a very good friend. I trust him implicitly.' He paused. 'Would you like me to come over and be there when you talk to her? Or perhaps have Matt with you?'

'No. It's kind of you, but I think this is something that I have to do alone.' As he spoke he wandered over to the window. Through an arch of battered clematis flowers, he regarded Kate, a lone dark figure, silhouetted against the sky. He felt like a traitor. 'Sam? If she refuses to go with me to see this Lawrence Hassel — which she might — what happens then?'

Sam said, 'If you remember, you dealt with this when you were a police officer. If concern is raised about someone's mental health, and if they are deemed to be a danger to themselves or others, we call a team of health professionals who assess the patient in a place of safety. This team would normally consist of a registered medical practitioner, an approved mental health professional like a social worker or a psychologist and a section twelve approved doctor, usually a psychiatrist. If they all agree on a diagnosis, the individual concerned will be found a place in a suitable hospital.'

'Sectioned, in other words.' Will sighed, recalling a number of pretty violent incidents during his time as a policeman involving people who had been sectioned. How had things got this bad?

'So, you can see how much better it will be if you can convince her to go for a private consultation voluntarily. It would be on her terms then. No one would be making decisions for her.'

'I understand. Perhaps you'd give me your friend's contact number?'

Sam gave him the phone number and the address. 'If she agrees, be there at eleven tomorrow morning. Lawrence will be expecting you.'

Will hung up with a heavy heart. This was the most difficult thing he had ever had to do, and he was filled with dread.

He was so entrenched in his thoughts that he hadn't heard the car doors slamming. Matt Ballard and DC Bryn Owen were at the front door. His first thought was that something else had happened at Emilia Swain's cottage. Until he saw their faces.

'I met Bryn while I was on my way here,' Matt said. 'You need to listen to what he has to say.'

'We've just had a call from a Captain Philip Fauve?' Bryn said. 'It seems his ward has gone missing.'

Will froze. 'Sophie? Missing? I don't understand. They're in London, aren't they? Has she got lost or something?'

'No, sir. They're staying at the Fenmoor Lodge. He said they changed their minds and drove up here this morning.'

'Here?' Will saw Matt flash him a concerned look.

'Well,' Bryn continued, 'as I said, sir, it may be nothing — the youngster might have just gone off with some other kids or something — but due to the recent tragedy in her life and considering her age, we're treating her as "at risk." Apparently, they checked in earlier than expected, and went to the pool for a swim. They swam for a while, then Philip had a call from his base. He took it in the swimming complex reception area, only a few yards from the pool. Sophie said she'd go and get changed and meet him in the foyer, but she didn't turn up. He had someone check the changing room, but Sophie had gone.'

'Jesus! I have to go there!' Will exclaimed.

'Hang on, Will.' Matt took his arm. 'Have they searched the hotel?'

Bryn Owen nodded. 'From the attic down, believe me. We need you to stay here, sir,' he said to Will, 'just in case she tries to get to you. You are her nearest relative in this country. She's just arrived, so she can't have made any friends yet, so that is what we think she might do.'

Will closed his eyes. A few moments ago, he had been worrying about how to tell Kate what he had arranged for her, now everything had been turned on its head by the disappearance of his young niece.

'The hotel is only four miles from here,' Bryn was saying, 'and we have officers out checking every inch of that area.'

Will began to collect himself. 'Have there been any sightings? How long has she been missing?'

'She has been gone since two fifteen, and no. No sightings, as yet.'

'What about her clothes? You say she went into the changing area. Did she actually get dressed?'

Bryn nodded. 'Her swimming costume was still in the changing room, and all her clothes were gone.'

'Could she have been abducted?'

There was an uncomfortable silence. Then the door opened wider. Kate was standing just inside, her mouth slightly open, her eyes wide and staring. 'Abducted?'

With surprising speed for such a big man, Matt ran forward and caught her just before she hit the floor.

'I warned you, Will! I told you it was too late. How much more "proof" do you need?' She spat out the words, then closed her eyes and slumped into Matt's arms.

Will hurried to her, lifted her limp wrist and checked her pulse. 'Matt, get her into the lounge. Lay her on the couch. I'll get a duvet. We need to keep her warm — she's frozen and her heart rate is far too low.'

Will ran upstairs and returned with the duvet. As he gently placed it over his wife, he heard Bryn asking Matt what Kate had meant by, "I warned you," and "it was too late." He looked utterly bewildered.

Matt glanced at Will before replying. 'I don't rightly know, lad, but don't read too much into it. As you can see, she's really poorly at present.'

'Is she anorexic?' Bryn asked.

'Something like that, and she's been overworking. Deadlines and such.' Matt almost shoved the young detective out of the lounge.

Will heard Bryn say that he'd better get back out and join the search. He promised to keep in touch via Will's mobile phone and handed Matt a slip of paper with the Fenmoor Lodge number. 'Captain Fauve needs Mr Stonebridge to speak to him, sir. The poor man is beside himself. Would you ask him to call as soon as Mrs Stonebridge has recovered?'

Matt accompanied him to the door. Will heard him say, 'You couldn't have a word with the powers that be to get Will's phone working again, could you?'

'Well, you know what they're like, sir. One word from us and they find twenty other priorities to attend to first. But I'll ring them by all means and explain the situation.'

Matt thanked him and hurried back into the room. 'How is she, mate?'

'She's sleeping, and her pulse is better than it was. She's freezing. You wouldn't make her a hot drink, would you, Matt? Lots of sugar. I'm afraid to leave her.'

Matt returned a few minutes later carrying a steaming mug. He set it down on the coffee table and stared down at Kate's diminutive form. 'How long has she been like this?'

Will took a deep breath. 'Since that fucking rowan tree came down in the storm last night. She believes that it was protecting us, and when it fell, we would pay for it.' He shook his head. 'God, I wish we'd never come here, or that she'd got to hear of all those missing Holland children!'

'Dead right!' said Matt. 'But I suggest we don't tell Philip Fauve any of that. The guy is probably out of his skull with worry enough without hearing the local tales about disappearing children.'

Will nodded, without taking his eyes off Kate. 'And by the way, Matt, I don't think Sophie will try to find her way here. If she hates this place so much, to the extent of having nightmares about it, she's not going to want to come here, especially not on her own.'

'Well, the alternative isn't too good, is it? You're saying there is a chance she's been snatched.'

'I know. That's exactly what I am saying. Poor little kid. After all she has been through, this is just not fair!'

Matt had no answer.

Having spent so many years in the force, both of them were only too aware that if Sophie wasn't found in the first twelve hours, the hunt for the missing child could easily become a murder enquiry.

* * *

Matt returned to the kitchen and rang Liz, asking her to come over immediately. He then made Will and himself hot drinks and tried to gather his thoughts. There was a good chance that this latest blow could send Kate over the edge, and in a strange kind of way, that might be a blessing in disguise. Matt wasn't sure how much more Will could take without breaking down himself.

He took the drinks into the lounge. Will was still sitting next to his wife, her hand in his.

'I can't get my head around this.' Will spoke so quietly that Matt could hardly hear him. 'I had just found the courage to phone Sam and organise her some help, and now my Sophie has disappeared. It's beyond belief.'

'You've got an appointment for Kate to see someone?' This was good news indeed.

'Tomorrow, at a clinic in Wainfleet. A doctor called Lawrence Hassel — he's a friend of Sam Page — but—'

Matt interrupted. 'I know what you're going to say. But take a look at that woman on your sofa. Kate *has* to be your first consideration. Half the police force are out looking for Sophie. Kate has only you, and hopefully, this Lawrence Hassel — if you can get her to him.' He looked Will straight in the eyes. 'I'll hold the fort here while you're away and keep you posted on any updates. But for her sake, you have to get Kate some help.'

'How can I leave Holland House while Sophie is out there somewhere, maybe taken by some pervert, or . . . ?'

'Slow down, Will.' Matt gripped his friend's arm. 'There are a dozen places she could be. Don't jump to conclusions.'

Will had an idea. 'I wonder if Lawrence Hassel would come here?'

Matt shrugged. 'Why not ask Sam? Oh, and then do ring Philip. Bryn said he's desperate to hear from you.'

Will reluctantly let go of Kate's hand and took his phone from his pocket.

The call was brief. 'Sam said he was sure he would if he could, but Hassel's severely disabled. He's in a wheelchair, and he never leaves the clinic.' He hung his head. 'And Sam said exactly what you did — not to cancel that appointment. He also said he's coming over in case he's needed.' He swallowed hard. 'Which means that when she wakes up, I have to break it to her that I have arranged for her to speak to a psychiatrist. After all I promised her. I feel like a traitor, Matt.'

'It's gone way beyond that now, Will.'

Kate gave a little moan, and Will gently coaxed her into sipping at her drink. Her expression was distant, vacant. As if in a dream, she drank the tea, seeming to be completely unaware of Matt's presence in the room. 'I'm so tired,' she whispered.

'I'll get you to bed, my darling.' Will gathered her up in his arms. Matt could see from the way he carried her that she weighed next to nothing.

As Will was putting Kate to bed, Liz arrived. Matt hugged her, muttering, 'God, this is such a mess.' He told her what had happened.

Liz finally released herself from his arms. 'Mattie! That's dreadful. That poor little girl! And Kate?'

He raised his hands. 'God alone knows. The only good piece of news is that Will has an appointment tomorrow morning for her to see a specialist.'

'*If* she agrees to go,' said Liz dubiously.

'She'll go, one way or the other. You didn't see her, darling. She was . . .'

'I get the picture, Mattie.'

'At least Sam Page is on his way over. I'll feel a whole lot better knowing that a proper healthcare professional is with her. We are so out of our depth. And Will doesn't know which way is up any more.' Matt sighed.

'Then stick with him.' Liz squeezed his arm. 'He's lucky to have such a good friend.'

'I feel like a fucking chocolate poker,' he said. 'What on earth do you say to a man whose wife is on the brink of losing her mind, and whose sister and brother-in-law just died, and now his little niece is lost and possibly abducted?'

'Nothing, Matt. Just be there for him, that's what he needs now. He needs to know he's not alone.'

* * *

By nightfall, Will was distraught. He knew that at the hotel, Philip Fauve was pacing the foyer, his eyes glued to the front doors.

Local radio and television carried news flashes showing a photo of the pretty, dark-haired child, and the chief superintendent made an impassioned plea for anyone who knew anything to come forward.

During the day, Will's kitchen had become a meeting point for the search parties that were scouring the marshes, but as night descended, they were called in for fear they might become lost themselves. There was no more to be done until first light.

Sam Page had sat with Kate, while Will, Matt and Liz had brewed teas and coffees for those who had been out searching. Two constables, Jack Fleet and Debbie Hume, were to stay the night at Holland House, just in case the child did turn up. The owners of the Tanners Fen village fish and chip shop had kindly delivered hot food for them all. Will, believing that he wouldn't be able to eat a thing, found he was ravenous.

Kate drifted, half awake, refusing food. She kept wringing her hands together like some Lady Macbeth.

Now, at nine o'clock, Will, Sam, Matt and Liz sat with her in the bedroom. An awkward silence settled on the room. Catching Sam's meaningful looks, Will realised that he could no longer delay the confrontation with Kate.

With a sigh, he moved from the window seat to the bed, and taking her hand in his, sat beside his wife. Looking into those large sad eyes, all his well-rehearsed lines melted away. Squeezing her hand, he told her that he loved her and asked her to forgive him for what he was about to say.

Kate listened without interruption. Will waited for her response.

The only sound in the room was the ticking of the clock.

After what seemed like an hour, Kate raised her eyes and fixed them on Sam Page. 'Did you put him up to this?'

With a gentle smile, he said, 'Yes, my dear, I did. You need help. And you are breaking your husband's heart.'

Will was certain she would turn on him, spitting venom and hurling abuse, but she simply said, 'Thank you for your honesty.' There was another pause, then she said patiently, as if to a child, 'But you are, of course, wrong. I don't need help, especially from the kind of doctor that you are suggesting. I am really quite surprised that you can't see what is going on here.'

'And what is that?' Sam asked.

She lifted an eyebrow. 'Three dead Holland children, Professor Page?'

She turned to Will and said, 'And, yes, I know about Elizabeth being taken from her playpen. I knew about it long before you tried to hide the website from me.'

Will's mouth fell open, but Kate was continuing, talking with more animation than he had heard from her in months. 'Actually, there are more disappearances, but the history is a little sketchy and the Hollands feared a witch-hunt.'

'And you believe that the house is responsible for all this, and indeed is still claiming young lives?' Sam's tone was even and reasonable.

'For God's sake! What more evidence do you people want? These are hard facts, those things you policemen are supposed to crave. No child was ever safe here. We should learn from history, Professor, but sadly, my husband didn't listen hard enough, and now his sister's child has joined the others.'

Once, when Will was a young constable, he had been present at the apprehending of a serial killer. He had been amazed at how ordinary this man appeared to be, how unassuming. He had talked lucidly to his captors, looking them in the eye and answering their questions quite candidly. He just lacked all emotion. He sensed that same lack of empathy in his wife.

Unintentionally, his own voice became cold. 'Sophie is not dead.'

'So, where is she?' She stared at him, her gaze cold as a reptile.

Unable to meet her eyes, he looked away. 'I don't know.'

'So how do you know she's not dead?'

'I *don't* fucking know! I don't know anything any more! I don't even know who my wife is!'

Sam's warning look was lost on Will. He took hold of her shoulders and shook her roughly. 'You are seeing that bloody doctor tomorrow if I have to drag you there! And we're leaving this detestable bog just as soon as I can get this dump on the market! Understand?'

Her face changed in an instant, assuming a look of pure hatred.

A strong hand pulled him away from Kate. 'That's enough, Will,' said Matt softly. 'Leave her now.'

Kate had fallen back on the bed, a flat, glassy expression replacing her earlier animation.

She turned slowly to Will, and in an empty, expressionless tone, said, 'Whatever. I'll see your precious doctor if you want. It really doesn't matter one way or the other. If he's so bloody good, he'll realise I'm right, then we'll see who looks the fool, won't we? But I'm not leaving here. I'll never leave here. You go if you want, but I'm staying. Understood?'

Will ran from the room.

He raced down the stairs and out of the house. Swifty and Debbie looked up in surprise as he dashed past them, out into the lane and into the reedy grass of the marsh.

He screamed her name, again and again. 'Sophie! Sophie!'

Somewhere out over the wild moonlit landscape, an owl took up his call, an eerie cry that turned his blood to ice. Slowly, he lowered himself down on to the soft spongy ground.

His wife was right.

Sophie was as dead as his little sister and her husband.

CHAPTER TWENTY-ONE

Will had not been prepared for Lawrence Hassel. He had thought they would be meeting with a "professor," a typical dry academic devoid of any shred of humanity. He recalled a psychiatrist who had once been called to collect an escaped mental patient they had apprehended. He had a goatee beard, half glasses, a tweed suit with a waistcoat and a faint German accent, and wouldn't have looked out of place in the Vienna of the early twentieth century.

A far cry indeed from the man now talking earnestly to Kate.

Although in his late sixties and suffering from some severe and obviously longstanding illness, Lawrence Hassel had a round and kindly face beneath a thick crop of silver hair. More than anything, he reminded Will of Father Christmas.

Kate had been uncommunicative and unresponsive, with a glassy stare and a fixed expression. Within half an hour, Dr Hassel had drawn her out, persuading her to talk — and listen.

Will could have listened to the doctor's voice all day. After a while, the doctor asked Will if he would mind leaving. There were coffee and biscuits in the reception area, and perhaps he would wait there until Mrs Stonebridge and he had finished.

Sam was waiting for him. They sat in comfortable chairs and sipped coffee. 'What do you think he will suggest, Sam?'

'I'm certain that he will want to keep her here. Whether or not she will agree, I can't say. It would be for the best if she did, you are far from well yourself, and with that poor child still missing . . .'

There was now a full-scale hunt in progress. The police were sifting through dozens of reported sightings, some possibly helpful, others obviously hoaxes or from disturbed people. Will felt ashamed. He had helped no one by totally flipping the night before.

Swifty and Debbie had dragged him off the fen, kicking and screaming like a madman. For a moment during her harangue about Sophie, his wife had become unrecognisable to him. It had been the final straw. A very large brandy had reduced him to tears, thereby restoring some normality. Sam, Matt and Liz had stayed, consoling him, until the early hours of the morning, and when he finally lay down next to his sleeping wife, he was drained, but his old self again.

Sam's voice interrupted his thoughts. 'You do realise that Kate would have to stay here voluntarily, don't you? He can't make her stay without sectioning her.'

'Er, yes, you said yesterday, but I'm sure she won't want to spend even one night away from her precious house. Do you?'

'I agree, but Lawrence can be very persuasive. He has a way of suggesting something to a patient that makes them think it was their idea. I have seen him calm some very frightening people in that manner. I think his secret lies in his disability. He too is damaged, just like them, so he doesn't represent a threat. People can relate to him.'

'Has he always been in a wheelchair?'

'Since childhood.'

Will mulled over the options that were available to Kate. She could be admitted as an in-patient for a full assessment and treatment. She could stay for a single day's observation, then be given follow-up outpatient care. Or she could leave on a wing and a prayer with a bagful of drugs that she would probably flush down the toilet. Once upon a time, she would have discussed these options with him, and they would have decided together. Now, well, he had no idea what she would choose to do. In a calmer moment before they had left for the clinic, he had managed to make her understand that he had been angry and upset about Sophie when he said he wanted to leave the fen, but he could not forget the look she had given him. There had been nothing in it but pure malice.

An hour later, Kate came out of the office, alone. She sat next to Will and calmly stated that she would be staying with Dr Hassel for a couple of days. She had decided that she owed herself a rest, she had been working too hard lately. She hoped he would understand. Without waiting for an answer, she stood, turned to Sam Page and said, 'Perhaps you would stay with Will. He is under rather a lot of strain at present, and I think you owe me that, don't you?'

Sam nodded equably, and said he would be happy to stay for as long as she liked.

She turned to leave. 'Sweetheart?' Will said.

She stopped but did not turn back.

'Please. I love you, Kate.'

Slowly, she swung round and looked at his face. She seemed to be searching it for something. 'No more talk of selling up?'

'Just get better, baby.'

'You didn't answer my question.'

'Just come home to me, Kate. You won't see any "For Sale" boards in the front garden.' He knew he was being evasive.

She kissed him coolly on the cheek and said she would ring him when she was ready to go home. 'The doctor wants a word with you before you leave.'

Will returned to the office.

'Mr Stonebridge, I am delighted that your wife is going to join us for a while. Perhaps you would be kind enough to fetch some clothes and toiletries for her. I am going to suggest that you leave her things at reception and do not visit Mrs Stonebridge. Oh, and no phone calls unless there is an emergency. We will get her comfortable in her room and start assessment immediately. Outside contact is discouraged during that time, it can be unsettling. I hope you understand.'

Will nodded, suppressing the urge to snatch Kate up and run away with her.

'Please don't worry,' the doctor continued. 'She will be fine here, and I see no reason why she shouldn't be home very soon. I will prescribe a drug regime that is tailored to her specific problem. I assure you that I can help her, Mr Stonebridge, and she seems willing for me to try. Good news, is it not?'

Will nodded, though he didn't trust Kate's sudden compliance one bit.

Sam drove them back to Fenchester. Will was silent, his thoughts running all over the place.

After some time, Sam glanced at him. 'It's for the best, old fellow. I know it's a dreadful thing to do, leaving someone you love in a clinic, but the care she will receive there is second to none. Lawrence is the best psychiatrist I know of, and I would be very surprised if Kate didn't respond to his treatment.'

Will drew in a deep breath. 'I feel much more relieved having listened to him. Now I'm worried about Sophie. The trouble is, Sam, I've seen so many cases like this. I keep thinking of Naomi Jones, and little Josh Wilkins.'

Sam nodded gravely. 'I remember them. I was actually consulted in the Jones investigation. Did you work on both cases?'

'Yes, I did. Poor little kids. I just cannot understand how these animals can do such terrible things to children. You know that the full details of what happened to the Wilkins boy were never released to the public?'

'I recall that there were a lot of rumours doing the rounds,' Sam said.

'I don't know what you heard, but they were probably all true. I was still a rookie copper then, and a PC James was on the case with me. A nice chap, real family man who had three youngsters himself. He left the force not long after it went to court.'

'Too much for him?' Sam said.

Will nodded. 'Totally. After the Wilkins case, every time he got a shout, he thought it was going to be another butchered child. Poor sod.'

'Do you have any thoughts about what might have happened to Sophie?' Sam asked.

They overtook a tractor towing a trailer piled high with freshly dug potatoes. Will stared at it, unseeing. 'For some reason, I can't look at things in the way I used to. Back then, I was able to distance myself from a problem and look at it clearly. Kate's wild imaginings must have infected my thought processes. I'm constantly coming up with different theories, but they all seem slightly mad.'

'It's no wonder you can't think straight. It's impossible to remain detached when it's your own family that's involved. And remember, you are still grieving for your sister. At least with Kate away for a while, you won't have one eye on the fen all day, trying to look out for her, or wonder what dark image she is creating behind that locked door.'

'That's true. Except that now I'll be scanning that damn marsh for a sign of Sophie.'

After another silence, Sam said, 'Maybe Matt or I should take Kate's things back to the clinic for you. It's probably a good idea if you don't go back there just yet.'

'Thanks, Sam, I won't argue. I appreciate your thoughtfulness.'

They fell once more into silence.

As they turned into the track down to Holland House, Will noticed two police cars outside Gerald Grove's cottage at the bottom of Tylers Lane.

'I wonder what is going on down there.'

'We'll soon find out,' Sam said. 'And look at that! The press, if I'm not mistaken.'

At the end of the lane a group of men and woman with cameras and microphones were standing around.

They were met by a couple of uniforms and a small gaggle of people in anoraks and boots, obviously members of the search party.

'Any progress?' Will asked.

'Not sure, Will.' A windblown sergeant was standing on one leg, endeavouring to get a piece of grit out of his boot. 'We had an anonymous call telling us to search old Berridge's place.'

Will frowned. 'We saw the cars there on the way in. Did the caller specifically say "Berridge's place"? That was what the cottage was called back in the old days.'

The officer shrugged. 'Think so.'

'Then I would assume it was a local that called it in. Berridge has been dead and gone for years now. Newcomers or strangers wouldn't know it as that.'

'Got a point there, Will. He definitely had a Lincolnshire accent.'

'So, have they found anything, Sarge? The guy who lives there is a nasty character, not quite the kind you want as a neighbour, I must say.'

'Oh, we know all about Grove, Will. But it rather seems that he was out of the area when the lass was taken.'

'Convenient.'

Sam interrupted. 'Look, William, perhaps we should talk to Matt and make arrangements to get Kate's things out to the clinic, if that's alright?'

'Sorry, Sam, of course, and I expect these guys could do with some hot drinks.'

While Sam called Matt, Will went upstairs to find some things for Kate. While he was hunting through her belongings for clothes and toiletries, he remembered her only request.

He had asked her if there was anything special she would like him to include, and she had said, 'Bring Elizabeth. I want the doll.'

Reluctant to even touch the thing, he picked up the doll from Kate's bedside table. At least the revolting object would be out of the house.

He almost threw it into the case, and closed it quickly, managing in his haste to catch the dress in the teeth of the zip. Cursing, Will opened it again, trying hard not to look at that hideous face. He pulled the doll out and turned it face down, flattening the material to keep it from catching again. He was just about to zip it up for the second time when he noticed something about the dress. There was a jagged tear in the back of the skirt, and a piece of the material was missing. He caught his breath, the alarm bells ringing.

He almost fell over his own feet in his haste to get to his side of the bed. He pulled out his drawer and rummaged through the contents. He found what he was looking for at the bottom. The two evidence bags from Emilia Swain's garden. He had meant to give them to Matt, in case the police thought they had relevance, but with all the angst with Kate, he had forgotten.

He ripped open the first one and stared at the small ivory coloured scrap of linen. There was no need to even place it against the tear in the doll's dress, it was so obviously the same material.

Will sat down heavily on the bed. He didn't understand. How had that shred of fabric got into Mrs Swain's garden? Kate?

A voice from the doorway caused him to look up in alarm. He must have looked pretty odd, this large man, sitting on the edge of the bed with his mouth half open, doll in one hand and the tiny piece of material in the other.

Sam Page stood over him. 'Did you tear it, my boy? What a shame.'

Will put the doll back in the case and closed it, hoping that the doctor hadn't noticed the tremor in his hands.

Taking the case, Sam went to the door. 'Get some rest, lad. You look exhausted. We decided that Matt was more use here, so I'll go and drop this at the clinic.'

Will managed a smile. 'Thanks for doing all this, and for going. Yes, I will try and have a rest.'

With a nod, Sam left the room.

Why hadn't he shown Sam what he'd discovered? He wasn't sure himself. He lay back on the bed and tried to make some sense of it. Could Kate have trashed Emilia's garden? And if she did, had she also killed the woman's cat and done those other things?

What was he thinking? For heaven's sake, she had been at home with him when the graffiti artist had been doing his work, and the fire bug. And by no stretch of the imagination could she have floored Matt with a chunk of wood! So what did it mean?

He could only think that she had dropped it when she stopped to talk to the old lady, which she did occasionally. She may have been invited into the garden to admire some botanical specimen or be given some of Emilia's strawberries. Will remembered seeing his wife wander the fens carrying the doll, so she could easily have walked down the lane with it. Probably the dress had snagged on a bramble or a rose thorn.

He lay pondering the mystery, until he heard voices below. He pushed the scrap of material back in the evidence bag, returned the things to the drawer and went downstairs.

* * *

'They drew a blank at Grove's cottage. He grudgingly let them in, but they found nothing. Must have been someone who didn't like the bloke and thought they'd stir things up a bit for him. And as that includes most people round here, I don't think we'll be spending too much time looking for our time-waster.' Swifty looked at Matt and Will and shook his head. 'This is really rough on you two, isn't it? I expect you'd rather be in my shoes right now, wouldn't you?'

'You can say that again, Swifty,' said Will. 'I miss you guys, I really do.'

Swifty kicked at a weed that had valiantly forged its way up between two paving slabs. 'The DI still wants you back, you know. I reckon we've got more ex-coppers than serving police officers in Fenfleet by now. If that arm improves, you get yourself back in the job. And if not, don't make strangers of us. We all still think about you, we miss you.' He directed a thumb to Matt. 'And this one. I've been trying to get him to have second thoughts and all. You should both come back.'

Will patted Swifty's arm. 'Thanks, mate. So, nothing at Grove's place?'

'No, nothing. God knows how the bloke can live in that rundown old shack. It's a wreck. No mod cons, so to speak, other than a telephone and electricity.'

'I've never been inside,' Will said, 'but you have, haven't you, Matt?'

Matt grimaced. 'It was pretty basic, alright. They did run electricity to it when old Isaac took sick. Up till then he'd used the old kitchen range to heat the place, plus an open fire in the sitting room, and oil lamps and candles for light.'

'You seem to know quite a bit about it,' commented Swifty.

'My grandmother used to send me out there to buy samphire from him. She used it for pickling. I was always a bit scared of him, though I never let on. The first time I went there on my own, he had a hare on the kitchen table and was skinning it. I'd never seen anything like it before, and I couldn't take my eyes off it. Little did I know I would one day be attending post-mortems — and still feeling sick.'

Swifty laughed. 'Well, it's worse than basic now. I wouldn't be surprised if the next high tide carried it away into the Wash. Still, we found nothing unusual, except for a computer, which was a bit of a surprise, given the rest of the place. He let Debbie have a quick shufti through his files, but it all seemed to be about insects and stuff. He told her that he hosts a website for other lepidopterists. They catalogue local stuff and post sightings of rare specimens. All seems to check out.'

'My wife seems to think he's some kind of expert.'

'I think she's right, Will. The place is stuffed with framed butterflies and moths. And the books! Really advanced volumes. Not a Beginners Guide to the Countryside to be seen!'

'I still think he's a slimeball,' muttered Will.

'Me too. Anyway, better get back out there, and . . . er, well, I'm really sorry about your niece, Will. We're all doing our best to find her.'

Will's throat constricted. Unable to speak, he nodded at his old colleague.

It felt odd to be on the other end of an investigation. Missing child's closest relative. He shivered. If he had been leading the investigation, he would be taking a very close look at the person holding that particular title. Four-year-old Josh Wilkins had been tortured and killed by his uncle, and the whole force knew that Naomi Jones had died at the hands of her father — they just couldn't find enough evidence to send him down. Not that it had mattered in the long run, because the bastard had topped himself, or so it appeared. Will was never totally convinced that he hadn't had a bit of help.

No, he would much rather be the one carrying a warrant card than the anxiously waiting nearest and dearest.

He saw a uniformed sergeant approaching him, talking on his radio. That familiar crackle made Will long to be part of it all again. He had been too young to retire, he missed the buzz, the excitement. It would have been different if Kate had been well, or if Emma had lived. Then he could have enjoyed a new life with his family. Right now, all he wanted was to be part of the action, chasing the bad guys. And not alone.

'The super has asked me to thank you for letting us use Holland House as a meeting point, and for all the cups of tea you've given us.' He paused, hesitated. 'It's now been more than twenty-four hours since Sophie went missing.

You, of all people, know that doesn't bode well for her. We've cast the net further, the nationals have been given her photograph and all the TV channels are carrying the story. I expect you've already seen the press hanging around, and I'm pretty sure you'll be inundated with them before long. You know what things are like these days — the powers that be want quick results, and we saw no reason not to enlist the help of the media straightaway. I hope it's not a problem to you?'

'No. The more people you can reach out to, the more chance of finding someone who has seen her.' Will was glad his wife wasn't there to see her precious garden trampled by policemen's boots.

'I've just heard from the station — a witness has come forward who thinks she may have seen Sophie.'

Will fastened his eyes on the burly sergeant. 'Yes? And?'

'She's only a kid herself, but she says she saw a young girl walking alone down a footpath across a field a mile or so outside the village. Seems she described her clothing in some detail. Kids are very clothes conscious, aren't they?'

'When was this?'

'Yesterday, at about two o'clock. If she was on foot, it would be about right, timewise, from when she left the hotel.'

Will's heart sank. It was too long ago. Anything could have happened to the child since then. He ran his fingers through his hair. But if it was her, then it did seem like she was heading in the direction of Whisper Fen. Yet, why come to the house that had scared her so badly? 'Nothing since then?'

'No. We've been to every house, farm, barn and derelict building for miles. No one has seen her, or anything suspicious.'

'Someone has got her, Sergeant.'

'We don't know that for sure, Will. We have to keep our hopes up.'

'I wonder how many times I've said that.' He smiled sadly at the officer. 'I was never brave enough to agree either.'

The man looked down at the ground. 'Kids have turned up after much longer than this. You know that.'

'And a good percentage turn up dead, don't they?'

Will's phone buzzed in his trouser pocket. Before he answered, he told the man that the kitchen was unlocked and his troops should help themselves to hot drinks.

Poor Fauve sounded ready to crack. 'What the hell is happening, Will? I'm a prisoner here! I daren't move from this damned hotel in case . . . in case she comes back. I only left her for a few minutes, Will. You do believe me, don't you? I'm so, so, sorry.'

'We've been over this, Philip. It's not your fault, okay? No one is blaming you.'

'Well, I'm blaming me!'

'Then you are the only one, man! No one could have expected such a thing to happen. Think of all the people who go out and leave their children alone half the night, or all damned night for that matter.'

'It doesn't help, Will. I love that kid and I've let her down. If some bastard has got her, I'll tear his head off, so help me! Oh God, I'm sorry, talking like this. I just wish Annette were here.'

Will felt for this man. Out of the kindness of his heart, he had taken in his best friend's orphaned child, and now this had happened. He must have felt that he had let everyone down, not just Sophie, but Eva and Guy as well, not to mention Will himself.

'Did I tell you that they are sending her doctor out, the man who has been counselling her?'

'No, Philip. When is he due?'

'Tonight. Not sure what time exactly. They reckon that when she is found, she'll need a specialist to debrief her, and she'll respond better to someone she trusts.'

If she is found. 'We have a special police unit that would look after her. They're trained to work with children who have been abused. Listen, Philip, have you got someone with you? Have you been assigned a liaison officer?'

'Yes. Nice woman. The hotel people have set a room aside for the police to use. She's down there now talking to some of her colleagues. I just needed to hear a friendly voice.' He paused. 'How is Kate taking it all?'

'Er, Kate has gone into hospital for a few days' observation, Philip. She needs help, and more than I can give her, I'm afraid.'

'I'm real sorry to hear that, Will. But sometimes you just have to throw up your hands and say, "Over to you." There is only so much you can do in the face of illness. I admire you for getting her the help that she needs. It can't have been easy, especially with all this going on at the same time.'

'I'm gutted, Philip, just gutted.'

'And here I am wailing to you like a baby. Look, you take care, and if anything happens here, I'll call you immediately.'

Will promised to do the same. They wished each other well and rang off.

Hearing the loud voices coming from the kitchen, Will decided to give it a wide berth and find himself something constructive to do. He went slowly upstairs and stopped outside Kate's studio.

He had to get a look at her latest work. She would have taken the key, of course, but just in case, he tried the door. To his amazement, it swung open. He stepped inside, feeling like a voyeur. He had been made to feel so unwelcome there of late that he kept looking over his shoulder in case he was being observed.

On her workbench lay copies of the finished illustrations for the Fairy Dreams book, the ones the courier had collected. He leafed through them. They were good, but that eerie and slightly frightening atmosphere increased as he progressed through the series. He wondered what Angela would make of them. Still, at least Kate had managed to complete them. He wondered if he should tell the agent of Kate's illness but thought better of it. She would be furious at his interfering.

Maybe after Lawrence Hassel had finished treating her, she'd be able to deal with Hubert herself.

His gaze wandered around the tiny room. Only the illustrations had been left tidy. Unusually for Kate, the place was a mess. There were artists' materials everywhere, plus sketches, half-finished plans and pictures, notes and screwed-up pieces of paper.

He turned to the stack of paintings that he had photographed but left them alone. Not those nightmarish illustrations, not today, knowing that his dear little Sophie could be lying out on the fen, like the subject of one of her deranged aunt's creations.

Again, he was struck by the horrible coincidences, the unexplained connections between all the events at Whisper Fen. He recalled that last picture, and Sophie's dream, followed by her disappearance. He had to see it again.

He pulled it out and stared at it. A yellow post-it note was stuck to the top right-hand corner.

I knew you wouldn't be able to stay out of my room, Will, so I didn't bother to lock it. And you have seen this before, haven't you? On one of your earlier visits? Ironic, don't you think? Or do you still believe that children are welcome here?

He stared at the frightened child. Perhaps he hadn't looked at it properly before, but the resemblance was clear enough now. Not to Sophie exactly, but to Eva, her mother. The look of fear had distorted the features, but the more he looked the more it became obvious. Kate had modelled that child on his dead sister.

He left the room feeling sick. Surely there was more to this than just grief over a lost baby. Emma had been his child too, and he had coped. So what had happened to Kate?

He shut the door and stood on the landing. The answer was all around him. Holland House had happened. Its miserable history had seeped into his lovely wife's fragile mind and taken it over. He descended the stairs, step by step. As soon as Sophie was found — alive, or . . . he couldn't bring himself to contemplate the alternative — he would ring the estate agents. He refused to see the rest of his life out in this dreary place. Kate could argue all she liked but they were leaving, and if she thought he would leave her alone in Holland House, she could think again. He'd burn it down before that happened.

CHAPTER TWENTY-TWO

Liz and Matt's concern over Kate Stonebridge had diminished somewhat, but as the hours passed, their fear for the missing girl mounted.

'Will is in a state of panic,' observed Liz, washing up yet another trayful of dirty mugs. 'If only there was something we could do or say to help the poor guy.'

Matt grunted. 'He's seen too much in the past, like we have. All the awful situations he had to confront in the force are probably running through his mind.'

'Add to that his worry over Kate, and the macabre history of the children of Holland House. The way she spoke so casually about there being more deaths. It had me wondering if she could be right.'

'I'd rather stick to the facts right now, wouldn't you?' Matt said. 'And fact number one is that that little girl has been missing for far too long and, frankly, I'm starting to panic too.'

'At least Kate's not here to see it all. Sam reckons that, if she is amenable, she'll probably be staying for about a week, or ten days.' Liz refilled the kettle.

'Don't you think it's odd that she didn't put up a fight?' asked Matt. 'I thought she'd protest like hell. Will said she simply agreed.'

'I think perhaps she was upset by having the police and a horde of strangers arrive on Whisper Fen,' Liz said. 'It was her special private place, and the search for Sophie would have been a colossal intrusion into her privacy. Maybe she needed to escape for a while. She obviously didn't think she needed treatment, so she might have thought she was using the situation for her own ends.'

'Maybe, Mrs Freud, but right now I'm not sure about anything where Kate Stonebridge is concerned.' Matt dried the last of the mugs. 'If it's alright with you, I'm going to suggest to Will that he and I go and join some of the guys out on the fen. It will do him good to feel useful. He has his mobile, so if anything happens here, you could contact us.'

'Go for it. I'll call if anything occurs.'

Matt went out to where Will was pacing around the garden. 'Come on, mate. Let's get out there and help. Liz has got everything covered here.'

Will readily agreed.

The light was failing, and clouds were forming in great boiling grey masses. Matt nodded towards the sky. 'If it gets any darker, they'll be calling everyone in. All we need is another bloody downpour. So, if you're ready, let's go over to Tylers Lane. If any of our old cronies are still there, you might get a chance to have a look at Grove's place.'

Donning waterproofs, the two of them set off down the lane.

They arrived to find a lone officer, another new lad, still on duty and checking through the shambles that had once been a garden. The old Berridge place had always been a hovel, and it hadn't got any better.

'Sorry. It's all locked up again. CID have left and so has Mr Grove, although I understand he is coming back later tonight.'

Will stood chatting to the young PC, while Matt clambered through the shrubs in an overgrown flowerbed trying to see in through one of the grimy windows. The interior was almost invisible through the smears, but he could just make out a jumble of boxes, books and other junk. The frames of the windows were rotten, the exterior walls decorated with damp patches and dangerous looking cracks. He wondered how an educated man could live in such squalor.

Will joined him, and they peered into the gloom. Matt commented that other than the electric light fittings, it was very much the same as when Isaac Berridge had stood at the table skinning his hare.

'They said he has a computer, well, I can't see it.' Will rubbed at the grimy glass.

'Maybe it's upstairs in his bedroom. There are only two rooms up there. One was a fair-sized bedroom, and the other a sort of windowless box room. Berridge used the small room for storing everything from dozens of jars of jams and preserves to seed potatoes and dahlia tubers. He even used to make his own carrot whisky and parsnip wine, oh, and a concoction that he brewed up and sold to the local eel men and fishermen to keep them free from the ague, whatever that was. The old men used to swear by it and paid a good price for a small bottle.'

'God, look at all this!' Will was gazing around the yard. An old mangle stood in one corner, its rollers, once bleached white by constant washing, now split and covered in green moss and greyish mildew. There were old brass pans heaped together around the iron legs of the mangle, and a pile of rusting pieces of gardening equipment spilled out over the stone paving. The skeletal remains of a small boat leaned drunkenly against the garden wall and some equally decayed lobster pots rotted quietly beside the outside privy.

'All Isaac's things,' Matt said. 'I remember when that boat used to be moored out on the other side of the sluice. His mother used to come out here every week to do his washing for him. I can still picture the old woman all dressed in black and with her sleeves rolled up, passing the sheets through that mangle. She had muscles on her forearms like a brickie's hod carrier. I was a bit scared of Isaac, but that was nothing compared to my fear of his mother.' Matt grinned at Will. 'The local children said she was a witch. She was covered in what looked like warts, although no one had the courage to get close enough to see for sure. Now I realise that the poor woman suffered from some dreadful skin complaint. No wonder she shouted and swore at the little horrors who were always pointing at her and calling her names.'

They hunted around the yard, looking for anything that shouldn't be there, anything that might relate to Sophie.

'I've no doubt the CID team have thoroughly checked the contents of Grove's computer,' Matt said, 'but all the same, I would dearly love to get the chance to see for myself what he has on it.'

Their external search of the cottage, and that of the constable, yielded nothing, so with the sky darkening by the minute, they made their way back down Tylers Lane towards Emilia Swain's place.

Little Anchor had a lonely and uninhabited air. Matt picked up a few letters from the doormat and they gave the cottage a cursory check. Nothing appeared to have been touched. Dust was gathering on the furniture and the old lady's collection of brass on the fireplace had taken on a dull, uncared-for look. Matt was glad that she hadn't come back, but he couldn't help being sorry that the homely cottage was beginning to resemble Miss Havisham's boudoir.

Back outside, Matt said, 'Look at those clouds. We'd better get back to the house before the heavens open.'

Will glanced up at the gathering thunder clouds and nodded. 'We can either run the gauntlet of the press, or double back out on to the fen and take the cattle track up to Holland House. What do you reckon?'

'The fen. It will only take a few minutes more and I'm really not in the mood to have a microphone thrust in my face.'

The two men struck out across the damp ground until they came to a well-worn path on their left. After five minutes or so, the shape of the fallen rowan tree could be seen in the back garden of Holland House, and in no time at all they were joining a milling throng of searchers all complaining about the dark. Matt and Will made their way through the sea of Gore-Tex jackets to where the sergeant was scribbling furiously in his notebook.

'Any news, Sarge?' called out Will.

The man snapped his book shut. 'Ah, Will! Yes. Liz was just about to phone you. A few minutes ago, we had another sighting, and it corroborates the little lass's story. A farmer was ploughing one of his fields when he saw a girl in a blue-and-white baseball jacket on the bridle-path leading to the fen road. That's about half a mile from where the youngster saw her. He didn't think too much of seeing her alone as he thought she had a dog with her. He now thinks it might have been one of the farm dogs. The timing is right, and we are now quite certain that she was heading here. She just never arrived, poor kid.'

'So, you are concentrating your search to this vicinity?' asked Matt.

'This is the most significant sighting, but naturally we're still trying to cover every avenue. The super isn't keen in putting all our eggs in one basket.'

Matt felt confused. 'But how could she have found her way here? There are so many footpaths and bridle paths. I was born here, and I can't remember all of them. Surely a child who is new to this terrain wouldn't have the slightest clue about where she was going?'

The policeman nodded. 'We've considered that point, Matt. We sent one of the officers brought in from the Humberside area, to see if she could find her way to Whisper Fen, just using signposts and asking directions. She had never set foot on the marsh before. She reckoned the child could have done it without even asking for help. All the fen walks and footpaths are really well signposted, and there is a big map of the surrounding area in the foyer of the hotel. Would you say Sophie was a bright girl, Will? Capable of reading a map?'

'*Is* a bright girl, Sergeant,' Will said sharply.

'Sorry. I wasn't implying anything.'

Matt threw Will a warning glance.

'No. It's me that should apologise,' Will said. 'I'm getting pretty frayed around the edges. Yes, Sophie can map read, in fact she enjoys it. Her father was sent all over the world and my sister said Sophie always traced his routes on the map. Plus, she is in the Brownies. She told me that she was doing her orienteering and compass work badge and she loved it. Sophie could have found her way to Whisper Fen with her eyes shut. It's *why* she wanted to come here that worries me.'

'Surely, if you're her only living relative, the answer is obvious,' the policeman said, puzzled.

Will looked at the ground. 'She only came here once, but the fen, and Holland House in particular, frightened her a great deal.'

The sergeant shrugged. 'You told us about that before. Well, it seems that the thought of seeing you again made her overcome her fears. We now have two almost certain sightings.'

A fine drizzle blew off the fen and coated Matt's cold face with a sheen of salty mist. 'It will soon be impossible to remain out there.' He gazed out across the miserable windswept expanse of marsh. 'Not just the weather, but the tide. I saw on the local news that we are expecting one of the highest tides of the year tonight.'

'What gets swept out invariably gets returned to us.' The sergeant's tone was grave.

'Do you think she just got caught by the incoming water? Swept out into the Wash?' Matt asked.

'Can't be sure of anything on this coastline. It certainly could have happened that way. I've even known locals get caught out.' The policeman paused, frowning. 'But I don't know, it just doesn't feel right. The coastguard and the Royal Air Force are out there and they've found nothing yet. No, my gut feeling tells me that there is more to this than a simple accident. Sorry, Will, I imagine that's probably not what you want to hear.'

Will glanced at Matt. 'We feel the same, don't we, Matt? Plus, we have a real lowlife living out here. Added to the strange goings on at Little Anchor, the whole thing stinks.'

'And don't forget the gruesome stories about Holland House,' added Matt. 'They might be fables and old wives' tales, but they don't help.'

'You can say that again,' Will said. 'They're certainly real enough to Kate — real enough to warp her mind, by the looks of it. Oh Lord. My poor Kate!'

Matt put a reassuring arm around his friend's shoulder. 'Come on, Will. She's in good hands. Better than being here, that's for sure. Let's go inside for a bit and let these chaps get on with their work. They'll soon come and get you if there's any news, won't you, Sergeant?'

'Of course. In fact, I'm expecting the boss and some of the top brass down here shortly, so I'd better make sure my finger is on the pulse, so to speak. Oh, and now that the search is to be concentrated here, I understand they are sending out some toilet facilities, arc lights and catering equipment. We really appreciate everything you've done for the men, but we'll be organising our own hot drinks and food from now on — you know, health and safety and all that.'

Matt smiled. 'Oh yes, I remember. A Portaloo, a Land Rover and a tea urn?'

'Most likely.' He turned to Will. 'But could we still use your garden as a meeting point?'

'Sure, and if the guv'nor wants to use the kitchen as an office, she's welcome.'

'I'll pass that on, sir. Naturally, they have an incident room set up at the station, but a warm, dry base out here may well be very appealing. Thank you.'

With a last look out over the fen, Matt and Will went indoors.

CHAPTER TWENTY-THREE

'The phone rang just now,' Liz called from the kitchen. 'I wasn't in time to get it.'

Will noticed the red light flashing on his answering machine. He lifted the receiver and heard the welcome buzz of the restored line. It was a small thing, but comforting, and made Kate seem a little less far away. Mobiles were great, but the fens were notoriously bad for coverage and he had been constantly afraid of losing the signal or forgetting to charge the battery.

They took off their jackets, and as they hung them up, Will noticed Mrs Swain's letters sticking out of Matt's inside pocket. 'Don't forget those.'

Matt pulled them out and waved one at Will. It was a smart cream envelope with an official-looking logo. 'This looks important. Must be a solicitor from the name and address on the back. I hadn't planned on forwarding anything until things had calmed down here, but maybe I should give her a ring. If it's urgent, I'll have to deal with it. If not, it can wait. She'll understand.'

Will suddenly felt guilty about the old lady, especially since his discovery of that piece of material from the doll. It could be completely innocent, or he could be withholding evidence. 'I'll ring her, Matt. I really should tell her about Kate.'

'Please do not concern yourself,' Emilia said at once. 'You have enough to worry about. We've been watching the news. It is your little niece, is it not? The little girl that is missing?' Her accent became more pronounced as her emotions took hold. 'The poor dear child! And Mrs Stonebridge? How is she coping with this tragedy?'

Will did not have the heart to go over the whole story again, so he merely said, 'She has gone away for a few days, Mrs S. It's like Victoria Station here at the moment, all too much for her.'

'I am sure. Her nerves are not good, are they, Mr Stonebridge?'

'No, they are not good at all.' He paused for a moment, his mind returning to the tiny piece of linen. He said tentatively, 'Have you ever seen my wife carrying an old Victorian doll?'

'No, I can't say that I have. She used to visit quite frequently but sadly, since my troubles began, I haven't seen much of her at all. Well, not to talk to, that is. I have certainly seen her on the marsh. She spends a lot of time out there, and on the fen paths. Maybe a bit too much? It's a lonely place, and if you have problems, I don't think you'll find healthy answers in all that solitude. Anyway, listen to me going on like a demented old fishwife! Forget the letter, Mr Stonebridge, just send it on when it's convenient to you. It will only be confirmation of a letter that I sent to my solicitor about putting my cottage on the market. I had asked them to deal with the sale if I do.'

'You're selling up?' Will said.

'I'm not sure yet, but I think I probably will. I should get a good price for it. It's in excellent condition for such an old cottage and as Liz said, if you like remote, it's in a lovely spot. I think it has retained its old-world charm, even with all the improvements my husband and I made to it.' She laughed sadly. 'Despite my objections, my dear husband always insisted on having the best of everything. Apart from the expensive heating system, even his garage has an inspection pit and a workroom. Well, at least it will help me get a fair price for it.'

Will felt the hairs rise at the back of his neck. Why was that? 'Have you told anyone else about this, Mrs S?'

'Only my friend here. Why?'

'I'm not sure,' he mused. 'Have you had anyone ask about the cottage? Anyone make you an offer for it recently?'

'No. I've not even contacted an estate agent yet. I am still not entirely sure if I will sell it in the end.'

'Then could you do me a favour and not mention your idea of moving to anyone just yet?'

'Of course,' she said, sounding puzzled, 'but I hadn't planned on telling anyone until I was sure in my own mind.'

Will ended the call and stood for a moment, staring at the floor.

'You look rather thoughtful,' Matt said.

Will looked up. 'Matt, the police haven't checked Emilia's place, have they?'

'They never said, but I don't think so. They know she's away and probably saw us going in and out and thought there was no need. Why?'

'Dunno.' Will was fighting his way back into his jacket. 'But something's not right there. Come on, Matt. We've missed something.'

Grabbing his own coat, Matt chased after Will, who was already halfway down the drive. 'What are we looking for?'

'I'll know when I find it,' Will threw back over his shoulder. 'So far, it's nothing but the old copper's nose, twitching like fury.'

Matt muttered something and then called out, 'Will! I've been through that cottage with a fine-tooth comb. There's nowhere left to look.'

The rain had come to nothing. Will thought they had about an hour before the twilight made it difficult to continue. They were lucky to escape the notice of the reporters.

Just as they approached the group of them waiting by the gate, two cars swung into the lane and the press ran off to catch a sighting of the arriving dignitaries. Will and Matt were able to slip into the garden of Little Anchor without as much as an eye turned in their direction.

'Okay. If you've been right through the interior, it has to be outside. The only thing I can tell you is that we're looking for something, anything, that would be worth forcing the old lady out for.'

'So, where outside exactly?' grumbled Matt. 'The shed was trashed, the summerhouse is empty, which only leaves the garage.'

'Then let's get out there now, before we lose the light.' They let themselves into the big empty garage. The fluorescent lights fluttered and steadied.

'Goodness! I've never seen a smarter garage, have you?' Matt looked around in admiration. 'Carpet?'

The floor was indeed carpeted. There wasn't an oily puddle or greasy rag to be seen. One wall was lined with cupboards, each carefully labelled with a list of the contents. At the far end hung every kind of tool a mechanic might possibly require. Each implement had been outlined so that it could be returned to the appropriate hook.

Will whistled, lifted a large adjustable wrench from its appointed position and looked at the carefully painted outline. He placed it back almost reverently.

They looked around but found only carefully stacked tins of paint, a lawn mower and shelves of car cleaning polishes and waxes. 'There's nothing here,' said Will. He had been so sure of finding something.

Matt stared around doubtfully. 'So, where is the workroom? She said there was an inspection pit and a workroom, didn't she?'

'Well, I suppose that is the pit.' Will pointed to a square outlined in the carpet. They rolled it up and found a long wooden slatted cover beneath it, which they slid back.

There were steps down into the pit. Will flicked a light switch to the side of them. They looked around, started to speak and fell silent. There, at the far end of the pit, was a door.

'The workroom?' Will said, his throat dry. It was completely invisible from above, even with the light on. You would have to actually get down into the pit to see it. He knew at once that this was the reason someone wanted Mrs Swain out of the house. But why?

Matt turned the handle. It was locked. 'Damnation! We need a key! The garage key ring, Will, is there another key on it?'

Will rummaged around in his pocket and pulled it out. A second, long, Chubb-type key hung next to the one marked "Garage." His hand shaking, he inserted it in the lock. It turned easily and the door swung open. A single hundred-watt bulb hung from the ceiling, and in its harsh glare the two men saw . . . an orderly and ship-shape workroom.

They gazed around in disbelief. Both had been certain that the missing child would be inside.

With an oath, Will kicked out at a cupboard door. Then, with a cry, he slumped down to the floor and sat with his head in his hands. 'I really thought . . .'

Matt grasped his shoulder. 'I know, mate. I did too.' He looked around. 'Very well, so we haven't found Sophie, but I think this is what you were looking for, don't you?'

Will raised his head and took a proper look at the room. It was about fifteen feet long, quite narrow and had a low ceiling. The fitted benches held expensive power tools — saws, sanders and drills. On one bench was a big vice and several handsaws. On closer inspection, he found drawers full of drill bits, screws, nails and an unused set of wood chisels. The late Mr Swain had obviously been something of a woodworker.

Apart from a walk-in cupboard, there were no other underground rooms, and no way out.

Matt picked up a chisel knife and gingerly ran his finger along the blade. 'Seems like our Mrs Swain couldn't bring herself to get rid of all this. And you'd think her husband was here only this morning, it's so incredibly spick and span.'

Will frowned. 'A bit hazardous, though, don't you think? There's no other exit. I wouldn't like to be down here if there was a fire, would you?'

'Perhaps that's one reason it's so orderly, and the electrics are all new by the look of it.' Matt looked around. 'And, see, two fire extinguishers and a fire blanket, one each end of the workshop. He evidently did all he could to minimise any danger.'

'It's a perfect hideaway for getting up to no good, isn't it? No one would ever know about this room, unless they went down into the pit, and with that carpet, you wouldn't even know it existed unless you were told. We've both looked through the windows before but we never realised that there was an inspection pit, did we?'

Matt shook his head. 'I had no idea. And how many garages do you know that have one?'

'Exactly. So, it's the perfect place to hide your stolen goods or print your counterfeit money.'

'I wonder who knows about it, other than Emilia herself?' mused Matt.

'I think I will have to ring her back and ask her, don't you?'

'Come on, Will, let's get home. And act casual with our media friends. We can't get lucky twice in one night.' They returned the keys and locked up the old cottage. Contrary to Matt's expectations, they walked past the gathering producing no reaction other than a few raised eyebrows.

To Will's surprise, they arrived back at Holland House to be greeted by Philip Fauve, with Swifty Fleet at his side.

'Will! I hope you don't mind. I couldn't stay at that hotel a minute longer. They told me that they were concentrating on Whisper Fen and, well, I had to come.'

Will accepted the outstretched hand and smiled at him, noting the hollow eyes and the lost expression on the man's face. 'You're welcome, Philip. Come on inside. And, Swifty, how are things going? Anything new?'

'Nothing else since the farmer saw the girl answering Sophie's description. I can't make head nor tail of it, Will. She must have been within half an hour of here, then she just disappears!'

Will took hold of Swifty's arm and held him back. 'There is something I need to tell you, strictly off the record. I'll get the others a drink, then perhaps we could have a quiet word somewhere out of earshot?'

Swifty nodded, giving him a quizzical look.

The kitchen was bustling with men and women, some in civvies and some in uniform. Swifty introduced Will to his new commanding officer, Inspector Michael Fenner. He was a tall, spare man with a slight stoop, which, together with his pronounced hook nose, made Will think of the grey heron that so often stood on the edge of the sluice.

He studied Will over the top of a pair of wire-rimmed half glasses, making him feel like one of Gerald Grove's rare specimens. He had the distinct impression that the inspector didn't like what he saw.

The man thanked him politely for his hospitality and offered his regrets that they had not made more headway in the search for his niece. All the while, that cold, steely stare bored into him.

Will was just deciding on the quickest means of escaping those piercing eyes when the door burst open and the sergeant made a dramatic entrance.

'Sir! I think we have something!'

'Sergeant Keene. Less of the histrionics, please. Now, calmly, what have you got for me?' Fenner's voice was as cold as his gaze.

'The girl was seen again, approximately twenty minutes after the farmer saw her. She was walking along Water Lane, with a man . . .' There was a distinct shift in the atmosphere. 'From his clothing and appearance, we think he is from one of the gangs that are working the fields up off the main road. He is probably from Mud Town, sir.'

'Mud Town?' Philip repeated.

Keene nodded. 'Yes, Captain. It's a group of old static caravans and huts used by the field workers, mostly Eastern Europeans these days. They're paid rotten money and are shipped from one farm to another, wherever they are needed.'

'Skip the lecture, Sergeant. Who saw them?' Fenner said.

'Sorry, sir. A BT linesman out checking a fault. Gave us a very clear picture of the guy. He was wearing a padded black sleeveless jacket with a knitted jumper underneath. The sleeves had stripes of orange, red, green and yellow. Should stand out like a beacon, shouldn't he?'

Fenner gave the man a withering look and asked if anyone had been deployed to Mud Town.

'Two cars are already on their way, sir. We're waiting to hear from them now.' As if on cue, his radio crackled into life, and following a few terse words, the sergeant confirmed that they were taking a Romanian man back to the station for questioning. He had admitted to seeing the girl and said that she was only asking directions.

Before Keene finished speaking, the inspector was on his feet. At the door, he paused and fastened his pale eyes on Will and Philip.

'This may come to nothing. Do not pin your hopes on this man being the abductor. The search will continue.'

He was gone before Will could utter a word. 'What a charming gentleman,' said Sam Page, who had just joined them. 'So warm and friendly.'

'Don't knock him, Prof.' Swifty grinned broadly. 'Bloke's got all the charisma of a frozen turd, but his brain is as sharp as a filleting knife.'

'I'm pleased to hear it. When exactly did he leave the storm troopers?' asked Sam dryly.

There was a muffled chuckle from one of the PCs, and the room once again burst into life.

'Where is the boss lady, Swifty? I thought DCI Anders would be here by now,' enquired Will hopefully.

'She's coordinating things at base. Plus, her and Fenner don't get on too well.'

Will smiled. 'Matt, where's Liz?'

'She's gone home, needs a rest. She still gets tired if she does too much.' Matt looked at him. 'How are you holding up, mate?'

'Worried sick. I think I might ring the clinic, just to see how Kate has settled in. Would you get everyone a drink, Matt?'

Will went out to the hall and rang the clinic. He waited for nearly five minutes before hearing Lawrence Hassel's deep voice.

'Ah, Mr Stonebridge. Good. Firstly, I am very glad that your wife consented to stay with us. You are aware of how poorly she is?'

Will assured him that he was. He warned the doctor that Kate's mood swings were pretty spectacular, and he was concerned that at any moment she might choose not to cooperate.

'I am treading very carefully. At present she seems happy with her room and has spent the afternoon in the occupational therapy department.'

'Painting?'

'Yes, Mr Stonebridge. Painting.'

Will waited for the man to go on.

'Professor Page was kind enough to send me some copies of her recent "dark" work, along with another colleague's art therapy report. They prepared me somewhat. However . . .' The psychiatrist seemed to hesitate. 'I have to admit to being rather shocked by what she produced today. I am unused to seeing evil represented with such technical mastery.'

'Evil? Isn't that rather a strong word?'

'You have seen her work, Mr Stonebridge.'

Will was forced to agree. 'I am sorry you haven't seen her earlier pieces. They were so beautiful and sensitive you wouldn't believe they came from the same brush.'

'I don't doubt it, Mr Stonebridge. Her talent is beyond dispute. It's the subject matter that is so shocking.'

'Doctor? Would you be able to send me an image of them?'

'I could, if you really think that's a good idea.' He sounded doubtful.

'If it's not too much trouble,' Will insisted.

'It doesn't make pleasant viewing, Mr Stonebridge, but I will attend to that straightaway. Now, I had better get back to my patients.'

'Thank you for your help, Doctor. I really am indebted to you.'

'Let's see how we go, shall we? It is very early days yet, but be assured, I will do everything I can for her.'

Will gave him their email address, hung up and switched on the computer. Sam would no doubt be interested to see Kate's latest tour de force.

Back in the lounge, his visitors were busy quietly discussing the latest turn of events. Before Will could tell him about Kate's new work, Sam asked if her studio was still locked. He would like to take another look at the dark work. Philip went upstairs with him, leaving Will with Matt and Swifty.

Swifty began at once. 'Alright. Spill the beans. What's eating you two?'

Will told him about the room under the garage floor at Little Anchor, and that he believed it to be the reason for the attempts to drive the old lady from her home. He then described how he had come across the torn doll's dress and the scrap of material from it, and how he believed that his wife had been responsible for wrecking Emilia's garden.

'Come off it, Will!' Matt sounded almost angry. 'Sure, she's been acting weird, but vandalism? That piece of material could have got there in any number of different ways.'

'Matt, it was clean when I picked it up. If it had been there before the garden was destroyed, it would have been muddy, dirty. I am certain it was Kate.'

'Listen, Will. Before you get your missus locked up,' Swifty said, 'we are pretty sure we know who is behind it. That petrol can was purchased by a kid whose father is known to us. He paid cash, but the girl who sold it remembered his flashy trainers and the red and white Adidas T-shirt he was wearing. From her description of the lippy little git, we reckoned it was one of the Hemmings boys. Their dad is a right nasty piece of work, do anything if the price is right. Naturally, half of Fenfleet are willing to swear he was somewhere else on all the dates in question, but we've got his number now and we are watching him. A hundred to one it's him, and I've nabbed him with a spray can once before, so now we just need to find out who he's working for. So, forget what you just told me about Mrs Stonebridge, okay? And I'll do the same. Let's get to the bottom of why someone wants the Swain cottage so badly, shall we?'

Relieved, Will nodded. He had needed to hear someone assure him that Kate couldn't be to blame. 'Thanks, Swifty. I feel better about it now. I guess I got everything out of perspective.'

'No problem. Look, I have to get back out there and help with setting up the lights. I'm not far away if you need me, and if I hear any news, I'll be in here like a shot. Oh yeah, and Gerald Grove will be back home tonight. We are going to be keeping a very close eye on that little shit. Knowing what he was involved in before, I find it very hard not to believe that he's behind all this in some way.'

'We feel the same. Just thinking about him gets my back up.' Will shuddered.

Swifty picked up his cap and left.

'Why didn't you tell me about that piece of linen before?' asked Matt softly.

'I only realised that it matched when I put that bloody doll in Kate's bag. I'm sorry, mate. Initially I didn't have the heart to talk about it at all, then with everything going on, I forgot until a few minutes ago.'

Heavy footsteps on the stairs announced the return of Philip and Sam. The doctor had brought one of Kate's paintings with him and with great care, propped it up on a side table. Then he dragged over a chair, picked up his brandy and sat facing the picture.

'I've got the same problem as you, Matt. Something is bothering me, and I can't quite put my finger on it.'

'Jesus! I hate that!' said Matt. 'It's like the other day when I got clobbered. Something someone said seemed significant, but I couldn't remember for the life of me what it was. I actually remembered tonight when we found that underground workshop. I was talking to that PC, Debbie, and she commented on what had gone on at Little Anchor. I said that the poor dear would never come back if things continued the way they were. And that was it, that was all it was. It had nothing to do with her being Jewish, nothing to do with neo-Nazis. She was simply being driven out because someone wanted her cottage for some criminal activity. I think the underground room kind of confirms it, don't you?'

'Mmm.' Sam was staring hard at the picture. It was the one depicting a creature descending the stairs into a cellar, clutching a child wrapped up in a bundle.

'Do you recognise something?' asked Will.

Philip too was staring at the illustration, horrified that such an abomination could have been created by the same person who had painted Sophie's birthday picture.

'Not the place, that's not it at all, but something is crying out to me, and I don't know what it is.'

Matt went and stood at his side. 'Do you know, Prof, I feel the same way when I look at that. I'm certain there's something there that I should be picking up on.' He groaned. 'Here we go again! Blast it!'

Heavily, Will sat back down in the armchair. He took a sip of his brandy and watched the flames lick at the dry bark of a log. He recalled their first days at Holland House, happy times with a Kate who was still childlike and enthusiastic. Days before they knew about the missing and dead children, before her acquaintance with that slimeball Grove. His thoughts strayed to the man's decaying shack. If only the man had stayed away until Sophie was found. Better still, stayed away, full stop. The house should be allowed to do as Swifty had suggested and just slip into the water. He wondered what on earth the man thought about out there alone in that dreadful old ruin. Well, he did have electricity, that was one thing, and a telephone. He thought of the new cable snaking up the crumbling brickwork . . .

Will sat forward with a start. 'Matt! There are two lines! At Grove's place!'

Matt dragged himself away from the painting and stared at him. 'Sorry?'

'Two BT lines. Why would anyone want two telephone lines?'

'Some business thing, like for his academic work maybe?' Matt shrugged.

Will was on his feet. 'No, no! You don't need two incoming lines. There was one line in on the ground floor — that would be the usual main BT telephone line. But I saw another separate line running upstairs. Did you hear them say who checked that house over? Because I think they missed something.'

'They just said CID searched it from top to bottom,' said Matt. Then he took a breath. 'Ah, but I wonder . . . ?'

'What?' asked Will urgently.

'There's a second attic area. Just a small space and it's accessed by a trapdoor in the box-room ceiling! They might have searched the main attic, but I doubt they will have even realised the other one is there!'

'We've got to find Swifty! They have to get back there before Grove does! Sophie could be there!'

'We'll come too.'

Will and Matt raced out into the night, with Philip and Sam at their heels.

CHAPTER TWENTY-FOUR

In the glare of the halogen lights, the garden had taken on an unearthly glow.

Jack Fleet was at the refreshments' vehicle, talking to the sergeant. 'Our turn to offer *you* a drink, I reckon.'

'Bugger the drinks! Swifty, you have to get back into Grove's cottage! I think you boys have missed something,' Will said. 'I'll explain as we go!'

Fifteen minutes later, the cottage door swung open and Will received a blast of the foul air from Gerald Grove's kitchen.

A PC on a ladder had traced the second line to the level of the attic.

'DC Kenwright has already been up there, Stoney. Said the dust was as thick as a carpet. Hadn't been used in donkey's years.' Swifty sounded worried. He had acted without calling it in and awaiting instructions, and if they failed to find anything, he would be in deep shit. Even so, they had a child missing, and suspecting her to be concealed there, her life in danger, he was within the law to enter without a warrant or Grove being present.

'Swifty! It's not accessed from the main attic,' said Matt. 'As Will told you, there is a tiny trap door into a branch off the main attic. It's in the box room.'

Leaving Sam and Philip outside, they mounted the creaking stairs two at a time and burst into the room.

'Behind all that stuff! Up there!'

The far side of the room was stacked to the ceiling with junk. The earlier search had shown up a century of Isaac Berridge's rubbish, along with heaps of empty removal boxes and hundreds of magazines and periodicals. It appeared that the detectives had given up just before they got to the tallest pile of boxes. These had obviously not been moved, and behind them was a narrow trap door. With a freshly oiled bolt.

Matt knocked the empty cardboard containers away and dragged a table to just beneath the small door. He looked up in dismay. 'Damned if I'll get through that tiny aperture!'

'Then you need a proper copper.' Showing remarkable agility, Swifty climbed through the narrow trapdoor and was soon calling down from the dusty loft above them.

'Nice one, Matt! This area is walled off from the attic proper. You'd never see this from the main hatch. And guess what? We have a mini office! Our man has a second computer! I wonder what this one has on it?'

Will groaned and whispered to Matt, 'But no Sophie.' He felt distraught that his niece had not been found, but relieved, too, that she hadn't been in the clutches of a man like Grove.

'No Sophie, but what will we find on that second computer?' Matt then yelled up to his friend. 'Don't touch anything, mate! Get back down here and radio for the SOCOs and an IT bod. And get your guv'nor back out here.' He turned to the others with a sigh of relief. 'I thought I'd blown it. I could just see Grove arriving back to find us in his parlour.'

'What on earth is that unsavoury man up to?' asked Sam.

'We'll soon find out. The station's techies will get that baby to cough up its secrets in no time. Now, I suggest we all get back to the house, while Swifty waits here for the scene-of-crime team.'

With the beam from the torch bobbing up and down in front of them, they made their way back to Holland House. As they went, they discussed the find in the attic and speculated on the nature of Grove's game. Whatever it was, it wasn't anything to do with pretty butterflies!

Around them stretched the black and endless marsh. Will saw Philip shudder. They must all be thinking of a frightened little girl and a long, dark night.

A light flashed, bright and diamond sharp, and was immediately swallowed up.

A fishing boat coming in on the high tide? Or maybe a freighter out in the Fenfleet Deeps. Will waited for another spark but saw nothing more. The clouds obscuring the stars moved away occasionally, and in the clear black sky a cluster of twinkling, brilliant, crystal points of light emerged. Kate knew the name of every star. His heart gave a lurch, and while the others moved on, talking quietly, Will followed in silence, full of thoughts of his wife.

'The press are up ahead, Will. Get ready to run the gauntlet,' Matt called back.

The line of cars, vans, trucks and reporters now extended from the road all the way down Tylers Lane and the track to his home.

In a tight group, they marched through the throng, ignoring the calls and shouts, the flashing cameras and the microphones. They practically fell through the front door, and slammed it shut behind them.

'Hell-fire! Where's that brandy?' They collapsed on to the lounge chairs swallowing their drinks gratefully.

'Will?' The round head of the sergeant appeared in the half-open door. 'Sorry to interrupt. DCI Anders wanted you to know that the Romanian seems to be in the clear. He said the girl had asked for directions to Whisper Fen. He walked along with her for about five minutes before directing her down the correct route to Tylers Lane. He said she was wearing a baseball jacket with the number thirteen on the back.

She told him her name was Sophie and she wanted to pay a surprise visit to her uncle.'

Philip's hand flew to his mouth.

'Then where is she?' Will was at breaking point. 'Where the fuck *is* she?'

'Sir, I'm just trying to keep you updated on what we know. I'm sorry it is so upsetting.' The officer backed out of the room, closing the door quietly behind him.

A dreadful hush descended on the room. Will sat by the fire, rocking backwards and forwards. Philip stared blindly into his glass. Sam resumed his seat in front of the picture, and a few moments later, Matt joined him. The only noises to be heard were the clock ticking and the crackle of a log shifting in the grate.

Sam Page said, 'It's something to do with certain items she's included that just don't fit with the rest of the picture.'

Will and Philip went and looked over his shoulder.

'That lamp, see? It's ornate, rather beautiful. What's it doing in such a filthy setting?'

They squinted, and could just make out the dim outline of part of an old oil lamp that had fallen on its side on the dirty floor of the cellar.

'That's it!' Matt's sudden exclamation made them all jump. 'That lamp belonged to Isaac Berridge. It has a particular design on the stand. Look, an anchor with plaited ropes extending down to the base.' He stared at each of them. 'But it wasn't in the old cottage tonight. It was definitely not there. I'd have noticed it. It always sat on the kitchen windowsill. It was a very fine lamp for a poor fen man. My grandmother said he had been given it by a "toff" in exchange for six bottles of his homemade tonic.'

'So, how on earth could Kate have painted it?' asked Will.

'I have no idea,' breathed Matt.

Will said, 'Matt, go and look at the other pictures again, there may be something else.'

As his friend turned to go, Philip held up his hand. 'Wait. Will, didn't you say that the doctor was sending you a copy of a new painting?'

They all hurried into the hall and Will sat at his PC. After waiting a few minutes for the image to download, they were gazing at Kate's latest work.

It was simply a dark room, but it seethed with menace. There was nothing obviously gruesome to be seen — no severed limbs, no decomposing body. But you *knew* that the huddled shape on the filthy floor was a child. That the huge shadow lurking just behind the half-open door was full of malice and evil intent. You could smell the fear.

Matt gripped Will's arm. Without a word, he pulled him back into the lounge and walked across to where his and Liz's "welcome to your new home" gift hung in pride of place above the fireplace.

'*Dying Light*. I could be wrong, Will, but I think I know where Sophie is.'

They stared at the picture of the cottage and the ancient mill.

'The mill?' asked Will. 'But they searched there, Matt. I heard the crew report in. They said it was dangerous, but they had managed to check it out thoroughly.'

'Were they locals or men drafted in from other areas?' asked Matt urgently.

'No idea. I'll ask. No, better still, I'll see if I can find them, and you can talk to them yourself. Matt, what do you know about that old derelict mill that they don't?'

'If they're locals, probably nothing and I'll have been mistaken. If they are outsiders, a *lot*. I spent many an idle hour in there when I was a kid, avoiding having to play sport. There's a lot more to that old mill than meets the eye.'

'And why do you think Sophie is there?' Philip asked shakily.

'Well, if I wanted to conceal someone out here on the fen, I'd choose the mill. Seeing that picture made me remember the old storerooms and the gallery chamber. But it would take an old-timer like me to remember the hidey holes we used to play in.'

'Forget the crew.' Will said. 'We have to get out there, now.'

* * *

Inspector Michael Fenner made them wait until he and Jack Fleet arrived from Grove's cottage, and then a convoy of cars took off along the lane that circumnavigated Whisper Fen. A wind had got up, blowing away the clouds, and the night sky was a deep indigo blue. Out beyond the marsh could be heard the sound of water rushing on to the boggy fenland shore. The mill was a black hump standing out in stark relief against the moonlit horizon.

The local force, shortly joined by an armed response team, surrounded the ruin. Matt Ballard had asked if there were any older local men among them that he could confer with. Sergeant Charles Palmer was a contemporary of Matt's, and the two of them worked out how best to search the old building. They knew that the main body of the mill had been scoured, as well as the outbuildings. Two small storerooms had been overlooked, as had the galleried reefing chamber used for servicing and access to the now absent sails.

Staring up at the dark, louring building, Will felt a hand on his arm. He turned to see DCI Charlotte Anders, who had replaced Matt Ballard when he retired. 'Good to see you here, ma'am.'

Her grip tightened. 'Hang on in there, Will, we're all rooting for you. Just because I've not been getting my shoes muddy out here doesn't mean that I haven't been moving heaven and earth to get her back.'

Will swallowed hard and nodded. Right now, he wished with all his heart that he could turn back the clock and be part of it all again.

Through a loud-hailer, the hollow disembodied voice of Inspector Fenner informed whoever was inside that the mill was surrounded, and they should come out immediately.

An eerie silence ensued. Fenner called again, asking the person, or persons, to identify themselves.

There was no sound but the sighing of the wind. A night bird screeched in the distance.

Several teams of officers were then deployed to search the building. Under instruction from Matt Ballard and Charles Palmer, the men swept into the concealed storerooms. They were empty. This left the chamber, high up in the body of the mill.

'This won't be quite so easy.' Rubbing his chin and frowning, Palmer looked up.

'Just tell us what to do, Sergeant,' the officer in charge said. 'If anyone is up there, they certainly know we're here. There is no chance of surprising them, so let's get on with it.'

Matt and Palmer led a group of men to an old scratched and peeling door on the outside of the mill. It opened to reveal an alcove and a flight of steps that led up inside the thick double wall.

Matt whispered to the first man ready to go. 'Be *very* careful. The room is a sort of gallery, a wide area called a reefing stage. There used to be a balustrade, but it was rotting away when I was a boy. Now I should think the floor just stops. In fact, the whole thing could have fallen in, so make sure before you step off the staircase that there is a floor at all.'

Three men prepared for the ascent.

'Go! Go! Go!'

Philip gripped Will's shoulder. Some time later, a radio crackled into life. Tinny voices shouted something unintelligible, then shouted again.

Will grabbed the Canadian's arm. 'What did they say?'

Philip's mouth worked, but no sound emerged.

Sam turned to Will in amazement. 'They've got her!'

'Is she . . . ?'

Charlotte Anders moved forward. 'Fenner! The girl?'

'We don't even know if it's her yet,' Fenner said. 'But whoever it is, she's alive.'

Everyone moved towards the black door.

'Get back! For God's sake, you'll frighten the kid to death! Go on — move back! Where's the child protection officers?' Anders called.

Two women in plain clothes moved to the front of the small crowd. Will found that he was standing next to the inspector.

'They're coming out!'

Everyone fell silent.

Will stood and watched. What happened next seemed to unfold in slow motion.

The black-garbed officer carried the child in his arms. As he gently lowered her to the ground, the policewomen rushed forward and threw blankets around her.

Will, his mouth slightly open, stared at his bedraggled niece.

He took a step towards her and her eyes met his. His Sophie! Safe! Alive! He opened his arms to her.

Her mouth rounded into a terrible, soundless scream. She pulled away from him, her eyes wild with terror. She looked around, as if searching for an escape route.

'Sophie?' Will said.

The inspector gripped his arm, holding him back. There was no need. Will had frozen to the spot.

Sam came running towards him, shouting. 'Hold on, old chap. We have no idea what she has been through. Let them get her to a place of safety and we'll ask questions later.' Sam stood in front of him, his hands on Will's shoulders, blocking his view of the distraught child and her rescuers.

'But her face! Did you see her face?' Will pulled away and tried to peer around him.

'William! God knows what ordeal that child has been through. Now forget what you saw! She is safe now. Hold on to that.'

Will let his head fall forward. He felt someone put an arm around him. 'Listen to what he says, Will,' Charlotte Anders said. 'She's alive. We'll take care of her.' Then, after a quick word with Sam, she moved away.

Will had seen the look on Fenner's face. Instructions from his training echoed in his mind: 'Always look close to home for the murderer or the child molester, PC Stonebridge. The father or an uncle are the most likely candidates.' Fenner must have had the same instructor.

'Where are they taking her? I want to see her, I've *got* to!'

'Calm down, lad. They're taking her to the family suite where she will be looked after. You know the drill, William. You know what happens next. None of us can see her, not yet.'

He did know, but none of it made sense. Why had she looked at him like that? She should have run to him. What did it mean?

Someone called out from the darkness above. 'Sir! Ma'am! There is something else. I think you should see this.' Inspector Fenner and DCI Anders moved swiftly towards the door in the old mill wall.

'No one else enters, got that?' the inspector said as they disappeared inside. 'Especially no civilians!'

Will stood with Sam. He felt strangely numb. The liaison officer had taken Philip with them to the hospital where Sophie would be treated. He would not be allowed to see her in person but would be on hand to provide the doctors with any information they needed about her. She would have a thorough medical examination and then, when she was ready, they would start the difficult process of determining what had happened. The Royal Canadian Air Force doctor was en-route from Waddington, where he had landed a short time before.

'Seal this place up until the SOCOs get here!' yelled DCI Anders. 'Where the hell are they anyway?'

'On their way from the Grove cottage, ma'am.'

Two more cars joined the melee. The scene-of-crime officers pushed through the blue-and-white tape, donning their white protective suits.

'Kenwright! Take a couple of uniforms and bring in Grove.'

'What's the charge, ma'am?'

'Distributing indecent images of children contrary to the Protection of Children's Act 1978, and Contravention of the Obscene Publications Act will do for starters, and from the look of what we've just found, there'll be a number of choice additions before long. Just get the bastard, will you?'

The detective constable and two uniformed officers ran to their car and sped away into the night.

Will stood motionless while around him the various players milled about. He felt trapped, caught in a big glass bubble. All the time, he was aware of Fenner's steady gaze.

The inspector stood apart from all the activity, staring at Will. After a while, he walked slowly across and stood before Sam and Will. 'We believe that Groves' computer has a lot of incriminating evidence on it, including emails to Holland about "deliveries." He clearly didn't think it would be found, as they were still in his inbox. A lot of stuff has been deleted, but IT are working on it now. There's little doubt that he is deeply involved in the importation of illegal material.' His eyes never left Will's face. 'I trust I will be able to find you at Holland House later? I will be wanting to talk to you. Right now, we have a number of loose ends to tie up. It looks cut and dried, but I'm not so certain.'

Will found his voice and asked what they had found in the mill.

'Videos, photographs, computer discs, magazines. Pornography. Boxes and boxes of the stuff.'

'And you think it's Grove?' Sam asked.

'With his history, Professor Page, and what I have just been told was found on his second computer, there's little doubt about it,' Fenner said.

'And the child?' Sam glanced at Will.

'You know I cannot answer that,' the inspector said. 'She is alive and apparently unharmed — physically. The experts will tell us more when they have examined her. You will be—'

'Sir! We've got a problem.'

A PC came running towards them. She said to Fenner, 'Sir, the coastguards have just notified us that this area is in danger of flooding within the next hour or so. There is a weather front out in the North Sea, coupled with a massively high incoming tide. They have advised us to get out of here fast.'

'Jesus! DCI Anders! We have to get that evidence out of the mill. Find me the SOCO in charge. We need them to sweep the place and bag everything they can, now!'

'Can we help?' Sam asked.

'Sorry, Professor, but I think you had better leave this to us.' He cast a speculative eye on Will. 'And you might want to make sure that Holland House is not in any danger.' With that, he turned on his heels and moved rapidly towards the old mill, barking orders to his subordinates.

'Come along, William, we'd best get out of here. We obviously aren't wanted, and we may need to batten down a few hatches at home.' Sam took Will's arm and guided him to their car, where Matt was waiting for them.

'What the hell kind of stuff do you think they found on that pervert's computer?' Will kept asking. 'I knew that filthy little scrote had something to do with it. It makes me sick to think that Kate was friendly with him.'

'I wouldn't like to even hazard a guess at what they found, although hearing what they found in the mill, I can imagine. But we mustn't let our imaginations run riot until we know for sure,' said Sam calmly.

Will shook his head slowly. 'I just can't take it all in.'

'Hardly surprising, lad,' Sam said. 'But the main thing is that the child is alive, and hopefully we got to her before anything, well, before anyone else did. There is a very good chance that she is just frightened and hungry. Let's hold on to that until we get more news, shall we?'

Will swallowed hard. With an effort, he turned his thoughts to the forecast high tide. 'This flood, Matt, do you really think it will affect our side of Whisper Fen?'

'No, I don't think so. Holland House and Mrs Swain's end of Tylers Lane are set further back, and they are on an incline that leads up to the new sea bank. Chances are that the old mill, and maybe Grove's place, because it's out in the marsh, will be the only properties in danger. We can check with the local authority if you like.'

'Of course. We have to know.' Will hesitated. 'Sam? Matt? Did you see the look Fenner gave me? He thinks I'm involved, and from the way Sophie acted, I don't blame him. What was that all about?'

They came to a halt at Holland House. Sam turned to Will. 'I really don't know, William, and it's no use speculating. We'll hear soon enough. There are a dozen reasons that would explain her actions, but right now we can only speculate, which is a waste of time and energy. Let's concentrate on the job at hand. We could all be under several feet of water in an hour if we don't get on that phone and find out what the devil is happening!'

CHAPTER TWENTY-FIVE

From the bedroom window, Will surveyed the scene below. Men were clearing equipment from the patio and dismantling the lights that had only been erected a matter of hours before.

Matt was busy talking to an Environment Agency officer on the phone, and Sam was talking to one of the police officers in the kitchen.

Will desperately needed to get control of his mind. He took a deep breath and stared into the night, where he saw the lights of a car out on the lane leading to Grove's cottage. How he hated that man. He had always distrusted Grove, and now it seemed he had been right. If he had child pornography in his possession, then the little shite was more than capable of taking his dear, sweet Sophie, and doing God knows what to her. And to think that Kate had defended him! Just how naıve — no, how fucking stupid could you get? He should have knocked the shit out of the slimeball long ago. Perhaps then he would have buggered off out of the fen.

'Will?' Matt called up the stairs.

'Coming.' He turned from the window and went down to find his friend. 'What's the news?'

'Well, as long as the bad weather out in the North Sea doesn't get worse, they are expecting only the mill to be affected. They are almost certain that the old building will go tonight,' said Matt.

'I hope Fenner gets everything he needs from it to nail that bastard Grove.'

'From the speed those chaps were working at when we left, I should think they will. And if all else fails, he could always do a King Canute. One look from him should be enough to turn back the tide.'

'Yeah, sure,' muttered Will.

'Don't worry about him, Will. He's a tough nut, but I'm sure he's a good copper. You have nothing at all to do with this kidnapping. It won't take him long to come to the same conclusion.'

'He doesn't like me, Matt.'

'I'd be very surprised if Fenner likes anyone.' Matt laughed. 'Especially the DCI, by the looks of it, so don't get ideas above your station. You heard the way he spoke to Sergeant Keene, and he's the most agreeable fellow you could hope to meet.'

Will remained unconvinced but dropped the subject. 'So, we are safe from the cruel sea?'

'It seems that way, though it wouldn't hurt to check the garage and outbuildings and make sure that nothing valuable is left lying on the ground. The high wind will most likely be the main problem, and if the dykes should overflow, we could get a bit of excess water draining through.' Matt wrinkled his brow. 'Liz was going to come back here, but I told her to stay put and keep an eye on Cannon Farm. We are quite exposed up there on Tanners Fen. Oh, and she sends her love. She's over the moon that they've found Sophie.'

Will thanked him. Whenever he thought of Sophie, he saw that terrified expression on her face. To distract himself from his thoughts, he asked about Emilia's cottage.

'That's even further inland than you, and it's a good bit higher. That's how her husband was able to put in the pit and that store without it flooding every time it rained. Her place should be fine.'

'I think maybe I'll let her know. She'll have seen the warnings, and at least I can put her mind at rest a bit, and tell her that Sophie is safe.'

'Well, don't tell her too much just yet, but if you are going to speak to her, ask her about that underground workshop. Find out who knew about it, if you can.'

Ten minutes later, Will, Sam and Matt sat at the kitchen table eating sandwiches that Sam had made for them.

'She says that other than a few of her husband's old friends, no one knew about that room. She really didn't think too much about it, and certainly not that it might be a reason for someone to want the house.'

'Well, I do. I think it's someone's main reason for wanting it. In fact, I—' Matt was interrupted by the phone ringing.

Will went to answer. He sat back down without a word. His half-eaten sandwich seemed to fascinate him.

'William?' Sam's voice drifted in as if through a mist.

After a while, Will spoke, his eyes still on his plate. 'That was Mrs Swain. She thought it was probably nothing, but she remembered one other person who had seen the workroom.'

Matt and Sam glanced at each other.

'It was Kate.'

Sam shrugged. 'And what is the problem with that? You're neighbours. Kate did spend quite a bit of time with the old dear at one point, didn't she?'

'Try to think like a suspicious copper, Sam. We have dealt with devious minds all our working lives. Yes Kate chatted to Emilia, she also spent a lot of time talking to Gerald Grove,' added Matt grimly.

Sam groaned. 'Oh, of course! Why didn't we see it before? It's so damn obvious!'

Will looked up. 'It's a fact that since we first came here, Grove has been ingratiating himself with Kate — confiding in her. He knew I was an ex-copper, so he turned what could have been a problem for him to his advantage. He saw how kind and gentle she is, and got in quick, telling her about his "troubles," how he'd been harassed, the "unjust" allegations against him. He helped her when she had a panic attack . . . oh, the crafty bastard!'

'And I'm betting he spent a lot of time listening to her as well,' Matt added. 'He's a naturalist, and a good one, he knows all about this fen and the countryside hereabouts. He knew that one day the weather would claim his hidey hole at the mill, and his cottage too, if some really hard weather hit—'

'And who owned the perfect property for his needs? A place with a secret store where he can hide his illicit goods.' interjected Sam.

'Emilia Swain!' said Will.

'But she is happy there, has no intention of selling her lovely home,' Matt continued. 'So, what does he do? He frightens the poor dear away.'

'With the intention of buying her cottage, most likely through a third party to avoid suspicion,' said Will.

'All ably assisted, albeit unknowingly, by your darling wife!' Sam raised his eyes to the ceiling.

'Maybe she assisted him more ably than you think, Sam. I believe it was Kate who trashed the garden.'

The doctor's mouth fell open. 'What?'

'I'm sorry I didn't mention this to you before, but you remember seeing me pack that evil doll in her case?'

He frowned. 'Yes. You had just torn the dress.'

'Wrong. I found that piece of linen in Emilia's garden, just after it had been destroyed.'

Sam was silent for a while. 'You mean you think she actually did it to help Grove? But that's preposterous!'

'I don't know what I think, Sam. I'm just telling you what I found.'

Sam rubbed his eyes. 'We certainly have plenty of questions for Kate, don't we, when she is well enough to answer them.'

'Too many. I hope Swifty brings us up to date on what's happening with Grove. I won't sleep until I know that the evil pervert is under lock and key.'

'They'll get him, Will. He must have been pretty damned confident that even if the mill was searched, they would miss that upper room. The place is so dangerous, and the way that door is set in the wall is perfect. It would have taken a real local to know about that. He was even confident enough to return tonight.'

'You'd think he would have stayed away a bit longer, at least until the furore had died down,' Will said.

'I suppose he couldn't risk it. I'm willing to bet that he knew about the abnormally high tide and, Sophie apart, he had thousands of pounds worth of pornography stashed away in that mill.'

'How could he have got away with that? The marsh is heaving with police!'

'It is now, but that area had already been searched. And Grove would have gone out after dark. He knows Whisper Fen like the back of his hand. I suspect he would have loaded up that old estate car of his and moved the stuff out under cover of night — or sent his helper, the guy who hit Matt. He also knows the fen.' He turned to Matt. 'You said he took off into the marshes like a jackrabbit after he hit you. And he knew the searchers would be called in at dusk . . .'

'What a risk though! The police would be watching him like a hawk,' breathed Sam.

'Probably, but with some outside help and his knowledge of Whisper Fen, ten to one he could have given them the slip,' said Matt.

'And Sophie?' Will asked.

'Let's not dwell on that, my boy. Right now, she is most likely curled up in bed with a hot-water bottle.'

'I hope.'

'As soon as the medical is over and samples have been taken, they will cosset that little girl like a princess. I know that for a fact.'

'And interrogate her and make her play silly games.'

'She's not in Colditz, William. Certainly, they will question her, they have to, but very, very gently. Okay?'

'Sorry. I'm sure you're right. I never had much to do with child protection or domestic violence in my day.'

'Mmm, nowadays they are usually dealt with by specially trained teams,' Sam said. 'But rest assured, she will get all the care she needs.

'Anyone want another brandy?' asked Will.

'I never finished the last one,' said Matt.

'Come on, let's see if the fire is still alight. There is nothing more we can do now until the dreaded Inspector Fenner's visit, or, please God, that of Swifty Fleet.'

Will threw more logs on the fire and tried, unsuccessfully, to rid his mind of worry about his wife and his niece. They were both hospitalised, both afflicted, one with troubles of her own making and the other a sad victim of man's twisted wickedness.

It was after ten when the bell finally rang.

Swifty almost fell in through the door. 'Sorry I'm so late. Bloody road is flooded on the outskirts of town, and still some flamin' idiots think it's cool to drive right through it, then they wonder why they break down!'

Swifty took off his cap. 'How are you doing? Worried sick, I'll bet.'

Will ushered him through to the lounge. 'You can say that again. Any news about Sophie?'

'Not yet. Inspector Fenner may have heard something, but it's not filtered down through the ranks yet. I came to tell you that we've got Grove.'

'Great! We'll all breathe a little easier now. Did the mill actually flood? And did you manage to get all the evidence you needed?'

'The mill was still standing when we got out, but the water was flowing in fast. By the time we drove away, the whole structure looked ready to cave in. But, yes, we got plenty, thanks. You should have seen it, Will. We unearthed cases full of CDs. Some were X-rated, hardcore movies, but there were others too — kiddie porn, all marked with just names — you know, Vicky, Daniel, Millie, Jessie. Turned my stomach to think of the poor little sods. Good thing it wasn't me that went out to apprehend Grove. I don't think I could have kept my hands off 'im.'

'You and me both, Swifty. Any chance he will crawl out of this, like he did before?'

'No way. Well, certainly not the distributing indecent images, or the obscene publications charges. He had dumped a load of stuff from his computer, but the IT lads resurrected most of it from the hard drive. There's enough there to send him down for a good long stretch, and that's apart from the fact that his sidekick, Hemmings, is singing like the dawn chorus.'

'And he's actually coughed to putting the frighteners on old Mrs Swain?'

'And to belting Matt. He's not daft, Will. He knows there are some pretty heavy charges being dished out, and he's giving us Grove, lock stock and barrel. He's admitting to the small stuff and throwing his boss to the wolves.'

'I do admire loyalty in a man, don't you?' Will said dryly.

'Well, DCI Anders sweetly explained what desperately deep shite he was in before she asked him nicely to cooperate, and suddenly he was delighted to help us with our enquiries. He was still squealing when I left.' He gave a short laugh. 'My mate said Anders scared the shit out of him. She's certainly got a way with words.'

'And Grove?'

'Threw up his hands to importing and distributing obscene publications and indecent images, but emphatically denied knowing anything about Sophie's abduction.'

'I suppose it's what you would expect,' Sam added. 'He would hardly admit to that — he'd want you chaps to try to prove it.'

Swifty looked fierce. 'And as soon as all the tests come back, I hope we'll have enough of a case to send him away for a very long time indeed.'

'Surely there is no doubt about that, is there?' Will asked.

Swifty shrugged. 'You know the justice system, better than most. If he gets a smart brief, it could be in the lap of the gods, and the crime scene may well be halfway across the North Sea by morning. That's a great help to the prosecution.'

Will began to feel uneasy. 'But Sophie will identify him.'

'The last child didn't, did he? That boy down in the West Country never admitted it was Grove took him. They're trying to trace him, by the way. If our man is convicted of Sophie's kidnapping, then he might just feel safe enough to tell us what really happened to him all those years ago.' Swifty was pacing the room, his hands buried deep in his trouser pockets. 'Or he may have chosen to forget the horrors of the past. Bad memories can get buried pretty deep, you know.'

'Well, at least Liz's investigation seems to have been solved off the back of this.' Matt smiled grimly. 'She's unearthed one of the outlets Grove used to distribute the dirty magazines. He's been supplying them to a village store. They're going out inside copies of the *Telegraph* of all things. You would not believe how lucrative hard-copy porn is! One of the vice squad boys told me that pervs are getting twitchy about Big Brother seeing what they are accessing digitally, and they are sourcing out old-style mags that they can keep under the mattress! Liz'll be chuffed to hear about his arrest.'

Swifty accepted the offer of a coffee and Sam went out to the kitchen. When he had left the room, Swifty moved closer to Will and in an urgent whisper asked his friend if Sam knew about Kate's demolition job on the Swain garden.

Will nodded. 'Yes. I told him earlier. Why?'

'Because Hemmings admitted to killing the cat, messing up the shed, spray-painting the walls, attempted arson and assaulting someone who tried to stop him, but not to running amok in the garden. He swore that act of destruction had nothing to do with him.'

'Which rather points to my wife, doesn't it?' said Will glumly.

'Rather. But I'm saying nothing about that. No one's going to take it any further, so I suggest we let sleeping dogs lie. Now, the interesting thing about Grove and his designs on Little Anchor is that he wanted it for more than just that underground room. The chatty Mr Hemmings told us all about the nice little smuggling racket dear Gerald had going on — porn and sex toys from Holland.'

Sam emerged from the kitchen. 'Kettle on. Come again, Swifty? Smuggling?'

'Yeah. He's not just the middleman either. He runs the whole enterprise. He has small boats bringing in merchandise from bigger boats. Real hardcore Dutch porn. Magazines, books, CDs, toys and S & M merchandise. You name it, if it has a market, Grove could get hold of it.'

'Well,' exclaimed Matt, 'that really is history repeating itself. Isaac Berridge did a similar thing, but in his case it was Dutch gin. Smuggling of that kind has been going on for generations, ever since they used to trade Lincolnshire fleeces for genever gin. That's how I knew about the second loft space. It's where he hid his contraband.'

It dawned on Will that the lights he had so often seen out in the Wash had probably been signals. 'So, he really needed Emilia's cottage. Otherwise he'd have had to move his business to another part of the coast.'

'Exactly.'

Matt smiled grimly. 'At least that's the reason for setting the fire by the coal shed. He wanted it to look like a serious attempt at burning the place down but not to cause any real damage. That's been bugging me and Liz ever since we saw it.'

Sam left the room, shaking his head and muttering something about jigsaw pieces. He returned a few minutes later with a tray of hot drinks. 'One thing still bothers me. As William said earlier, why did he store his contraband in the old mill, and not at his cottage?'

'Damp. It was ruining his precious merchandise,' said Swifty.

'But surely the mill was as close to the water as his cottage?' Will said.

'Well, that's what he told us, just damp.'

'I think,' said Matt slowly, 'that he may have been right. That room was right up high in the body of the mill. There was a free flow of air and it was always dry. Plus, if anyone did decide to pay him a visit, the cottage was clean — with the exception of that computer. Which reminds me, how come your detectives didn't pick up two telephone lines on his bill?'

'Because the second line was ex-directory and listed under a different name — Mr I. Berridge.' Swifty looked at his watch. 'I'd better get off home. My wife will be worrying. I'll call back tomorrow, and in the meantime, I hope you get some good news about Sophie. And get some kip, guys, especially you, Will, you still look like shit!'

Will thanked his friend for all his help. He walked with him to the door. 'We still haven't had our promised visit from your boss.'

'He and DCI Anders were taking it in turns to terrorise Grove when I left, but if he said he'll come tonight, then I'm sorry to say, he will. Perhaps you won't get to bed so early after all.'

'Until I get news about Sophie, I won't be able to sleep anyway.'

Swifty nodded and grasped his arm. 'She'll be okay, Will. That Canadian doctor arrived earlier. They are pinning quite a lot of their hopes on him. She has the best around her, honestly.'

'It's the not knowing, Swifty. What happened to her? Why was she coming here? How will this affect her? Just how much is one little kid supposed to take? It was bad enough losing her mum and dad, but this? It beggars belief.'

'Go on inside and try to relax. I'm sure it won't be long before someone has some news for you, even if it is Fenner.'

Will grimaced. 'I would even open my arms to him if it meant that I was getting some news.'

He closed the door, weariness washing over him. He longed to crawl into bed and sleep for hours, days even, and wake up in his wife's arms, knowing that she was well and happy, and that Sophie and her parents were safe and happy too. But his sister was dead. Guy was dead. He had no idea how much damage had been done to Sophie. And then there was Kate. A woman he no longer knew, full of secrets and dark thoughts.

He was on his way back to the lounge when he heard another car draw up. He glanced out of the side window and saw Fenner getting out of an Alfa Romeo. He didn't think that mere inspectors of police were that well paid.

He opened the door before Fenner could ring the bell and invited him to come in. He refused a drink but accepted a chair close to the fire. Will wondered if it would make him melt at all.

'I do have some news, Mr Stonebridge, although it's of the "good news, bad news" variety. Firstly, your niece was not sexually assaulted.' He paused, watching Will's reaction closely.

Will found himself fighting back tears. 'Thank God!'

'She is unhurt — that is to say physically, other than being stiff and cold.'

'How was she restrained?'

The inspector regarded Will with some interest. 'Why do you ask?'

Will looked bewildered. 'I wondered if he had hurt her. If she is like her mother — or me for that matter — she is a mouth breather. A gag could have caused her great distress.'

'Another baffling element about this strange case, sir. You see, Mr Stonebridge, she wasn't restrained.'

No one spoke. Matt took a sharp breath.

As Fenner was obviously not about to volunteer more, Sam finally broke the baffled silence. 'I don't understand. Do you mean she wasn't kidnapped at all? She was just hiding there, not bound or fettered in any way?'

'Until she tells us something, we don't know. But we still believe she was taken by force and was held there without her consent.'

'But how?' Sam said.

'Fear, Professor Page. We don't know what he said to her, but he frightened the life out of her. She was so scared that she didn't even cry out for help when the first search party checked the ground floor of the mill. Not even when the building was surrounded by police and I used the loud-hailer. Remember the last case Grove was involved in? The boy never spoke about what happened — well, not to tell the truth. Which brings me to the more negative news. So far, Sophie has not spoken a word. She will not, or cannot, communicate with our team or the doctors, including the specialist from Canada.'

'I don't believe you should be overly concerned by that,' Sam said. 'It is only a matter of hours since she was found. Unwillingness to talk about what happened should be expected. It will be some time before she feels safe enough to let go.'

'I'm sure you're right, Professor. I am just passing on the information that I have been given. Naturally, I am hoping for something concrete that will incriminate Grove. I don't want that man to get away with anything, anything at all. He avoided prison once before because of lack of evidence. I don't want that happening again.' Fenner leaned closer to the fire and held out a hand to the heat. Will noticed that it was white and slender. 'I don't know how you feel about this, Mr Stonebridge, but it has been suggested that as soon as we can allow it, the child should be sent home to Canada. Her own doctor believes she should be reintegrated into the family environment as soon as possible. Captain Fauve has agreed to accept a permanent post in Saskatchewan so as to give her the stability that she will need.'

'That is one hell of a lot to ask of the Fauves when she's not even their own flesh and blood,' Will said.

'No one is asking it of them, Mr Stonebridge. They have offered it freely. Are you objecting?' The gaze wrapped its icy cloak around him.

'No, of course not. It's just that, well, she is all I have left of my sister. In fact, Sophie is all I have left of my entire family. Maybe I hoped that she would want to stay here — not now, not after everything that has happened, of course. I just . . .'

'I think you know that your niece will never set foot on this fen again, don't you? Something here has petrified her, and all I can hope is that Canada is far enough away for her to be able to forget it.'

'Whatever is best for Sophie. That is all I want,' Will said weakly.

'Good. Now I need to go. And I'm glad to see the flood stopped short of Holland House.'

Will wasn't so sure. He was starting to wish that the North Sea tide had swept it off the fens.

The car purred off. Will returned to the living room, massaging his arm. The pain was radiating in short sharp bursts right down to his fingers. 'I have to turn in, guys. I've had enough for today. Help yourselves to another brandy. I'm going to take one up with me.'

The doctor nodded. 'Please. I don't think I'll need any rocking, but perhaps the cognac will help soothe my overactive brain.'

'I think it would take morphine to soothe mine,' muttered Will.

'She's alive, dear boy, just hang on to that. Children are remarkably resilient. You said yourself how brave she was. I'm willing to bet she'll surprise you. Just give it time.'

Matt yawned. 'And I must phone Liz and ask her to pick me up. I daren't drive with two brandies inside me and all these coppers in the vicinity. What a day!'

* * *

In the early hours of the morning, Will woke up in tears. They hadn't stopped an hour later when he finally drifted back to sleep.

CHAPTER TWENTY-SIX

At breakfast the following day, Sam told Will that he had risen early and taken a walk to the remains of the mill. There was still a police cordon around the building, which had sustained significant damage. The tower had completely caved in, scattering rubble and other detritus across the boggy ground. He had not been allowed too close, but one particular scrap of debris had caught his eye. Along with some other pieces of rubbish that had been collected up by the officers and piled in a heap, was the broken remains of Isaac Berridge's oil lamp.

They concluded that Grove had taken it from the cottage to the secret storeroom at the mill to provide a source of lighting. To have noticed the lamp, Kate, at some time or another, must have gone there, either with Grove, or alone. Will had seen her walking near the mill many times, and was inclined to believe that she had watched Grove, and then after he left, gone inside herself. Surely he had far too much to hide to risk inviting a copper's wife into his Aladdin's cave, although after one of his consignments had arrived, he would have shipped it all out as soon as possible, so maybe she'd found the gallery room, and there was nothing incriminating to see anyway?

Will went to phone the clinic. Thinking of Kate wandering the marsh made him feel terribly lonely. He missed her and longed for her to be back with him. With Sophie safe and Grove in custody, he could concentrate on his wife and her recovery.

He was told that Lawrence Hassel was with a patient and unable to come to the phone. Will said he would ring again later, but apparently the doctor was doing assessments all afternoon. Perhaps Mr Stonebridge would leave it until the evening, or better still, the next day? He was assured that his wife was settling in "just fine," but they would prefer it if he didn't speak with her for a while. 'She has just started Dr Hassel's medication regime, sir. It would be very unsettling for her. I'm sure you understand.'

He said that he did and hung up, realising that he had needed to talk to her for his own sake, not hers. He wondered how Sophie was. Had she slept? Had she had nightmares? Would someone have stayed with her through the night? He hoped so. He was concerned that he had heard nothing from Philip Fauve.

'It must have been like bedlam at the hospital yesterday,' Sam said, reassuring him. 'It's no wonder the poor chap didn't call. I've been involved in something like this before, and the man would have been inundated with questions. They need to know everything they can about Sophie, in order to assess her properly. He probably didn't get any rest until the early hours, if then.'

Will nodded miserably. 'I don't like to bother him. He has enough on his plate right now. I would just like him to know that I am thinking of them. I wish we could go there.'

'Not a good idea. We wouldn't be allowed within a mile of the child. I'm sure he'll ring when he can. Meanwhile, I suggest we keep busy. Give me some jobs to do, young man. Cleaning, shopping, anything you please, just to get me moving.'

Will looked around him in dismay. The house was a tip. The laundry had overflowed its basket and lay on the bathroom floor. Dust had gathered on every surface and dried mud from the boots of countless policemen caked the carpet and the kitchen floor. How could it have got so bad so quickly?

'Come on, lad. The two of us can get this sorted by lunchtime. It'll do you good.'

* * *

By half past one, the washing machine was on its third load, and the house was looking acceptable once more. Sam was busy ironing shirts and doing a perfect job of it. This was nothing less than a miracle considering that a year ago he had been shot and badly injured. To see him now you would never have known it had happened.

Will was checking the fridge and making a list of the provisions that Sam had volunteered to go and fetch that afternoon when the phone rang.

Will was slightly disappointed to hear the guttural tones of Emilia Swain. This soon vanished amid her exclamations of delight that his niece had been found safe, and that the man who had been the cause of all her distress had been apprehended. She confessed to missing her home and was planning to return the following day. 'I will give it another chance, Mr Stonebridge. See how I go, as they say. At least there is no permanent damage, I must be thankful for that, and with those awful men behind bars, maybe I'll be able to regain my old love for the place.' She took a long breath. 'Although I doubt the garden will ever look quite as good again in my lifetime. I don't know. You nurture it and feed it, and then some animal tears it to shreds.'

Will said nothing of Hemming having denied any involvement in that beastly act.

'And Mrs Stonebridge? Is she feeling better? I am sure that now your niece has been found, her problems will ease.'

'She will be away for a bit longer yet, Mrs S. I need to get this place back to rights before she comes home. To be honest, I don't think Holland House is good for her. I am hoping to convince her to move away from here.'

'Oh dear. That is not something I would relish tackling! She is very attached to the house, very attached indeed.'

'Overly, if you ask me,' he said. 'Her love for this place is not what I would call healthy.'

'You are right, of course, but let me just say that you will have to be extremely careful what you say to her. Tread warily, Mr Stonebridge.'

'What has Kate said to you about this place?'

There was a pause. 'Everything and nothing. She simply lives and breathes for Whisper Fen. She can speak of nothing else. But as I said before, she had become rather distant over the past few weeks. Before I left, it was all she could do to even wave to me.'

Guilt? It seemed far-fetched but the old lady had frequently spoken of the garden as her "baby." Could that be the reason for Kate's act of destruction?

'I'm sorry, Mrs S. She hasn't been herself for some time now.'

Emilia clucked in sympathy. She must go, she said, and hoped that he would call in and see her when she returned.

Promising he would, he hung up. Immediately the telephone rang again. This time it was the call he'd been waiting for.

Philip Fauve sounded tired and anxious. 'Jesus, Will. This is just terrible. I'm sorry I haven't been able to reach you before, but what with the police and the doctors . . . and there is still nothing to tell you. Sophie has just clammed up. "Gone inside of herself" as they say.'

'Have you seen her?' Will asked.

'Only through an observation mirror. They won't let me in. She has someone with her constantly, but they are making little progress.'

'Sam here says this is natural. It takes time for someone to be able to talk about a trauma such as the one Sophie underwent.'

'Yeah, they say the same here, but there seem to be other symptoms that they're not happy about. And every case is different, everyone reacts differently to trauma. God, I feel so helpless!'

'We all do, Philip. Can I ask you something?' Will was still haunted by the look the child had given him. 'Are the people with her all women?'

'Except for her Canadian doctor, and one family support officer, yes. Why?'

'Did she react badly when she saw the male doctor?'

'She didn't react at all, Will. It was as if he wasn't there.'

Will had been hoping that the dreadful look she had given him had merely been a general fear of men caused by her ordeal. But there were plenty of other men around at that moment. No, that panic-stricken gaze had rested on him and him alone. 'They say that she needs to get home, and that you are going to get a permanent post there.'

'My boss has offered me an excellent position at the base, and I would be a fool not to accept it. Life is too short, Will. We've all learned that recently, from Guy and Eva. I want to be with my family for as long as I possibly can.'

'You're a good man, Philip.'

'Nah, just a family man. I love my wife and my kids, including Sophie. I'd do anything for them.'

'I want to offer my support, but it seems that all Kate and I have done is bring more grief down upon your heads.'

The Canadian sighed loudly. 'We just need to get Sophie back home. Françoise and Annette will do more for her than any doctor.'

'I'm sure you're right. The police just have to nail the bastard who took her, for the sake of other innocent kids.'

Philip said he had to hang up. The doctors wanted to speak to him again.

'Keep us posted, Philip.'

'Sure thing. As soon as there is any kind of breakthrough.'

Call ended, Will went to find Sam, who was about to leave for the supermarket. When he had gone, Will found himself alone for the first time in what seemed like an age. He wandered from room to room, picking things up and putting them down again. He finished up in Kate's studio, looking out over the deserted fen.

All trace of the search team had gone from his garden, leaving a lone car parked by the house. The high tide hadn't claimed it after all, and even the outbuildings had escaped the rising waters. He heard the phone ringing downstairs.

'Mr Stonebridge? The Linden Clinic here, sir. Could you hold for a moment? I have Doctor Hassel on the line for you.'

Will tensed.

Then the psychiatrist's deep voice was telling him not to worry. 'It's not bad news. There is just a slight problem that is preventing me from proceeding as I would wish. Your wife is somewhat concerned about a tree that came down in the storm?'

'The rowan,' Will said.

'The rowan, yes. She seems terribly upset about it and needs to know that you will deal with it for her. I'm sure that once her mind is put to rest on that score, we shall be able to make a bit more headway.'

'I forgot to call my gardener. A fallen tree was the least of my worries.' He knew he sounded waspish, but he felt aggrieved.

'But it is of great importance to Mrs Stonebridge. Now, this is what she would like you to do. Please have your man reduce it to pieces of a manageable size and drag it out on to the fen, where it should be burnt. She is emphatic that it is to be committed to the marsh that supported it during its life.'

'Forgive me, Dr Hassel, but my young niece has just been rescued from the clutches of a paedophile, we have just suffered a flood on the marsh, and the police are crawling over everything, and you want me to play games with a tree? You're joking, aren't you?'

'I am most certainly not, Mr Stonebridge. I would hardly waste my precious time with this if it were not of the utmost importance for your wife's treatment.' He sounded almost as cold as Inspector Fenner.

'Why?'

'Is it such a great inconvenience to comply with her wishes?'

'I suppose not.'

'Exactly. And it will make Kate happy.'

'Alright. Tell her that I'll attend to it for her, just as soon as Barry can fit it in.'

'You are not just saying this, are you? You will do it for her? After all, she will know when she gets home again.'

'I will do it. Okay?' Will paused, collected himself. 'I'm sorry, Doctor. I've been under a lot of stress lately. My niece . . .'

'I am delighted to hear that your niece has been found, but right now, Mr Stonebridge, your wife is my sole concern. The matter of the tree may seem trivial to you, but we cannot move forward unless it is dealt with.' His tone became kindlier. 'I do understand what a difficult time you are having, and I do sympathise. I assure you that as soon as your wife begins to make headway, I can be there for you too, but initially, she has to come first.'

After a second muttered apology, Will asked when he might be able to see his wife, or at least speak to her. The doctor was vague. 'I have high hopes that you'll be able to visit fairly soon. Let's just get a few more days under our belts.'

'Give her my love.'

'If she asks about you, then of course I will. Have patience, Mr Stonebridge. It'll be worth it in the long run.'

Will hoped that it would, because this was agony. He called Barry, who said he could get a lad to him the following day and would ten o'clock be convenient.

How refreshing it was to hear nothing about his recent troubles. If only everything were so simple. When would life return to normality?

Absentmindedly, he began looking through Kate's old paintings. He selected one entitled *A Meeting of Fairies in the*

Forest and stood it on her workbench. He then took one of her most recent works, a grim and forlorn depiction of dark shapes trudging across the marsh at twilight and stood it beside the first. The two paintings had absolutely nothing in common.

He put the later picture back with the others, its face to the wall, and left the joyful woodland dance on the bench. He remembered her finishing it — her joyful smile when he had declared it her best to date. He had picked her up and swung her round. How he had loved her! He saw them not long after they had moved in, chasing each other through the house and giggling like two children.

Would they ever be like that again? He tidied her brushes up and straightened some sheets of paper. He doubted it but swore that he wouldn't give up hope.

* * *

Days passed. Sophie remained silent, locked inside herself. Kate, he was told, was slowly responding to the drugs and the therapy.

Matt and Liz spent a lot of time with him, mainly trying to resurrect the garden after the damage wrought by all those policemen's boots. They prepared nourishing meals, Will having no appetite for his own efforts.

He and Matt helped Emilia move back into her cottage, and he resumed his twice-daily walks there, just to reassure the old lady that he was around should she need him. They also provided a good excuse to get out of Holland House.

Although there was precious little to report, Swifty kept them abreast of developments in the cases against Grove and Hemmings. Every day had brought new evidence to light about the indecent images of children and the pornography racket. It had been a big, well-organised business and Grove had been much more than just the go-between on the marsh. Offshore accounts traced back to him showed up a lot of money. The cottage on the marsh for the "reclusive entomologist" was just a temporary and useful base, being situated so close to where his delivery boats came in. They also discovered that he had other properties scattered around the country. The business had yielded him rich pickings and, apparently, another year working from Whisper Fen would have seen him ready to cash in and disappear abroad.

Despite all this, evidence proving that he had also abducted Sophie was much more difficult to find, and with the child unable to help, the police were growing increasingly frustrated. The boy Grove was alleged to have kidnapped some years ago had disappeared without trace. There was nothing suspicious about this. The young man had taken to the streets the previous year and had not been heard of in months.

Bryn Owen finally admitted that there was a real danger that Grove would get away with abduction again. They were still sure that he had taken her, but proving it was a different matter. So far they didn't have nearly enough evidence for the CPS. He would certainly go down for all the other crimes, but most likely not for taking Sophie.

Tempers were running high at the police station, and patience wearing thin in the family unit where Sophie was being looked after.

And on Whisper Fen, time stood still.

* * *

The following weekend, Sam, who had been staying on to lend Will his support, announced that he needed to go home. He had mail and messages to attend to, and he ought to make sure that his cottage was okay. He promised to return the following Monday.

On Sunday evening, at the end of a miserable, drizzly day, Will had a visitor.

Will was shocked by the change in him. Philip Fauve looked as grey as the weather. He had visibly lost weight, was unshaven, and his usual buzz cut had grown out. Will was reminded of Kate's abrupt change from a healthy, vivacious brunette to a lank and dreary stranger in scruffy clothes.

They went into the lounge, where Will poured him a large scotch and they sat facing the log fire.

'How is she?' Will asked.

'They say she is improving, but I can't see it,' Philip said.

'Have you been allowed in to see her?'

'Yes. Yesterday they let me sit with her for almost an hour. I talked to her about all the things she loves — the Brownies, the animals, and what Françoise has been up to. I even told her funny stories, but there was no response. Nothing at all.'

Will's heart sank. 'So, what's next?'

'Getting her home,' Fauve said.

'Ah.'

'That's why I'm here. They are moving her to the psychiatric wing tomorrow. They'll do some tests there, and hopefully release her into the care of Dr Abrahams, the air force doctor. We could be airborne a week from today.'

'That's good, isn't it?' Will asked.

'Yeah.' Fauve hesitated. 'Thing is, Will. I know that you're her only relative, and . . . and I'm real sorry about this, but they don't want you to see her before she goes.'

Will felt like a bucket of freezing water had been thrown in his face.

'It's to do with associations,' Philip was saying. 'You know, she associates you with the fen, and then, obviously, with what happened to her.'

While he had been alone, Will had been indulging in various fantasies in which he and Sophie were happily reunited. He had pictured himself in Canada, spending days at the lake with her, rowing, swimming, fishing. It was never going to happen.

'Could I see her through the one-way glass, do you think?' Will asked hopefully.

Fauve avoided his gaze. 'Sorry, Will. Look, as soon as she is better . . .' He stood up. 'I have to go, things to organise. Will, I am so very sorry.'

'Look after her, Philip.' Will stepped forward and hugged him.

'I'll keep in touch, Will, I promise. And tell Kate we are thinking about her. Good luck.'

Will closed the door, turned the key and drew the bolt.

* * *

In the weeks that followed, the news from Canada was fairly encouraging. Back with her family, Sophie had emerged from her shell. But there were subjects that remained taboo, and sadly he was one of them. According to Annette, she was improving daily but there was little trace of the child that had embarked for England. She was nervous, moody and prone to rages that were followed by periods of black depression. Nevertheless, the doctors at the military hospital, where she was being treated as an outpatient, remained tentatively optimistic. It would just take time. She had never once mentioned her ordeal, or even her trip to England. It was as if she had never gone.

* * *

'You may come and see Kate if you like, Mr Stonebridge. Tomorrow at two, if that is convenient?'

He chose his clothes with care, feeling like a youngster going on a first date. It had been three weeks since Kate had gone into the clinic. He had spoken on the phone with her a couple of times, but this would be his first visit. He longed to breathe her special scent of flowers.

He checked the time again.

This was it. He smoothed down his trousers and picked a piece of cotton from his sleeve. Reminding himself to stop on the way and buy her flowers, he locked up and headed for the car.

* * *

Darkness had fallen. His smart clothes lay in a heap where he had thrown them. It was nine o'clock, and he was well into his third scotch. He had meant to ring Matt, or Philip, or Sam, or the Samaritans — he wasn't sure which — but in the end he had called no one.

He had spent nearly half an hour with some stranger, a poor imitation of the woman he had married. Kate had sat there wearing a smile that he didn't recognise, her hair brushed into a style that wasn't hers.

Before he went in to see her, Lawrence Hassel had advised him that she would be subdued, and perhaps a little forgetful or confused. This was only the effect of her medication and he was not to worry. It would soon begin to wear off as she became more accustomed to the powerful drugs. The good doctor had neglected to mention that Will would not actually be seeing Kate, but some badly put together doppelganger.

He had cut short his visit and left without saying a word to anyone.

The last thing Will remembered about that terrible day was the clatter as the whisky bottle slid from his grasp and struck the floor.

CHAPTER TWENTY-SEVEN

Will sat on the bench and eyed the latest crack in the wall. A few had appeared since the fen had flooded for the second time and they had called in a surveyor, who had assured them that there was nothing to worry about. *Pity,* thought Will. He still hated the place.

When the man went on to admire the house, calling it a "sturdy old building, well designed and constructed to withstand the elements and the soft Lincolnshire soil," Kate had smiled, taking the compliment personally.

They had now lived there a full year.

In the end, Lawrence Hassel had worked wonders. Kate was, to all intents and purposes, back to normal. Except that she could not paint. Both the skill and the desire had gone, and her work for Angela's eighth volume had been rejected. As Will had feared, the illustrations were far too dark and frightening for a children's book. Her contract had been terminated.

To his immense sadness, he soon discovered that along with her desire to paint, Kate had also lost her passion for life. Only Will seemed to notice that Kate had become a pretty shell, an empty husk. Of late, he had sensed her drawing even further away from him.

The last time he had felt close to her was a few weeks after she had left the clinic. He had done as she requested and had the rowan tree dragged out on to the fen, where he had burnt what he could of it. The great pyre had lit up the sky for days, and by the time Kate returned, some of the charred trunk remained. He had taken to using the spot for burning garden rubbish that was too big for the incinerator. On that particular day, he had taken out a dead conifer and along with some other garden waste, had built quite a substantial bonfire.

She had stood with him, her arm through his, and they had watched the fire consume the dead fir tree branch by branch. After a while she had gone indoors and to his surprise, returned carrying the dark paintings, which she had committed to the flames.

Then, from under her jacket, she had produced the doll and with a kiss, consigned that too to the pyre.

He had held her tightly, told her that he was proud of her, and kissed her with all his old passion. They had gone up to their room and, tenderly, made love.

The following day her feelings seemed to have cooled along with the ashes, and from that moment on, she began to drift away.

While the news came from Canada that Sophie was improving and becoming stronger, Kate seemed to wane. Every day she became a little more transparent, less substantial.

He gazed at the figure silhouetted against the horizon. He could just make out her red windcheater. She had left at breakfast time, and it was now just after eleven o'clock. He had sat on the bench, daydreaming, unable to force himself to move. He was tired of trying to work out what to do about his wife. He couldn't bear to think of life without her, but life with her was becoming unbearable too. He really should ring Matt, or maybe Sam, but he couldn't muster the energy to even make a call.

He stood up and stretched. He had heard the postman earlier but hadn't bothered to check the mail. It would only be bills. No one ever wrote to them these days. At least Philip phoned regularly. Those calls were the only bright point in Will's life. Sophie was back at school. She was still receiving therapy, but she was much recovered. There was even talk about her going off to camp again. Philip and Annette had trudged through the mountain of required paperwork and were well on the way to becoming Sophie's legal parents.

He went to check the post. Among the bills he found a letter, the address written in a clear, childish hand. The stamps told him it came from Canada.

Will turned it over in his hands. After a few moments, he took the letter outside and with a beating heart, tore the envelope open.

Dear Uncle Will,

You may never get to read this, and it feels really spooky to be writing when maybe what I say will only get lost or screwed up and thrown away. My therapist says I should write out my most worrying thoughts, then burn them, letting the sparks fly up to Heaven to be purified. Weird, or what!

Do you remember the rabbit? It ran away last week, and we caught it under Mr Bloomfield's car. It was lucky we got it out, it could have been run over. I think Mr Bloomfield was more worried about his brake cables, whatever they are!

I have a new mum and dad now. I expect you know that. I hear Annette and Philip talk to you sometimes, they always say it is someone else, but I know it's you. They will never take the place of my real mum and dad, but they are very kind to me, and I am sorry because I think I have been horrible to them. Dr A. says it is not my fault, it is because I have been ill, and they still love me. I hope so. Dr A. says my therapist is right to tell me to write things out, so I decided to write to you.

The thing is, I don't want to remember the bad thing that happened because it frightens me, but Dr A. reckons if I talk about it just once, I can forget it for ever. That would be really neat. Françoise is pretty cool about everything and if I start to get freaky she just goes, 'Oh Soph, chill out will you, you're upsetting the dog,' or something like that. She has great clothes by the way and says I can borrow them but she's bigger than me which is a shame. So, as I want to forget the bad thing for ever, I thought I should tell you that I really should not blame you for what Auntie Kate did. It was not your fault. I know that now, and I also know that she did not mean to hurt me. She was just trying to protect me from the house. See, when Philip left me by the pool that day, I suddenly remembered all the fun Mum and Dad and me used to have. I missed them so much I thought my heart had broken. So, I needed you and I went to find you. I knew that I could do it and I did. But I met Auntie Kate down the lane, and she said it was really dangerous for me to go to the house. She said that I should never have gone to the fen. She hid me somewhere smelly and told me to wait for her. She said that only she could save me. She told me lots of things, Uncle Will, about the horrible things that happen to children out in the marsh. She told me that I must not go to anyone, that the marsh monster could change into anything it liked, even into you. She said I must hide, and if I saw you, it would be the marsh monster in disguise. But she didn't come back to save me, and she wasn't there when the men took me away, so I thought they were all monsters.

Well, that sounds really silly, doesn't it? and I hope Dr A. is right because now I've written it out, that means that I can forget it for ever.

I love you, Uncle Will, but I think Auntie Kate is pretty sick. Maybe Dr A. would talk to her? Anyway, it was good about the rabbit, wasn't it?

Sophie XXXX

Will read the letter again, then a third time. He folded it carefully and tucked it into his shirt pocket. He placed a hand on the arm of the bench, thinking briefly of all the times he and Kate had sat there together.

The tiny silhouette was still out on the skyline. He pulled himself painfully up and began to walk down the path towards the sea bank. His thoughts were clear for the first time in months.

It was Kate who had left the child in Grove's vile storeroom. High up on a decaying, rotting floor with no safety rail, just a long drop on to the stone flags below. Alone with thousands of pounds' worth of filth, involving children of

Sophie's own age. Had left her in a state of terror, sufficient to bind her to the spot as securely as if she had been chained.

She must have known that one day Sophie would be well enough to speak of what had happened. And as she left the house that morning, she must have seen that letter, lying as it was on top of the rest. Or had Kate simply erased the memory of what she'd done, just like Sophie?

And Grove. The man was scum, yes, but in this case, he was innocent. Kate had been perfectly happy for him to take the blame for the child's abduction.

She wasn't far away now, standing on an old wooden pier that overlooked the deep drain, and the fast running waters that gushed out into the Wash. She half turned to him. Caught in a shaft of sunlight, her thin face seemed to be made of purest alabaster.

He blundered into a glutinous patch of boggy ground. Oh, Lord, what was he going to say to her? What could he possibly say?

He thought he heard her voice, soft and whispery. Love, she was saying, "love," and "Bear."

He extricated his foot from the mire and looked up to where she had been standing. The wooden pier was empty.

He ran along the sea bank, calling her name.

At first, he saw nothing but the swirling greenish brown waters, then a flash of scarlet broke the surface. A white hand reached out to him.

He slid down the bank, shouting her name. Seeing a slimy mooring post, he grabbed it with one hand and jumped into the fast-flowing drain. The arm, red sleeve clinging to it, emerged through a circle of frothy bubbles. He snatched at it, almost losing his hold on the wooden post. The soaking material fought to free itself from his grasp, but he held firm.

He had her. He tugged at the sleeve and her white face burst through the water, her long hair forming a wide dark corona around her head. Frightened, imploring eyes stared up at him.

The eyes of a child.

Will froze. Sophie!

The jacket was slipping from his grasp, while he saw the terrified child being led up the dark stairs to that awful room. He saw her shaking as night fell and the shadows gathered.

He knew what those eyes were asking of him. He relaxed his aching fingers and opened his hand. Gently, he pushed the beautiful face under the water. There was no fight. She simply disappeared.

It took all his strength to drag himself from the drain and up the bank. He flopped down on to the muddy path and stared, wide-eyed, out over the silver expanse of water, searching for a tiny splash of red.

He stayed there, watching, for what seemed like an eternity. She had always said she would never leave Whisper Fen. Now she had her wish.

The fragrant scent of flowers drifted back to him from the sea. Lilacs! Essence of Kate. He had always thought it might be lilacs.

He dragged himself up, his wet clothes heavy, and turned his back on the Wash. Unconsciously, he took the soaked letter from his pocket and as he walked, ran it gently over his lips. Salty tears met with the river water and blurred the carefully written words.

Will smiled forlornly.

Yes, it was good news about the rabbit.

* * *

Some quarter of a mile away, up on a high part of the sea bank, Matt Ballard lowered the binoculars. It took him a few moments to realise that he had stopped breathing. He drew in air. He had to have been mistaken. Surely . . . ? Matt closed his eyes and, for a brief moment, fervently wished he had never noticed Kate Stonebridge standing by that rotting wooden pier.

Matt swallowed hard, then pulled out his phone and dialled 999. In a voice he hardly recognised as his own, he reported a terrible accident.

Then he was running, his lungs burning, to where Will now sat slumped on a wooden bench that looked out over Whisper Fen. His closest friend had just lost the love of his life.

But as he ran, he wondered what he had really witnessed. She fell, didn't she? Will jumped into the water to try to save her, didn't he? Of course he did! What he thought he saw, well, it had to be a trick of the light. Didn't it?

THE END

ALSO BY JOY ELLIS

THE BEST-SELLING NIKKI GALENA SERIES
Book 1: CRIME ON THE FENS
Book 2: SHADOW OVER THE FENS
Book 3: HUNTED ON THE FENS
Book 4: KILLER ON THE FENS
Book 5: STALKER ON THE FENS
Book 6: CAPTIVE ON THE FENS
Book 7: BURIED ON THE FENS
Book 8: THIEVES ON THE FENS
Book 9: FIRE ON THE FENS
Book 10: DARKNESS ON THE FENS
Book 11: HIDDEN ON THE FENS

JACKMAN & EVANS
Book 1: THE MURDERER'S SON
Book 2: THEIR LOST DAUGHTERS
Book 3: THE FOURTH FRIEND
Book 4: THE GUILTY ONES
Book 5: THE STOLEN BOYS
Book 6: THE PATIENT MAN

DETECTIVE MATT BALLARD
Book 1: BEWARE THE PAST
Book 2: FIVE BLOODY HEARTS
Book 3: THE DYING LIGHT

STANDALONES
GUIDE STAR

FREE KINDLE BOOKS AND OFFERS

Please join our mailing list for free kindle crime thriller, detective, mystery, and romance books and new releases, as well as news on the next Joy Ellis mystery!

www.joffebooks.com/contact

Thank you for reading this book. If you enjoyed it please leave feedback on Amazon, and if there is anything we missed or you have a question about then please get in touch. The author and publishing team appreciate your feedback and time reading this book.

www.joffebooks.com/contact

Follow us on Facebook, Twitter and Instagram
@joffebooks

We hate typos too but sometimes they slip through.
Please send any errors you find to
corrections@joffebooks.com.
We'll get them fixed ASAP. We're very grateful to eagle-eyed readers who take the time to contact us.